ONE MAN
TWO VOTES

Swept into the exploding, sleazy side of Washington politics, Robert Carlton has become a target. There is no option to walk away. Every agency has been infiltrated. He must find the killers behind this conspiracy, or watch his friends become its victims. Weaving past corrupt politicians, ruthless NSA operatives, and destruction of the nation's democratic system, Robert's family, career, and friends land in the crossfire.

J RUSS BRILEY

ONE MAN
TWO VOTES

LRP PUBLISHING

Liz Russel Productions L.L.C.™

One Man Two Votes
Copyright © 2015 by J Russ Briley
Revised Edition 2017

Excerpt Two Dirty For D.C.
Copyright © 2017 by J Russ Briley

Liz Russel Productions L.L.C. and
the LRP Publishing logo are Trademarks of
Liz Russel Productions L.L.C.

Written by J Russ Briley

Edited by Liz Russel

ISBN 978-1-943882-02-1 (Paperback edition)
ISBN 978-1-943882-03-8 (eBook edition)

www.jrussbriley.com

Dedicated to my gorgeous wife
without whom this novel would not have been possible.

ONE MAN TWO VOTES

Chapter 1

"Mr. Trask?" Andy set his fly rod on the rack of his open top jeep, extending his hand to the man exiting a rental car.

"Call me Alan. You're Andy?" Trask's accent carried a Texas twang, sounding odd in the clear Wyoming air.

"That's me. First time to Jackson?" Andy's calm Jackson Hole manner matched his comfortably worn jeans.

"Yep. First time fly fishing, too." Trask answered.

They shook hands briefly. Trask stood six inches shorter than Andy and looked older with his silver hair. Pale skin, sunglasses, and stiff new hiking boots branded him a tourist. "Well, you picked the right place to start," Andy assured him. "We'll fix ya right up. You'll be a pro in no time."

"Come on in the house and let me show you around." Andy invited, climbing the steps to the porch of the weathered ranch house. "Don't worry about your gear. We'll get that when I take you out to your cabin."

"Where is everyone?" Trask asked, looking around.

"Beth is getting supplies in town." Andy headed up the steps.

"Just the two of you here?" Trask queried.

"Off season like this it's just us. You have my undivided attention," Andy smiled, turning toward Trask. His face changed when he saw the gun in Trask's hand. There was no delay as the trigger pulled back. Andy crumpled forward off the steps and into the dirt.

"Good." Trask, real name Alex Hunt, rolled Andy over. The blood stain grew in the center of Andy's chest, spreading through his flannel shirt.

Hunt sent a quick text on his phone. A pickup truck came down the long dirt drive, dust billowing behind it.

The man who got out matched Andy's description. The woman getting out on the other side matched his wife's.

"She's at the store." Hunt was all business. "Put him in your truck and get out of sight. Drive over that ridge toward the river."

They moved quickly without a word. The new Andy grabbed the shoulders of the dead man, while "Beth" lifted his feet. They tossed the body into the bed of the truck. Hunt scuffed dirt over the small blood pool as the pickup drove off.

Hunt waited a few more seconds, then spread another layer of dirt over the spot. Satisfied, he stepped up on the porch and sat facing the road in a rocking chair, waiting.

<u>Chapter 2</u>

Edward Bradley saw where the turbulent water rose up, then fell behind a boulder on the upstream edge of a deep swirling pool. He'd entered the river just below the "Y" where two streams converged. One crisp, clear stream came down a wide valley, rushing over smooth, round rocks. The other cascaded down a deep ravine in swirls, brown from mountainside runoff. The fish, preferring to swim in the mixed water, would come to the junction and feed on the insects and worms washing down from the mountain rains. In this late fall weather they were getting hungry, and stocking up for the winter ahead.

Edward stood in the murky brown water. The trick, he'd been told, was to fish just over the clear edge. He should cast his fly onto the brown water so that it would float over to the clear side where the fish would see it.

Facing the big boulder, Edward reviewed what Andy had talked about the previous evening. Below the largest rock, the biggest fish in the lower stream would be hiding. "At least twenty-four inches long," Andy had said. Edward edged closer to the drop-off. The rocks had been carved out over the centuries by the water, forming a ledge around the pool. The boulder was a good fifty feet beyond that, just between the converging waters. For Edward, it was a very long cast. He looked up and saw Andy pointing toward the rock, waving at Edward to cast toward it. He nodded at Andy, and turning, stepped nearer the edge. Andy climbed higher up the bank and looked out over the water.

Edward pulled his line backward forming a smooth "D" loop behind him above the water. Andy had taught Edward the single-handed Spey cast the previous evening. It was much harder than a roll cast, but Edward felt he had mastered the steps. He pulled the line into a curved shape, then used an arched swing to send the line and fly rushing past to curve up behind him. With everything he had, he cast forward. Giving a flick to his brand new Orvis ZG Helio rod, he let the Royal Governor fly land gently onto the water.

The floating yellow double-tapered line took the carefully tied fly downstream over the wavelets, but the fly had fallen short by at least ten feet. His target would require a much longer cast.

"If I could just use my straight line overhead cast I could make this," Edward mumbled to himself as he slid his booted feet forward over the slick underwater rocks. But he knew the shoreline and scrub brush behind him were too close for a straight cast. He had to make this Spey cast work.

Sliding his boot as far as possible out in front of him, he tested his footing by tapping the extreme edge of the drop-off. The ice-cold water rushed into and around his legs, trying to knock him down. The soft rubber of his waders held, but the rocks felt tenuous at best. He couldn't see his feet with all the silt washing down from the mountain. He had to step by feel.

Edward knew he wasn't a great fisherman. He had just enough experience to get by. His guide, Andy, was an incredible fly fisherman. He'd put Edward on the track of some beautiful holes the day before. Andy had recommended the Royal Governor fly as a start. If that failed to attract fish they'd switch flies, based on what seemed to be hatching in the area. Edward was looking forward to their evening trip downstream, and to trying out a Brown Drake Andy had tied for him.

Edward impatiently cast his fly out onto the water again. He'd been enjoying this trip, but if it had been up to him, he wouldn't be here. He'd be in his office. He was here because he'd been told that as the Attorney General he had an obligation to stay healthy, both physically and mentally. He was standing in this icy fall run-off strictly because of his doctor's orders to "Relax." Those orders had been specific: one week with clean air, relaxation, lots of sleep and no cell phones, texts, or e-mails. The doctor had not required cold water or impending winter. Those came as a bonus with the clean air and isolation.

Edward's doctor had said that Edward was bucking for a bleeding ulcer, and with that came a host of other problems. The country didn't like illness in their officials—especially now. Edward's predecessor had worked as Attorney General for only two years before dying of cancer, leaving the Department of Justice in relative chaos as a new administration transitioned into office. Edward had been brought in as a conservative supporter of the President. His confirmation had gone well, and he'd moved into the job with acumen, but recently there had been tension between him and the President. The President said Edward was too rigid in his interpretations. Publicly he supported Edward's decisions, but privately the stress between them was running as high as this river ran fast. Arguments, discussions about Homeland Security, and the country's economic problems were making Edward's new and old relationships brittle. Edward's doctor's orders came at a good time for taking a break.

Edward made another set of sweeping motions with his fly rod, casting the fly out onto the river. Short again. He pulled up on the rod, and swept the line into the air another time. He tried to concentrate on his technique, reciting his casting lesson to himself.

"Lift...2/3 and sweep...2/3 and deliver...and drift."

Edward concentrated as he focused on the power stroke, accelerating smoothly, but quickly to the 11 o'clock position, and holding there, looking over his shoulder to see the line straighten out behind him. He followed the line down with the rod tip for a gentle presentation of the fly on the water. The bright colored line, pulling the leader and fly with it, landed gently one more time on the water about forty-five feet away. It was closer to his target rock, but still short. To succeed with the big fish, he'd have to place the fly "on its nose". Edward played out the line as it was pulled along with the current. Sitting on top of the muddy water the fly wouldn't be visible to a fish, but its shadow might be. Edward tried to re-focus on relaxation as he watched his fly float down the river.

"It really is a beautiful spot," he mused, looking up at the mountains and clear blue sky. "Gregg was right."

Senator Daniel Gregg, Chairman of the Senate Rules Committee, was also Chairman of a task force that included Edward as a member. They'd chatted, and as soon as Edward mentioned that he was looking for a vacation spot, Gregg had recommended this place.

"Andy's Private Fishing Guides, Jackson Hole, Wyoming. That's where you need to go, Eddie. There's no better spot anywhere, and no better guide." Gregg was the "go-to" guy for everything in Washington, and had an unsurpassed reputation for living well, if expensively. Edward hadn't hesitated to follow his advice.

Andy, watching from the shore, observed Edward getting closer to the edge of the deep pool. He turned to move up the slope toward Craig Davidson.

Agent Davidson was hovering above the shoreline, watching Edward and everything around him. Craig came with the Attorney General job, heading up Edward's security detachment of three men. Craig paced along the rise, dutifully checking the three hundred and sixty-degree view. Eric, the second man on the detachment, stayed with the truck and communications gear. Larry was the night man, asleep back at the cabin. Craig was the only member of the prior Attorney General's security team to remain on this assignment. The others had moved to new responsibilities, and he was now the agent in charge. It had been a nice promotion for the 28-year-old. Serving as security to the A.G. had been his only assignment since graduating from training, and he took the job very seriously.

Watching as Andy moved to the top of the bank next to him, he still surveyed the river. Moving closer to Craig, Andy explained where the next fishing hole was located. Both men looked up the river briefly, as Andy pointed out the landmarks they would soon be nearing. The bending view turned Craig away from where Edward stood for a moment as his eyes followed Andy's hand.

High on a hill above the river, a camouflaged observer watched Andy and Craig. Without moving his binoculars, he reached down to a radio controller. At the moment Andy pointed upstream, he pressed a button. The button turned on a green LED light held in the hands of a diver coiled deep in the water hole below Edward's feet.

Edward had failed at two more attempts to cast to the rock. His frustration was building. Mustering all his strength he began the sweeping tempo to propel his line further. He took half a step forward, his booted toes hanging over the rocky ledge where the rushing water tugged at his foot. He shoved the rod and fly forward with an audible, "umph," propelling his line out across the waves. He watched as the line arched outward, the fly racing along with it. Leaning precariously out, stretching as far as he could, Edward tried to get one foot farther. He didn't notice the black-gloved hands rising from deep in the pool, sliding over the rock and his boot. The hands deftly slipped a line around his ankle, looping the line back onto itself and clipping it with a dull green D ring. Just as Edward's arm reached its full extension and his fly settled on the surface, the underwater line went taut.

Edward was yanked off the slippery rock, and down into the pool. He disappeared instantly, his short yell choked off completely in the sound of rushing water. The ripples of his fall were barely discernable among the hundreds of churning wavelets. His fly rod and hat floated half-submerged in the murky water. Drifting rapidly down river, they faded quickly from sight.

Andy finished discussing his detailed fishing strategy with Craig, and the two of them turned back to the river. Edward was gone.

"Where is he?" Craig asked, his eyes scanning up and down the river.

Andy squinted, looking in the same direction as Craig. "He must have moved down river," he said, pointing toward the bend.

The river bend and scrub brush hid the view around the corner. Craig moved down to the water's edge, trying to push his way around protruding brush with Andy right behind him. A multitude of sharp branches hung far out over the water, forcing Craig and Andy to climb back up the bank to go around.

In the bottom of the dark pool, well below the water's surface, Edward's body was screaming at the sudden shock of ice-cold water. The rush of frigid water into his waders froze him to the bone. His mind flashed to stories of fishermen who drowned when their waders filled with water, and he reached for the suspenders to release them. He couldn't see the light. How could he be so deep in this seemingly shallow stream? Fumbling for the clasps he could feel his chest cramp from the cold, his air running out. The current knocked him into the rocks repeatedly, and he couldn't tell whether he was moving downstream or stuck in a whirlpool. He had no sense of direction, and couldn't tell up from down. Bubbles in the water swirled in all directions. They were no help even if he could see them. The line around his ankle strained against his movements, but in his shocked state Edward couldn't feel it. The line held taut against his struggles, anchored around a boulder at the bottom of the pool.

The diver, clad in a dry suit with a bubbleless rebreather tank, watched silently. He sat in the comparative calm of the eddy, in the upriver edge of the pool. The diver's booted feet were held firmly by nylon loops fashioned to climber's cams, and locked in the boulders. He had every advantage as he watched his quarry struggle in the murky water.

Craig had quickly climbed up the bank beyond the brush. Andy clambered after him. Craig stopped, scanning upstream, ignoring the bleeding scratches on his face and hands caused by the bramble.

"Where the hell is he?" Craig bellowed at Andy. 'Where could he have gone? He couldn't have disappeared!"

Andy was standing with his hands on both hips, looking up and down the river. "Didn't you find him?" He yelled back over the noisy river. "He's got to be here somewhere."

Craig shook his head "No," and waved for Andy to look farther upstream.

Edward was out of air. Cold sank steadily into his arms, making them weaker each second. He managed to release the suspenders, and reached down to pull the waders off. If only he could get out of the water-filled waders he could reach the surface, but his soaked clothes clung to the rubber.

The surging current constantly spun Edward around, disorienting him. Up was down, and down was up. The waders would not come off. His muscles were cramping with the cold, and his fingers had lost all their strength. Unable to see, and unable to pull down the waders, he thrashed at the water. The line held tight. For the first time, Edward felt the line around his ankle and realized he was snagged. Bending at the waist he reached for the tied ankle, his lungs burning; screaming for air, and his body temperature was dropping.

The diver moved in.

Edward's movements were becoming sluggish and weak. His hands reached the line and the securing D ring. His numb fingers fumbled with the unfamiliar clasp when he felt something knock his hands away. A sudden thump to his stomach robbed him of his last oxygen. Gulping in ice-cold water, his mind blurred, and his vision clouded. He gasped for air, taking in more icy water. His body convulsed, then went silent. Edward's eyes stared lifelessly into the dark water, mouth open. His body bounced against the rocks, tugging at his ankle tether, limp and lifeless. Deep in his chest, his heart gave its last faint beats and became still.

The diver made several tight wraps of aged and tangled fishing line around Edward's loose ankle, then pulled back into the shadows and waited.

Craig came back from searching down river.

"Nothing!" he declared.

"Me, either," Andy replied, panting as he ran up. "I'm sure it's nothing. He's probably just taking a break." He assured Davidson.

"What are you talking about?" Craig was sounding frantic.

"You know, he's probably just gone to 'see a man about a horse'," Andy smirked, sounding more confident than he felt.

Craig muttered something unintelligible, and ran up the trail toward the trucks, searching through the scrub on both sides. He yelled into his radio, alerting Eric. Andy followed.

As soon as Craig and Andy turned away, the observer's hand pressed the switch on the transmitter again.

The light on the diver's remote flashed several times, then went dark. The diver unclipped the D ring and released the line. Edward's body floated to the surface and began to drift down river, face down. Detaching his own securing lines from the rocks and coiling them neatly into a rubberized pocket, the diver followed along with Edward. He looked like a shadow in the water as the current pulled them along. Around the bend Edward's body headed toward the shallows. The diver glided between deep pools, disappearing far downstream.

<u>Chapter 3</u>

Without a breeze to break the cool stillness, the multicolored trees along both banks of the inlet gave the air an almost claustrophobic feel. The cold water rarely moved, reflecting the trees in mirrored perfection. The dense undergrowth absorbed every sound. Even the insects were quiet.

Sitting on the porch of the secluded Maryland crab shack, Blair slowly drank his beer. The slight chill in the air caused a cloud of steam to rise from six hot, newly served Old Bay-coated blue crabs. A large stack of destroyed crab shells lay on the other side of the brown-paper covered table, along with a pile of mutilated paper towels. The flavor of the spices clung to Blair's face and hands. A corner of his index finger, where the cuticle was split, was stinging from the peppery mixture.

The little restaurant was a locals-only kind of place, buried in the trees, and overlooking the water from the winding bay. The autumn temperatures were becoming cold, but Blair appreciated the change from the humid summer weather. Come winter, he would like to sit here by himself as the locals huddled inside. But he'd only visit once; he never went to the same place more than twice a year.

This crab shack's specialty was a black pepper seasoning of the cook's own creation. Blair didn't order it, preferring Old Bay's classic mustard and spice blend. The tasty paste covered everything; shells, paper, wooden mallet, his face, and hands up to the wrist. He had removed his watch as part of the traditional preparation ceremony used for eating crabs Maryland style.

The man across the bench from him was slower in his consumption, with half as many crabs eaten. He was a blue crab rookie, still wearing his watch. His Texas accent was somewhat faded, like his hazel eyes and silver hair. He knew the job he'd been hired to do, and knew how to do it well. The crabs were an awkward distraction.

"Wyoming go smoothly?" Blair didn't look up from his crab.

"Perfectly."

"Your operatives spotted by any locals?"

"No, the feds buttoned up the property tight for the investigation. The first night without witnesses we burned the house. The fire eliminated the owners and all traces."

"No traces?" Blair was skeptical.

"Ashes. Not even a bone."

"The feds spent time with your operatives." Blair reminded the man.

"They'll lay low, now."

"A loose end. You need to plan better." Blair preferred his own plans. "Is the next phase ready?"

"Everything is in place." His voice was quiet, further disguising the East Texas twang. It had faded from years on the road, but the accent remained. "The informant removal plan is in place. Our man inside knows his role, and we have leverage to prevent him from changing his mind."

"Make sure he doesn't." Blair's low voice came back hard and unyielding. He had no accent, sounding generically American. His dark, almost black hair had no distinctive style, and neither did his clothing. He could blend into any crowd easily, except for his black eyes. But there was no crowd to blend into here. It was early, and with the restaurant almost empty no one sat near them. Blair preferred being isolated.

The Texan continued. "The observation of the player has begun, and the informant will be fed just enough to get him started. I have someone close to him to drop the appropriate hints."

"That's the part I don't like. I would prefer a more reliable source to feed the player." Blair's words carried a silent threat.

"It will work out."

Blair crushed another crab claw and pulled the meat out with his teeth. "You have a man assigned to the player's security?"

"It could go one of three ways, and I have a person for each possibility. I think it will go to the Secret Service, and I have an Agent we've used before set to be assigned."

"I agree. The Secret Service is most likely. His father will push for that. Make sure the player stays on the track we laid out, and on schedule. Don't help directly unless he strays way off the mark. I don't want any chance of him or anyone else recognizing the setup. These guys aren't stupid. They could pick up on something if you're not careful."

"Sure. I know that. I've got it under control." The accent seemed more noticeable. The Texan was becoming defensive, even nervous.

Blair continued as if the older man had not spoken. "Only get involved if your man can't make it happen within the schedule. Understood?" His eyebrows pulled together, frowning in a decidedly unfriendly look, but he didn't look up.

"Understood."

After a long gap in the conversation while cracking crab shells, eating, and washing down the food with some beer, the Texan moved to the next item. "The informant removal plan is ready. It looks real good." His stocky fingers played with a decimated crab in front of him.

It was Blair's plan. He knew every step. "Just keep within the schedule."

"Understood," the Texan repeated. His voice was showing the strain. "It will work. There will be no trace. None."

"Make sure." Blair used his foot to push a small black gym bag sitting under the table across the deck boards.

Feeling the bag hit his leg, the silver haired man's shoulders relaxed a little. His confidence returned. "Yes, Sir. I know. It will go smoothly."

Blair stood up. "I want to start on the player the second the investigation declares the drowning an accident."

The Texan started getting up.

"Sit down and finish your crabs. They're too good to waste." Blair ordered. The deep voice and glowering eyes were uncompromising. He placed four twenties on the table under his beer bottle. "You know our time schedule."

"I've got it. Don't worry." The Texan sounded better as he dutifully sat back down, cheered by the indication that the conversation was concluding.

Blair put a hand on the table and leaned toward the Texan for a final low-volume admonishment. "I shouldn't have to remind you that this is an important one. Timing is key. Your foot is leaning against the first half of your payment. If you fail, not earning the second half is the least of your worries."

Blair walked away, leaving the Texan with a knot in his stomach. He knew it was unusual for Blair to meet with him like this, face to face. It meant that this operation had to be flawless. Not a single mistake could be made, and no one could ever know anything had happened when it was over.

The Texan dropped the crab he was holding back onto the table. As good as they had tasted, he'd lost his appetite.

Chapter 4

Setting his coffee mug on the counter next to the computer tablet, Robert Carlton pulled his Burberry coat closed and tied the belt. Today's headline was on the economy...again. The last big story had been about the drowning of the Attorney General, Edward Bradley. The headlines had been huge: "Attorney General Drowns," and "Attorney General Mourned." It had been quickly ruled an accident, and just as quickly the story had been relegated to page four of the political section. That article, when Robert finally found page four amidst the ads in the online newspaper, coldly speculated on the possible ripple effects within the government. Robert's name was mentioned in the last paragraph, so he left the page up for Tracie to see. He hit the print button, and heard the wireless printer in the office crank out a copy. Tracie would save it in his scrapbook. She kept every noteworthy mention about him. She kept hers, too, in a separate scrapbook.

Tilting his ear toward a raucous noise emanating from upstairs, Robert listened to the boys whining and fighting about going to school. Andrew was bellowing the usual, "I don't feel good," or maybe it was, "I don't feel like it." James was starting to sound just like Andrew, so Robert realized it could be his voice. Either way, it wasn't a surprise. Both kids were going through what seemed to be a permanently obstinate and spoiled phase. Robert felt that they had a bad case of entitlement, and that it, along with their lack of respect came directly from Tracie's deficiencies in the art of discipline. Robert wondered why they had to go through this every morning. He detested it. He also knew that the situation wasn't going to change. Tracie was too wrapped up in her own sense of entitlement and social ambitions to take on the uphill challenge of changing the boys' attitudes. Robert didn't notice his own lack of proactive attention to the matter.

He checked his Panerai watch, wondering if it was time to leave. He had never been sailing, but he liked the image the watch presented. Like his car and clothes, the watch was a symbol of what he wanted his friends and colleagues to think about him. He and Tracie shared an understanding of that, at least.

The Westminster chimes of the antique grandfather clock in the hall struck seven, and the doorbell rang. Immediately Robert heard the key turn the lock in the front door, and the alarm system made a brief chirp, signaling the door opening. Alicia, their household assistant, was right on time to pick the boys up for school. Alicia was always right on time. Robert wondered if she waited out front until the clock chimed, to make sure she was punctual. Then again, maybe she was savoring each moment of freedom before the clock demanded that she enter their house and take charge of their children.

"Alicia is here! Don't forget your ID cards!" Tracie called out as Andrew and James cavalcaded down the stairs past Robert without a word, racing to Alicia's car. Andrew yelled, "Shotgun!" while simultaneously texting something on his phone.

"No fair! You had shotgun last time!" James snapped back, still playing his handheld Nintendo.

"Did not!" Andrew's next comment was cut off as Alicia pulled the door shut, taking over the child rearing for another day.

Robert heard Tracie leave the upstairs hall for the master bedroom, heaving an audible sigh as she went. She would be coming down the stairs in a few minutes to say goodbye to him. It was a habit she'd kept over the years, except after very late nights. She used to have the kids in tow to say "goodbye" to their father, back when they were too little for school. In those days she'd follow up Robert's departure by taking the kids shopping, to the doctor, to see relatives, or to organized events—all the usual soccer mom activities. That seemed longer ago than just a few years to Robert. Other things had changed since then, and he wondered why. Tracie's goodbye kiss was shorter, and the list of things she gave him to do was bigger. Tracie's bathrobe was full-length, now, and thicker.

Picking up his briefcase, Robert headed down the tastefully decorated hall to the garage door. As always, the guest powder room door stood open, showing the perfect towels, scented soaps, and silk floral arrangement on display. The family wasn't allowed to use that bathroom. Tracie insisted that Robert and the boys always "messed it up." The bathroom had become a symbol of the things in their lives kept for appearances.

Each of Robert's steps echoed on the immaculate, hardwood floor. Right on cue Tracie came up behind him, and stood at the door to the garage. Her soft Prada slippers disguised her quick steps. The long Coco Channel robe with its beaded collar was draped and tied gracefully. She looked crisp and wrinkle free. Her dark blonde hair was nicely arranged, although Robert was sure she wouldn't have agreed with that assessment. Robert thought that except for the lack of makeup, no one would guess she had just awakened. She looked beautiful and elegant as ever, and quite proper in every way. Robert felt he should appreciate that more.

His Washington Post and Wall Street Journal were in her hand. They were the traditional papers needed to complete the look of a Washington DC politician or lawyer, and he was both. These were part of his appearance statement. He never read the papers, preferring to get his news electronically, by RSS feed, or by podcast.

"You remember we have the Barrys' dinner next Friday, and the Quezadas' on Saturday?" Tracie reminded him.

"Yes." He answered, well aware that she'd remind him at least four times between now and then. His smartphone would be equally annoying with its reminders.

"I just wanted to make sure. And my car needs to be inspected, the oil changed, and that squeak fixed. Can you pick up your laundry? I'm going to be going in the other direction today, and Alicia will be at the boys' after-school activities until six."

"Yes, I'll take care of it, and I'll get you an appointment at the dealership."

"Thank you. Not for Thursday, though, I have a luncheon." She smiled sweetly. "Are you going to check again on when they will make your promotion public?"

Robert's jaw muscles flexed as his teeth clamped together. His response was carefully neutral. "You know that takes time, Tracie." Every single day she asked. She would keep asking each day until she got the answer she wanted to hear. Robert was beyond being tired of it. Her question felt like an attack; a personal attack that he dreaded. Heaven help him if he didn't get the job.

"I know, but there is so much to plan, and I can't arrange most of it without a date. I need at least three weeks advance notice."

"Of course, but they haven't scheduled any of the preliminaries, much less appointed me, yet." Sometimes Robert thought she wanted...no, *needed* the title more than he did; and *he* needed it. Really needed it. "I'll check on it today." It was a lie. He knew he'd asked too often already. Plus, Bradley's body was still warm, politically speaking.

Tracie noticed the flexing jaw, and felt the irritation in his voice. She had seen his eyes narrow. "I'm sorry; I don't mean to be pushy. I won't bring it up again." Her smile was as thin as her voice. Her apology sounded artificial, and was as untrue as her promise to stop asking.

"That's okay, I don't mind." Another lie. He offered a half smile. "They'll get to it. Oh...I was mentioned in the Post article on Bradley. I left it on the counter."

"Did you print it?"

"Yes."

Her eyes brightened. "Well, congratulations! I'll clip it out." She didn't know, or care whether it was a positive mention. Any news was good publicity in her mind.

Handing him the papers, Tracie reached for the doorknob, neatly managing a brief one-way hug, and light kiss. "Bye, Honey." She smiled prettily. "I hope you have a nice day."

"Bye, beautiful." Robert responded automatically. "I'll call if I'm running late."

Tracie waved as she pulled the door closed behind him, before too much cold air could rush in from the garage. He heard the alarm system being armed as he headed toward his car.

Climbing into his BMW, Robert punched the built-in remote garage door button. After pulling out, he patiently watched as the door closed completely before he began the commute to downtown Washington, D.C., and his office in the Justice Department. The office of The Associate Attorney General of the United States of America.

Chapter 5

Winter was coming on fast this year. The warmth and color were being sucked completely out of DC. A few colored leaves held onto their limbs in grim defiance, while their brown relatives tumbled past in the wind. The gray season had begun in the Capital.

The commute was awful. Bad weather had socked in the area overnight, and Robert was completely unprepared. He never watched the weather reports, believing that weather reporters mostly guessed at the forecast. He shuddered at the cold pouring off the car windows, feeling chilled despite having started from a warm garage. A heavy cloud bank loomed in the northwest sky.

Robert drank more coffee and took more vitamins in the gray season. He wore brighter shirts and bolder ties. He did everything he could to counteract the effect the dark days had on his personality. Not long ago simply driving past the Lincoln Memorial would have been enough to lift his spirits out of the gloom. The sight of the nation's monuments had inspired him with national pride. Now his feelings of patriotism were clouded by pessimism, and darkened by a need for personal recognition. He struggled with knowing that his capabilities were well beyond the duties he performed. He wondered whether it was recognized in the Executive Branch of government that he could achieve more. His aspirations were focused on his rise through an elite circle, and he wanted some indication that his career was keeping pace with his drive to excel.

Robert pulled into the secured garage, and eyed the "Deputy AG" parking spot that he hoped would soon be his.

The elevator came quickly, but not quickly enough to outrun the cold air sweeping over Robert. The chill rushed in between the stainless steel doors, surrounding him. Still, the tepid warmth the elevator held after the doors closed was welcome. Robert paid no attention to the few people who got on at the first floor, and they paid no attention to him, either. They each issued the mandatory

DC, "Good Morning," without making eye contact, as if an empty space was being greeted rather than people.

Exiting the elevator Robert passed through the wide marble corridors. The hallways always harbored chilly temperatures. It was a welcome feeling in the humid, sweltering summers, but at this time of year the marble seemed unnecessarily Arctic. Occasional bursts of heat from the vents provided a reminder that somewhere in the building a higher temperature existed. Robert was quick to reach the AG office suite door. He rapidly pulled it shut behind him.

Passing his assistant, he heard her customary, "Morning." Robert reflexively answered, "Morning," in return, as he went to his office. He automatically thumbed through the stack of messages on his desk after discarding his coat. The pink pages did nothing more than prioritize the electronic mound of voice mail, e-mail, electronic meeting invitations, and register of dockets. Most would be answered with e-mails, the de-facto standard for office memos. Some he'd handle with texts.

Amidst the pile of actions, he could delegate were a few items that needed his immediate attention, and which might be politically smart to address. Robert didn't look forward to attending to these chores. They'd require the usual frustrating, drawn-out con-calls, meetings, phone calls and above all else diplomacy; endless, innocuous, superficial diplomacy. Plus, each call he made tended to generate two more. It seemed to him that the issues he dealt with became more tedious and less interesting each day. He'd made a habit of scanning everything for the important names first: his boss, the cabinet secretaries, or the occasional governor. Lately, those had been few in number. The office had been uncomfortably quiet since Bradley had died. It wasn't a good omen for Robert's career.

Lorraine, Associate Administrative Assistant during the last seven Attorney General's reigns, brought his second cup of coffee in about nine-thirty. She was the most experienced admin, but not the highest in rank. No amount of good work or efficiency could make up for Lorraine's lack of political skill, so she'd stayed at the same desk while nine political animals who'd served as her supervisors came and went. She scooped up the contents of Robert's outbox, and was out the door before Robert had time to reach for the cup she'd set next to him.

Robert stretched in his high backed chair, accidentally sweeping a number of the remaining messages onto the floor. As he picked them up, three caught his eye. They were all from an old prep school friend, Chris Stoker.

Chris had been calling for two days, and Robert had been ignoring him. The calls were a low priority among issues from more influential people. Chris wasn't connected enough to make any of Robert's lists. In fact, he wasn't connected at all, but that didn't stop him from trying to get Robert's attention.

Robert and Chris had spoken about a month before, and Robert wasn't anxious to pursue their conversation. Chris seemed to have what amounted to a conspiracy theory, but he wouldn't divulge who or what the conspiracy involved. He just kept insisting that Robert should share his concern.

Everyone in Washington had at least one conspiracy theory, but Robert felt that Chris was becoming consumed with his. Chris' thoughts had been jumbled and scatter-brained when they'd last talked. Robert hadn't been able to make sense of what he'd said, but he hadn't tried too hard, either.

Now it appeared that Chris had begun calling almost every hour, piling up voice mails and messages. In doing so, Chris had found a way to make himself Robert's immediate priority. He knew Lorraine would tire of the calls, and that she'd soon begin harassing him to return them. Robert dialed voicemail to hear Chris' messages.

Chris' voice began normally enough, but devolved into a nervous, insistent plea for Robert to return his calls. In his last message he reminded Robert of a meeting time they'd agreed upon;

a meeting Robert heartily regretted accepting. He'd completely forgotten about it, and hadn't canceled it as he'd intended. It was the last thing he wanted to do.

Talking to Chris on the phone was one thing; meeting with him was a waste of time. It might give Chris the idea that his conspiracy story had validity, or was interesting to Robert. It was annoying as hell.

"Why did I let him push me into this?" Robert thought. He kept looking at his smart phone calendar as if he could make the glow on the bright screen disappear. He'd agreed to meet Chris that day, and Chris had insisted on meeting him outdoors, on The Mall. Never intending to keep the appointment, Robert hadn't considered the possibility of lousy weather. He should have cancelled yesterday.

He should have been able to dodge Chris' request, but he felt trapped by a sense of obligation, which was an increasingly rare feeling for anyone in DC. He and Chris had been close in school. After college they had seen each other less and less as Robert climbed the ladder of politics, but they'd kept in touch. Chris had adapted to the "connected Y generation" with enthusiasm, delving into a computer driven life. It hadn't furthered his career, but it kept him employed. He'd ended up buried in the middle-management levels of the National Security Administration. He was in a good position, but not, by Robert's standards, an important one.

When Chris had originally pressed him into meeting, Robert had been surprised at the urgency in his voice. Robert had offered an office meeting, but Chris pushed the idea away quickly. Robert had concluded that Chris must have some personal legal problem, probably concerning a divorce. Chris and Anne had never seemed to be an ideal match, and it had been some time since Robert had seen them together. Robert hated giving legal advice; particularly free legal advice outside his area of expertise. He'd agreed to the meeting anyway, later discovering that Chris's paranoid theories were going to be the topic of discussion.

Robert was in no mood to try to crush Chris' unfounded, disjointed conspiracy theory. He dialed Chris' office number to cancel the meeting. Getting Chris' voicemail, he hung up. Looking through his listings he found Chris' cell phone, and tried texting him. "Can't make meeting." An auto text responded immediately, "Chris Stoker is not available."

"Damn!" Robert exploded. He attempted a phone call to Chris on his cell, only to hear Chris' voice say he wasn't able to take calls at that time. For a Gen Y connected guy, he certainly knew how to disconnect from the world. Obviously he did not want to be reached, or in this case, stopped from attending their meeting.

Short of standing Chris up, which would probably result in more nagging calls, Robert would have to see him.

"I'll make it quick," Robert assured himself, grabbing his coat. He also took a spare scarf and gloves from the closet. He decided he'd have to be firm about crushing Chris' suspicions, whatever they were.

Lorraine looked typically composed as he marched past her. She concentrated on her computer screen.

"I'll be back in about an hour." Robert barked as he yanked open the door.

"Yes, Sir." She answered, never missing a beat in her typing rhythm.

Robert yanked his gloves onto his hands as he pulled the door closed behind him. He tramped down the hall, still irritated. "I can't believe this. It's going to be freezing out there!" He mumbled audibly. A look out the glass entry doors confirmed that the weather had gotten worse. A snowstorm was moving in. His gabardine coat was fine for the underground parking lot, or for a quick sprint to lunch, but not heavy enough for standing outside in blowing snow.

Passing security at the building's main door, he pulled up his gray cashmere scarf before pushing against the door and the wind. As he'd expected, it was freezing outside. The temperature was dropping fast. No other person was in sight. His icy stroll would be a lonely one. Robert didn't rate any personal security, and wouldn't even if he officially got his promotion. He walked alone toward The Mall.

Chapter 6

In good weather the trees, ponds, and grassy expanse of Washington DC's Mall were inviting, and would be covered with tourists from the Capital to the Lincoln Memorial. On this day it was a barren wasteland of wind and cold. A few tourists braved the weather for short bursts of photography, but most were sheltering inside the museums.

Chris Stoker stood next to a huge old tree. Frigid swirls of wind rushed over the grass, tossing leaves into shallow piles around his feet. Those that found a protective eddy from the wind would soon be sprinkled with ice crystals. The storm had not yet started producing actual flakes. The sudden cold front was okay with Chris. He had on an old blue parka, ski hat, and gloves he kept in his car all the time as part of his emergency bag. A candle, matches, cat litter and candy bar completed the kit. His commuting car was nondescript, old, and a little worse for wear, so he felt better being prepared. He occasionally wondered if he should buy a newer vehicle, but always decided that it didn't pay to have a nice car for commuting. It would just get banged up and rusted.

Chris hardly felt the onrushing cold air. Winter seldom bothered him. Today the sudden cold front was keeping everyone inside, and away from him. He was fine with that. The fewer people around, the better, as far as he was concerned. He leaned against the old tree, watching. Adrenaline kept him warm as he anxiously scanned the area.

His vantage point was down The Mall, away from the Capital, and close to the Washington Monument. He had picked a spot within a reasonable walking distance from Robert's office. He stood away from the road, outside the concrete path that expanded in an arc from the sidewalk's main path to a stroller's turnout of sorts. There, two pale marble chip encrusted terrazzo stands held a span of plain concrete between them, making a bench. He knew the bench's surface offered no comfort, and with no back, it offered no shelter, but its advantage was clear visibility. Chris watched Robert Carlton walk up to it and sit down.

Robert sat huddled in his stylish overcoat with his back against the wind, facing the street. He was freezing in the bitter cold, and regretted every second he sat there. He had no hat, and his ears were starting to go numb with cold. Vanity always overrode good sense with Robert. He wore hats only if he absolutely had no choice. They flattened his hair.

Chris watched Robert tug at the gray cashmere scarf around his neck, futilely trying to cover his ears.

"Why in the hell did Chris pick this spot?" Robert wondered, as his muscles quivered in a short, shivering spasm. He looked longingly toward a red neon sign in the distance advertising espresso. It was too far away to read, but he knew the place, and right now anything warm looked like heaven.

Chris was still leaning against the oak tree just out of view. He wanted to make sure it was safe to meet Robert. He watched for anyone looking toward him, or following Robert. Chris was naive about most things outside his small office, or beyond his family life in the suburbs. He knew he might be followed or watched, but his knowledge of spies and secret agents came from the movies. He carefully surveyed two people scurrying by, coat collars turned up against the wind. Despite the distance between him and the buildings across the street, he scanned office windows for peering eyes. What he hadn't noticed was a gray sedan that had followed him. He didn't see it now as it sat in plain view. The car had rolled past him as he'd parked, going around the corner, and taking up a position a few yards away. The dull color of the dirty car blended with the city's winter landscape and grimy stone buildings.

The driver of the sedan was crouched down in the seat. His head was level with his seat's headrest, effectively hiding him from sight. When Chris had first crossed the street, the driver pulled down the visor, opening the vanity mirror from which he'd already removed the tiny light bulbs. Now he reached up and adjusted the mirror, pulling his hand out of sight afterward. A special convex mirror replaced the original, giving the man a wider field of view. He spotted Robert's arrival easily, and waited.

Chris scanned back and forth nervously. Eventually, seeing no one he deemed a threat, he walked over to join Robert on the bench.

Robert's freezing face looked up at the sound of Chris' heavy shoes crunching leaves.

"What's this all about, Chris?" He asked loudly, sounding as annoyed as he felt. "Let's go get some coffee, instead of freezing to death out here." He glanced significantly toward the distant espresso sign and started to get up.

"No. Wait! I'm sorry Robert, but I can't take any chances." Chris kept his voice low and glanced both left and right. He sat down heavily on the bench trying to position his body casually, as if he were simply a chatty stranger. He kept talking. "I had to know you weren't followed. Try not to look at me while we're talking. Act like we're talking about the weather."

In the car the hidden figure viewed them in the mirror through small, powerful binoculars. He watched the two men talk. Reading their lips as easily as most people read street signs, he repeated each word into his Bluetooth earpiece, recording what was said on his smart phone recorder app. The binoculars contained a video camera recording the scene. It might have been a lucky coincidence that Chris had chosen to meet outside and that Robert sat facing the street, but the man knew Chris's habits. Chris was nothing if not predictable.

Robert looked like he thought Chris had lost his mind. "Followed? What are you talking about? Why would anyone follow me? I'm sitting here with my new shoes covered in dust and leaves. It's starting to snow. There are a thousand good coffee shops around here, and you want to sit in the great outdoors playing 'Nanook of the North.' Nobody in their right mind would follow me out here!"

Chris' face was drawn and thin. To Robert he looked ten years older than the last time they'd met. "He's really scared about something." Robert thought. He suppressed his frustration to try to get Chris talking. "What's going on, Chris? Just tell me what this is about."

"They're going to take control of OPOV!" Chris blurted out. His nervous eyes showed the dark patches of days without sleep. He glanced nervously from side to side as he spoke. "Your boss was on to something, and he died because of it. He must have known, and they knew he knew."

Robert felt the surprise pass through his rapidly numbing body. Last time they'd met, Chris had been vague about his conspiracy theory. He'd kept referring to something he'd found that was suspicious, but wouldn't elaborate. Now all of a sudden it was OPOV, and Bradley was murdered? He stared at Chris in disbelief. "Bradley?" he said slowly, "you think Bradley was murdered?" He frowned, shaking his head. "Ed Bradley's drowning was an accident, Chris. The investigation team made a complete report for the President. I saw it before it went into his hands. There was no question about it."

"*He was murdered,* Robert." Chris punctuated each syllable, while still scanning the area. "It wasn't a fishing accident."

"Why?" Robert paused, waiting for more, and remembering this was just another conspiracy theory. He took a calming breath. "Why would anyone want to kill Bradley?" Okay, Robert had opened a can of worms with that one. Threats against the Attorney General were almost as commonplace as with The President and Vice President. He paused, hoping Chris would pass by it. Chris seemed hesitant to go on. "Come on, Chris, you don't seriously think he was killed in some plot?" He prodded.

Chris finally looked directly at Robert. "I don't *think* it. I *know* it. It's all connected to OPOV. We've been working—I've been working on the security of 'One Person One Vote' since Congress voted to fund it. We've got it working ahead of schedule, but it can be compromised. I know how they will do it."

Robert had an intimate knowledge of the One Person One Vote project, too, commonly referred to as OPOV. He'd been on the original concept committee. He had also been part of the President's campaign team that had developed the plan, and he'd participated on the oversight committee that followed.

"Chris, I know everything about how OPOV works. What makes you think it could be compromised? That's why the security is with you guys at the NSA in the first place, to keep the system tightly controlled. And you still haven't explained what Bradley drowning has to do with any of this." Robert shook his head. He was beginning to think Chris's brain had snapped from stress, or maybe just long hours and bad television. He wasn't making any sense. "Chris, you shouldn't be talking like this. You'll lose your security clearance. I hope you haven't..."

Chris cut him off. "They plan to take over the vote through the OPOV system." Chris insisted. "The vote. All of it! We would think we are voting; doing the democratic thing, and that the results would be tabulated accordingly, but that's not the case. The vote wouldn't be ours!" Chris' voice had gotten louder. He had forgotten his casual pose, and was leaning toward Robert, intent on making his point. "It's a perfect setup, Robert. After all those election fiascos in Florida everyone's been anxious for voting reform. The President made campaign promises to 'Give Back the Vote.' Give it back to 'The People,' directly, and cut out the so-called 'representation' we've got now. And he wanted to make the whole system easier, better, and more efficient. You guys came up with OPOV, all electronic, fast, efficient, low cost, and everyone loved the idea. Well, the voting public liked the idea, anyway, and it put the President in office. Then we all built the system. Now they've got it running, but it is set up to fool everyone. First, 'the people' win a few votes to build confidence, and then these guys take control of the voting issues that matter to them—the close calls that they want to swing their way. That's how it will be at first.

You know they'll get bolder later. We'll never be the wiser. Next thing you know, POOF! Democracy will be gone! The system will be less representative than it ever has been, but no one will know that. It's perfect. And it's already been built right into the software. A few powerful people controlling everything—and we'll think it's all legal."

Robert waved a hand dismissively at Chris. So this was the heart of Chris' conspiracy theory. He'd already heard numerous, unfounded concerns about OPOV. "Chris, I've been in on this thing from its inception, even before you got a look at the plans. I was on the development Commission; remember? I've seen all the security reports. The system is protected. There's no way the votes can be changed after they're entered. Plus, there are checks; balances. It can't be done."

"You haven't seen the code, Robert—and you and a bunch of Senators wouldn't understand it if you did see it. I've seen it. I can read it. I know how the architecture works. You've only viewed the reports, and they tell you what you want to hear. First the reports showed a few glitches, then a few big cost overruns, but eventually everything worked—and ahead of the deadline. Don't you think they know how to play this?" Chris slowed down, and looked intently at Robert. "What I'm telling you is that I can prove it. They have complete control without any security breach showing up. It's in the code, or at least it will be, and I can prove it."

Robert felt more impatient than ever with Chris. "No one's taking over OPOV." Robert told him condescendingly. "The final test runs worked flawlessly. Everything is in place for the first vote. Security on the system is the best ever created, and it's monitored constantly. There are too many checks in the system for anyone to change the results."

"Can't you hear yourself?" Chris was becoming more agitated. "That's exactly how it will play out. You're not listening to what I'm saying. Remember Bradley? He was running a special investigation. You and the Deputy A.G. weren't in on it. He was getting close to the answers—too close. They had him killed. One of my programmers started asking questions after he'd been working on the software code. He hasn't come back to work after taking an unplanned vacation. No one seems to know where he is—and nobody seems to care. I'm right about this, Robert. So, here's what I'm going to do: I'm going to get you the proof, but I need you to agree that you'll look into it. You! Not somebody who works for you, not going through channels; just *you* doing the leg work."

"Chris, we've been friends for years." Robert began, thinking he needed to calm Chris down.

"Don't blow me off, Robert; I know what I'm talking about." Chris snapped, jabbing his finger fiercely at Robert's chest.

"I'm not. Just let me finish." Robert tried to dredge up something to say to defuse Chris' conspiracy theory panic attack. "I believe you're sincere, Chris, and that you've run across something you don't understand. It's making you question the system. You're too worried about the people around you. You have to admit this sounds a little wild. No one can possibly..."

"They can." Chris cut him off again. "They already have. Look, I'll get everything you need to verify this from your end. Real evidence. They won't be able to deny it when the facts are in front of them. For now, just understand that the OPOV system was *designed to be compromised*. It's built into the software. I can prove it, but I need you to find out who's behind it. You have to find out who's pulling the strings from outside the OPOV team at NSA, and stop this from happening."

Robert hadn't been listening to most of what Chris had been saying, but now his words were finally getting through. "Wait— you've actually got *proof*?" Robert tried to do a reality check. Could this be possible? What would proof look like? Could Chris actually have substantiated evidence that someone had compromised the system?

Chris' mind was swirling in disbelief. Robert hadn't been taking in what he'd said! Why couldn't Robert trust him on this? Why couldn't he see how obvious it was? Chris had been obsessing over the problem for weeks, and had thought through every angle. It was obvious—it should have been obvious to everyone from the beginning. He had spotted the flaws months before, but his ideas to fix them kept getting shot down. In fact, from the day the architecture and code had been given to him by his boss Bill Karlovich, he had seen the improper connections of files and data packet calls. An idiot could see how it could be done, but when he showed Bill, his boss had passed it off as a minor problem. Sure it was there, but there was another team covering that door. Chris didn't believe him. He never had trusted Karlovich; the guy was too glib. He was sure Bill was hiding something.

Chris was too entrenched in what he'd been studying for months to understand that he hadn't communicated all of this to Robert. "Robert, haven't you been listening? Am I wasting my time with you? I wouldn't be coming to you if I didn't have the data. I know that you can't do anything without it." Chris' eyes were glazed, and his adrenaline was higher now that he realized he finally had Robert's attention. "I'll get you everything I've found, but the files are time-coded. They'll know when I download them, and when I send them. There's no way to take them out on a thumb drive or disk. I get one shot at this, and I have to know you'll be ready. Whoever is behind this has powerful connections. If you don't catch them they'll just cover up everything again, and I'll be another 'accidental' casualty."

"Can't you talk to your boss?"

Chris' hands jumped to the sides of his head in fists. His eyes squinted and he shook the fists at the air. "No! He's in on it. You aren't listening!" He still hadn't realized that it was impossible for Robert to hear all of the conversations going in Chris' own head which explained his conclusions.

"Seriously, Chris. You guys have procedures. How about his boss then, or a coworker?" Robert had overcome the trickle of doubt that momentarily assailed him when Chris invoked the word "proof." It seemed unlikely that one guy at the NSA could uncover an actual conspiracy. How could it get past everyone else there?

"Sure, I'll try that...NOT." Chris answered sarcastically, shaking his head. "Sometimes you live in a fantasy world, Robert. You think passing the proof around to my coworkers, or going over my boss' head will fix this? Did you hear the part about Bradley being killed? Or when I said one of my coworkers who spotted this is missing? Don't you think I know what's going on? I'm in there—inside the building. I need someone outside covering me if I don't want to end up a disappearing act. *You* need to cover me."

"Okay, Chris. Just send what you've got to my personal e-mail, and I'll have it checked out. I'll give you the address I use at home," Robert said calmly as he pulled a business card from his pocket. He figured the only way to defuse this conversation was to read whatever Chris had and shoot some holes in it.

Chris exploded. "No! Don't be stupid about this, Robert! They can trace that e-mail. Hell, my daughter can trace that." He fought to lower his voice, again scanning around the area. "You don't understand." He continued, making his voice more intense, and speaking slowly. "I don't know who can be trusted, and neither do you. This thing is ready to go. They've bought the people they need. They have them everywhere. Why do you think I came to you? Jesus, Robert, how can you be this dense? This isn't a game. My missing programmer and Bradley got too close. If these guys find out about me, I'm next."

"Okay," Robert figured that no matter how crazy it sounded, it wouldn't hurt to look into what was bothering Chris so much. If there were problems, they would need to be straightened out. Maybe the OPOV programming had been pushed along too fast, and the agency had taken a few precarious shortcuts. It wouldn't be the first time a government program had glitches. He wasn't buying

Chris' story on Bradley, or the programmer, though; that had to be paranoia. "I'll look into it. When do I get the details?"

"I'll call you," Chris responded, looking away.

"Well, at least tell me who is in on this," Robert demanded. He had no idea who Chris could be referring to, when he talked about "powerful connections."

"There's no time." Chris was already preparing to leave. "It'll all be in there. I just have to know you will back me."

Robert's eyes narrowed, his skepticism renewed. "Chris, you either have the evidence, or you don't. If you've got it, come up with it. If you don't, then stop this nonsense."

"I'll get it to you as soon as I can. That's the best I can do." Chris insisted as he stood up. "After I send the files to my home computer, I'll put it on a memory stick that has a hard password keyboard built in. We'll meet somewhere, and I'll give it to you. That way they can't track anything to you. I have an encryption plan they won't detect—at least not the first time I access the system, but they'll know I sent the files. I can't override that. That will tip them off if they're looking, and I'll bet they are. I'll have to disappear. I put in for vacation to cover my absence, so maybe they won't notice the file transfer for a couple days. You'll need someone sharp who can read the OPOV program code, and to help you with the encryption key I'll give you. Someone you can trust completely. Robert, this is *my life* we're talking about. I've got to know you're going to make sure they don't get away with this—that you'll make sure they can't cover it up."

Chris had been speaking in a rush of words. Robert stood up, completely frustrated with Chris' statements. "Damn it, Chris, I don't even understand what's going on, yet!"

Chris stopped, turned, and moved close to Robert's face. "Do you care about this at all? Do you want OPOV to be a total deceit? I'm asking now, Robert: do you care about the survival of this country? You did once. Does the fact that I'm putting my life on the line matter to you?"

Robert paused, looking Chris straight in the eye. He was still dubious, but something in Chris' face made him stare. Chris looked haggard and anxious, but there was a conviction behind his eyes that Robert couldn't deny. Chris believed what he was saying. After a moment Robert sighed, resignedly. "Yes. I care. I'll help. I'll make sure this doesn't get buried—if you've got the proof."

"I'll call." Chris quickly walked away.

Standing at the curb, Robert watched Chris as he walked across the road. Rumors, innuendo, even threats against the President and his programs were commonplace. Robert heard about them every day. This was different. He could feel a twist in his gut that told him Chris' concerns might have some foundation. Robert had a hundred thoughts going through his head. Could OPOV have been perverted to serve special interests? He didn't see how that could happen. There were too many checks; too many security layers. Who would have enough power to try something like this?

Robert shook his head. Whatever was going on, it scared Chris. There was no doubt about that.

Robert suddenly shivered. For a moment he had forgotten he was freezing. A sudden gust threw sharp ice crystals into his face and eyes. Drawing up his scarf, he looked up at the dark clouds. Winter was looking more ominous than he'd expected. He stepped off the curb. His path led him away from Chris, toward shelter. He needed some hot coffee.

Chapter 7

As Robert and Chris parted, the concealed observer picked up his cell phone and dialed.

"They're leaving."

"Excellent," Blair's strong, low voice responded. "Did he say he's got proof?"

"Yes."

"Did he give specifics?" Blair's plan didn't include Chris giving more information than was necessary.

"Some...almost everything you listed. He promised to send the information. Want the removal now?"

"Yes." Blair liked to be sure that action was necessary; timely. Now he was certain.

"Confirming removal." The other end of the phone went dead. Quickly sending the text message "now," the driver darkened the phone screen and set it on the console. Sliding up into his seat as Chris moved beyond him toward his parked car, he watched in the side view mirror. The phone screen popped on with an acknowledging 'thumbs up' icon.

Chris, fumbling with his gloves for his keys, dropped them on the ground next to his car. "Damn." His breath puffed out in a frozen cloud. Bending over, he clumsily grasped the keys and tried to push the remote unlock button with the thick leather fingers. Finally biting the fingertips and pulling off his glove, he hit the button again. The car locks released with a beep, and he jumped in, slamming the door behind him.

The engine started despite the cold, sluggish battery. "The last winter for this battery," he thought. He used the windshield wipers to brush away leaves and fine snow crystals. He had left the defroster switch on and it quickly fogged the lower half of his view. Chris was used to it; despite the cloudy windshield, he pulled out of the parking spot and made the turn onto Constitution Avenue. He didn't notice the gray sedan pull out behind him. Using the sleeve of his jacket, Chris wiped the fog away as he signaled to turn onto ninth. As he made the turn, the sedan followed.

Chris got onto "Indy," as the Marylanders called Independence. The street became a one-way road out of Capitol Hill, and commuters seemed to think of it as their personal high-speed racetrack. Chris hated the aggressive drivers, but he always went this way. The NSA was up toward Fort George, Maryland, and Chris lived a little distance beyond it.

He had traveled several blocks when the sedan passed him, moving in front of Chris' car. Chris was close behind the car as they passed Lincoln Park. The sedan suddenly stopped right in front of him. Before Chris realized that he was too close, his car slammed into the sedan. Wham! The jolt of the bumpers meeting threw him into the steering wheel, making a red mark across his forehead.

"Ummmf! Jesus Christ!" Adrenaline rushed through his hands and neck, flushing him with heat, and sending blood rushing through his body. He hardly noticed the darkly dressed man leave his car to come walking back toward him. When he finally focused on the guy, he saw what looked like a typical DC businessman. The man gave the bumpers a cursory glance as he proceeded back to Chris' door.

Knocking on the window, he moved his hand in a circular motion. Chris complied by rolling his window down an inch or two.

"We seem to have had a little problem here," the man said.

"Yes, I'm sorry." Chris responded, "I don't think your brake lights are working." He hid the anger that threatened to flare up, still feeling the shock of impact. "Damned idiot," he thought to himself, "Driving with no tail lights."

"Let's get off this main road and exchange information." The man pointed at the next intersection, and to a street that led off to the right.

"Fine." Chris acknowledged with a nod, rolling his window back up.

"This is just great," Chris mumbled to himself. "This had to happen now." He watched as the man got into his car, pulling slowly forward with his right blinker on. He turned the corner. Chris followed a short distance until the sedan pulled onto a secondary road and stopped. Brake lights glared through Chris' windshield.

"God damn it! I know those weren't working before." Chris put his car in park, and leaned over to the pocket to get his insurance card.

"As if I didn't have enough to worry about." He grabbed the papers and sat back up thinking, "What happened to my airbags?" He noticed movement by his left shoulder. Turning he saw the man was standing outside his window. A blue steel pistol with a huge barrel was pointed directly at his head. Chris' eyes widened and his mouth opened as a shot went off with the airy pop of a silencer.

The pulverized safety glass blasted into Chris' face, falling like tiny ice cubes over his legs. In one smooth motion, the pistol with its long silencer slid back into hiding. The man reached in through the smashed window to stop Chris' dead body from slumping forward into the car horn. A remorseless push sent the lifeless form into the passenger seat.

The assassin took a look around. No one seemed to be in the area, which wasn't surprising at that time of day, or with the onrush of bad weather and cold. Even if there had been, it was unlikely anyone on a back street near D.C. would want to get involved, or admit to seeing anything. There would be no witnesses. Going back to his vehicle, he pulled his car away smoothly. Five blocks and several carefully planned turns later, the nondescript sedan pulled into an alley, entering an open garage located under a dull rental flat that had seen better days.

The door closed as the car entered. Two men began pulling off the tires and taping the trim before the assassin had turned off the engine. In two hours a black car with booming stereo, bright chrome wheels, and a different license plate would pull out. The paint would be aerosol based, and totally dry. It only had to last for the drive to West Virginia, where the car would be stripped down to the last nut. No part of the car would remain. No one would ever find the switch on the dash that had turned off the brake lights.

Chapter 8

Robert stomped down the hall to his office, trying to knock off the leaf and snow debris from his new shoes. Wisps of steam rose from his damp shoulders. He passed by the darkly stained doors, each with a department name etched on a brass plaque, and most with a full-sized standing American Flag on the left. Senators and Congressmen had state flags on the right. The Attorney General decreed that placement of the Department of Justice flag would also be on the right.

Robert's toes felt the sting of each footfall on the marble terrazzo floor as he passed the doors. The cold numbness was wearing off, and feeling was coming back. He started to notice dampness touching the balls of his feet. The first trace of snow had been just wet enough to seep into his shoes. They were new, soft, black leather Ferragamos. He knew Tracie would screech at the sight. Tracie always stressed that it was "important to look a touch better than your position if you want to move up." For dress events she had purchased him a pair of Berlutis, which would be his daily shoe upon his next promotion. She mapped everything out years in advance. Robert was convinced she already knew what accessories they would need if, and when, he made it to the White House.

Robert, on the other hand, could remember when his favorite shoes were his worn out running shoes—the broken-in ones with the grass stains. They'd always felt great, despite the fact that they'd been cheap knock-offs. Robert hadn't worried about designer names in those days. He'd bought what he liked. His appearance had been less important than his work. It was a distant memory now, but somehow Robert had a feeling he had been happier then.

He reached the end of the hall and turned the knob on the heavy door, pushing harder than he intended. The door hit the wall with a solid thud. Lorraine, as professional as ever, and only slightly startled, looked up. Robert pulled the door shut again and walked past her, ignoring the new stack of message slips that waited for him. He headed straight into his office.

Pulling off his gloves, scarf, and overcoat, Robert dropped them on the nearest chair. He moved to the far side of the heavily used mahogany desk, and sat in the tall burgundy leather chair. Lorraine came in with a cup of steaming coffee, setting it on his desk coaster, then moved silently toward his coat.

Robert needed a moment to regroup and think about Chris' comments. A long sip of the coffee made him warmer, but it didn't enlighten him; nor did it convince him that Chris had stumbled onto a real problem of fact, rather than paranoia. Still, he had to consider the possibilities.

Next to the mug, Lorraine dropped the latest stack of messages.

"Thanks, Lorraine." Robert barely looked up. He'd never paid much attention to how well Lorraine did her job, but it occurred to him that he did, in fact, appreciate her efficiency and discretion.

Robert had grown up in a wealthy family. While both he and Tracie had been trained to be polite, they took paid service for granted. Occasionally he realized that he should do more. He made a mental note to acknowledge Lorraine's efforts more often. Maybe he'd take her to lunch next week, if he could find a break in the schedule.

"Will you be needing anything else, Mr. Carlton?" Lorraine asked over her shoulder as she gathered up his coat, and hung it in the closet. She placed the gloves neatly on the shelf above the hangers.

"No, Lorraine. That's fine for now. Hold my calls."

"Yes, Sir." She left, closing the door behind her.

Robert tried to order his thoughts. Was Chris right about a conspiracy existing, and about Bradley being killed after he stumbled onto it? What could Chris have to gain from telling such a wild story?

Okay, think it through, he told himself. Robert couldn't imagine how Chris could get anything out of this. Chris had everything to lose if the NSA decided he was *compos non-mentis*, or worse yet, trying to bring down OPOV. Homeland Security wouldn't hesitate to act, and the consequences would be harsh. Chris could be imprisoned for treason. Was it likely that Chris had become involved with some activist organization? Robert shook his head. Chris had never had self-serving political interests, unlike most people surrounding Robert. He wasn't a joiner either, disdaining clubs and social groups equally. He had minor aspirations, middle of the road opinions, and usually avoided getting involved in any DC issues, political or otherwise.

Robert was racking his brain for answers, but they weren't coming. After turning over the facts a dozen times, he finally concluded that Chris was overreacting to something he'd discovered. There might be some thread of truth that had triggered Chris' panic. Truth that could be easily explained. This had to be a simple case of excessive imagination.

Robert felt good about this conclusion. He hoped that Chris' imagination wasn't a developing case of mental illness. Schizophrenics could be very convincing with the stories they wove around their paranoid theories.

Having defrosted in the warmth and normality of his own office, Robert was quickly dismissing any chance that Chris' fears were real. There was a bright side: if Chris managed to come up with any factual information, there could be an opportunity for visibility. It might be a chance for Robert's star to shine. Uncovering a flaw in OPOV that hadn't been noticed, but which might easily be corrected, could bring Robert some notoriety. It might be just what he needed to push his promotion into gear.

Before Robert bought into any of Chris' story, he needed to find out what Bradley had been working on before he died. Picking up the phone, he connected to Lorraine.

"Yes, Sir?" she promptly answered.

"Lorraine, I need to follow up on what Bradley was working on, in conjunction with any reports or files regarding OPOV." Robert told her. "Recent work. The last six months."

"Right away." Lorraine responded.

"Thanks." Robert hung up.

Bradley's files would be a good place to start, but Robert was sure that if Bradley had found any evidence of an OPOV breach, or possible breach, Robert would have been notified. There wasn't much point to going through the regular, official files on OPOV again. Those documents wouldn't give the insider details. They contained only the facts that eventually would become public.

Robert realized that he was going to need help on this. He needed viewpoints from someone who understood OPOV, but who didn't have a conflicting agenda. Someone who was accustomed to research assignments handed down from The Hill.

He searched his memory for the best fit. Robert's staff was usually the perfect choice for internal and interdepartmental research. The problem was they all had their own political agendas, and would love to be responsible for cracking open an OPOV flaw, since it was an extremely high profile program. Robert needed an outsider, but one who could access all resources while not using the opportunity for his, or her own benefit. Robert wondered whom Bradley might have used, since clearly it hadn't been Robert or his staff. Bradley had played his sources close to the vest, and the odds were good that there wouldn't be a specific reference in his notes.

Robert mulled his options. Like all Washington insiders, he had his private allies and resources. Those resources were closely guarded, and never "loaned out" to other camps. Robert had contacts scattered throughout various government sectors, in special interests, and even in the opposing party. Robert considered his alliances to be "connections."

Robert wanted tight control of this research. He didn't want rumors. He couldn't go directly to the commissioners; they might delegate a request, or steal Robert's thunder, if thunder there might be. They all could use the boost. He decided that the best choice for this job would be one of his associates who had been on the commission that had overseen OPOV from its inception.

Robert mentally shuffled through the list of members and their associates. The Treasury was still vying for jurisdiction over Federal level fraud in the form of voting, so someone from that department might be interested. The military members were only interested in the issues of technology, security, and the military applications that could be derived. An aide had represented each military branch secretary, but two of these were pushing to become generals, and had political aspirations. The Coast Guard aide was too junior. That left one choice: Grady Barlow.

Grady was Robert's occasional link to the intelligence community at the Pentagon, and he was a rare commodity these days. An Air Force Academy graduate who practically had the honor code tattooed on his chest, Grady was a throwback to the old school. Integrity was everything to the guy. Grady had begun as a pilot. He'd climbed through the ranks, gaining a reputation of being a straight shooter who understood discretion, with no apparent desire for political office.

Robert had worked directly with Lt. Colonel Barlow when he'd first started in Justice. Robert liked and admired Grady. Actually, Grady was the kind of guy everyone liked. While he wasn't a regular "connection" for Robert, they had a good working relationship. He definitely struck Robert as someone who wouldn't start rumors, and who wouldn't use this as an opportunity to further his own interests.

After a quick contact search on his computer for Grady's number, Robert came up empty. He picked up the phone.

"Lorraine." He paused suddenly, reconsidering. It might be best to keep his contact with Grady under wraps. If this thing turned out to be a wild goose chase, it would be better not to have anyone think he was chasing conspiracy theories.

"Never mind." Robert hung up. Lorraine went back to her filling, unruffled.

Robert remembered that he could look up the phone number on the computer contacts listed under "Office of the Under Secretary of the Air Force." He found Grady listed, and hit a couple of keys on the computer keyboard to start it dialing the number. Placing a wireless earpiece in his ear, Robert listened as the phone rang.

"This is Lieutenant Colonel Barlow's voicemail box. I am in meetings today, but will return your call as soon as possible. Please leave..."

Robert hit the 'end call' button. Having decided to keep this under the radar, he didn't want to use voicemail. This situation called for something more interactive, but less documented—and definitely not official. Face to face would be better, he decided.

"How do I catch him informally, and still have an opportunity to talk privately?" Robert wondered aloud. He stared down into his coffee cup.

"Coffee!" Remembering a dinner conversation with Grady, Robert recalled that Grady had confessed to a regular espresso habit. He'd discoursed avidly on virtues of Arabica versus Robusta beans, and the abundance of premium coffee stores in the DC area. Grady had even recommended a place that was his habitual stop each morning. A more local, less national coffee spot, he'd said. Robert had gone by the place a couple of times, even bumping into Barlow twice, right at seven-thirty in the morning. Robert had stopped going when Tracie bought a one-touch, eight-hundred-dollar automatic espresso machine. Instead of stopping for coffee, Robert now used the machine. Robert wasn't sure he liked the coffee as much, but he felt the expense needed to be justified, and it was, admittedly, convenient.

The idea of catching Grady at the shop suited Robert. He normally didn't want much to do with people early in the morning. Coffee shops were too energetic; too full of noise, too early in the morning. Grady, on the other hand, seemed to get as much out of the coffee shop experience as he did from the coffee. Unless he was out of town or had a broken leg, Grady would be at his ritual brew joint in the morning.

Decision made, Robert turned to the stack of interruptions on his desk. His usual turkey sandwich with lettuce, tomato, provolone cheese, spicy mustard, no mayo, and iced tea showed up on his desk for lunch.

"Iced tea." Robert shivered and rejected the cold beverage, leaving it untouched. "Consistency without external feedback," he thought. It was true he'd told Lorraine that iced tea was his standard choice. He wondered if he should consider changing that for winter.

From there the afternoon lumbered on.

At three-thirty, his computer calendar popped up an appointment warning. Without the warning, he would have completely forgotten the reception he was supposed to attend. His iPhone chimed in moments later with the same warning, "ABA Recept—W.H." American Bar Association representatives from several states were attending a reception at the White House, and Robert never missed a White House invitation. His father had taught him that rule.

On his calendar, he also spotted his commitment to meet for a few minutes with the Secretary of Commerce, Carl Hanson. He had some NAFTA related questions he wanted to go over just prior to the reception.

The intercom beeped. "Mr. Carlton." Lorraine's voice came over the speaker.

"Yes?" Robert responded over the speakerphone.

"I wanted to remind you. You have a reception at the White House."

"Yes, thank you, Lorraine. I'm packing up." Robert clicked off the speaker. He took a few minutes to review his messages. Checking the stack of message notes again, he didn't see anything urgent. He pushed them aside onto an older stack for future action. The IT department had set up Robert and Lorraine with electronic messaging, so if any of these became critical she could type in the message and it would appear on his computer and cell phone simultaneously. She could also connect a caller directly to voicemail, which would show up immediately. They both hated the system, since it seemed to add to the chaos of each overloaded day, but it had its uses.

Pausing for a moment, he turned to pull open his file cabinet. Robert had his personal notes and custom reports on OPOV there, from his work on the committee. Several agencies also had made reports on possible problems during the OPOV set up, and Robert had copies of these. He chose "Recent Campaign Investigations" and "OPOV Security Checks" from the file drawer, and tossed them into his briefcase. Some of these documents were on his computer or in his e-mail, but the hard copies were part of the filing process, required in the legal documents system. Lorraine did the physical filling efficiently, which made them easier to find than searching his electronic files. Closing the drawer and spinning the combination lock on the file cabinet, he flipped over the green "Locked" sign, and turned to the computer to shut it down. After waiting for the interminable Windows shut down, he undocked the laptop, and slid it into his briefcase. Taking a quick look around the room to make sure he hadn't left anything, Robert walked to the closet, and grabbed his coat, scarf, and gloves.

"Lorraine, if anything important comes up, I'll have my cell phone with me. See you Monday morning." He passed by her, and opened the main office door.

"Yes, Sir." Lorraine acknowledged to Robert's back, keeping an eye on the hall door closing behind him. She watched until she was sure the door had closed, keeping out the cold hallway air, and returned to her typing.

Stepping out of the elevator and into the parking garage, the chilly air and dirty gray concrete reminded Robert of his cold meeting with Chris. Robert tried to push the thoughts the meeting evoked aside for now, but the look in Chris' eyes lingered in the back of his mind.

<u>Chapter 9</u>

Claire and her grandson Kelvin trudged past the police cars scattered along the road, blocking the street. Back in the fifties this had been a nice neighborhood. Over the years the block had deteriorated. It had gone from being tolerable to an all-out war zone. She ignored the cops as they went about their business. The flashing lights and sounds of more sirens approaching barely drew a glance from her, and garnered only mild curiosity from the twelve-year-old boy. Some white guy was being dragged out of a car and hoisted onto a stretcher. It was none of their business.

The police were chatting amongst themselves, their cold breath puffing back and forth in clouds of steam. She heard them say something about a carjacking gone bad, or maybe a drug deal. Either way, the sickly reddish-brown splatter of drying blood on the inside of the passenger window told her more than she wanted to know. Looking down, she saw Kelvin staring idly at the blood-splattered glass. Grabbing her grandson by the arm, she lurched up the filthy steps to the cold-water apartment.

On the street, the dead man's body flopped carelessly onto the stretcher. His blue parka made him look bloated. The man's blood-soaked ski hat slowly oozed out its burden onto the white sheets. No steam rose from the blood, only the workers' breath and truck exhaust could be seen. Everything else had lost its heat in the icy air. An arm fell limply over the side of the gurney. No one bothered to pick up the hand as it bashed into the angular steel doorframe of the ambulance. The EMT finished some paperwork and handed it to one of the policemen, while Chris' body was pushed unceremoniously onboard. The grinding noise of the tow truck winching up the damaged car marked time to Chris' death, minus the fanfare. It was enough noise to block the sound of the ambulance pulling away.

Chapter 10

Robert still couldn't clear his mind. He kept going over the meeting with Chris as he drove out of the secure underground parking area. He thought about the sound of Chris's voice as he merged into traffic, and as he became one of the masses headed down the road. Both directions were packed. He inched along with the snarled rush hour traffic, glad that it was a short trip to The White House.

The guards at the gate were attentive, and better suited to facing the public than most. Their demeanor was that of brighter individuals who could handle more complex conditions. Each facet of the Presidential zone was just slightly more refined. Still well below the standards of regimental military splendor at Buckingham Palace or the Kremlin, it had disappointed Robert when he'd first realized the differences. He'd felt let down by the lack or military spit and polish. There were Marines within, but D.C.'s finest at the gate seemed to be short on dramatic presence.

Still, the exterior area was cleaner than the other government buildings. The grounds were tidier, well-manicured in good weather, and tended to be quiet.

In stark contrast, the West Wing offices were filled with the noise and congestion of people constantly bustling about, overwhelming any uninitiated visitors. The offices were cramped, and people spoke rapidly, expecting swift answers. No sense of royal deference or awe infiltrated the intense atmosphere. It was a political hub, filled with every deadline and pressure point of the busiest offices in a Wall Street trading firm.

Robert hardly noticed the confusion around him. He'd visited the West Wing many times. Making his way to one of the break areas, he grabbed a bottle of water and swallowed a third of it along with a vitamin B pill. He always carried them with him. The B complex of vitamins would block most of the effects of the alcohol he'd be consuming, keeping his mind sharp. Tracie had taught him the trick, and it gave him an edge at cocktail parties. His political adversaries often drank and talked too much.

Looking down he noticed the disgraceful condition of his new shoes. He gave them a quick buffing with the motorized shoe valet in the nearby cloakroom. They'd never be the same, but they were better. He proceeded up the stairs and down the hall to the reception area, where Carl Hanson was to meet him.

The conversation with Hanson went well. There were some minor legal questions surrounding a section of NAFTA being revised, which had all been reviewed, allowing Robert to easily deal with Hanson's concerns. Still, the conversation took almost an hour. Robert had to hurry to make it to the reception.

Walking along the colonnade connecting the West Wing to the White House, Robert paid little attention to the fact that he was in the President's residence. The thrill he'd felt when he'd first been invited to the hallowed structure had been lost over the past year. He no longer took the time to reflect on the presidents who had passed through these halls; his thoughts centered strictly on business.

Of the four state reception rooms in the White House, Robert liked the Red Room best. Its Empire style somehow suited his vision of elegance. It seemed a bit small for this gathering, particularly with Senator Gregg in the room. Gregg, Chairman of the Senate Rules Committee, and heir apparent to the Appropriations Committee Chair, was a large and important man. Robert knew he would have to make a point to speak with him. There were some other notables expected whom Robert hoped to see, and it was thought the President might make an appearance. Robert quickly mapped out his approach for spending a few minutes with everyone he knew in the room.

Shaking hands with several State Bar representatives, Robert made his way around the Red Room, and through the adjoining Blue Room, opened for this gathering. Selecting a scotch from the steward's tray, he headed back into the Red Room. Robert progressed determinedly toward Gregg's corner, where the Senator was holding court. Gregg was one of the most accomplished politicians in D.C., polished, smooth, and extremely influential.

"Senator Gregg, how are you this evening?" Robert offered his hand to the Senator through the tight gathering, getting a firm shake from Gregg in return.

"Mr. Deputy Attorney General...I hope you don't mind me calling you that. It is, after all, only a matter of time." Gregg's smile was complimentary, but at the same time, Robert thought he heard condescension in the deep voice. Gregg was adept at giving compliments, but he could also subtly send unspoken messages. Robert wondered if he'd just been on the receiving end of one.

Robert could be adroit, as well. "You honor me, Senator. I certainly hope I can live up to your expectations someday." He continued with a safe objective, "Would it be possible for us to take a moment to discuss the review on ethics? I would like to propose some procedural adjustments for the committee. I think it could help streamline the process flow." Robert knew that without Gregg's support, no changes would be considered. He also knew that his ideas would not alter much, but having his name attached to government streamlining would be perceived as positive. It would have the same effect for Gregg.

"Of course, Robert. I welcome any discussion that can reduce waste in any form." His broad smile conveyed confidence and trust. It was a clever disguise for the consummate politician. Gregg swung his six foot one, two hundred and eighty-pound frame around, bringing his arm heavily across Robert's shoulders. "There's a subject we should touch on, first."

As Robert turned with Gregg, a stocky man suddenly appeared at Gregg's elbow. Gregg glanced at the man's name tag, then smoothly brought him into the conversation. "Robert, I'm sure you already know Alex."

The stocky man took over, saying, "Senator, it's always a pleasure to see you, but I don't believe the Deputy Attorney General and I have met. I'm Alex Hunt; Texas Bar Association."

"Robert has reminded me tonight that he's not yet the Deputy AG, Alex." Gregg interjected. "We're both a little premature in our congratulations on what apparently is still in the 'state secrets' category," he added with a knowing wink.

"That may be, Senator Gregg." Hunt nodded with a smile. "But it's such a well-known secret that I'm sure you'll be wearing the title soon enough," he told Robert. "It's very nice to meet you." His Texas accent was somewhat faded, like his hazel eyes. His silver hair was subdued next to Gregg's shock of pure white hair. Still looking at Robert, Hunt asked, "I wonder if I could pull you aside for just a moment? I'll be glad to return him to you in a few minutes, Senator," he told Gregg.

Robert was used to this two-step, Texas or otherwise. "Certainly Mr. Hunt. I hope you don't mind, Senator?"

"Mind? I'm delighted, since it gives me the opportunity to refresh my scotch." Gregg patted Robert on the shoulder before he headed toward the bar steward. The corner now belonged to Robert and Hunt.

"I believe we share a common interest." Hunt began.

"What would that be?" Robert put on his politician's look of interest.

"We all want OPOV's first vote to come off without a hitch. I'm sure y'all have covered all the bases, and that there will be no problems. We have every confidence in your ability to insure that, but if anything should come up, I'm available to help. Here's my card. I want you to consider me a willing and able resource for whatever you may need—anything at all. Feel free to call me anytime." He didn't wait for a response before adding, "Perhaps you'd like to do a little fly fishing, or maybe some dove hunting one of these days? Any time you'd like to go, just give me a call. Hang on to that card."

Before Robert could speak, an announcement came from the side door. "Ladies and Gentlemen, The President of The United States." Robert turned toward the door as The President entered. The President was wearing his usual room-encompassing smile, seeming to catch each attendee's eye as he worked the room.

Once the President had finished his handshaking, Robert turned to where Hunt had been standing. He was gone. In fact, now that Robert thought about it, Hunt hadn't been there when the President had shaken his hand. Robert was dumbstruck. Not only was that the shortest conversation he could remember having at one of these events, it also seemed to be pointless. He checked the card Hunt had given him. It had nothing on it except a phone number.

Looking around the room, Robert also noticed that Senator Gregg was gone.

<u>Chapter 11</u>

Pulling out of The White House parking lot, Robert was tense. The careful conversations and undercurrents running through the seemingly idle chitchat had made his neck as stiff as a board. Like most events of that kind, each visitor had an agenda. Robert could have ignored all of them, like most politicians, but that was one skill he hadn't mastered. Each question seemed to come with a request or a direct link to something on Robert's to-do list; his very long to-do list. While he hadn't picked up any action items from the lawyers in the rooms, he none-the-less felt increased pressured about his own overloaded job. He needed to work off some tension, and forget the job for an hour, but the drive home was only increasing his stress level. The few miles down Constitution Avenue and across the bridge to 66 took longer than the twenty miles into the suburbs.

Robert could feel his spine compressing, and his jaw clamping down. The bands on the sides of his neck felt like rods of steel, penetrating his skull. He reminded himself that all of Washington was stressed, but he felt no joy in the fellowship. Everyone he knew downed prescription happy-pills, chugged coffee, and swilled more alcohol every day. Most of his friends had diet problems, thinning hair, hormone imbalances, or prostates that were about to explode. The obsessive exercise and health food regimens of the nineties had faded—not that they'd ever been that popular in DC. Bars, not health clubs, were the habitual retreats of politicians and the thousands of government workers.

Robert knew he'd end up with a health or drinking problem if he kept having days like this one. He hadn't been able to get Chris' assertions off of his mind. They'd been nagging at the back of his brain between reminders of tasks left undone. That meeting with Hunt bothered him. Senator Gregg had glanced at Hunt's name tag, as if he hadn't quite remembered him, but to Robert it seemed that Gregg had arranged for the introduction to take place. Robert still couldn't figure out what purpose Hunt had in seeking the introduction, or why Gregg had sounded just a bit condescending about the Deputy AG title. And certainly Hunt had the oddest business card Robert had ever seen. Hunt may have some connection to a special interest group or lobby, he decided. This was probably a clever maneuver to get Robert's attention. Robert figured he'd be hearing more from the guy sooner than he'd like.

By the time Robert pulled into the back driveway of his two-story, mock colonial home, he'd developed a headache to go along with the stiff neck and compacted back. He felt like he could have ripped the leather off his briefcase with his teeth from the frustration he felt.

Inside the home there was no sanctuary. The house was a war zone. James and Andrew raced by shouting something unintelligible as they collected their karate paraphernalia and hand chopped all the furniture.

"No kicking!" Robert yelled, as the stair rail took a side kick from Andrew.

Tracie could be heard upstairs giving Alicia instructions about the boys' schedule through bedtime. Tracie's voice had a high-pitched, harried tone. Robert decided to lay low downstairs in the study. It had been his private office, but when Tracie got her appointment as European Hostess to the Kennedy Center it had to serve double duty for them both. Her father had arranged the elite position for her. It wasn't a job. Nothing in Washington worth having was. The salary, or lack of one, was meaningless. Everyone made their money from side deals garnered from their new connections. Tracie's appointment was strictly on the volunteer level, but she treated it as being as important as any job Robert had.

Robert heard Tracie making a final checklist for the kids with Alicia. He heard her come down the stairs, and through the hall. The study door opened.

"Robert?" her head peeked through the door. Seeing him sitting at the two-sided banker's desk, she came into the room. "I thought I heard you come in. I have a dinner with the German delegation to set up the visit from the Chancellor." She spoke in a continuous string of words. There was no point in Robert responding. He was just supposed to listen.

"Isn't it wonderful? This is really a fabulous opportunity!" she continued. "There'll be a reception, small classical concert, and then there's a formal dinner at The White House." Her speech flew by at high speed as she ticked off the events on her fingers. The last three words were emphasized with a flourish. "They'll handle the dinner, of course, but the rest is mine. Isn't it great? I've got to rush now. Alicia put something in the Sub-Zero for you. Don't wait up for me." She left the room and hurried down the hall, her heels tapping loudly on the hardwood floor.

Robert rose from the desk and reached the hall in time to see Alicia closing the door behind her and the boys. The door slammed shut and the alarm activated with a chirp. None of them had waived, or even yelled goodbye.

"Fine, honey, how are you and the kids? Me? Oh, it was a normal day, the government is falling apart, my old school chum may have gone around the bend, and the debt will enslave all of us, but the coming civil war should fix everything." He commented sarcastically toward the vacant hall. Robert went back to his study. The sudden quiet of the house was startling, but he felt a sense of relaxation. It was as if the house could now breathe a sigh of relief. The silence was broken only by the cold wind causing a leafless tree branch to lash at the window behind him. He was left isolated with his thoughts.

Rubbing his eyes, Robert replayed the day's events in his mind.

What data was Chris going to give him? Why had Gregg slipped out of the reception so quickly? And what about Hunt? Was he actually a member of the Texas Bar? Robert snapped his laptop into the docking station. Jabbing on the power, he absentmindedly toyed with the mysterious "Mr. Hunt" card in his pocket.

A familiar tune signaled the computer boot cycle was complete. Robert punched in his ID and password, and pressed his thumb to the sensor device plugged into the USB port. It read his print, and began flashing the second phase of IDs and passwords as well as opening several programs in sequence across the screen.

Clicking on the Intranet global data warehouse icon, Robert continued clicking until he reached the Federal and State Bar Association listings. Selecting The Texas State Bar Association, he scanned several pages, coming to a short list of lawyers named Hunt. None had a first name of Alex, or any variation of that name. Robert paged through them. One after another went by, complete with photographs. Not one looked even vaguely similar to the man he had just met. Robert rocked back and forth in his chair. Perhaps Hunt had only recently passed the bar? Unlikely, he decided. Hunt's age and invitation to a White House function precluded that notion. A quick search of the web for the name Alex Hunt turned up a number of people, but no lawyer was among them. The phone number also came up empty. White House security would have kept him from getting a pass into the White House reception if he wasn't legitimate somehow, Robert mused. He'd check with them in the morning, but the information they'd release would be limited. White House security didn't share readily. The real question was whether Hunt was connected to Gregg. Gregg didn't spend time with people he didn't have a use for, so Robert knew there had to be a link. He printed out the list of all licensed lawyers and bar associates with the last name of Hunt.

While that was printing, he headed toward the kitchen, thinking he'd pour a glass of wine, and see what concoction Alicia had left for him to microwave.

Pulling a nice, drinkable Cabernet from the wine rack, Robert selected an appropriate glass. He opened the bottle and poured, then set aside the glass and bottle to breathe. Opening the refrigerator he saw the note stuck to the side of a rectangular plastic container. "Roast – heat in microwave for two minutes, turn two minutes, add vegetable container, heat for two minutes" it read.

He closed the door without removing the containers. Picking up the wine glass, he headed back to the study. The printer had run out of paper, so he put in more and hit the flashing orange button.

As he stood there, Robert looked up at the wall. His diplomas, certificates, and picture shaking hands with the President were framed and hung in the corner above a tall, narrow frame of his successive business cards. The rest of the wall was covered with pictures of Tracie with every dignitary she had met since she had become a Kennedy Center Hostess. The wall used to be a showcase of every important event since she and Robert had met. Their French winery tour, bridal photos, wedding portrait, baby pictures, and each yearly family photograph had originally adorned the space. Robert wondered what she had done with all those pictures. He decided they'd been relegated to the attic with the other family shots. Tracie's new sense of interior design did not allow family photos in the public areas, or in their showcase bedroom for that matter, since it was on the tour during parties and dinners. Only politically impressive images and the occasional sign of family wealth remained. It was a collection of yachts, clubs and dignitaries.

Robert reflected that beneath the apparent chaos of their days, there was always an order to everything. His life and Tracie's had been well planned from birth. His father was one of the highest-ranking oil company executives in the country; the kind you never saw on TV, but one whom Washington insiders wanted to know. Robert had been given everything necessary for success, including private tutors, influential friends, and straight teeth. His life had been orchestrated to be picture perfect. His career had begun with ideal credentials. Magna Cum Laude from Brown University, Summa Cum Laude from Harvard Law School, published in the Harvard Law Review, and a beautiful, debutante wife who was well educated at Swarthmore, and came from a family listed in the Social Register. The photo wall reflected their latest levels of connections and power.

Robert's accomplishments had allowed him to move smoothly through the political landscape. Opportunities came looking for him. A friend had sought him out to help with the campaign to re-elect Senator Tom Baxter. Six years later he had distinguished himself as a regional campaign manager, helping to achieve the Presidency for Senator Baxter. When Baxter stood to take his Presidential oath of office, Robert stood three rows back, and fourth seat to the right during the ceremony. Two days later he became the United States Associate Attorney General.

The printer finished and Robert sat down to look through the list. He rested his forearms on the desk as he thumbed through, occasionally taking a sip of the wine. Hunt seemed to be a common name amongst lawyers. It was a very long list.

Robert's head jerked up from the desk, the noise of the slammed garage door still echoing through the house. Blinking the film from his eyes, he ignored his expensive watch and poked the face of his phone to see the time: it read eleven-thirty. He remembered briefly waking when Alicia had brought the boys home and put them to bed. He'd only cracked one eye open, hoping they would fall asleep and be quiet. Then he'd promptly fallen asleep again—the exhausted sleep of the overworked. Somehow being that tired made his solid wood desk feel comfortable. Now, looking up, he realized that the screen on the portable computer read, "Timed Out – Disconnected". The wine in the half full glass sat next to his hand. A saliva oval, where his mouth had rested, had sunk into one of the pages below his face. He could hear Tracie going up the stairs to the bedroom.

Giving up on finding a connection to Hunt, he remembered that he'd groggily turned to searching the government archives and public domain for OPOV security references and inferences. Yawning more and more often during his search, he'd come up with little more than the overblown political rhetoric and public hoopla that surrounded any government program. He found a lot of bloggers whining about "big government," or "privacy implications" in both new and saved links, but no unusual information.

Numerous texts droned on about the missteps of previous administrations, and how, as the information age took hold, the government of the United States continually implemented and then retreated from problem-laden programs. Most writings focused on apocalyptic consequences, extravagant overspending, and "pork barrel" appropriations. Others discussed public election debacles, or theorized alternative approaches to democratic processes and programs. Most of what Robert found was typical of the battleground between self-professed "conservatives" and so-called "liberals," with a dash of political academia and lobbying added for spice.

The compilation only emphasized why the public had embraced the idea of OPOV. As economic conditions had worsened, and the divide in party politics had ignored the average citizen, the people had lost trust in the representative voting process. They became anxious for a change. OPOV offered One Person, One Vote on an Internet-based user interface, with a government-controlled, dedicated electronic communications backbone for best-in-class security. In addition to local and state votes, federal voting would be conducted on the system, and delegation actions such as the archaic and political favor-laden Electoral College would be abolished in favor of each citizen's choice. The reality of every vote counting in the election of the President would be achievable.

In fact, each vote and each election would be more accessible, and more accountable. The program would streamline a number of government intermediaries by dispensing with them. It was a rare moment of both parties having desires align in the reality of reducing unnecessary government, while allowing each citizen to be heard.

Of course there had been obstacles. Voting through delegates or the Electoral College had been created to tackle the issues of a widespread public lacking timely access to voting centers and the country's leaders, the problem of illiterate citizenry and common language issues, and the impracticality of leaving farms and businesses for political matters, as well as slow or nonexistent communications. While these issues had, for the most part, been conquered in U.S. society, the Electoral college and delegates had no wish to lose the benefits of their positions—and those who appointed them were loath to lose the leverage and reward system. Politicians had mounted fear campaigns against OPOV, and decried its reliability, but the idea of seeing each vote become more meaningful, and thereby holding politicians more directly responsible for their representation had won out. Immediately the system in DC had begun to see changes, including lobbyists' attention being redirected to the public.

In President Baxter's Senatorial campaign, he'd declared that politicians were not the solution. He'd sought to change the role of government, touting a reduction in federal and state governments alike. He had surrounded himself with young visionaries, as well as established scholars, who worked jointly on rebuilding the role of government. They concluded that installing a structure, which would give people the power to choose how they would be governed, was not only necessary, but also possible. They had come up with the simple and brilliant OPOV.

For the Internet "connected" public, the promise of One Person, One Vote was an addictive drug of power and participation. It was the ultimate social media, and an expression of narcissism. OPOV was the opiate voters could not resist. They couldn't see the implication of responsibility that came with it; they only saw the ability to be heard. They eagerly voted for Tom Baxter, the man who would make them the most important American voters in history.

Action had followed the Senator's induction as President. Once the software had been put in place, regional tests of OPOV had been flawless. The software was still in beta-mode, but the national trial was now at hand. It was to be tested on a minor bill currently before the Senate. The issue itself, although relatively insignificant, would affect each voting district in the country. Everyone would have easy access to consistent voting methods and measurement. It was the first chance to see if it was truly workable to have the people actively participate in legislation. The operation had been running smoothly to this point.

Robert's long trail of distracted thinking was suddenly snapped in two.

"Robert!" Tracie's voice broke in from the hall. "Be a dear, and unload the car for me. I've just got to change out of this dress." Her voice trailed off as she climbed back up the stairs, still talking. "Tonight went beautifully. Everything came together so well. Did Alicia get the boys back? Are they tucked in, and asleep? I wonder if they had a good..."

He couldn't hear the rest, as her voice trailed off somewhere in the house. He sat up with some difficulty, shaking off the effects of the awkward nap and wiping off the wet side of his mouth. The car trunk was probably full of table ornaments or place cards. Mementos that dignitaries wanted to keep, but felt too important to handle themselves. The custom was to discreetly ask the hostess to send the object to them. Tracie always had a load of this stuff to mail.

"Yes, your Highness." He muttered as he stood slowly, feeling the stiffness still in his neck. The imperious air Tracie carried after these events irritated him. The good news was that they'd both drop into bed soon, and he wouldn't have to deal with it for long. Opening the trunk he found four hideous table centerpieces and a dirty dinner plate. With a sigh of resignation, the acting Deputy Attorney General of the United States of America began unloading the collected junk. It was a great way to spend a Friday night. Just as he finished unloading, he remembered he'd forgotten his promise to pick up the laundry and make Tracie's car appointment.

Chapter 12

Blair's dark eyes peered through the night vision binoculars, watching the women's dormitory. The grounds were quiet. The darkness was broken here and there by a few lights, bleaching the landscape beneath them, and shining over Utah's crystalline snow.

Blair's phone alarm chimed and he lowered the glasses. He spoke clearly to the two young looking men sitting behind him in the car. "Seven. She should be heading back from dinner. The kid in the adjoining room will be going to her evening yoga class. Follow the plan. Improvise only if necessary. Got it?"

"Yes, Sir." The men answered.

"I don't want any deviations. You two make sure you fit in. This is going to go quickly, and quietly. I want to see smooth execution."

"Yes, Sir." The two men exited the car. The fuse for the interior lights had been removed, making their departure from the car virtually unnoticeable. As they walked past a small U-Haul truck, they appeared indistinguishable from the other college students coming and going from the dorm. Their ski parkas, jeans, and general attitudes fit the scene. The Friday evening activity was light. Students not already on dates or leaving for parties were holed up in their rooms with computers and televisions.

Another man inside the lobby doors at the main corridor pathway stayed in Blair's view. He, too, was dressed like the dorm kids. Leaning against a wall just inside the main lobby door, he seemed to be waiting for a ride. His backpack sat on the concrete garbage receptacle nearby.

Two minutes later he picked up the backpack, following the girl headed to yoga class. His job was to make sure she didn't return unexpectedly.

Blair watched as his two other operatives timed their entry with that of an arriving coed. They passed through the pitifully inadequate security with her, holding the door for their unwitting accomplice after she punched in the dorm code. Good move, thought Blair. She'll think they're nice Mormon boys. He turned over the engine, rolling slowly toward the U-Haul, keeping his car's lights turned off.

Christen sat at her desk in her room. The frosty air falling off the windows made the floor cold, but her burley wool hiking socks were cozy. She tapped a pencil to her music mix as she tried to get into reading her class assignment. The room around her lacked personality. She was new at the school, and so far she'd only collected some candles, mugs, and a poster for décor. The orange and yellow retro beanbag chair was her pride and joy.

There was a scratching at the door, almost a metal sound, but it was so faint it didn't capture Christen's attention. Her ear buds were playing loudly, drowning out the noise of typical dorm activity. Christen didn't react at all as the door handle turned and the latch clicked open. She noticed the door swinging open from the corner of her eye. Thinking she must have left it unlocked, she wondered which friend was dropping by. She turned, smiling, and saw the two young men walk in, quickly and quietly.

The smile dropped from her face as she jerked up from her seat. Her chair rocked back on two legs, threatening to crash to the floor, as she asked, "Who are you?" She could tell from their faces that this was no "friend of a friend" drop-in surprise. One man clamped his hand to her mouth, locking his shockingly strong arm around her. The other swiftly closed the door, then deftly moved to catch Christen's chair, setting it upright.

Christen spun on the ball of her left foot and brought her right knee up sharply into her assailant's groin. It had no effect against his protective cup. It did affect his reaction to her. Her quick spin had placed her face to face with him. His arm behind her clamped down hard across the base of her shoulder blades, pinning one of her arms. His free hand grabbed her by the hair and crushed her face into his chest.

Christen flailed at his back and legs with her free hand and feet, but she was too close to strike hard, and she couldn't reach up to attack his face.

"I see you've had some training." He whispered into her ear. "So have I." Yanking her hair and head back harshly to the point where her throat could barely draw breath, he pulled her neck ever so slightly further backwards, his eyes burning down at hers. Her air was cut off and her knees buckled and bent under the pressure. "Now, Miss Torrance, you need to listen to what I'm going to tell you." Christen's eyes widened in pain. His partner grabbed her hands and pulled them behind her with a twist of her elbows.

A weak gasp came from her collapsed throat.

"We're not here to hurt you." He continued in a quiet, deliberate tone. "Cooperate, and we won't have to. We're going to walk with you outside, and put you into a car. You're going to walk normally, and say nothing. You will hold my hand, and this gentleman will hold your shoulder. We will not hesitate to hurt you if you cause trouble. If you behave you will be brought back very soon, as if nothing ever happened. Nod if you understand."

The severe angle of her neck continued to cut off Christen's air. She could hardly do more than grunt. Christen nodded as much as she could, her eyes tearing.

"Fine. I'm going to slowly relax my grip, and I don't want you to make a sound. Don't move. I don't want to even hear you breathe." As he raised her head, he pressed his forehead into hers, staring into her eyes. "Understand?"

Again Christen tried to nod.

"Good." He slowly let go of her hair as he moved his head away. "Put on your shoes, coat, and gloves, and we'll go." His harsh eyes contradicted his youthful face, making him look severe in the fluorescent lighting.

When he loosened his grip and let her go, Christen made a lunge for the door. Instantly she felt the air knocked out of her, and her body thrust backward into the other man. The lightning fast impact against her sternum left her helpless, her breath coming in short spasms. Her legs lost all strength, and she sagged.

"That was the last chance you get, Miss Torrance. Next time you won't leave here standing up." The other man pulled her back and down into her chair as she collapsed. She gave no resistance as he put on her shoes and pushed her into her coat.

Christen was no longer fighting back. She did as she was told. She walked beside the first man, her hand held in his strong grip, as his partner followed behind her down the stairs with one hand clamped on her shoulder. The light blue sedan sat almost invisibly under the deep shadows. The two men took Christen to it, opened the door, and pushed her into the front passenger seat. Deftly, they used two plastic tie wraps to bind her hands together behind her and then a third around a rope secured about the seat. Fastening the seat belt across her chest they acknowledged a nod from Blair and stepped back, closing the door.

Blair calmly jabbed the needle of a small syringe into her left thigh. Her weak scream faded as the warm drug swept through her body. Her head rocked backward and she was out.

The sedan pulled away without lights. Blair left them off until he was out of view of the dorm. Christen's abductors went back into the dorm, quickly and efficiently removing all of Christen's belongings from her room, and loading them into the U-Haul. All the surfaces in her room were wiped clean. The key to the door was left sitting on the desk.

Lew checked his watch, and left the corridor outside the yoga class. He headed toward the Student Union building's coffee house and one of the Internet terminals. He had Christen's official forms ready to transmit from her e-mail account to student housing and the administration, explaining her departure and directing applicable refunds to her accounts. There was an e-mail thanking the Residence Advisor for her time, and a few to new acquaintances.

No one would miss the quiet freshman. The grey days of winter were a common time for homesickness to set in. Her departure would be attributed to the all too common "winter blues" that regularly affected new students.

Blair headed down Foothill Drive, away from the University of Utah, taking care to not ride alongside another car, or to get caught next to a vehicle at a light. The slow, cautious driving looked normal on the slick, frosted roads.

They were well beyond Salt Lake City, and headed east on I-80 when Christen slowly began to regain consciousness. "Why are you doing this?" Christen's voice was thick and garbled. Drool oozed from her lips, and water pooling in her eyes blurred her vision. "Why?" She couldn't maintain her thoughts, and drifted back into the drugged sleep.

Blair ignored her, watching the road as he drove.

Despite the snow and ice, the drive time was under an hour and a half. They'd traveled a little over fifty miles. Christen's hands had long since lost their feeling. She had been leaning against them the whole trip, the plastic straps biting into her delicate wrists. She had become half-conscious a few more times, but her unintelligible protests were ignored until she kicked at Blair sluggishly with her foot. His response was to stop the car and put a strap around her ankles.

Nearing a side road outside of Henefer, Blair dropped the car's speed, and switched off his headlights before making the turn and approaching a small cabin. He also flipped a switch that deactivated the brake lights as he drove. He proceeded slowly, using the moonlight to judge the road's edge through the blanket of snow. Nothing but trees surrounded three sides of the cabin. The trees extended for more than a quarter of a mile, but Blair moved toward the building cautiously just the same. It was dark and tiny. No sign of life came from it. Even when Blair stopped by the door and it opened, no light shone outward. A large woman with black hair stepped out and opened the car door. Without a word, she released Christen's safety belt, pushed the girl forward, and with a pair of dikes clipped off the tie wrap that held Christen to the seat. Pushing her arm in between Christen's elbow and body, she pulled the girl up and yanked her bodily from the car. Christen's tied feet dropped to the ground. Noticing the bound legs, the woman shoved Christen into the snow. She then turned to push the car door quietly, but solidly shut. Christen watched through her blurry eyes as the car pulled away, snow crystals flying into her face from the tires. The woman dragged her into the cabin, her ankles banging against the threshold.

It was pitch dark inside. Christen couldn't see a thing, but her captor seemed to know exactly where she was going, and what she was doing. Christen could feel the warmth of a heater, the soft cushions of a low couch or futon and the cold steel of a handcuff on her right wrist snapping shut. The plastic tie wraps about her wrists were now completely clipped off and her arms fell forward to her sides.

A strangled scream gushed from Christen's throat as her cramped shoulders seem to pop out of their sockets, and the blood rushed into her released wrists. The woman ignored her groans.

"Why are you doing this?" Christen asked. She was recovering from the drug rapidly now. The shock of snow and cold air outside had snapped her awake.

A surprisingly soft voice responded from the dark. "Sit still."

Christen's tangled feet awkwardly crossed each other as the strap around her ankles bit in. She could see the woman's silhouette as she approached the open door and closed it. When she switched on the lights, Christen's startled eyes had trouble adjusting.

"What are you doing to me? What did I do?" Christen began sobbing uncontrollably.

The woman's short jet-black hair sat unkempt on her head, her clean pale skin gave a startling background to her dark brown, almost black eyes and heavy eyebrows. Looking directly at Christen, she said in that eerily soft voice, "You'll be staying here until a job is finished, then you'll be released. You will call me Mary. I will call you Christen. You will sit or sleep where you are sitting. The chain will give you plenty of movement between here and the bathroom." Christen looked toward the bathroom and saw that the door was open, or that it might have been removed.

"Pay attention!" Mary's change in voice tone snapped Christen's attention back, as Mary's hand grabbed her jaw and twisted her head back to face her. Mary let go of her face, and continued, "If you feel the need to exercise you may use that bicycle machine. If you cooperate, you may use the TV. Your chain won't reach my bed or the kitchen, only this room and the bathroom. I am a talented fighter. I can give you real pain without damage, so don't test me." Mary leaned down, her face closing in on Christen as she raised her right arm. With a lightning fast blow from the heel of her hand, she hit Christen solidly at the base of her sternum.

Christen was launched backward into the sofa cushion, her breath gone once again. It seemed impossible to catch. As she sat there gasping for air that would not come, Mary stood up tall, this time with what seemed to Christen a demonic smile of pleasure.

"Do you understand now?"

Christen frantically nodded her head as her gaping mouth clawed at the air for breath.

"Good. We'll work out the finer points of living together later."

Chapter 13

"Good evening, Bernard."

"Good evening, Senator. I trust the day went well."

Senator Gregg handed his overcoat and hat to his butler. "It was excellent, thank you. The dinner was successful." His gloating smile indicated he'd had a sumptuous meal laced with deal making that had been particularly in his favor.

"Would the Senator care for a drink this evening?"

Gregg briefly glanced at the aging butler. "Yes. Any messages?"

"Yes, Sir." Bernard turned to the antique hat stand and raised a small silver tray. It held a heavy glass of expensive single malt Scotch, and a small piece of white paper folded in half. Turning back to the Senator, he offered the contents of the tray. "Your room is prepared, as well, Sir," he commented in his very precise British accent.

A satisfied smile came over the Senator's face as he picked up the glass and note. After reading the note, he placed it back onto the tray. It was from his wife, Evelyn.

"Tell Mrs. Gregg I will be flying out to the ranch next Friday for the weekend. I'll see her at the airport. Please give her my flight schedule."

"Very good, Sir."

The Senator turned. Leaving the elliptical entryway, he headed up the curved wood and iron stairs to the bedrooms of his impressive townhouse.

"Will that be all, Sir?" Bernard asked from the entry.

"I'm not sure, Bernard," Gregg called over his shoulder. "I'll ring if I need you." With that, the conversation ended. Bernard watched as the Senator slowly scaled the finely finished stairs, framed by the delicate, ornamentally carved wood wall panels. Putting the silver tray back on the stand and checking the locks on the heavy mahogany side lighted beveled-glass entry door, Bernard proceeded to the stainless steel and marble trimmed kitchen in the back. He shredded the note into ever-shrinking, precise halves between his fingers as he walked.

Finally upstairs, Gregg took a deep breath and pushed open the door to the master bedroom. It had been remodeled into a suite with an opulent bath, keeping as much of the historic Federalist high styling as possible. The home had been finished in several different period styles, as each section had been added to the original building with its own character. Antiques filled every room, sitting on tapestry rugs and framed by heavy brocade drapes wherever the style permitted. The townhouse bedroom was trimmed with dark woods, ornamental plaster, brass, opulent materials, and deep green leathers. Old aromatic cigar smoke and cedar sticks from the fireplace filled the air. The room was dimly lit, with only firelight and a patch of hall light flowing in from the door and its Palladian transom. Pulling off his coat, Gregg hung it on a brass valet stand in the corner.

"Mr. Senator." A sultry voice wafted from the shadowy far corner of the room. A statuesque woman stepped forward.

Gregg, without turning, switched on a green glass floor lamp that added a glow to the room. He began pulling off his tie. "Are you ready for me?" He turned to look at her.

"I've been waiting for a man like you all my life." She said huskily.

Turning his head to the side, he looked her up and down, memorizing every curve and texture. She was very tall, perhaps five-foot eleven, with a magnificent figure of curves. Her full, shapely hips rose to a small waist. Smooth, tapered legs looked unbearably long on top of four-inch heels, and the tops of her black, lace-trimmed stockings could be seen through the high slits on either side of her long black satin gown.

"How are you this evening?" he asked her.

"Wonderful now, Senator." She smiled. "I always feel good around a powerful man."

Gregg smiled. Moving over to the big green leather wingback chair, he sat down. Years ago, he had been a football athlete, but his two hundred and eighty pounds were no longer distributed nicely across the shoulders, legs or arms of his six-one frame. Good living and better scotch had taken their toll, and provided him with a substantial girth.

The woman came toward his chair, slowly pulling a strap of her gown off each shoulder as she walked. The thin satin slid gracefully down her body, gliding softly over each curve, caressing her full breasts and erect nipples as it slipped silently to the floor.

She moved closer, her breasts pressing toward him. They were perfectly round, almost too perfect. The Senator liked them that way. Sliding her hands up the sides of her naked body, she ran her fingers up through her elegant champagne blonde hair, emphasizing its shimmering glint in the light. Pulling her hair back, she shook it as though she were in a shampoo commercial. Her breasts hardly moved, and his eyes never moved from them.

Stepping out of the black gown lying around her high heels, she bent over and placed her hands on his thighs, kneeling down in front of him. She looked up for a moment, her light, almost gold colored eyes daring him to look up from her breasts. Resting one on each of his knees, she slid her hands up to his belt and began to unbuckle the Spanish leather. He didn't move to help her. He liked watching her struggle with his pants and silk boxers. Slouching back into the chair he gave her full access to his body. As the woman went to work on him, he congratulated himself on deciding months ago that this one would be worth having for a return visit.

The phone on the table next to the chair toned quietly with the sound of a fine chime. He reached over to it and answered. "Yes?" The girl never broke stride.

"Everything is complete." The deep voice responded.

"No problem with the package?" Gregg asked somewhat more attentively.

"None," came the answer.

"Good." Gregg hung up the phone. Placing his hands on the woman's head, he thrust his fingers into her hair, pulling her face up to look at him. Then he pushed her head forward again. "Now where was I? Oh, yes, you were showing me how you love powerful men."

Chapter 14

It was six a.m. and dark when Robert's alarm went off. Tracie stayed in bed, and so did the boys. The boys had the day off from school, and Tracie was planning a spa day with a girlfriend.

After showering, Robert headed downstairs to the kitchen where he turned on the espresso machine. While the unit heated up, he mixed a chocolate protein shake. He used too little water and had to choke down the thick shake along with a handful of assorted vitamins. He went back to the espresso machine, dropped in a "pod" of ground espresso and watched the machine exude the dark liquid with its rim of crema. Another "pod," this time of milk, was placed in the machine. The machine went through another heating cycle, then Robert hit the steaming button. The machine was quick and easy, and the pods were a high-end version of cheaper, more popular machine-cups, but as Robert sipped the drink he thought the flavor was flat.

He watched a couple of minutes of recorded stock market news recorded on the DVR, then went back upstairs to dress. With one last check of hair and attire, Robert left the bathroom. Seeing Tracie's hand emerge from the bed covers he went over and mechanically kissed the hand goodbye. Then he turned off the hallway light as he left, and was on his way well before seven.

The weekend had gone by rapidly. Tracie had gone to a dinner at the Kennedy center, leaving at two-thirty Saturday afternoon to make sure everything was perfect. Robert had not seen her again until she woke him up getting into bed late that night. Sunday Robert had worked in the home office while Tracie took the boys to some activities and shopping—a rare occurrence since they'd hired Alicia. Occasional bursts of noise from the family's pit stops and uniform changes at the house broke the silence, and distracted Robert from his overflowing desk. Busy as he had been, both days left Robert largely bored. In a way, Robert welcomed the return of his weekday routine. At least his weekday irritations were interesting.

Monday morning's traffic was lighter than usual. Robert arrived at Grady's favorite coffee house around seven-fifteen.

Now Robert sat fiddling with a latte, wishing he'd ordered a mocha instead. The sugar would have given him a boost. The serotonin bump from the chocolate wouldn't have hurt, either.

He had chosen a stool at the counter that lined the front window. From there he could watch the parking lot, and not miss Grady. He clutched his latte a little tighter. It had turned bitterly cold overnight, sinking below twenty degrees. Winter was in full swing outside, and the cold created a draft that seemed to roll in waves down the window onto his hands. Right now anything hot felt good. He bought a low-fat raspberry muffin, which he ate too fast. He toyed with the paper it came in, and the idea of getting another, but gave it up in favor of keeping his carbohydrates in line.

One caffeine addict after another came into the coffee bean den. Customers arrived with mixed expressions. Some looked grouchy or angry; others seemed irritated or sleepy. A few looked hopefully toward their temple of the caffeine god for deliverance. Those leaving with their treasure caressed it like a lover. The relief and gleeful smiles on their lips were universal. Even before the first taste, the drug's effect was clearly visible.

Robert picked up his phone and punched in Chris' cell number, as he'd done half a dozen times over the weekend. There was still no answer. Chris hadn't said when he'd send the information, but Robert was getting impatient. Chris' assertions had been bothering him all weekend. Why would Chris contact him if the need wasn't immediate? He'd assumed that Chris would be sending the "proof" right away. Looking at his watch he realized how early it was, but he was still bugged about Chris not calling.

His attention turned back to the door. Not given to paranoia, Robert only occasionally became aware of the vulnerability of his position in government, and the possible dangers he might encounter. In some foreign countries a man in his position would have several bodyguards. In the U.S. Robert was considered to be comparatively safe. He hadn't thought much about hanging out in this crowded place, or whom he might run into, but the incessant flow of people began to make him uncomfortable. Who could tell if these people were nuts for coffee, or just nuts? Worse, they could be lobbyists. He did his best to avoid them. There was a guy in the corner who had arrived shortly after Robert, and was taking way too long to drink his coffee, but then, so was Robert. There was a college-age girl frantically texting on her phone, and a salesman-type working on his laptop. Robert's fingers began tapping the counter.

Out of the corner of his eye he spotted a uniform. Grady was heading in from the parking lot. His long stride was athletic and self-assured. He burst through the door with an air of extreme familiarity. With a simple wave and acknowledgement from the barista, his order was placed and brewing.

"Good morning, Barry!" Grady called to the man who had worried Robert. Barry raised his mug, but not his head. The colonel looked around the room and spotted Robert. "Well, good morning, Mr. Carlton. Decided to return to the embrace of my favorite coffee haunt?" With two long strides Grady stood next to Robert and was shaking his hand warmly. Grady was tall. His uniform fit impeccably over his fit build, and his dark skin appeared young and firm. He had a look that instantly attracted women. It attracted men, too, but for different reasons. He was pleasing to the eye, likable, and confident. Robert had many friends and associates, but none of them had a universal appeal like Grady. The guy had charisma.

"Good morning to you, too, Grady. And what's with the 'Mr. Carlton' routine?" Robert tried to emulate Grady's warm enthusiasm. He wanted to set a casual tone to the conversation.

"Just respecting the office, Robert. May I join you?" Grady asked.

"I wish you would." Robert gestured to the stool next to him.

Grady smiled as he sat down. "It's been a long time, Robert. How are you enjoying the job?"

"It has its challenges and rewards," Robert answered carefully. "And you?"

"Outstanding... Where's that espresso?" Grady looked over his shoulder. "Slow this morning." Turning back to face Robert he asked, "Good latte?"

"Fine; thanks," Robert responded, wondering how to begin explaining his request to Grady.

"'Fine?' They use the best beans here! They're great! I'll have them make you a better one." Grady turned and raised his hand but before he could speak, Robert grabbed his arm and pulled it down.

"No, really, it's great." Robert turned the stool to face Grady more directly. "Frankly, I was hoping you would come here this morning. I tried your office Friday, and you weren't in. Rather than leave a message, I thought I might find you here." He felt awkward. He still wasn't sure how to present his query to Grady.

Grady cocked an eyebrow at Robert. "Well, you were right, but it must be important to go through that much trouble."

"It is, but there are too many people here. I'd rather discuss this in a less congested environment."

Grady reached up to grab his 'eye opener' from the girl who had hand-delivered the libation. Grady's to-go cup contained four shots of espresso with a splash of milk and froth. It came with a particularly enthusiastic smile from the attractive barista. "Thanks, Beth," Grady said. Taking a big gulp, he let out a satisfied, "Ahhh, delicious!" She laughed, turned, and almost skipped back to her duties.

"I'd like to find that less busy location now, Grady," Robert said in a low voice, staring hard at Grady. Grady's surprise momentarily quelled the pleased expression on his face. He stared back at Robert for a moment. "Okay. You've got my attention. You've also got me wondering why you didn't go through channels." He said, gravity creeping into his voice.

"Can we just get out of here?" Robert looked around, feeling ridiculously paranoid. "How about we go to your car?"

"Sure." Taking another swig of his hot coffee, Grady slid his stool back noisily and stood up. "Let's go."

"What about the check?" Robert asked.

"I have an account." Grady pulled the keys to his Jeep Cherokee out of his pocket, and marched through the door.

The alarm "cheeped" as he deactivated it and jumped into the 4X4 SUV. He started the engine as Robert got in the other side.

Robert put on his safety belt while Grady stacked old coffee cups to make room for the new one in the cup holder.

"Where to?" asked Grady, glancing at Robert.

"Around the block." Robert looked around the parking lot as they left.

"Okay... so, you want to tell me what this is all about, Robert?"

Robert took a breath, and launched into his speech with less finesse than he'd intended. "I need you to check out something for me, Grady. I need to know if there is a way to break into the OPOV system; to compromise it, or control it."

"We already did that report, Robert. Every agency in the government did one." Grady looked slightly bemused at Robert's request. "Hell, you're more in-the-loop than I am. You have all those reports. What's up? You don't need me to track down information you've already got. What do you really need?"

Robert sighed. He wasn't handling this well. Grady had seen right through him. "You're right, those reports are fine. That's not what I need."

"I didn't think so," Grady said, cocking an eyebrow at Robert. "Are you going to tell me what is?"

"I need you to look at it again, unofficially." Robert mustered up his most commanding posture. He knew what he was asking could put Grady in a tight spot, but he needed Grady to agree to do it. "I need to know if our own agencies can break the system from inside."

Grady gritted his teeth, the muscles under his smooth, dark skin flexing back and forth. "So, what you want to know is whether any branch, CIA, FBI, NSA, Military, whoever, could break in and modify OPOV, or worse, use legitimate access to compromise it? You know we checked that already, too, Robert." Grady looked over at him, his brows drawn together, and his deep brown eyes searching Robert's. "We checked all security breach scenarios. And it's the NSA's and FBI's job to do that."

Robert felt frustrated. He was communicating badly. He was also beginning to think he might have to tell Grady more than he'd intended. "What I'm trying to say is, if someone on the inside intended to compromise the system, or was attempting to make it easy to do so later, could they? Could you spot it if they had already succeeded?" Robert looked forward, avoiding Grady's eyes. "If the NSA, for example, had done it, they wouldn't say so in their own report, would they?"

"You're kidding, right?" Grady asked in disbelief. Robert didn't answer. "You're suggesting...no...testing the idea that there could be espionage from the inside; probably with multiple layers of conspirators, and no checks or balances stopping it because the infiltration is internal. You want me to figure out how they could do it from out here?"

"I'm not asking you to break into the system. All I need to know is, theoretically, if it can be broken into, changed, or controlled in any way from the inside without anyone finding out." Robert held his breath for a second, then released it. "Grady, I need to know if the vote can be rigged by somebody on the inside. And if it can, is the system set up in such a way that no one will ever know that it happened?"

"You think someone is trying to do that?" Grady was incredulous and perplexed.

Robert paused just a fraction of a second too long. "No, I just need to know if it can be done. If it's possible, then..." Robert didn't quite know where to end that sentence.

"OK, easy answer. Anything is possible. You happy now?" Grady pulled back into the coffee place's parking lot.

"All right," Robert realized he should have seen that coming. What he really wanted was an answer from Grady that would convince him Chris was wrong. The only way to get that would be to explore every possibility. He thought for a minute before going on. "The system is as good as we can make it. The reports said so. So what are the best ways to break in, internally? Can you tell me that?"

"Sure, I can give you a list of the best methods. Everyone who's seen a movie knows most of them. So do the guys who built the OPOV safeguards. You just can't do it with so much security, and so many people watching the system. Not unless you're James Bond."

"Fine, give me that list, and I'll start there. But I need you to help me check this system out, Grady. I need you to go deeper. I need you to assume someone has already succeeded. I have some information that I have to check out, but it has to be kept quiet."

Grady took a moment, then asked, "So if you think someone has already done it, why can't this be an official investigation?"

"If everyone knows we're looking, they will shut it down. They'll wait until we aren't looking anymore." That was more than Robert planned to say.

"So, it's already been done. Or you think it might have been." Grady looked as unhappy as he now felt. "That's reasonable, I suppose," he said slowly. "If there is an insider compromising the system, an investigation would tip them off. All right. I've got a few contacts. I'll check it out for you, Robert, but don't expect me to go too far without this thing becoming official. I'll do what I can." Grady knew that snooping around wasn't likely to achieve anything but resentment and suspicion from other departments. He might not be able to keep his research quiet. Even if he was extremely discreet someone was bound to notice.

"Okay if I tell my boss I'm doing a project for the AG office?" Grady continued. "He won't ask questions. He just likes to keep track of resources, and set priorities if something hits his desk."

"Sure, and thanks." Robert stepped out of the car.

"Hey, how should I get a hold of you?" Grady asked.

"Don't. I'll call you." Robert, paused, rethinking that idea. "Wait—on second thought, here's my cell number." He wrote it on the back of his card and handed it to Grady. He turned and walked off toward his car, leaving Grady staring after him.

Flipping over the card, Grady read the number. He wondered if Robert's promotion was going to his head, and if he was just flexing a little muscle. "Give a guy a big title…" Grady muttered, shaking his head. Yanking the steering wheel, he pulled the jeep out of the parking spot.

Chapter 15

Robert got back in his car, started the engine, and clicked on the heated seat. Winter was two days old, and he was already tired of being cold.

Robert had thought that talking to Grady would make him feel as though Chris was suffering paranoid delusions, but he realized that the conversation had provided the opposite effect. The idea of OPOV being compromised from the inside was beginning to sound all too possible. He started driving but changed his mind about going to the office. Instead, he headed for the Treasury Building.

Pulling into the secure underground parking of the Treasury, he flashed his ID, but the guard wanted a closer look, plus a second form of ID. Then he wanted to look in the back seat and trunk, examining every inch of the car.

"Thank you, Mr. Carlton. Visitor parking is on your left after the first turn." He said, finally waving him in.

"Thank you." Robert's tone was acerbic. Once again the delay of his promotion irked him. He was sure that if he'd received the title, his treatment would have been different. Out of sheer obstinacy he pulled into a space reserved for special visitors, marked only as "Reserved B".

Getting through building security was quicker. He arrived on the second floor without running into anyone he knew. He was avoiding the big brass on this trip, hoping for some information from the trenches.

The outside of the imposing Treasury building was designed to instill confidence, respect and awe. Inside was a different story. The second floor had a few bits of woodwork, narrow, vinyl-clad halls, and small offices. The building was worn and out of date. It was a remnant of a long gone federal spending spree from a forgotten administration. Robert found the office he was looking for, rapping twice on the door before opening it.

Phil Davidson sat surrounded by stacks of paper on his desk. The paperwork was arranged to form paths on the floor. His office had become a rabbit warren of reports and printouts, overwhelming the shelves, desk, floor, and even the chairs. Robert expected to see the file cabinets burst open at any moment. It was one of the largest offices in the building, but entirely claustrophobic.

Phil looked up at the sound of Robert's knock. "Mr. Carlton," he acknowledged, setting aside some paperwork he'd been reading. "Come in, please."

Phil's dull brown sweater covered most of an ancient beige knit tie. His graying hair had thinned long ago. Permanently pale skin and reading glasses completed a scholarly, if somewhat shabby picture. The intellectual vibe was very much in character with his personality, but his dress and office suggested a lack of interest in everything else.

Phil's appearance and office didn't match his spotless record. He had numerous awards, probably buried somewhere beneath the office clutter. Phil had a low political profile, but was a key go-to guy at the Treasury. His plain demeanor hid a "can do" attitude. He had been a field officer when he was younger. These days he was more of a living archive and think-tank information disseminator. His opinion was sought as much as any presidential advisor, yet he was unassuming and approachable. Phil was also blunt. It was part of his non-political personality. "What can Treasury do for the Justice Department, today?" he queried.

"Right to the point, aren't you, Phil?" Robert said appreciatively. "I need to ask you a couple of questions."

"Sure, fire away," Phil responded.

Robert grabbed a stack of reports off the guest chair, and set them on the nearest pile. Phil watched each motion, mentally cataloging the new file location. Robert pulled the chair closer before sitting down, his shoes bumping the next stack of papers.

"You remember our discussions about jurisdiction and OPOV, right?"

"Of course...I still think that the Secret Service holds..."

Robert held up his hand, deciding to get straight to his question. "Yes, I wasn't going there. What I was working up to was: if a department wanted to monitor the system, how would they go about it?"

"Hmm...the first step should be to contact the responsible agency, but we never resolved that completely, did we?" Phil asked.

"No, too many people wanted a piece of the pie, and got it. Oversight by committee." Robert was not a big fan of the Commission's result of compromising on dotted line management. Progress sometimes required concessions and sharing, but their decision had left the ultimate responsibility for OPOV to a diverse committee.

"Well," Phil continued, "I would say they should go to your department to cover their legal ass, and then tap into everything that could be construed as public. If they want to go deeper on monitoring, I'd guess they should go to the House Committee on Oversight and Government Reform, or to each individual State Board of Elections. They could also go through channels and request the NSA's statistical reports on a regular basis. If you wanted to personally monitor the system, you'd have to be part of the Oversight Committee."

"I was thinking of getting further into the nuts and bolts of the system." Robert pressed.

"Well, now you'd be talking software and the actual development group. I think for security issues you'd have to be going into the system past the firewalls, and getting into the software code. No agency would do that. It would cross the NSA's boundaries for encryption. The military has that expertise, but under normal circumstances, and unless formally asked to do so, they wouldn't go near the actual system code—if for no other reason than it would introduce security issues. In order to monitor, there would have to be data exported, and that means another open port. That means more potential flaws and access points. It just wouldn't be smart."

"Okay, instead of monitoring the system, how about testing the system? Would you use the same techniques needed for hacking-in?" Robert probed. Phil's responses were helping him think this thing through. He was mentally thumbing through other possibilities as Phil spoke.

"Sure, if the purpose was to test external security protection and resilience. The usual thorough vector testing used on the software during development is built from the inside out, acting like a hacker works from the outside in. But those tests have been done in excruciating detail. There are always experts testing by trying to break in—and before you ask, we don't simply test our own work and call it good. Neither does the NSA. Everyone has a separate 'third eye' looking for weaknesses."

"Of course," Robert said reassuringly. He knew he could easily tread on some nerves here. This kind of thing gave Treasury people nightmares, even as it ignited passion for their jobs. He leaned back in his chair, trying to look more relaxed. "I'm just performing a final check on all the possibilities. Devil's advocate; it's my job, you know." Robert conjured up his most casual smile.

"Right." Phil's demeanor relaxed. "I don't think we need to worry," he added. The wheels of Phil's mind were turning, though; he was still considering the question.

The two men sat quietly thinking. Phil spoke first.

"If I were an adversary, I'd try to buy somebody at NSA, and get in that way. It sounds a little like cold war era spy tactics, but that would be the easiest way to get into the system. If you couldn't buy someone outright, you could get a little treachery going by calling in a favor on some seemingly simple grey-area request, then impose some blackmail to get into the system. Then you could falsify vote results, or flood the Internet with fake votes, nullifying the actual vote count, or crashing the system and creating an invalid situation."

"You don't 'mince' words, do you, Phil?" Robert was a bit taken aback by this sudden flood of insight. "You've been thinking about this for a while."

"Devil's advocate. It's my job, too, you know." Phil smiled.

"Okay, let's go with your complete scenario." Robert leaned forward onto the arms of his chair. "I understand the spy thing, and inside manipulation through coercion. I can grasp falsifying votes, although I think ballet stuffing would be easily spotted on a recount. But what good would crashing the system do?"

"Well, if you can't swing a vote your way, the next best thing is to stop votes that are going against you. Make the vote invalid, and you give yourself time to rally favorable results." Phil smiled. "I wouldn't discount ballot stuffing. It's worked before. But each of these possibilities has already been considered. There are safeguards. You'd have to buy a lot of people at the NSA, and make sure no one investigated when the problem surfaced. I think you're wasting your time."

"Thanks, Phil. I wanted to go over this one more time, and I knew you'd be the guy to bounce it off of before we go live." Robert stood up. "After all, it's been over a year since we finalized the program. A refresher was in order." He moved over to the desk, and reached across the pile of papers to shake Phil's hand. "Good seeing you, again, Phil. Mind if I call you if another question comes up?"

"Certainly not. Please call anytime. Do you have my card?" Phil began shuffling through the piles on his desk, looking for one.

"Don't worry, I still have your card. Thanks, again." Robert stepped carefully toward the door of the office.

Phil noticed a report he had uncovered. "So, that's where that went." He sat down and began reading it avidly, forgetting Robert's presence entirely.

Robert was feeling satisfied that due diligence had been done. If he didn't get something compelling from Chris he'd probably call off Grady's research. He looked at his watch as the elevator doors closed. With a shock, he realized that the day was half over, and he still hadn't heard from Chris. He pulled out his phone, but couldn't get a signal. He would have to wait until he drove out of the garage to check for messages.

When he got to his car, he noticed a yellow paper wedged under his windshield wiper. Snatching the paper from his car, he glared at the form. It had a series of check boxes. A big black check mark was next to box number two, which read, "Illegally Parked," with an added note reading, "This parking space is reserved. Your tag matches a registered vehicle. The infraction certificate will be mailed to your immediate supervisor."

Cursing, Robert pulled out his keys and hit the button to unlock the car. In no time he was out of the garage, leaving the guard standing with a wad of yellow paper in his hand.

He pulled out his phone and pressed the button to activate the voice recognition. "Call office." It dialed.

"Hello, Mr. Carlton," Lorraine answered, noting the caller id.

"Any calls for me?" Robert asked.

"Yes, Mr. Carlton. You have two: Senator Gregg's office, and one from Mr. Hunt." She responded.

"What did Senator Gregg want?" Robert asked.

"It was his assistant. She asked that you call as soon as possible. She didn't have any more information." Lorraine sounded uncharacteristically annoyed. She didn't like having incomplete information.

"OK, connect me with the Senator." Robert wondered what Gregg wanted. Gregg's call was timely, since he chaired the Senate Rules Committee. They had an obvious connection to the Federal

Election Commission as part of Rules Oversight. Robert decided he could use a little Q&A time with Gregg. He heard the various clicks and snippets of on-hold music, as Lorraine maneuvered past the gauntlet of secretaries and assistants that ran interference for the Senator. Navigating government offices could be a challenging business.

"Robert, are you there?" Daniel Gregg's voice boomed on the line. He sounded confident and comfortable, exactly as he did when speaking to his constituency. Gregg generated trust, sincerity, and authority with that voice. He was the kind of politician people loved, but he wielded the kind of political power that intimidated his opponents and compatriots alike. "Where are you, Son?" Gregg asked.

"I'm on a cell phone, Senator." The political world had long since learned the risks associated with wireless communications. It had become customary to warn callers. Cell phones provided great convenience, but no security.

"We need to get together. What's your schedule looking like?"

"Lorraine keeps my calendar, didn't she...?"

The Senator interrupted. "How about in forty-five minutes. My place."

Robert recognized the Senator's power play; it smacked of LBJ with his intimidatingly tall desk and short guest chairs. Robert had learned the hard way to never meet on someone else's turf— especially when unprepared with information about why a meeting was taking place. "Sorry, I'm on the wrong side of town." Robert parried. "How about halfway? Shall we say the Round Robin? I'll buy." Robert knew the Senator was a regular at the Round Robin inside the Willard Intercontinental Hotel, and a sucker for lunch when someone else was buying.

"All right, Robert, I'm happy to help out. The same forty-five minutes from now?" The Senator asked.

"See you there." Robert waited for a couple of seconds then hung up. Suddenly he had the feeling that this was all a little too convenient. Robert felt less comfortable about his research on OPOV. He dialed the office again. "Lorraine?"

"Yes, Sir." She answered.

"I'm going to meet with Senator Gregg for lunch. Anything from Chris Stoker? He was supposed to call." Robert tried to sound casual.

"No, Sir. Just Mr. Hunt, and some new calls regarding the current Supreme Court Docket." Lorraine told him.

"Thanks. Did Hunt leave a number, or say what he wanted?"

"No, Sir. He said you have his card." The note of annoyance was still in Lorraine's voice.

"Yes, that's right. I have his card in my briefcase. Thanks, Lorraine." Robert said.

Robert hung up. At the stoplight he fumbled through the pocket section of his briefcase, and found the strange card Hunt had given him. Robert figured he'd better face the music and find out what this guy was all about. He punched in the number and waited. Placing the cell phone in its cradle, he activated the car's hands-free link features. The telltale sounds of a phone transferring came over the stereo speakers.

"Mr. Hunt's office." A woman's voice answered.

"This is Robert Carlton returning Mr. Hunt's call," Robert told the voice.

"I'm sorry, Sir, but he has stepped out of the office. May I take a message?" the woman asked.

"Tell him I called. He can reach me in my office after three," Robert, annoyed, hung up before she could ask any questions. Who the hell was this guy?

Robert's drive to the Willard didn't take too long, but he'd had an odd feeling of being followed on the way there. Washington was easy to navigate between rush hours in the winter, and the hotel was close by, but he took a couple of extra turns around the block to make sure he was alone. Seeing no one behind him after the second turn, he turned back toward the Willard. As Robert pulled into the Valet parking section, he chastised himself for being paranoid. Snatching his phone back from the cradle, he gave his key to the uniformed attendant and went into the bar, briefcase in hand.

A plain brown sedan pulled up to the curb across the street. The driver watched Robert go into the hotel.

Chapter 16

Marty sat at his keyboard staring at the twenty-three-inch flat panel monitor. Displaying four normal-sized screens at once, the monitor flashed multicolored characters and graphs across the screen. Instant messages and WebEx notices from his meeting schedule nagged him from the left-hand side. His second monitor held his current project on a split screen of software and its underlying machine code. Marty leaned forward, squinting at the characters. He had a smaller, old monitor above the first, full of scrolling data from the server running a self-diagnostic. Marty had been struggling with the decision of whether to get a fourth monitor for a month. Most of the team had four, but it just seemed to make them more ADHD than they were before. Marty loved high tech stuff, but four monitors seemed to stretch the human limit.

Marty was a true geek when it came to computers. On everything else he had average interests, and average knowledge. He could talk sports, but he didn't follow particular teams or events. He liked the Olympics, but passed on most pro football games, all basketball, and baseball. Too boring. He wasn't big on yard work, car maintenance, or home repairs, either. They all fell into the "only if necessary" zone. He liked movies, a few video games, and relaxing on a warm beach once a year.

"Marty! You going to lunch?" Terri called from over the cubicle wall.

"It's cold outside." Marty answered, "I'll just grab something in the cafeteria."

"Oh, yeah. Mystery meat. How appetizing," she commented sarcastically, but with a laugh in her voice.

"It's not that bad." Marty didn't pay much attention to food. Whether the cafeteria was good or bad was irrelevant, as long as it existed.

"Oh, come on," Terri coaxed. "It'll be good to get out."

"Okay, okay." Marty didn't really care about going out, but he knew from experience that Terri wouldn't let up until he agreed. "I'll go, but no more Tex Mex, or Chinese buffet. I want something warm, with low carbs and low fat. You know...a burger with fries," he quipped, with an attempt at humor. He put his computer to sleep, activating the password lock, and stood up, while grabbing his coat. "I hate this, Terri. Fifteen minutes to check out, and twenty to check in. There's no time left for lunch. Can't you girls ever eat alone?"

"No, and it takes two of us to go to the bathroom. Now shut up, and let's go." Terri smiled at Marty. They had been lunch buddies for over a year now, but he still complained every day.

Marty huffed irritably and set a fast pace toward the door. As they passed Chris Stoker's office cubicle, Marty asked. "Where's Chris these days?"

"He went on vacation," Terri answered.

"Oh, must be nice. But he needed it. Come on, let's move it before the line starts." Marty hated the process for getting in and out of the facility. The line through security could get long. "It's bad enough going through the search without the long wait."

"I think it's kind of fun. All that touching, feeling, and looking through your clothes. It's kind of kinky." Terri's eyes sparkled with impish humor.

"You get off on the weirdest things." Marty had a hint of a smile. He wasn't oblivious to Terri's humor, or her charm. She always made his day a little more fun.

Terri had been with the NSA for eight years, but it had taken her six to get to this security level. It had taken another year to get invited to work in The Crypt. She was sharp, one of the best cryptologists around, but in The Crypt she was still considered a rookie.

They reached the aluminum and glass exit. The door, walls and ceiling were polished and buffed like a brand new airplane. Six people stood waiting.

"We're too late, Terri. This will take forever," Marty gruffed at her, turning to leave.

She grabbed him by the arm. "Come on. You can make it. It's only a couple of minutes. They're moving pretty quickly today."

They watched as the employees approached the door and the framed glass plate next to it. Placing the right hand on the plate for scanning, each person walked through the door alone. It was the first stage of "the Airlock." A handprint got you into the booth, which took a full body and retina scan before letting you go out the other side. It also scanned magnetically, and once a week, employees got reference scanned with ultrasound. If you had a new tooth filling put in, they would have to adjust your file to match before you could get through. If you failed the test, you were locked in. Security would interrogate the individual before releasing him or her. That happened to Marty about once a month. For some reason, the machine hated him.

No employee could take anything in or out. No car keys, change, wallets, belt buckles, or jewelry were allowed through the door. All of that stuff had to stay in the outside lockers. Most employees kept separate glasses for the work side, just to avoid hassles. Marty wore a belt he had modified to use Velcro instead of a metal buckle to hold up his pants. The whole thing was a pain in the butt. Plus, he had never gotten used to the guards looking at him naked. The images were much too clear for his liking. They were so clear that an electronic blur they jokingly called, "the grape leaf" had been added over the groin area. The female guards looking didn't bug him as much as the males. Terri seemed to get a kick out of it.

Terri did comment once that it was disappointing to never meet the guards who did the visual checks. They were in some back room, or maybe even in a different building. The guards by the door had other functions. The employees had no idea who saw the images, or where they were sent. "It's kind of like having your picture on the Internet," Terri said. Marty found that irritating.

Terri went first, then stood in the outside lobby waiting for Marty to come through.

"Damn thing takes longer every time," he groused.

"It does not. You just like to bitch. Here's your stuff." Terri handed Marty his keys, and wallet. Since they usually arrived at the same time and left at five on the dot, they had exchanged locker combos to speed up their departures. First one through the airlock got the personal effects.

"Thanks. Whose turn is it to buy?"

"Mine...I'll drive." Terri took the lead. Marty grimaced. She had a lead foot and the roads were slick. This was always a test of his nerves.

"I tell you what. I'll buy if you let me drive." He tried.

"Chicken. No way. You know the rules. The driver picks the place and I know just where we're going. It's something new." She had a big smile on her face.

She wasn't fooling Marty. There weren't that many restaurants within ten minutes, and even with an hour and a half lunch, time was precious. So it had to be one of the usual spots.

Terri didn't scare him too badly at first, only sliding once in the parking lot. Marty was forty-three and Terri was thirty-two—almost thirty-three, but sometimes she seemed like a teenager when driving. As she came past the last stand of trees and turned into the strip mall, Marty's life passed before his eyes. This time it wasn't from her driving. It was the "Grand Opening" banner and the name over the restaurant.

"Mongolian Fusion? Not a chance, I'm not going in there!" He wasn't sure she'd pay any attention to his protest, but he knew he didn't want to try out another stomach churning batch of weird food.

"It just opened. According to the rules I drove, and you have no choice. You set up the lunch deal."

"Well, I'm not eating anything." He insisted.

"Oh, yes, you are. Get out of the car, Marty. You'll love it." Terri slammed her car door, and crunched through the frost toward the red doors of the restaurant.

"If I die, it's your fault," Marty called after her, following.

"I'll buy you some Tums, or Geritol, or whatever," Terri called back.

"It's no joke. Wait 'til you turn forty. No spicy food without antacid pills, no spicy body without diet pills, and no spicy sex without blue pills. You'll see."

"Promises, promises." Terri giggled.

Marty was divorced, and Terri had never found her "Mr. Right." She and Marty had started this flirtatious, teasing repartee the first day they'd met, but had kept it strictly in the joking category. Marty was a little on the shy side. He was attracted to Terri, but didn't know how far he should take their flirting. For all he knew, she was just toying with him. That made sense, given her age, and since they worked together every day. He tended to let Terri deliver the winks while he played the stiff, awkward role. It came naturally.

Lunch went surprisingly well. Despite his protests, Marty could handle almost anything except jalapeños, and they weren't on the menu. He had a weird chicken with pineapple thing that sounded better than it tasted, but it didn't attack his stomach. Their conversation was lively, as always, if a bit one sided. Politics, movies, and even the latest cable shows came up. Terri did most of the talking. His knowledge of most subjects was limited anyway. She did have a knack for hitting things he knew something about, like the latest episode of whatever he'd watched on cable. It was good to talk about anything but work. Work was top secret, and rarely went past the airlock. They both had a standard set of non-work subjects to fall back on.

Terri only gave him one or two adrenaline rushes driving back to the building. Unlike NSA headquarters the building they worked in was little known, and off the beaten track. Heavy trees formed a natural screen around the facility, and the tall metal fence within the trees seemed invisible. Only the automated entry gate with its badge check was visible. That was pretty common for company entrances anymore. The wide-open parking lot made security very controllable. Passersby would never notice the heavy electronic warning systems, or cameras that tracked every deer and stray dog, or the ground sensors that noted even the lightest footfall. The trees helped provided a natural visual shield against optic infiltration.

As they entered the lobby Terri handed Marty a pack of Rolaids.

"Hey, don't you care about my calcium?" Marty joked.

"They didn't have Tums, so get over it." Terri started to say something else, but the guard interrupted her, looking at Marty.

"Dr. Torrance, you have a message. The Director asked to see you immediately." The unemotional face of the guard told him nothing.

"Thanks, Don." Marty sighed. Karlovich had a habit of wanting one of his employees the minute they all left for lunch or the bathroom. The rest of the time they didn't know if the Director was even in the building.

As always, conversation went to zero at the airlock. By the time they both got through the hand scan, the body scan, or the occasional cavity search, no one could remember what they had been talking about anyway. Marty entered first and went straight to the Director's office.

He was only gone a few minutes when he came out and stormed straight to his desk, plopping himself into his chair.

"What's wrong?" Terri peeked over the cubicle wall.

"We don't get the extra headcount to support OPOV. Damned politicians have us on a resource freeze. They have no idea how complex this project is. They'd rather spend billions on bailouts, drones, and pork." Marty spun around in his chair to look at Terri, who was hanging over the top edge of the wall. "They constantly underestimate the man hours it takes to do this job right."

"Drones and pork? Would that be pigs flying? Jeez, the way you were acting I thought it was something serious, or at least something new. Speaking of new and serious, has Christen found a lover at school, yet?"

"That's not funny, Terri. Just wait till you have a daughter." Marty often felt that Terri related more to his daughter than to him.

"One like Christen? That would be great! She's indestructible; reminds me of me." Terri smiled. "So, no more headcount, eh? Well, don't worry about it. We got the system running this far without help. Besides, it's too close to the first nationwide run. We don't have time to train a newbie." Terri sat back into her chair and typed in the pass code to her workstation. "So, how's that lunch settling?"

"I already upchucked."

"Bulimic. I knew that's how you kept your figure!" Terri quipped back.

Chapter 17

Lt. Colonel Grady Barlow had been walking the halls of the Pentagon all morning. The numerous passages went on forever—seventeen miles, so the guidebooks said. Grady figured he could wear out a pair of shoes and never pass the same door twice—and that was only the above ground office levels.

Descending below ground under the Mezzanine, Grady entered the basement. It was cold and dim all year round. He always needed a jacket or a sweater down here, and running shoes would have been a plus. The Pentagon had been built during WWII when the government had been trying to save as much metal and money as possible. With that idea in mind, they'd put in ramps instead of elevators—but these hadn't been just any ramps. They were ten-lane super highways, stretching hundreds of feet, and sloping from floor to floor in one long straight shot. Grady's polished leather shoes slapped the hard vinyl flooring, his footfalls echoing off the bare walls. He assumed the government had saved money on air ducts, too, since the place had a suffocating lack of circulation.

Grady spent plenty of time at the Pentagon, as did most rising officers. Being Air Force, much of Grady's time was spent near corridors eight and nine. High-tech innovations were forcing government agencies farther underground for better security, so a lot of his work was on these basement levels. Since windows could allow laser microphones to tap conversations, the military spooks were down deep in the building—mostly out in rings F and G. Grady wondered how people worked in these offices year after year. He found the atmosphere depressing; like gray and white rectangular caves.

Surrounded by webs of copper wire, Tempest Qualified operations like the one he was visiting today blocked vibrational, RF, electronic, and visible signals from penetrating or escaping their rooms. Faraday Chambers were only part of their precautions. Grady knew about a few of the spy defeating materials inside and outside the walls that were constantly being updated from within.

Some rooms had oil-dampened floors which effectively blocked low-frequency vibration detection. Buried here were the gurus of technical espionage—the top of the espionage pyramid. No leaks of any kind could be tolerated in this group.

These weren't the glamorous spies of the movies. They were more like scientists scratching out formulas. They were laborers of listening, deciphering, and reading to find hidden meanings, and developers of technological security. The Colonel was seeking the working class spies who went unnoticed. These were the members of the invisible intelligence community who seemed to be typical U.S. citizens. They commuted home to hug their spouses, yell at and love their kids, and mow the lawn like everyone else.

Grady's problem was that these people were used to keeping their secrets to themselves. Everyone was paranoid down in the basement. People talked very little, and shared even less. Grady knew he could approach only those people who had worked with him in the past. Trust was earned, and hand-to-hand referrals were the only way to meet new people.

Grady passed one door after another marked with obscure department names. "MVCD," branded one nondescript doorway, which Grady knew was the Mantle Vibration Communications Division. "SOSUS Sound Surveillance System" labeled another. It was probably a spill over office from the Navy.

Grady opened a plain gray door. Its appearance could have indicated it was a closet except for the old-style bumpy glass, and the label that read "PSC." Grady translated "Phase Shifted Crypto" in his mind as he entered a lifeless, tiny room, housing a dull gray desk and dark green vinyl padded chair. There were some stacked boxes in the corner. The chair's arm pads were torn, with shreds of aged yellow foam showing through. The gray, rubbery writing surface of the disused desk showed years of dents, scratches and abuse. Completely bare now, the desk had once been a secretarial post before headcount reductions. The advent of computers, e-mail, and secure networks had changed the landscape. Government secretaries had nearly been rendered extinct.

Like most of these reception areas, this one had been repurposed into an oddly designed entry and storage area. Grady opened another door, and continued down a narrow hallway leading to several unmarked offices. The first held gray metal shelves of supplies, and a coffee maker. The darkly stained glass pot made the coffee sludge appear unappealingly black. It smelled burned. Grady's lips curled as he flipped the hot plate switch off.

"Anybody here?" Grady called out.

"Down here." The voice came from the very end of the hall, where one door was ajar. "I'm in the last one on the right."

Grady strode down the hall and pushed open the door.

"Grady! It's been a long time." John McGarrity stood up behind his desk, simultaneously pushing a file drawer closed, and spinning the combination lock. Security was a mandatory habit in this area, no matter who visited. John offered a wide smile and his hand.

"It really has been a long time. Sorry about that, John." Grady responded with a solid handshake and equally warm smile. "The schedule always seems so full. How have you been?"

"Same as always. I don't think I've seen you since we were on that Pakistan 'what-if' communications task force. So, what brings you to the dungeon?" John's gesture indicated which chair Grady could safely use, as he sat back down in his seat. "What department are you in these days?" John inquired casually.

Grady smiled. These guys would never discuss anything without knowing which branch they were speaking to. "No change. I'm still in the same Military Intelligence group."

"You know your job's a contradiction in terms, don't you?" John laughed.

"Yeah, I know. Oxymoron—just like 'jumbo shrimp.' Not much different than your job." Grady agreed with a smile, pointing at John's division "Internet Security" plaque on the wall.

"Too true." John nodded. "Still flying?"

"Only to keep my qualification rating current. I had a 16C up last month." Grady answered.

John cut the pleasantries short, and got right to the point. "It's good to see you, Grady, but what's up? Why are you here?" He asked, easing back in the chair. The worn springs allowed the chair to lean almost to a reclining position.

"I'm just doing a little feasibility survey," Grady said easily. "Last minute check before the big day. I need to know if the OPOV system can be cracked."

John rocked in his chair a little, only to fall back into the reclining position again, his hands clasped behind his head. "You came to the right place, but the reports on that have already been done. Why did you really come all the way down here?"

Grady smiled and waited. He knew John would rather decode the puzzle himself than be given all the answers. He'd be reading between the lines, anyway, no matter what Grady told him.

"I would guess," John explored, drawing out the words as he put the answer together himself, "that since security has been tightened around OPOV, you're here to ask whether OPOV can be broken by someone who is inside the safeguards. How am I doing so far?"

Grady smiled wider, but said nothing. John loved a good deduction, and Grady enjoyed watching him reach his conclusions. It was a game they'd played since they'd first met.

"But that particular question was asked and answered in the reports. So why would you be asking it again?" John continued, rocking forward. He placed his elbows on the desk, gripping his hands together. "Someone," he reasoned, "is double-checking a rumor. Must be someone high up, or you wouldn't be here. Let's see...whether it's for personal or ideological gain isn't really the issue, is it? What you're concerned about is something more specific. Obviously, any system can be compromised from the inside, as long as the perpetrator has enough access, and is smart enough to cover his or her tracks. So, what you're really asking is, if OPOV is compromised, can the break be detected? Is there some way to find out, and can we stop it before the vote occurs, or at least know about it afterward?" John stood up, and began pacing behind the desk. "Well," he continued, "NSA has the system operators, the security managers, the remote site operators, and the software coders. They're all human, so we must assume that any of them could be had for a price."

Grady's face turned grim. He never liked hearing that someone who'd committed to a trusted position could be bought. It felt like a degradation of the whole system that he had pledged his life to protect. His jaw clenched, the muscles in his cheeks flexing involuntarily.

"Hey, I'm only telling it like it is, Grady. If you didn't want to hear my opinion, I know you wouldn't have come to this office." John said flatly.

Grady's eyebrows eased, his eyes becoming clearer. "Sorry. Treason gets under my skin."

"Not everyone's an Academy grad, and not everybody feels like you do about their job, and their country," John pointed out, remembering Grady's background. "Most people don't have an honor code that's as clear cut as yours. You know as well as I do that almost everybody has his or her price. Some prices are higher or have a different structure than others, but there are breaking points for just about everyone. Bribery, extortion, torture—they're realities. And you can't discount what it can do to someone's mental state if they have an ailing relative, serious financial problems, or a compulsive habit. Kids—now there's a big one."

Grady wasn't looking convinced. "John, I understand that the people in the positions we're talking about have problems, like everyone else, but they are in special circumstances in their positions. Plus, they are background checked for flaws and vulnerabilities."

John shook his head. "Grady, the government does periodic checks, but we've got a lot of dissatisfied people in this country right now. The government scene is no different. The brass is making unreasonable requests without regard to cutbacks in departments, pay grades, or what their employees are dealing with in this austere economy. Only a few of the higher ups show any respect for their employees. Most of them like to remind the plebeians that they can be replaced at a moment's notice. That tends to lower ethics and personal price tags. Treat people like furniture and they'll respond with their own negative brand of rebellion. Maybe for you, death would come before you'd break your word or commitment, but not everyone feels that kind of loyalty to what they consider strictly a job. Any kind of trouble at home can compromise their already weakened ethics."

Grady lifted an eyebrow, and gave John a long, appraising look.

John shook his head, looking amused. "Sorry...I'm on my soapbox."

Grady sighed. "Yeah, I know. I know, John. I hate this kind of investigation. It makes me feel like everyone is suspect. It's too easy to judge someone guilty before all the facts are in." Grady stood up, feeling uncomfortable. His strong frame filled his tailored uniform as he straightened his back. "But, a little reality every now and then is good. The idea of an insider being bought has been discussed before, of course, but we didn't see any way that the system could be compromised without discovery. How do you buy a whole department? If we suppose that it could happen, then what I need to know is the mechanics of breaking the system, and how we'd spot it. How could they do it? What could they do once they are in? Can a breach occur without detection?"

John's shoulders relaxed. "Now that's the tricky part...not getting caught. That depends on what you want to do once you're in. Come with me. I want to show you something."

John walked past Grady to the office across the hall. Grady found a room full of old and new contraptions; electronic boxes, old fashioned colored light panels, strange keyboards, and a mix of electrical smells and machine oil. "Welcome to my laboratory." John's wide gesture encompassed the comparatively small room. "Here's what I want you to see. This is an interesting gizmo. Recognize it?" John pointed to a typewriter looking device in a wood box.

"Enigma?" Grady asked.

"Right! Very good. It's a working facsimile of an actual Enigma device from Nazi Germany used in World War II."

"I saw a mock up Hollywood version in a submarine movie somewhere along the line." Grady loved war movies.

"Correct. Most of the Enigma ciphers were captured by the British off submarines." John loved old gadgets.

"And a purple box?" Grady looked a bit skeptical.

John picked up a small purple painted box. "This is an electronic clone of the Japanese Purple cipher, or AN-1, also from WW II. The real ones weren't purple, of course; that was the code name our black chamber guys gave it."

"Did they call it that in Bletchley Park, too?"

"Very good. Yes, the Brits as well. You *have* been watching the movies, haven't you?" John motioned toward the equipment again. "Everything in this room is an obsolete coding-decoding device. They work as well or better than the new stuff designed to replace them. In fact, we'd still be using them if their codes hadn't been broken. Or I should say, the Germans or Japanese, or whichever country developed them, would be using these devices. OPOV is basically the same thing. It captures the message—in this case, a 'vote' or tally of votes—transmits it in code, then decodes it on the other end. The part voters see are the electronic keys and screens, which replace paper ballots. The tough part is behind the scenes. You want to wreck the system? You have to break the code."

"So you have to think the way the people who broke these machines thought." Grady offered.

"That's absolutely correct. In reality, most of these weren't broken at all. Someone captured the device and the decoding book, or the transmitter made a mistake, like adding, 'Heil Hitler' to the end of too many messages. So, with OPOV, who can get their hands on the device? Or, In this case, who has access to the software code? Or will they make a mistake that we can catch? I would guess the enemy doesn't want to just listen in on the transmitted code; he or she wants to change the outcome. They could forge votes that add to the count, lose votes to reduce the count, or flip votes from one side to the other."

"Flipping makes more sense to me. That way the total would still tally." Grady offered.

"Yes, but there's more to consider." John's eyes focused somewhere behind Grady. "I'd like to bring Pat and Gail in on this."

Grady nodded his approval. "As long as they realize that this is a discreet and very unofficial investigation."

"Hey," laughed John, "we don't have any other kind."

In moments, John had returned with Gail. She was in her late forties, attractive, and a little on the heavy side. Her dark, warm eyes were friendly. Pat came in close behind her, his sixty plus years showing in his walk, but not in his toothy grin. They were civilians, as was commonplace in the Pentagon.

"Gail, Pat, this is Lieutenant Colonel Barlow, from M.I." John introduced.

"Pleased to meet you," they said, almost simultaneously. Grady noticed that Gail spoke with a faint South American accent. They all shook hands.

"I think we should start with a baseline," John said. "Colonel, care to do the honors?" John offered a marker to Grady and gestured toward the white board on the wall.

"No, no. You're doing fine." Grady declined. He figured he'd do better to let these three brainstorm while he listened.

"Okay..." John took a breath. "We're reviewing the idea of breaking the OPOV system, how it might be done, and where it could be spotted."

Grady listened as John reviewed what they had already discussed. Soon the three abandoned the board, and were talking in a circle. The information seemed to be a rehash of the obvious to Grady, but Gail and Pat looked decidedly intrigued.

"History is replete with examples of corruption in the voting process so let's not concentrate on that." John interrupted at one point. "Keep in mind that the existing voting method has a multitude of holes and problems. Remember Florida in the early two thousands? The system became a joke, and nothing until OPOV had any hope of restoring the public faith in voting. One Person, One Vote. The electronic system would never have been such a popular idea if the current system wasn't so flawed. My opinion."

Pat nudged Gail with a grin as she said laughingly. "Hey, just cause your guy lost, John, doesn't mean the system is a total waste."

"School's out on whether that was a win for us, or not." Pat shot back at Gail.

"Okay, let's get back on subject." John admonished them both.

"Yeah, sorry; back on track." Gail thought for a moment. "Okay...so, in steps Senator Tom Baxter with his revolutionary platform based on getting us back to One Person, One Vote.

OPOV becomes a critical factor in his election. He wins. The system is built, and it's about to go online, which brings us to this point."

"Don't forget that if it works, the new administration has promised to extend many of the voting duties of The House and Senate to the people, and to do away with the Electoral College completely. States may follow with some delegate systems," Pat added.

"That's an urban myth; although many would like it to be true." Gail argued

"Myth?" Pat shook his head. "Bull! Baxter said it."

"Myth or not," John chimed in, "motive to break the system is easy to come by. Plenty of people and special interests have reason to not like the concept. Let's stay focused on the process flow. Not the motive."

Gail scooted back in her chair. "As I understand the OPOV process, individuals use either their own computer, or public voting connection. They input their voting pin id, and place their vote. I see a bunch of software, hardware, and transmission weak points with that plan. Then the vote gets summed at a central county server; another software and hardware weak point, and all the county servers go to the state server and get summed up again. Once again, we have software, hardware, and transmission weak points—especially if the systems aren't all on fiber. Then the national server sums all the states. That's all the same problem again. Up until the transmission from the state to national, the whole thing is done through SSL 'secure' Internet, which is public domain, and anything but secure, so that's a huge conglomeration of weaknesses."

Pat leaned forward. "There are too many possible ways to connect with the Internet. Nobody can control all the possible lines between the individual voter and the county servers. Too many companies now control the certificates and SSL systems to call it secure from our viewpoint. Hell, it's hard just keeping the routing within the US. Truth is, there are so many weak points that the sheer volume of connections would overwhelm a perpetrator. The value of that much work would be doubtful except with a robot virus, and a virus would be too visible; too obvious. Low return on investment, if you ask me. The scope is far too large. What you want is a method that stays hidden, and is therefore reusable. This is, after all a multi-use proposition, right?"

Grady wasn't paying attention as well as he thought, suddenly realizing the question was directed at him. He jerked forward a bit in his chair. "Yes, I suppose that's true....yes...multi-use. Why would you want to change just one election, when you could manipulate them all?"

John agreed. "I'd agree with that. Why would a manipulation method be created for only one pass? The first time you tried it, the system would probably be testing, or the subject would be a vote of relative unimportance. Some future vote would be the target. So, you'd want to be able to control the vote anytime. You'd want control over the issues you care about."

John was quiet for a moment before continuing, "It's the subtotals that are important. It's all a game of percentages. Where you get the most return for your effort is the issue." Pat noted Gail's nod of agreement. "The connection of state to national can be on controlled lines. Fifty or so are manageable; in fact we have plenty of those now. The packet of information transmitted would be relatively small, since we would only be dealing in subtotals."

"Right." Pat interjected. "That makes software at the servers a likely target." John stood up to the whiteboard again. "So," Pat continued, "who wrote the software?"

"The NSA." Gail said. "They wrote the summing and Intranet software code, too."

"They're in charge of all the Crypto?" Gail asked.

"All of it." John stated. "They won't let anyone near it." John pointed to Pat with his marker. "So, it's safe to say the NSA is our number one technical weak point."

"Yes," Pat answered, "and no one agency gets to monitor everything they do. We all get a piece of it."

"They used quantum cryptography with coherent states, right?" John asked.

"Right." Gail nodded.

Grady positioned his hands in the shape of a capital T. "Whoa...time out. You've lost me with that one."

Gail turned in her chair to face him. "Have you read the white paper on *'Security of coherent state quantum cryptography against collective attacks in the presence of Gaussian channel noise,'* by Heid and Lutkenhaus?" she asked.

"Sorry, I must have missed that one." Grady wondered if they caught the light sarcasm in his tone. They all looked dead serious about Gail's question to him.

"Quantum Cryptography," Gail continued, "is all about stopping eavesdroppers. Simply put, honest users are limited by available technology. Bad guys aren't. We have to do a worst-case analysis here, so we must assume that only the laws of quantum mechanics limit the bad guys. This is somewhat restrictive, since we still can't generate controlled streams of single photons. They, like us, have to rely on weak pulses with strong vacuum components to enhance the safety of the transmission. You follow?"

"Only very generally," Grady had to admit.

"Let me try." John chimed in. "A quantum system assumes an eavesdropping attempt creates channel errors. Not errors in data; errors in phase, amplitude, and so forth. The amount of information leaked depends on both the system and the eavesdropping strategy. The ability to interject information is even more difficult, so small changes in the header or scrambler code introduce so much error that no matter how advanced the bad guy's equipment is, the laws of quantum mechanics, or physics, are against them all the way. The bottom line is, once it's on the controlled transmission lines, particularly fiber, they don't have a prayer." The room went quiet. "So that's it!" John smiled.

"What's 'it'?" Grady asked, perplexed.

"The answer," Pat responded. "It's in the software."

"Right." Gail had a big smile on her face. "The summing software is the most vulnerable spot, with the biggest gain for the effort made. That's the most likely spot for the breaker to make an attempt."

"There you go, Colonel." John placed his marker in the tray.

"Thanks," Grady answered, wondering how this had gotten him any further in his search. "Now what?"

"Well, that's it. We've pinpointed the most likely opportunity. Now all you need is a smoking gun. This," John pointed to the NSA letters on the board, "is the most likely place for the crime to occur."

"That's a lot of territories." Grady insisted. "What I was hoping to hear is how they could do it, so we can head off any attempt."

"That's the fun part, isn't it?" John told him. "Everybody will be watching the obvious hacker routines, and espionage plays. There could be a flaw in the crypto, but as you've heard that is highly unlikely. We can help there, of course. Gail and Pat would love an excuse to hack at NSA."

"We'd be glad to." Pat stood. "Crypto is our business; particularly this kind. Besides, any complex system has inherent flaws. National security is one of our charters, so it's in our purview. The easiest way to spot possible hacking is to actually hack the system. That's also how we'll find out how to spot the hacking. I get a kick out of doing it to the NSA."

John butted in, giving a look to Pat. "Not that we've ever done that, officially." John walked over to shake Grady's hand. "Give us a month on the cryptography. We should have something by then, but software and a software operator...that's the sweet spot on this deal."

"A month? I need something sooner, John. How about a week?" Grady asked, disappointed in the time frame. Neither he nor Robert had considered the time involved in a project like this. Plus, the software deduction wasn't an answer; it was just another question.

"You don't want much, do you? I guess we can get something for you in the next week." John relented. "But we'll have less to tell. I doubt we will be able to nail your target operation source."

"Rome didn't burn in a day." Gail chimed in.

"They didn't have the right flammable mix. I suspect your group here carries a little more fire power." Grady shook each of their hands. "I really appreciate all your help. Of course, I'd appreciate your discretion on this..."

"Keep it quiet?" John offered.

"Yes. Here's my card with a secure number."

"We never call," said John, "it's best for you, and for us. You can call me on this number." John showed him a small plastic key chain. "It will work for thirty days from when I sync it."

Grady watched as John held the thin plastic case against a gray plastic box on the desk. The small LCD display on it flashed all zeros then all eights.

John handed it to Grady. "The display will flash a ten-digit number for sixty seconds, followed by a six-digit number that will stay on for thirty seconds. You call the first number like any telephone. When you hear the beep, punch in the second number. It's similar to a VPN ID number system, but more advanced telephony. It is always scrambled between where I am and the closest military switch to wherever you are. Just a toy I cooked up."

"Military grade VPN?" Grady had not seen one of these.

"Well, it's *my* Virtual Private Network. Maybe this enhancement will make me rich when businesses want the same protection," John joked.

"It should, John, but not with Uncle Sam watching." Grady put the key chain in his pocket.

Grady reflected that he'd just involved himself more deeply in this project than he'd intended, and more seriously. He no longer wondered if this was a paranoid waste of time. Now he was worried they wouldn't find the weak point in time to protect the system, and he wondered who might be behind a plot to corrupt the voting. He also felt now that there was something Robert hadn't told him.

Grady headed for his office to call Robert.

Chapter 18

The Round Robin was steeped in tradition, and famous for having introduced properly made Mint Juleps to Washington. D.C. Insiders knew that it also maintained one of the finest selections of single malt scotches in the city. Robert's appointment with the Senator would be expensive, but meeting in one of Gregg's preferred hangouts might give him the edge he wanted.

Robert sat in the noisy bar watching tourists flow in to order the famous drink. At fifteen dollars each, the juleps were generally a single-drink experience. There were more economical offerings in other bars, which caused the sightseeing populace to move on in relatively short order. The locals filtering into the Willard were easy to spot. They largely shunned the Julep for Scotch, or for a glass of wine.

Robert was enjoying the Pittyvaich single malt scotch he was sipping. The waiter had recommended it for nose, tongue, and value, and it was living up to his endorsement. None of the Willard's scotch offerings were inexpensive, but some had a little less impact on the wallet, with the same big results on the pallet.

Robert navigated quickly through the e-mail on his smartphone, looking for noteworthy messages or names. He had finished half his glass, and completed several e-mails by the time the Senator came in and sat down in front of him.

"Hello, Robert. Glad you could meet on such short notice." He took off his scarf and gloves as he spoke.

"My pleasure, Senator," Robert answered. Robert was not a small man, but whenever he shook hands with the Senator he felt dwarfed. The Senator's oversized form carried a full head of white hair, with forceful eyebrows framing and emphasizing dark, penetrating eyes.

"Robert, we've known each other for some time. I think you can call me Dan when we meet like this." The Senator winked as he spoke. Gregg's deep voice was comfortable, but commanding. His broad smile was ingratiating.

Robert was well aware that while the Senator could be intimidating and domineering, he preferred to lure in his victims with charm. He seldom spent time with anyone on the Hill unless there was something to gain. It occurred to Robert that the Senator's agenda could encompass the entire lunch. He decided to dive in.

"So...Dan," Robert began, "what can Justice do for you?"

"Straight to the point. I like that," Gregg nodded. The waiter came by and the Senator ordered a drink. "Single malt, one of your finest...let's say a Lagavulin 21. Do you have the sherry cask still? He's buying," he chuckled, motioning toward Robert.

Robert felt a small twinge. That drink would cost him at least forty dollars. He had an expense account, but it wasn't unlimited.

"Of course, Senator; and you, Sir?" The waiter asked.

"I'm fine. Thanks." Robert acknowledged his half-filled glass with a gesture.

"What are you having?" the Senator inquired.

"Pittyvaich," Robert answered, glad that he'd taken the waiter's advice, and not settled for the cheapest choice.

"An excellent scotch for the price," the Senator approved. "One of my favorites."

"The waiter recommended it highly." Robert put his phone on vibrate and tucked it into his jacket breast pocket.

"Let me ask you, Robert, what do you consider to be the greatest threat to Homeland Security today?" Gregg seemed to be watching Robert's eyes to see his reaction.

It was obviously a leading question, so Robert fed back the approved party line. "Terrorism, the Middle East unrest, China, Russia certainly, and the economy." Robert waited for the inevitable rebuttal that would narrow the focus to Gregg's concern of the day.

"Dangerous, I'll admit," Gregg answered. "But, not the single biggest problem. The greatest threat is apathy."

Politicians were inevitably predictable, Robert reflected. Every question was designed to create a speaking platform. Now would come the pitch. Robert waited for the opening lines.

"Robert, men of influence like you and me need to speak for the silent majority. Nixon was right about their existence, and they're still out there. We need to wake them up, speak with one voice, and empower democracy. Drown out the narrow-minded screamers with their small grasp of the world, and smaller minds."

Robert said nothing. Gregg paused as the waiter delivered his scotch. He took a healthy drink out of the glass before continuing.

"We have a responsibility to the people," Gregg resumed. "The public is busy caring for their families. They have entrusted us to protect them and their way of life. If we become complacent, apathetic...well, you see what I'm getting at."

"Yes, of course." Robert wasn't sure he did, but that was the correct response.

The Senator sipped again before going on. "They need to be confident that we are in control; that they are safe."

"I can't agree more," Robert interjected. So far, this was political rhetoric. It seemed that it would be late into their lunch before Gregg got to the point. He decided that he'd move things along by getting some food ordered. "I put our reservation in for lunch, would you like to move to the table?"

"Excellent idea." The Senator raised his glass toward the bartender, silently ordering a second scotch. Draining the remaining contents he stood up. Robert tried not to wince. How Gregg could possibly taste the expensive libation drinking at that speed was beyond Robert's comprehension.

As they walked toward the dining room, a waiter delivered Gregg's fresh drink into his hand. "Outstanding service here." Gregg approved.

Taking their seats in the sumptuously decorated dining room, Gregg waved away the menu offered by the waiter, and ordered his "usual." Robert followed suit by ignoring the menu and ordering the special: a grilled salmon with dill béarnaise and mango chutney. Since this was one of the city's best restaurants, walking distance from the White House, and catering to a prestigious clientele, Robert was sure any choice he made would live up to expectation. Robert waited patiently as Gregg finished off his drink and ordered another round. After the waiter left, the Senator leaned his forearms against the edge of the table, looking directly at Robert.

Here it comes, thought Robert. He was about to find out why he had suddenly become the focus of Gregg's afternoon.

"I wanted to talk to you, Robert, because the Senate Rules Committee is concerned about next week's referendum vote. We want to ensure that the public remains aware of the return of their voting power, and that they understand we are the ones returning it to them. It's important that your office reassures the country of the effectiveness, safety, and importance of the system. We want a high rate of voter turnout."

Robert nodded as if he understood Gregg's concern, his mind moving quickly. He knew that this couldn't be the reason that Gregg had requested a meeting. The voting issue surrounded a binding nationwide referendum to redistribute funds earmarked for underground nuclear testing to individual states. The money had been left in the budget year after year since testing had stopped, and was being used as a slush fund. The problem was that there were no more categories in research or spending that legally were connected to the use of that money.

When Robert's office had been consulted about the matter, he'd immediately recognized the issue as an opportunity to test OPOV. The government had to close the fund anyway, why not let the population vote on it. Politically, it was always popular to return tax dollars to the taxpayers. Robert had recognized this as the perfect marketing tool for the system. A referendum could allow each state an equal share of the money, based on population, in effect returning taxes to the people through use in their states. As part of the One Person, One Vote reform, the President had agreed. He'd declared that this was exactly the type of Congressional vote that should be returned to the people.

The issue was neither groundbreaking nor controversial. If anything about the referendum was significant, it was that it would be the first nationwide vote using the OPOV system. There was some concern that since it was a popular referendum, and sure to pass, voter turnout might be low—but surveys had shown that most people were eager to try the new system. Younger voters were expected to vote in droves, since they couldn't understand why the system hadn't been in place earlier. Older voters were torn between a desire to experiment with the technology, and an interest in denouncing it, but either way, they said they were going to vote.

So, Robert wondered, where was Gregg going with this?

The Senator leaned back as the salads arrived. "We don't want the system itself to be seen as a problem."

"Pepper, gentlemen?" The waiter asked

They both accepted, delaying the conversation while the multicolored peppercorns were ground over the garden greens and vinaigrette.

"What are you asking my department to do?" Robert was a little too direct. It was a slight faux pas, but he figured this lunch was already costing him a couple weeks of his expense account budget.

Taken aback by this abrupt breach of protocol, the Senator frowned, and took a slow sip of his drink.

"Again, you come right to the point, Robert." He crunched a mouthful of salad and dabbed his mouth with his napkin. Robert waited for the next sentence.

"We'd like you to scrutinize the voting system during the upcoming pilot. Monitor it, verify the results, and erase all doubt as to its accuracy and effectiveness. This test vote has to go off without a hitch."

It took effort on Robert's part to control his facial features and maintain a bland expression. Certainly, it was a bit coincidental that Gregg was discussing monitoring OPOV, he thought. What was going on here? "Of course, Dan," he responded, "but aren't plenty of agencies monitoring it now?"

"Yes, but the Justice Department carries legal validity, and we want maximum confidence on this every step of the way. I'd ask the Attorney General, but..." Dan looked intently at Robert, waiting for agreement.

Robert decided that what Gregg meant was that they were looking for maximum CYA. Robert wondered if the rumor of infiltration into OPOV had somehow reached Gregg's ears. Had Chris mentioned it to someone else in the government? If something, or someone really was compromising the system then Gregg, as chairman of the Senate Rules and Administration Committee, had just handed the responsibility, blame, and problem to Robert. In his position, he was too powerful for Robert to refuse. Robert had to accept. He seemed to have played right into the Senator's hands.

Trying for a lesser commitment, Robert was about to say, "Absolutely. We'd be glad to assist the NSA in overseeing the operation," when Gregg jumped in with, "And you don't need to worry about authorization or protocol. Naturally, I got Jack to agree to let you help us before I called you." Gregg smiled as he stabbed more salad with his chilled fork.

Robert thought bitterly that he should have known that Gregg would be two steps ahead of him. Robert hadn't seen his boss in days, but Gregg apparently had. Jack Crain, the current Deputy Attorney General had been so busy since Bradley's death that Robert literally had only received a handful of messages from him—

and no personal meetings. The confirmation hearings for Jack's promotion had him completely tied up. Even as the presumptive successor, his examination at those hearings was intense. Robert had no doubt that he would find a voice mail confirming the agreement between Jack and Gregg waiting for him when he got back to the office.

"You should head the effort, personally." Gregg smoothly added, making the command sound as though it was a tribute, rather than a way to hold Robert accountable.

Robert swore silently. A step ahead again, the Senator had pre-empted any attempt Robert might have made to delegate the job. So, he wants me trapped, Robert surmised. He had no choice other than to agree, and to sound positive about doing so.

"I'm happy to do so, Dan. Of course, you realize that my calendar is extremely full—if I'm going to add this monitoring to the schedule, I'll have to keep you apprised of my activities through voice messaging, memos, or e-mails," he tried. He knew that the Senator would try and tie him into regular meetings to update the committee. Reporting that information would be the final step in making him the fall guy for any problems that occurred in OPOV.

"Yes, we're all overloaded these days. Considering the importance of this program though, Jack and I agreed that you could clear your calendar if need be." Gregg chuckled, "Of course you know Jack, he also said he was sure you would find a way to fit the time into your schedule."

That was typical of Jack, thought Robert bitterly. He always expected the impossible without any consideration for anyone's overburdened schedule. "Just squeeze it in" was his standard answer to everything. "Yes, that sounds like Jack." Robert shared the Senator's smile, but not the humor in it.

"The country is depending on us, so consider me your partner. Keep me informed at every step. My staff is at your disposal. You tell me what you need, and I'll make sure you get it." Gregg's attention was drawn away by the arrival of food.

They ate their opulent lunches with only occasional comments, appearing to concentrate on the excellent meal. Robert's enjoyment of the food was limited. Although he paid a few compliments to the luncheon, and to the Senator's good taste, Robert was busy reviewing what had happened in his mind.

The Senator had committed everything, even himself, to getting Robert involved in the examination of the OPOV system. Committing others to projects was commonplace, but allowing Robert direct access to his staff was rare. Gregg wanted Robert to be openly culpable for OPOV; he wanted him exposed, and reporting personally. Robert had to assume that somehow the Senator had found out he was already looking into the system. Robert's encounter with Hunt at the White House through Gregg's introduction was becoming increasingly suspicious, but the purpose behind it was, as yet, unknown. Robert decided to explore that a little.

"Dan, I got a call from Alex Hunt, but he left no message." Robert paused, wondering how much he could fish for information without sounding suspicious. "I thought he was an interesting fellow, but I can't imagine why he'd be calling me. Can you tell me more about him?"

"Good man." Gregg was quick to respond. "Good at finding things out; handy in a pinch. You know, he's been a consultant and researcher for the bar in almost every state. He could be a great resource."

That answered why Hunt was not on a state bar. He probably never needed to be, as a consultant in multiple states. But why would Robert need him? That was unanswered, but it would be awkward to press Gregg further about Hunt. 'Good man' was commonly used in DC to avoid committing to any particular character judgment. "He's a great guy," would have meant even less commitment. Robert racked his brain for a way to pursue the line of questioning, but couldn't develop a path that wouldn't send up the Senator's radar.

Cappuccinos were served, which Robert appreciated after the orders of Scotch and food. They threatened to make the afternoon one in which he'd have trouble staying awake. The Senator was looking even more relaxed. "I can't tell you how much better I feel with you on the team, Robert. This is a turning point in our history. Indeed, in the history of all democracies. We need our best on the job."

Oh, yeah, fluff my pillow. Make me glad to be set up, Robert thought cynically. He tried to figure out how he could squeeze just a little elbow room into this situation.

"I'm sure you realize the importance of needing to maintain tight control on our communications," Gregg added.

There it was, the confidentiality clause. Robert knew he should have seen that one coming. That little remark was supposed to keep Robert from involving other departments. He'd have to control the press, and report only to Gregg. That's my opening, thought Robert.

"I'd like to work with a couple of the cabinet members. Their resources would be important." That should give me a little room to flex, Robert thought, mentally congratulating himself on a crafty maneuver.

"Definitely. I agree. I'm sure the President would like to hear of our efforts, also. We want to present a united front. Just don't incite undue public concern, or alarm the press. After all, nothing is going to go wrong." Gregg smiled.

Robert almost choked on his espresso. This was a shocking turn of events. Senator Gregg on the same side with the President? Why? They had been at each other's throats since the President had taken the oath of office. Now, suddenly, it's bipartisanship? Robert always thought of that term as a nice phrase to indicate a legal conspiracy. Obviously, Robert had just been made a co-conspirator, but of what?

This new angle gave Robert a chip in the big game. If he played it right, this was his chance to make a big move up. Robert turned the question of how to play it over in his mind, and came to the conclusion he'd have to cooperate Gregg's way. The Senator had been ahead of him in every phase of their conversation, so he really had no choice in the matter. If Gregg and the President were on the same page, then Robert had better be, too.

As he paid the enormous tab, Robert wondered how much this lunch was really going to cost him.

Chapter 19

It had been a pretty typical day, Marty reflected, walking into his modest ranch-style home. He'd worked on software code all morning, lunched with Terri, and lost any chance of getting additional headcount in the department. Yep, all in all, it was another typical damn day.

He liked coming home, and leaving the NSA behind. He liked the solitude of his place. He could get away from everything here, especially stress. The house sat on a nicely wooded three acres, with almost no grass to mow, and very little formal landscaping to maintain. There was a path that meandered through the trees with a couple of tall stumps, a bench or two, and a large gazebo. He always thought he would spend time there, or invite friends to play cards on a warm summer night, but he never did. In the winter, when snow was on the ground, his daughter wanted him to put up little white Christmas lights on the path and structure. "Like fairies in the woods," she said. He thought maybe he'd get around to that someday.

The neighbors' houses were far away behind the trees, and he was lucky that they had quiet dogs. Marty had no pets, and no hassles. He lived a bachelor's life, and he liked it. He didn't have many friends since the divorce. His ex had taken most of them, along with the good furniture. He tended to fill his nights by watching movies, web surfing, or playing the occasional online shooter game.

Marty's kitchen was utilitarian. A microwave, an over-under freezer/refrigerator, and a small chest freezer nearby suited his needs. Pulling a package of frozen lasagna out of the freezer, he peeled off the box and popped the food tray into the microwave. He switched on the TV, drank the last of his water bottle, and poured himself a glass of Chianti Classico from the plain bottle on the counter.

Glancing at the answering machine he saw there were no calls. His remote mailbox sensor indicated that the box was empty. Yep, he thought again, it was just another average day. By the time the food was ready, he'd placed a paper napkin and fork on the coffee table, selected a movie from his streaming video choices, and was ready for dinner. As he walked across the floor with his hot lasagna, a bright light flashed across the front window. A car had come up the driveway.

"Who the hell could that be?" He wondered.

There was a knock at the door and Marty was already standing behind it, peering through the peephole. It was only six-thirty, but it was already dark outside, and he couldn't make out any details. "Damn, I thought I replaced that light," Marty mumbled to himself. He could see a silhouette against the car lights behind the figure. He hesitated for a minute then unlocked the deadbolt.

The knob spun in his hand and the door slammed open, knocking him to the floor. He scrambled back on all fours as two men rushed inside. The first one grabbed him by the collar and lifted him bodily, sending him sprawling into the couch. The coffee table, wine, and lasagna crashed across the floor.

"What do you want?" Marty yelled.

"Shut up!" The man yelled back. He pulled a huge pistol from his coat and pressed it to Marty's cheek. "I don't want to hear a sound from you."

Marty lay perfectly still.

The two men wore black overcoats, black knit ski masks, gloves, and black wingtip shoes. Their collars were pulled up tight, so he could see nothing underneath their coats. Their pants were both dark blue, one with pinstripes. They didn't look like burglars. The second man went to close the door. The first man leaned closer.

"Sit there, and keep quiet. We'll be waiting here a few minutes. Move."

Marty did as he was told with the help of a forceful fist twisted into his shirt, and the gun still at his head. He moved awkwardly across the couch away from the pressing gun barrel, the wine-soaked carpet squishing underfoot.

"What do you want?" He tried again.

The man's left hand drew back and shot forward striking Marty in his stomach. The oxygen burst from Marty's lungs. He almost blacked out from the shock. He gasped pathetically for air.

"I said, 'keep quiet!' Do you have a problem understanding English?" The man growled.

Marty's head wagged back and forth, his mouth wide open, panting as he held his stomach. His eyes bugged out like a fish lying on the bottom of a boat.

"Good. Just sit, and wait." The second man pulled a cell phone from his coat. The phone had a thick device attached to its back and a cable plugged into the earphone jack. "When the call comes, you won't speak until you are told to. I will hear everything you say."

In the secluded cabin, Mary checked her watch, re-calculating the time difference between Utah and Maryland. The phone would ring soon. She walked over to Christen, who had been sitting on the couch watching another mindless TV game show. The contestants were jumping up and down again while the audience screamed. Noticing Mary's approach, Christen instinctively shrank back.

"That's good; you should be frightened of me. Don't forget that, and you won't get hurt." Mary reminded the girl.

Christen tugged at the chain attached to her wrist. "Why are you doing this to me?"

"Just be quiet and listen to your instructions," Mary instructed, ignoring the question. "You can speak into the telephone, but only when you are told to, and you can't touch it. Break any of these rules and I'll smack your face. You know how quickly I can hurt you, so don't try to blurt anything out. Do you understand?" Mary asked harshly.

"Yes," Christen answered, trying to shrink farther away.

Mary showed Christen a cell phone. It was larger than normal because of a strange box attached to it. "This is a scrambled phone. We will use the speaker, and I will hear every word that is said. If I let go of this button on the side the connection will be dropped. Don't make any moves physically, or verbally. It will only get you and your father hurt. Do you understand?"

"My father?' Christen was startled into asking. What did her father have to do with this?

"Do you understand?" Mary asked again, more harshly.

"Yes," answered Christen, not daring to show the anguish she felt, or ask why she was getting to talk to her father. She was terrified to show how torn between fear and excitement her emotions were. Were the kidnappers asking her father for ransom? Was it possible that she could be released soon?

"Good," Mary responded. "Now, we'll wait."

Seconds later the phone rang with a harsh electronic sound. Mary answered it with one word, "Ready." Moments later the connection to Marty was made. The multiple transfers were designed to confuse any customary tracing techniques. A man's voice at a base station, or somewhere in between all the routing connections spoke.

"Dr. Torrance," the voice said.

Marty answered, "Yes?"

"Dad?" Christen said spontaneously. The response was immediate. Mary's palm slammed into the side of her face knocking her against the arm of the couch. She gasped in pain. Marty heard the smack, the gasp, and flinched himself, but said nothing. The man in front of him had already raised his hand to strike.

The base voice came on again. "That was foolish. You both know the rules. Punishment will increase with each infraction." He continued in a deep, cold tone. "Answer 'yes' or 'no.' Dr. Torrance, do you believe your daughter is alive, and that we will hurt her if you don't do exactly as we say?"

"Yes." Marty's voice quivered. He could hear Christen crying quietly, and he hoped they wouldn't hit her again.

"Miss Torrance; answer 'yes' or 'no.' Do you believe your father is alive, and that we will hurt him if you don't do exactly as we say?" The voice was calm, but full of malice. The speaker was obviously enjoying the situation.

"Yes." Christen sobbed.

"Good. Tell Dr. Torrance what he will do. The call is over."

Both phones went dead. Mary walked away without comment as Christen collapsed into the sofa crying uncontrollably, her body convulsing with the sobs.

Marty stared at the dead telephone as it was slipped back into the coat pocket, feeling his brain go numb.

"All right, Dr. Torrance. At your workstation tomorrow, you will download and save a copy of the JPEG file 'christen.jpg' from your last year's Facebook pages. In that JPEG picture you will find a copyright watermark. We know you understand how to work with watermarks, so don't waste my time with denials. In this watermark is a very long polynomial. We know you can handle algebraic expressions, too, Doctor. You will take that polynomial, written in HEX code, and place it in the client contact control file that's outside the firewall for the OPOV program. Make it a remark line. Is that clear?"

"Yes, but..." Marty cowered as the man raised the gun as if to hit him with it.

"Yes, or no only, Dr. Torrance. Comments are unnecessary, and will only result in pain for you, and for your daughter. Speak out of turn again, and you will be reminded by my actions."

"Yes," Marty responded, trying to gather his wits.

"Good. Remember that your daughter will be released when we are finished. This will take some time, so get control of your emotions, and keep your mouth shut. We know you can do that."

Marty could tell the man was smiling behind the mask.

"Do this right, and you won't hear from us again. If we detect any file changes, we'll be back. After you perform your task, keep the program stable and unchanged. Don't alter the normal movement of the file's IP addresses and server locations."

The man ceased speaking, and stood. The two men backed out of the house, got into their vehicle, and drove away.

Marty sat staring out the door. He was in shock but his mind was feverishly going over his instructions. Whoever they were, they knew what they were doing.

They knew that nothing could be taken in or out of the office. That prohibited any foolhardy disk or memory stick file transfers. Sending the polynomial hidden as an image watermark would hide it from normal security scans, and apparently they knew that, too. The web filters would ignore Facebook since everyone had access to it as one of the trusted external sites.

Marty had protested this type of access at one time as being a security risk, but had been overridden. During his computing career he had marveled at what was allowed and not allowed, just because someone higher up the ladder wanted access to stock prices, or a grandchild's pictures. So, even if his action with Christen's picture was noticed, his boss wouldn't think it was out of the norm.

Placing the polynomial in the OPOV program file would register only as a single copy command, instead of a long string of keystrokes that might indicate a significant change was being made, meaning that wouldn't get much attention either. Additionally, they seemed to have a good idea which OPOV file was the most useful. The client contact control program file was the only file outside the protective firewall that would allow some measure of access to all the servers.

These guys knew that the only way to spot a file sitting on the Internet quickly and easily was to know the name, location, or something absolutely unique about it. NSA file names and locations were secret, and moved frequently by switching the server and IP address. That still left the possibility of searching for something unique. Typically that would be the code sequence or check sum of the program itself. That, too, would be changed frequently by adding little non-functional bits of code. That was the key, and somehow these guys knew it. A unique complex polynomial would fit the bill perfectly. They knew he could put in non-functional code, and since it was written in HEX and hiding as a remark line, it would be very difficult for the host system to detect it. If the host system found it, it wouldn't spot it as a problem. Whoever was behind this would be able to find the program anywhere on the net easily, and anytime they wanted.

Marty knew that they wanted to watch the activity on the file to make sure it was genuine, while letting it move around as usual. The polynomial would sit there like a homing beacon.

Marty searched his mind for a way out of this mess, and an answer to who these guys were. How did they know so much about him? They knew he had access to the files. They knew he had the top security clearance needed to make program changes. They had Christen, and were using her to get to him. They were sure he could pull it off. Would any of the security measures catch them? Or him? Marty didn't think so. He wondered what they would do if he got caught. For the first time, Marty worried that the security system *would* work. He didn't know what to do if it did.

What about Christen?

He stared at the dark front porch through the still open doorway; at the porch light bulb lying on the ground, and he couldn't move.

<u>Chapter 20</u>

Robert sat in his office the rest of the afternoon, waiting. While his phone rang constantly, the call he wanted never came. Demand for his time was at an all-time high and no one, it seemed, could wait for his attention when it came to his or her special project. Each caller pulled him farther away from what he wanted to do.

Leaving the office at six-thirty, Robert was frustrated, short tempered, and no closer to a solution than he had been Friday, when Chris had dumped this potential problem on him. Solution...hell, he didn't even have a clear idea of the problem, yet, but Gregg had made it absolutely necessary to check out Chris' story. There was still was no word from Chris. Robert had kept trying his cell phone, to no avail. Grady hadn't called, either. Too many possibilities, theories, and suppositions were racing through his mind. What he needed was a silent moment to think; someplace quiet where the phone wouldn't ring, where he could jot down some notes, and maybe figure this out.

Robert soon discovered home wouldn't fill that need. The house was insane, with the kids running and screaming, and Tracie out at some dinner event. Alicia handled dinner, then cleaned up and was gone. The boys were now fighting over a video game. It was impossible to tell if they were swinging the controllers as part of the game, or to try and break everything in the room—including each other's faces. When Robert finally put his foot down, he had to yell to get their attention. Then he had to yank out the power cord to the video game to get them to stop swinging the controllers. Robert and the boys spent the last part of the evening sulking. Each sat in a separate room, each wore ear buds, and each ignored everything outside his microcosm.

Thinking that his random thoughts might come together in a pattern, Robert tried writing down his ideas on paper with circles and lines connecting them. All he achieved was plenty of wadded up paper. Every page had begun with Chris, Senator Gregg, and OPOV on them, but each was crumpled in turn. There just wasn't enough to work with to continue diagrams or columns. Deciding to get some rest, Robert trudged upstairs.

From the boy's bedrooms came the sounds of bickering. When Robert got closer, he realized they were in their shared bathroom. With their ear buds in, neither was actually hearing the other's complaints. They seemed to be arguing for the sake of it, rather than for any good reason. Pushing and shoving would soon ensue.

"You two had better be in bed by the time I count to ten!" Robert barked down the hall. There was no response. Flinging open the bathroom door, Robert's sudden appearance caught their attention.

"Take out the earplugs!" He yelled. They responded reluctantly, slowly pulling out their earbuds. "Did you brush your teeth?" Two nods. "Good. You have to the count of three to be in bed. One!" The frantic look of the boys grabbing up water glasses, trying to hide iPods and video toys while bumping into each other was amusing, but Robert held his firm expression.

"Two." They hopped into their beds.

"Now put away the electronics and go to sleep. Both of you!" There were no good night kisses or hugs, just the sound of Robert firmly closing their doors. He knew that it would only be a couple of minutes before the darkness would be illuminated with electronic entertainment from under the sheets, but he didn't feel like pursuing the matter tonight. When he took time to be honest with himself, he realized that all he cared about was getting them quiet.

After getting in bed, Robert read over some emails on his smartphone. He deleted most of them, and answered a few. He fell asleep, propped up against several pillows with the phone in his hand.

A sound from the master bathroom abruptly woke him. Raising his head from its awkward position sent a sharp pain through his neck, and he grimaced over the stiffness in his arm. Tracie came out of the bathroom, unaware that she had awakened him. The clock read 1:26 AM.

"Kind of late, isn't it?" Robert's words from the dark made Tracie jump, and utter a little shriek.

Tracie recoiled from the nightstand, trying to catch her breath. "You scared me!"

"Sorry," Robert answered, not feeling particularly sorry.

"For Heaven's sake, Robert! What are you doing up?" Tracie sounded flustered, and annoyed.

"I wasn't, actually." He answered. "You woke me. Why were you out so late?"

"Late? It's not that late." She flicked on the bedside lamp. The light made Robert squint uncomfortably. "Oh, well, I guess it is later than I thought."

"I'd say 1:30 qualifies for being late." Robert leaned up on one elbow. "Alicia said you had a dinner tonight, but didn't know what for. I didn't have it on my calendar."

"Oh, I told her." Tracie seemed to be preoccupied with putting her jewelry away. She was already in her bathrobe, having undressed and removed her makeup in the bathroom. "It was a dinner with the Spanish Military Attaché."

"Another NATO delegate party?" Robert asked, wondering how there could be so many pre-dinners before a dinner.

"Yes. They'll be coming next month." Tracie answered absently.

"I suppose Garaurd was there," Robert asked pointedly.

Tracie seemed to hesitate. "Of course."

"Seems there are a lot of NATO visitors these last three months. It's a good thing Garaurd is around to help coordinate them." He found himself deliberately dragging out the man's name. He knew he sounded irritated, despite his effort to disguise it.

"Yes, he is very good with the diplomatic aspects," Tracie answered neutrally.

"You two seem to be working together a lot." Robert pursued.

"I suppose." Tracie took off her robe, revealing a Calvin Klein t-shirt styled nightgown, and climbed into bed. Robert didn't know whether she seemed edgy, or if she could feel the tension in him, and was responding to it.

"It's nice to have made friends so quickly." Robert continued, in spite of himself. He knew he was pushing the topic too far, but he couldn't help it. It annoyed him that the smooth-talking Garaurd seemed to have dinner with Tracie more than Robert did. He tried to quell his sarcasm and add something positive. "Helps with the job."

Tracie reached up and turned out the light. "He's just a friend, Robert. You don't have to worry about any impropriety," she said with some indignation.

"I wasn't worried." Robert felt Tracie rolling over on her shoulder away from him. It was true that he hadn't been concerned a month ago, but he was becoming increasingly aware of Tracie's late nights. She was also showing less interest in being near him, and more interest in looking good at these events.

"Well, it's been a long day." Tracie told him, ending the conversation. "I know you have to get up early." She snuggled into her pillow.

"Yes, I have to get up at six." Robert pulled the covers over his shoulder.

"Good night, Honey." She said. She didn't offer a good night kiss, but then, she rarely did.

"Night." Robert was not going to fall asleep quickly. He was thinking.

Chapter 21

At seven a.m., Robert was sitting in his car at a stoplight. Robert felt the heated seat gradually warming. He rubbed his eyes. They felt gritty and half open. Tracie had ignored him this morning. Not only had she skipped the goodbye at the door, she hadn't even stretched her hand out from under the covers for him to kiss. Robert had no trouble conjuring up an image of Garaurd, based on the time they'd met, standing tall and dark in his military tuxedo. He'd looked like a Hollywood star. Black wavy hair framed his deep eyes, which never seemed to leave Tracie's face. The uniform was dashing even amongst the many lavish Attaché uniforms. Robert wasn't happy about the memory. It was a bad start to the day.

The light turned green, and he accelerated to the next red light. Robert's thoughts moved between what he knew and what he guessed, at home and at the office. Each carried the same frustration of unanswered questions.

To flush Tracie from his mind, Robert turned on the radio and forced himself to think about Chris. Chris had said he needed Robert's position, protection, and credibility to expose the information he had about OPOV. Robert wondered why Chris couldn't go to his boss. Did Chris know who wanted to control the system? Was his supervisor at the NSA involved? Was the Director a suspect?

He pulled into his office parking area, the security bar lowering as the heavy steel and concrete barricade rose up from the ground behind him. Robert couldn't help himself. He stared angrily at the reserved spot for the Deputy Attorney General one more time.

The elevator was again as cold as the parking garage. He could barely feel the warm air from the building when the doors opened upstairs.

Lorraine was early as usual. She handed him his messages as he passed her desk, his slamming of the office door still echoing behind him.

Placing his laptop into its docking station, he powered it up. The boot cycle connected with the external monitors, keyboard, and mouse. It requested his login and he pressed his thumb to the sensor. The remainder of the cycle connected the LAN, RSS feeds, e-mail, news wires, CNN, The Wall Street Journal, Washington Post, his online broker with real-time graphic ticker display, and his portfolio positions. The thumb scanner was a lifesaver for remembering his "favorites" and logins. While it worked, he twisted in his chair to face the desk. Leafing through the stack of messages Lorraine had left for him, he found invitations from several lobbyists. There was also the usual pile of questions about the Supreme Court docket. The red light on his phone "voice mail" glowed steadily, indicating more messages.

Robert liked computers and cell phones, but he hated voicemail, instant messaging, and texting. Thanks to them "time management" had become a fantasy. Robert missed the days before electronics had managed to make everyone feel as though they had Attention Deficit Disorder. He felt nostalgia for the old movie images of secretaries and receptionists handling communications and mundane tasks. Most of his career had been spent in the "technology age," where he'd been lucky to have a single assistant.

In his desire to have "staff" running interference for him, Robert forgot how lucky he'd been to get Lorraine as his Administrative Assistant. He took for granted the many small duties she performed for him each day without complaint, only noticing those she did not handle. Other assistants refused to be associated with getting coffee, ordering lunch, or hanging up coats, and they didn't like being treated as though they were receptionists. Those were the jobs interns were generally assigned. Lorraine had accepted his edict that she handle his communications and messages as much as possible. Robert's only complaint had been that she didn't deal with all of it.

Lorraine had experienced those "old days" of secretarial duties personally. She had her limits, and while Robert preferred to have a staff running interference, she had no desire to revert to the past, or to train and manage transient interns in lower-level duties. The pace of the office gave Lorraine neither time nor inclination to become Robert's slavish "Girl Friday." Senators and Congressmen juggled multiple assistants using Admins to manage them, but there was no budget in this office for additional paid assistants.

Lorraine walked into Robert's office with his morning coffee, and put away his coat, scarf, and gloves. These were two concessions that didn't bother her. She liked to keep everything as organized as possible, and getting coffee meant that Robert wasn't making a mess of the machine.

"Did I get a call from Chris Stoker, or Colonel Barlow?" he asked.

"No, Sir. I gave you all the messages." She responded.

"If they call, interrupt me no matter what I'm doing," he told her.

She nodded and left, closing the door behind her.

Where the hell was Chris? Robert wondered for the thirtieth time. And what about Grady? He was presumably looking into the nuts and bolts of how this could happen—if it could happen. Robert knew that once he had that information, the challenge of figuring out who could be behind it all should be a little easier. This wasn't Robert's biggest worry. If Chris's fears turned out to be valid, the real problem became keeping it confined as an internal investigation. A public investigation could become a nightmare.

Would Chris's evidence support an investigation? Robert shook his head. He was getting way ahead of himself in guessing that Chris had a smoking gun.

The day wore on. Still he had no call from Chris, or Grady. Robert crunched through his usual stack of calls and e-mail, only to watch the stack rise again. He went out for lunch, and came back to more messages. Only one interested him. It was a return call from Mr. Hunt. All it said was, "Urgent."

He tried the number several times, only to get voice mail each time. Robert's tension kept rising.

Something was bothering Robert about the sequence of events that had occurred in the last few days. The more he thought about it, the more Robert felt led around by the nose. Each step seemed to have been planned...or perhaps "anticipated" was a better word.

He shook his head. Maybe he was being paranoid. He got back to thinking about the problems of motive and opportunity. He hoped those were the keys that would lead him to who could benefit, and where this was all going. With Chris' information, and with some help from Grady, it should all become evident.

The telephone rang. Hitting the speaker button, he said, "Yes?"

Lorraine's voice announced the incoming caller, "Colonel Barlow calling."

"Put him through." At last, Robert thought.

"Grady?" Robert found himself feeling uncharacteristically anxious, waiting for Grady's response.

"Robert, I've had some success. I went downstairs..." Grady began.

Robert cut him off. "Let's get together." If this was going to be an unofficial investigation, he decided, there should be minimal opportunity for leaks.

Grady was taken aback. Slowly he answered. "Okay...where?"

Robert thought quickly. "Remember where we had lunch? The football game?"

Grady thought for a minute. "Yes...the playoffs, I remember. It was at the Marriott."

"Yes. Can you be there in an hour?" Robert asked.

"Sure, less actually," answered Grady.

"Good, see you there." Robert hung up.

Getting up, Robert glanced quickly at his new e-mails. Nothing caught his attention. His cell phone would get any new ones that popped up. He put his computer to sleep, and released it from the cradle. He then buzzed Lorraine. "I'm going to a meeting. I'll have my phone if you need me."

"I have a call for you, Sir." She paused slightly before continuing, "It's Mr. Carlton."

"Thank you," Robert answered mechanically, frowning.

The red LED flashed, marking the line where his father was holding. What did he want? His father rarely called him, and never just to chat. Robert wished he'd told Lorraine to say he was out. He finally snatched up the phone.

"Robert Carlton," Robert said, as neutrally as possible, as though Lorraine had not announced the call.

"Robbie! Glad I caught you in the office. Is your day going well?" His father asked, sounding upbeat.

"Busy as always." Robert hated to be called Robbie, and instantly adopted a hurried tone. He wanted to get this call over with as quickly as possible.

"Glad to hear it." His father said easily. He clearly hadn't noticed, or wasn't going to acknowledge Robert's tone and implication. His father had something on his mind. He probably hadn't even heard Robert's response. Robert figured his father would have said the same thing if he'd said he'd had a car accident that morning.

"I've heard that your department is looking into security around OPOV." The senior Mr. Carlton continued, "I just want you to know that, at some point, an indictment could be useful. Even better, arrests would be very beneficial."

Robert sat down hard into his chair. His head reeled. How had his father found out about the OPOV issue? He gave himself a moment to breathe. What the hell was going on? Okay, he reasoned, the truth was that his father always seemed to be a little too well informed. So, the better question was: how was it that this information had reached him so quickly, and why was he making these statements about indictments and arrests? As yet there was no criminal action, and in fact, Robert was still hoping to preempt any action.

Robert was thinking fast. The simplest explanation was that the President must have mentioned the matter. His father and the President lunched fairly regularly. Gregg had mentioned his apparent bi-partisan discussion with the President, so that had to be the answer. His father must have misinterpreted the situation in mentioning arrests.

"Father, I can't talk about any official activities. You know that." Robert tried his best to shut down where this was going.

"Absolutely," his father agreed. "I understand this is still *un*official. Now, here's the way I see it..." he was continuing.

Robert couldn't believe it. Here he was, the Associate Attorney General of the United States of America, and his father was still telling him what to do.

"I can't talk about unofficial possibilities, either." Robert cut in. He wanted to get off this call fast.

"Of course." His father continued, undeterred. "Now, Son, you've got a perfect opportunity here to get good visibility with the public, the press, and the President all at once. The press likes nothing better than espionage; spies and drama—that's their bread and butter. The public loves to hear that their government is keeping them safe, and as Tom says, 'Any press...'"

"...'Is good press.' Yes, I'm familiar with President Baxter's maxims on publicity, Father." Robert said sarcastically. Did his father ever think about whom he was speaking to, or did he just love the sound of his own thoughts too much to care?

"That's right, Son." Once again his father recognized the interruption only as an acknowledgment of his own point. "If you could find a way to get this wrapped up quickly, and publicize it properly before the test vote, it would be a big boost to your career. And of course, the timing couldn't be better with Jack being confirmed."

"I understand that. You know that this is all confidential, and that I can't..." Robert rushed back into the conversation, and then paused and repeated incredulously, "Jack is being confirmed?"

"Yes, yes," his father said impatiently, but sounding pleased that, once again, he'd trumped his son's knowledge base. "I know you haven't heard, yet, but the confirmation will be in shortly. Jack will be announced as the Attorney General. This is excellent timing for you. It's a real opportunity to shine. Just keep after it, Son. Tom would like to see you get this one, but keep the whole situation very quiet. If you can't pin down those responsible outright, don't let it get out that you missed. You got that?"

Robert's brain was seething with frustration. His father had known about Jack Crain's confirmation before the information became public; possibly before the committee had made the decision. It was also clear that Robert's promotion wasn't as probable as it was merely possible. No pressure there. He noticed also that his father didn't skip a beat when giving him more advice, along with managing to get in a little dig.

Robert reflected that this was just like getting "advice" from Senator Gregg. He was supposed to listen and keep quiet. Typical politics, he thought. Publicize victories; bury mistakes. Remember that there's always someone who is closer to the inner circle than you are, he thought bitterly.

Robert decided to wrap this up. "Good to hear from you, Father. I have to get going."

"Certainly." His father answered jovially. "I've got a meeting I need to get to, so we'll have to finish this up. I'll talk to you later, and check on how things are going." He hung up.

Robert replaced the phone thinking how typical his father's calls were. He always had to have the last word, while looking busier and more important than whomever he was speaking with into the bargain.

Once again, Robert was left feeling a little stunned about his father's connections to everything and everyone. Yes, he was connected at the highest levels, but did he really have to know everything before Robert did? He felt like a puppet, with his father pulling the strings. Robert had understood the connection of government and big business since early childhood, but he was still amazed at how closely tied his father was to politics.

"Only the public is foolish enough to think puny public servant salaries can keep the power of big business under control, Son. Big government is all about big business," his father always told him. He should know, Robert thought; his father was big in both.

Robert was feeling pretty angry about the call. He punched the intercom button hard. "Lorraine, I'm leaving now."

"Yes, Sir." She responded blandly.

"If either Chris Stoker or Colonel Barlow calls, forward them to my cell phone." He ordered.

"Yes, Sir." Lorraine's calm seemed impenetrable.

Picking up his computer, Robert stuffed it in its case and headed back to the car. He didn't say another word to Lorraine as he passed her on his way out.

Pulling out of the parking area, he tried to block his father from his mind by replaying his lunch meeting with Gregg, and by turning up the radio. His father's words nagged at him. He'd indicated that there were specific individuals to find—perhaps a specific person pulling the strings? Wait...his father hadn't actually said that. He'd indicated, "arrests would be beneficial." Putting that together with Gregg and Jack giving Robert the "fall guy" position, did his father mean that Robert better find evidence and someone to pin this situation on, quickly?

Either way, Robert suddenly realized with a shock, his father had indirectly verified what Chris had been trying to tell him. Chris Stoker wasn't paranoid. He was onto something. This was no longer a "what if" study. The President and his father had clearly been discussing the situation as an infiltration of OPOV. Now it was an investigation.

As such, it should seem straightforward, but it seemed that he'd been manipulated into a very visible corner. Gregg had attached him to the committee, which, in effect, put him on a leash. He'd be fed only the information Gregg wanted him to have. Plus, Gregg had cut off any outside agency connections by telling Robert to make it all "unofficial." Gregg was hiding some agenda. No surprise there, Robert thought. Gregg always had an agenda. But what was on it now?

This time, as Robert pulled away from the office, he noticed the plain brown sedan pull out behind him.

He didn't think much about the car; he just noted it. But soon casual observation became a concern. He tried to glance in the mirror through the side of his eye, careful to avoid moving his head as he realized the car was staying close to his. He was only a few blocks down Constitution Avenue when he pulled over to the far right lane and turned. "I'll make four right turns. Odds are he won't be following me after that," Robert thought.

He completed the first turn and watched as the brown car went by. It didn't slow down as it continued down the road.

"See? It was nothing. Calm down," Robert told himself. "You're becoming paranoid like the rest of these guys." He made the next three turns cursing the delay he'd caused himself, then came back onto Constitution heading back toward the George Washington Parkway. He kept checking the mirror.

Making it across the Roosevelt Bridge, he felt more at ease. He watched the Potomac disappear in the rear view mirror as he left DC behind. He relaxed. He didn't spot the brown sedan pull onto Constitution from 22nd street and fall in five cars behind him.

Chapter 22

The Key Bridge Marriott on sixty-six had a good beer and ale selection. It was a quiet bar designed for businessmen. With an upscale atmosphere and a flat screen behind the bar, it wasn't much of a sports bar, but more of a business traveler hang out. Being on the far side of the bridge it tended to be half-empty. There was always a seat available, even during big games. Robert pulled into the hotel parking lot. The brown sedan stayed back, going around the building before entering, and parking well away from Robert's car. It was still close enough for the driver to watch Robert go inside.

Robert saw that Grady wasn't there yet, so he chose a stool at the bar across from the entrance. From there he could face the door without being seen from the lobby area. He smiled at the cute waitress as he ordered a draft. She would be hard not to notice in that tight black dress. Robert wasn't the type to hang out at bars regularly, but he could see that this place had its attractions. Grady arrived a couple of minutes later, and made straight for Robert.

"What's with all the cloak and dagger?" Grady laughed. He seemed pleased with how the day was going.

"Let's switch to a table," Robert spoke in a restrained tone. He walked to the back of the bar where several small, secluded tables stood. "I think this is more serious than I realized."

"Really? Why?" Grady's interest perked up. He still looked like someone ready to enjoy himself, but he definitely was paying closer attention to Robert's careful attitude.

"People are suddenly showing an interest in this situation—and at higher levels than I would ever have expected," Robert told him. "I think we have less time to investigate than I originally thought. What did you find out?"

The waitress delivered Robert's beer, and Grady ordered an amber ale. He watched her walk away, appreciating the view before turning back to face Robert.

A new customer walked in and sat at the bar, facing the television. He took no notice of the waitress. His right hand, tucked under his left arm, held a black rod about 5 inches long. It looked like a pen, but it contained a directional microphone. An earpiece, resembling a Bluetooth headset, allowed the man to listen while simultaneously recording Robert and Grady.

"I'm glad I haven't wasted my time, then. I have a team working on it." Grady was saying.

"Who?" Robert asked directly. He was tired of vague answers.

"Crypto," Grady answered cautiously, eyeing Robert. He was now the one being cautious, since he didn't like talking about the Crypto team in public.

"Crypto...?" Robert interrogated. He needed solid answers.

Grady leaned closer and lowered his voice casually. "Cryptography. Codes and ciphers, and the guys who make and break them. They were probably more interested in trying to break through the NSA's security than in helping me, but who cares? They've already determined that the fastest way to infiltrate the system would be to have somebody on the inside, or to control someone there. That person would have to find a weak spot in the system. They're looking into it further, but the most obvious weak spot is in the software on the Internet side at one of the summing points. It may even be at the main collection point at the NSA itself. In any case, all those systems are designed by the NSA, so that's the place to start."

The conversation abruptly stopped as the girl delivered Grady's ale. The cut of her dress showed off her cleavage as she leaned over. She knew how to draw looks and tips. She set down a bowl of bar munchies with the drinks.

"Would you gentlemen like anything else?" She smiled nicely right at Grady as she placed her hand lightly on his shoulder.

"No, we're good. Thanks." Grady returned her smile, managing to keep his eyes on hers.

"Let me know if you need anything. My name is Shannon." With a smile, again directed at Grady, she turned and walked away.

There was a pause as the two men took a drink of their cold beers, and let their testosterone surges dissipate.

"Now, that's a problem," Robert commented into his beer.

"The girl? It's the uniform. It won't happen again." Grady joked.

"No; the NSA," Robert said with some frustration.

"The NSA? Why?" Grady said, picking up his beer and draining half of it.

"If it's the NSA, or someone in the NSA, it's a problem," Robert answered. "They have their own internal controls. They don't like people coming in and meddling. Even if we find some definite link they won't make it easy to resolve the problem, because we will already have trespassed on their turf. Not only is it adversarial, it's also not in the spirit of working on this project together. And, if we're right, and it's someone inside, they look incompetent."

"And I can understand it," Robert continued. "If they, the CIA, FBI, or for that matter, the Pentagon allowed interference, they'd never get anything done. They'd be addressing everyone's concerns and investigations all the time. Their security would be compromised constantly. But it does make our job more complicated. If I try to investigate with, or without their help, I'll be warning whoever's behind this just by showing up."

"I don't know about that," Grady said after a minute or two of thinking about the problem. "Most people don't really see you guys as investigators or cops. Your department seems very administrative. Lots of lawyer talk and paperwork hassles."

"You might be right about that, Grady," Robert said, "but they'll sense some kind of problem's coming if I approach them." He sighed, and took a drink before continuing. "Even if your Crypto people figure out how someone could do this, we've still got to find the person or people behind it. I don't know if you can nail down anybody's specific job in the NSA to the 'how.' They undoubtedly have multiple people checking each other. And I certainly couldn't spot someone doing whatever it is by looking over reports, or job titles, and functions. I doubt anything would stick out that obviously. If we approach the NSA, no matter how diplomatically we try to pursue it, we'll be putting them on alert. Everyone will be cleaning up their section." He paused, trying to gather his thoughts.

"Damn it, Grady!" Robert swore in frustration, curling his hand into a fist, and softly hitting the table. "The truth is that I don't even have a crime, yet. Just speculation that a crime is being committed—but there's too much interest in what I'm doing to call this 'a possibility' at this point. So much for jurisdictional power! Nobody has done anything that I know about or can prove, but now I'm expected to find a crime. The Attorney General's office isn't like that movie, 'Minority Report,' for God's sake. We can't foretell the future, and I can't stop crime before it happens if I don't know what I'm looking for." Robert tried to smile at his own joke. It was a good smile, but not charismatic like Grady's.

Grady frowned. He hadn't seen the movie, so Robert's attempt at humor was lost on him. "Robert, I'm sure that's a good reference, but not one I know. Look, I thought you had an informant, or some evidence. You seemed to think some crisis was at hand."

"I do have an informant," Robert told him, "but the evidence is forthcoming. The contact seems credible, and I've had some outside conversations today that seem to confirm what I've been told. But until I get the proof, we're still talking theory and speculation here." Robert continued, trying to shake off his frustration. "We have to establish probable cause, and have an investigative team assigned. This investigation is going to have to become 'official,' or we're going to get nowhere. Another problem

I've got is that right now all I have is a request to ensure that couldn't happen, but I'm going to have to find a way around that."

Grady shook his head, mystified. "Don't you have anything concrete? Is this person reliable?"

"I don't have anything, yet, other than a lot of big problems," Robert answered, shaking his head. "But I've known this guy for a long time. I didn't believe what he was telling me—now I wish I'd taken him a lot more seriously when he first mentioned it. And, in the continuing theme of one complication appearing after another, I haven't heard from him since Friday morning."

"Robert, who is the informant? Look, you're telling me that you've got reason to believe this thing is happening, but it seems to hinge on getting one guy's evidence. Does it make sense for everything to hang on one person?" Grady asked keeping his gaze steady on Robert's eyes.

Robert hesitated. Grady was right. What if Chris never came through with his documentation? Maybe Robert needed to talk about his with someone he could trust, and certainly the only person that fit that bill right now was Grady.

Grady pushed. "Well?"

"You have to keep this confidential." Robert insisted.

"What do you think I've been doing?" Grady frowned. "Robert, I don't go in and ask the Crypto guys to help me dig into the NSA every day. I've been taking this seriously. You should recognize that I understand the meaning of 'confidentiality.'"

Robert paused again before speaking. "It's Chris Stoker." He still wasn't sure he should be telling Grady. Legally, he'd just made Grady as responsible as he was if this thing didn't go well. Now he was going to implicate Grady even more. "He's a software guy at the NSA. We went to school together."

"Well, that changes things." Grady shook his head. "You can't go into the NSA holding hands with one of them. His job would be gone, and Homeland Security would jump in big time. Now you really need to have more than a hunch before you talk to the NSA. If his evidence isn't rock solid you're screwed." Grady knew that once a whistle blower was involved, all bets were off. The agencies would descend on the issue like flies, coming in from every direction.

"I can talk to the NSA." Robert said. "That's not the problem. What I need is something significant to talk about. Obviously, I can't mention Stoker, or even hint that I know him." Robert sighed. "How long before your crypto team might have something?"

"A week. They wanted a month, but I think they were padding the time." Grady answered. "What makes you think somebody won't make the connection between you and Chris? Those guys connect dots for a living." Grady took a drink of his beer. "Robert, I doubt that my guys will come up with anything that points to any one person actually manipulating the system. That leaves you with your guy's evidence." Grady was losing his enthusiasm. He felt he'd been sent on a wild goose chase. "I have to tell you, this doesn't sound good."

Robert wanted to reassure Grady. He knew he was going to need him to get a viable idea of how the control would be possible. "I'll get the hard evidence, Grady. It could be that Chris has had a problem removing it, but I know he's determined to get it to me. I'm sure whatever it is will give us a better picture of where, and who our problems are. In the meantime, we absolutely need to find out how OPOV could be manipulated. I had hoped our controls were tight enough to prevent that from happening, but after some of the calls I've had today, I'm not so sure."

"So, that's it." Grady eyed Robert ponderingly.

Robert swallowed most of the contents of his glass before answering. "Believe me, Grady, I wish I had more. My career may be hanging in the balance on this, good or bad."

"How high does this go?" Grady asked.

"Too high. And that doesn't make much sense, either. I just barely found out about it from Chris, so is it a coincidence that suddenly people who shouldn't, know something's up? Obviously, there is more going on here. And I can't shake the feeling I've been followed twice since I met with Chris."

"Followed?" Grady seemed startled.

"Twice, maybe more." Robert reiterated. "It sounds ridiculous, I know. I've found myself circling the block a couple of times since this started." Robert shrugged, and ran his hand over his head. He felt like an idiot for saying any of this out loud. He couldn't look directly at Grady.

"Hey, just because you're paranoid doesn't mean they aren't out to get you." Grady smiled, but there was a little crease between his eyebrows. "Maybe we need another beer." Grady offered.

"Next time." Robert shook his head. "I need to get to my computer. I'll be in touch."

"I'll keep pushing on the guys. You'll let me know when your friend delivers, right?" Grady asked.

"Grady, I've told you more than I should have about this thing, but I guess I owe you whatever explanations come out," Robert said.

They finished their drinks and left. Neither noticed the man at the bar leave just before they did. He tapped out a few commands on his phone, transferring the recording from his directional microphone pen as he headed for the main entrance.

Robert checked his mirror a few times as he drove out of the parking lot. He saw nothing except the overcast sky, which was getting darker fast.

Grady didn't notice as the brown sedan pulled out of the parking lot behind him. It soon fell back behind several cars.

Chapter 23

Robert decided to vary his habitual route home. Coming from the hotel changed his drive, but that wasn't the only reason he took a different course. He was definitely feeling as though someone was watching him. Voicing his suspicions to Grady made the feeling stronger. He looked in the rearview mirror more often, noticed the drivers in cars next to him, and left the distracting radio news off. The feeling got more intense. Twice he detoured, hoping to expose a car that might be behind him, while at the same time trying to rationalize his concern as paranoia rather than reality. He made a circuitous trip through narrow, older roads lined with forests. He might have enjoyed it another day, but right now his stomach was too tight.

The Virginia roads meandered like the cow paths they originally followed through the thick woods. Trees crowded the shoulder, closing in around him. Robert maneuvered around several sharp turns, going into and out of hidden gullies and over narrow bridges. The BMW handled the turns beautifully, but Robert didn't spend much time thinking about his car as he drove.

These roads seemed to Robert like trails through the wilderness, appearing deserted and void of humanity. It was an odd sensation, since the road was surrounded by homes hidden behind the trees. In summer, the deep green forest was calming, and had a hushed sound all its own. Warm days, and fall's crisp, brilliant colors made Robert wish for his old convertible. During the gray season the barren trees emphasized the cold, and the evergreens took on a dull shade of green with fewer needles. The ground was a montage of fallen dead and drying foliage. Patches of white and brown dotted the landscape all winter.

Frigid air crept down his driver's side window. Despite the BMW's excellent heater, his left shoulder felt chilled. The bleak view seemed to fit Robert's increasingly cheerless mood.

No cars seemed to be following him. Occasionally he had to swerve away from oncoming cars as they both hugged the center too closely. The narrowest roads had no marked center line and Robert's incessant mirror watching made staying on his side inconsistent, at best. By the time he pulled into his driveway Robert was ridiculously tense, and convinced that he was being foolish. He almost laughed at his own paranoia. He still carefully checked the shadowed driveway before parking his car in the garage.

He punched in his security pin as soon as he entered the house, and felt better hearing the reassuring chirp of the alarm system re-locking. Only a few lights glowed in the dim house. Tracie was saving energy with dimmers on the timers. She had one running on at least one light in every room, to confuse thieves.

"Hello? I'm home." Robert called out. There was no answer. Tracie's light system was working; even Robert couldn't tell if anyone was home. He walked into his office and laid down his briefcase. Hanging his coat on the rack, he went out toward the dining room.

"Anybody home?" He called again. Coming around the corner into the dining room he saw candles flickering brightly in a candelabra. The polished platinum-edged, black china was laid out on the table, with sterling silverware and black linen napkins. There were place settings for two.

"Tracie?" He called, wondering if he'd forgotten something.

"I'm in the kitchen." Her voice was light and happy sounding.

As he went past the table he caught the aromas of hollandaise sauce and asparagus. He could hear the water running, filling a pot. He knew a special dinner was being created. As he entered the kitchen he saw Tracie standing over the cooktop with a huge stainless steel pot. The pot filler water tap mounted to the tile backsplash above the stove was filling it with pre-heated water.

"I thought we'd celebrate," Tracie said, turning to greet him. She looked beautiful and shapely, in all of her five-foot-five height. In fact, she looked much like the debutante he'd married. Her skillfully highlighted hair suited her, and her dainty features disguised her aggressive blue blood dorsal fin. She was a shark in sheep's clothing. She had a nice shape, pleasing to the eye. He would have liked a little more bust to fondle, but she had the complete package, and she fit nicely when folded into his arms. He loved the way her long slim fingers would run along his back when they had one of their all too few lovemaking encounters—and they were getting fewer with every passing year.

The pot began to steam, while on the counter nearby two lobsters awaited their fate. Coming toward him, the long black negligee flowing with her motion, Tracie stretched out her arms to clasp his neck and kiss him. It was a nice kiss, even though the butterflies of their youth had long since fluttered away. Replacing the blend of curiosity and shyness was sensuality, and a sense of being comfortable with each other.

"The kids are staying at Alicia's, and we have the place to ourselves," Tracie told him. "I thought we'd have a little celebration. Would you get the wine?"

"Sure," Robert replied, wondering what the occasion was. He ran through the calendar in his mind quickly scanning for a match between today and any important dates. He focused back on her eyes and forced his smile a little wider.

She kissed him again then released her hold to return to the stove. Robert headed toward the refrigerated wine cabinet to fetch a good Chardonnay. As he twisted in the corkscrew, he asked, "So, how was your day?"

"I got the Turkish dinner assignment!" She called out brightly.

He hadn't forgotten a special date. She was just happy about getting the official dinner. Robert's tension evaporated with relief, and an audible exhale.

"What did you say?" She asked.

"I said...that's great!" Robert was feeling better, and prepared himself to be interested in her achievement.

"Can you believe it?" Tracie was, in fact, giddy with her achievement. This was a victory she could notch into her political gun grip. She sounded extremely pleased with herself.

Robert handed her a glass of wine, knowing it wouldn't take too much encouragement to keep her spirits high. "Of course I believe it. You're great at this! When is it?"

"The twenty-ninth of next month." She answered. Tracie babbled for five minutes about the event. Robert didn't hear a word. He knew there was some drivel about place settings and menus, but nothing about which he needed to make more than a few sounds of agreement. Garaurd, the ever-present, ever helpful NATO stud, was on his mind. Undoubtedly he would figure into this dinner, too. Trying to pass that situation off as unfounded jealousy wasn't working for Robert. He tried to remind himself that she was celebrating with him, not Garaurd, and cooking a romantic meal on top of that. Surely that meant something.

"So, how was your day?" She dropped the lobsters into the hot, steaming pot and put the lid on. When she turned toward him, her negligee flared open, exposing the sheer black lace and satin trim of her teddy. The legs were cut extravagantly high and the sweetheart neckline showed off her breasts to the best advantage. Pushup pads enhanced her cleavage. The line from her stomach to her thighs was smooth and firm from all her Pilates work.

Robert pulled himself back to the conversation in time to say, "Fine. Just fine."

Tracie immediately noticed Robert's distraction. Knowing it was her physical presence that had him captivated, a feeling of power coursed through her. She pulled the negligee open farther, and put on her best coquettish smile as she raised her long leg, her toe pointed to rest on the handle of the lower oven door. Robert's gaze focused on the underside of her leg as it curved upward. His passion aroused, other concerns in his mind faded. The days when

Tracie felt sensual had become rare, and his animal instincts were unfamiliarly near at hand. He swept forward and wrapped his arms around her narrow waist, his hands pressing against her back and pulling her breasts into his chest. They kissed again. His lips moved to the side of hers, across her cheek and down her neck. As he moved one hand around to her breast, his lips descended to touch her nipple as it pushed out from under the lace. Her head went back, arms opening as she almost dropped the potholder. The buzzer went off, its raucous noise abruptly ending the moment.

"Mmmmm." Her murmur faded as she turned away to pull warm bread out of the oven. Robert had to move back quickly, or get burned by the door.

Tracie clearly hadn't been swept away by the moment. Her focus was still on her achievement. "I just can't believe I got the job. You know the girls will be beside themselves when they hear about it." She didn't skip a beat.

Robert felt the air escaping from his body, leaving him deflated. She was much better at turning on and off in rapid succession than he.

Tracie gave the prepackaged hollandaise a stir and checked the asparagus for tenderness. "I think we're about ready." The fifteen-minute timer on the lobsters was counting down. "Could you put on some music?"

The hunger that had built up in Robert fell away as quickly as it had rushed in. He walked off to the stereo. Pushing a few buttons and spinning the display with his finger, he selected a collection of light jazz from the stored playlists. His libido had sufficiently recovered to tactfully pursue this possible romance. He turned the volume to a soft level, filling the house with sound from multiple speakers in almost every room. Going to the cabinet, he pulled out the wine bucket for the table. It was a sleek design that would keep the Chardonnay chilled. He heard the timer go off.

"The lobsters are ready. Could you help me with these?" She called.

He went back to the kitchen and grabbing the steaming pot, lifted it into the sink where Tracie snatched the lobsters out with a pair of tongs. Safely on the plates, corn on the cob and pale green asparagus with creamy yellow sauce framed the bright red lobsters. Sourdough bread finished the table array as they each carried their plates into the dining room. Robert pulled her chair out, looking down her décolletage, with its teasing view of lace and skin. His hand caressed her shoulder, his fingers gliding forward down her exposed neckline.

Her head tilted slightly back, her eyelashes sliding gracefully closed. "Oooh, that's nice." Then her eyes popped open again. "Come on. Sit down and eat before they get cold." She leaned forward and grabbed her napkin.

On and off again with blinding speed, he thought.

Robert obediently took his chair at the head of the large table. Tracie sat at the far end. There was only one leaf in the table, but still, he wondered how romantic this dinner could be over the distance of a six-foot table? He reflected on how, in the past, passion would have let this meal go cold; or, at least that was what he vaguely remembered. He knew the passion could return after the food and wine were consumed, but lukewarm lobster, on the other hand, was a sin.

They mimicked clinking glasses without toasting, and went to work on the lobsters. With hands prying and shells cracking, the lobsters were a messy meal, but they tasted great dipped in the hot, clarified butter, with just a hint of lemon.

Tracie seemed to eat daintily, despite the barbaric shell cracking. She also ate quickly. Her voracious appetite had always exceeded Robert's. He chuckled to himself. She couldn't talk as much with her mouth full, and he could tell she wanted to keep talking. He knew there would be no touching until the meal was over, the dishes put away, the kitchen clean, the remains deposited outside in the garbage, and last but most important, their hands washed…several times. Robert ate a little faster, in anticipation of a little sensual exercise.

The plates had been cleared away, and what was left of the wine was poured into the glasses. Robert stood leaning on the counter as he watched Tracie. Her long legs moved back and forth under the lace as she chattered about how great her event would be, and what dignitaries would attend. Tracie was putting the smaller pots in the dishwater when the phone rang.

They seldom answered the phone, preferring to screen their calls through the answering machine, and checking the caller i.d. Robert walked into the office to hear who might be calling, just in case it was important. The machine finished its message and beeped. The caller spoke. It was Lorraine. She sounded upset.

"Mr. Carlton. This is Lorraine…"

Lorraine rarely called him at home. Robert picked up the handset wondering what could be wrong. "Lorraine, what's the matter?"

"Mr. Carlton. I'm glad you're home. I know you've been expecting a call from Chris Stoker, so I thought I should call you as soon as I heard."

"Yes, Lorraine, I'm glad you did." Robert thought she sounded uncharacteristically anxious. "What is it?'

"I just saw a report on television talking about crime in D.C. I'm so sorry, Mr. Carlton. Your friend Mr. Stoker's been killed."

"Killed?" Robert was stunned. "Chris Stoker? Are you sure?" He asked, knowing that Lorraine didn't make mistakes like this. She would never have called him without being positive.

"Yes, Sir. It happened Friday. They were interviewing his wife, Anne Stoker."

Friday? He'd seen Chris on Friday. It couldn't be him, Robert thought. But Anne was Chris's wife's name all right. Robert slumped down into his chair, feeling disoriented.

"Who is it?" Tracie stood posed in the doorway.

"It's Lorraine." He answered. "Chris Stoker's been killed."

"Who?" Tracie looked confused.

Robert waved off the question with a feeble gesture, and turned his attention back to Lorraine.

"Mr. Carlton?" Lorraine was asking, "Is there anything you'd like me to do?"

"Thanks for letting me know, Lorraine. I'll pull up the news online and see if I can catch the report. I'll let you know if I need anything tomorrow. Oh, which channel were you watching?"

She gave him the number of the news channel. He thanked her again, and hung up.

"Who has been killed?" Tracie queried again.

"Chris Stoker," Robert answered shortly. He was still taking in the idea that Chris was dead. He didn't think he was up to explaining anything to Tracie at the moment.

"He was that friend of yours from school, wasn't he?" Tracie remembered.

"Yes," Robert replied distractedly, opening his computer.

"How did it happen?" Tracie asked.

"I don't know. I'm going to see if I can catch the report on the news." Robert had opened the browser and was typing in the station to search for its web site.

"Will you be long?" Tracie asked.

"No, I just need to hear this." Robert was completely distracted.

"I'm going upstairs," Tracie told him, leaving the study.

Robert didn't seem to notice.

Robert sat reading the report on the news station's web site, while the video loaded. The site gave limited details, but there was

Anne on the video turning away from the camera as tears filled her eyes and her voice failed. He gleaned that homicide had been called in to investigate, but there was little information beyond that. The story was about many crimes, and the growing number of murders in the city.

Picking up the phone, he called Grady's cell phone, but he got his voicemail.

"Grady, Chris Stoker has been killed. It looks like it might have been a carjacking but I have a really bad feeling about this. Call me. And watch your back." He didn't know why he added that last part. Surely there was no connection to Grady, or to him…was there?

Robert checked the alarm system on the house, made sure the blinds were closed and went back to the computer, surfing several channels, hoping to find expanded coverage about Chris. Washington considered it just another murder. It was on the Metro Police "MPDC Unsolved Homicides" page already. More than an hour passed before he stopped looking. Grady hadn't called back. Robert grabbed his cell phone, and headed toward the stairs.

As he passed through the hallway, he caught a glimpse of the kitchen garbage bag tied up by the doorway. Tracie had cleaned up the dinner, and the lobster remains would definitely need to leave the house. Grabbing the garbage bag, he headed for the garage. The alarm chirped as he turned it off, and he dumped the bag in the bin just outside the door. Re-locking the door, he activated the alarm.

Everything in order, he grabbed his cell phone again and finally headed upstairs.

Only one light was left on. Tracie was asleep in lobster fed bliss. He went into the bathroom, brushed his teeth, undressed, and climbed in bed. He switched off the bedside light. Tracie, with a sigh, rolled over on her side toward him and opened one eye.

"Did you take out the lobster?"

"Yes." He said quietly.

With her arm draped over him, they cuddled, which was unusual, and nice. Her breathing returned to a slow, deep rhythm. He was still holding his phone when he fell into a restless sleep full of questions.

Chapter 24

Grady had been driving for fifteen minutes before he noticed the lights following behind him. Immersed in freeway traffic, and then the crush of commuters going home through the suburbs, he'd thought little about the car that seemed to be trailing him to the 'burbs until he got closer to his house. Once he got past the newer developments, the houses got smaller, older, and the lot sizes got a little bigger. The area was thick with mature trees. Hills and valleys kept houses separated, and small streams had narrow bridges over them. With more curves in the road, it made it more obvious that a car was keeping pace with him.

Grady became more suspicious with each turn. Watching the lights, he deliberately drove past his house and went toward the shopping area where he usually bought groceries.

Pulling into the parking lot, Grady casually drove through as if looking for a parking spot. Under the lights he could see that the car was a basic sedan. Brown, or maybe gray in color. The parking lot lights made it hard to tell. Reaching the far side, he pulled back out onto the main road. Seeing the car follow, he stomped on the gas and took the nearest turn. Barreling down the neighborhood streets, he kept turning. He knew the area and avoided the dead ends. Concentrating on driving, he didn't look back right away. When he did, he was pleased there were no longer any headlights in his mirror. Continuing to move through the neighborhood at a much slower speed, Grady kept an eye out. Though he had managed to lose sight of the car, he was still uneasy. To test the situation, Grady came out on the main road, and then ducked off again. No one followed him, so he headed back, eventually coming out well away from the shopping area where he had started. He had not seen the suspicious car lights again.

Feeling triumphant, but also a little bit stupid for being paranoid, he made his way back home. "Ridiculous," he thought, "nobody is following me."

With few major intersections in the area, the only road that headed directly home took him past the same grocery store. He didn't see the brown sedan as it pulled out of the parking lot, well after he had passed it.

What Grady didn't know was that his tail didn't have to follow him anymore. He had turned back to wait in the parking lot once he'd realized Grady was aware of his car. He'd only followed Grady to find out if he was meeting with someone else. His associate would be quietly parked a few houses down from Grady's. He started dialing the associate's cell phone, but realized he'd lost his signal.

When he pulled up behind the other car, he got out and walked up to the passenger door. With a look through the window, he got in.

"I saw him come home." His associate said.

"Yeah, he didn't stop anywhere after the bar."

"Any word?" The associate asked.

"No, nothing. I had a signal before, but not here. You?"

"No bars on the phone," the man answered, "but the orders were plain enough. Make sure he makes the connection between Stoker and the NSA. Barge in, and demand to know what he has learned. Rough him up a little and tell him to back off."

"Yeah, well, I think they made the connection while they were at the bar." The first man told him.

"So, we're still on, and no new orders?" The associate confirmed.

"That's how I read it, but I don't like going forward without confirmation."

"You want to tell him you decided not to do what he said?"

"Nope."

"Me, either. Give it another fifteen minutes and let's get this done." A sneering grin crept across his face.

"Roger that." The man answered.

Grady's house was like most of those along the narrow road. Built in the sixties, the brick-sided house had a small front porch. The garage was an add-on near the kitchen, and the trees on the property were large and mature. The house sat on a rectangular acre. A low rock wall bordered the property, running along the road. Grady parked in the center of the two-car garage. The left side was cluttered with yard equipment and woodworking tools. The right side was dedicated to his 1999 Yamaha Road Star, the first model year the big cruiser came out.

Grady got out of the Jeep and started to walk out of the garage when he noticed that his security light was off. Reaching over next to the door opener button, he flicked the security light timer switch off and on again. "Damn thing. Five-year guarantee, my ass." He'd have to get a new timer. He punched the button that closed the garage door and went into the house.

Chapter 25

Grady sat watching TV. The bone of a grilled steak lay on a plate next to the empty skin of a microwaved potato. Nothing was on TV that interested him, so he turned on the news. Grady's fantasy football team was already set for the weekend, but there might be some update on the Redskins. Most nights he would eat, then work. If he got home early, he would exercise first, eat, and watch TV the rest of the evening. The routine was getting pretty dull. He looked over at the picture of his wife sitting on the roll top desk. She had died of cancer three years earlier. She had been smiling at him as he'd taken her picture, the big red hibiscus flowers from their honeymoon lanai in Hawaii framing her face. Most nights he would look at her picture and re-read the inscription below it.

> *"I think of you nightly*
> *From a distance too far,*
> *And smile at the memories*
> *That became who you are."*
> *Love, Keisha*

"Hey baby," he said, toasting her with the last of his beer.

"Love at first sight," his friends had kidded him, but it was true. They had met at an Academy Senior's party and within a few short months, they were married. It had been a massive wedding, the day after his graduation at the Academy. It had taken place in the cathedral-roofed, stunningly designed Air Force Academy Chapel, complete with dress uniforms, drawn sabers, and the Corps of Cadets in attendance. Keisha's dark skin had glowed, enhanced by her off-white lace, classic Grace Kelly inspired gown. It had been storybook all the way.

Grady's fighter pilot training had been followed up by an overseas assignment to Germany, and fast promotions. Keisha's elegant smile had charmed everyone they met. They'd been the perfect team.

The cancer had come on suddenly. He'd been able to take leave, and was with her every minute of the final two months they had together. The first month they lived a lifetime of travel, flying to beautiful places, and seeking out sand and water. The last weeks were crippled with pain and drugs.

They hadn't seemed to have enough time to talk about children. Grady was glad for that during the painful last days; sad for it, now that she was gone. The nights were longer when he thought about her.

The newscaster on the TV had been talking about growing crime in Washington D.C. when Grady heard, "Chris Stoker was shot and killed in an apparent carjacking gone wrong. We interviewed his wife, Anne..."

Grady stared at the TV.

"Mrs. Stoker, can you tell us anything about what happened?"

"He was just headed back to work from a meeting downtown." Anne Stoker told the reporter. "I don't know anything about what happened except what they told me. It makes no sense. He just...it makes no sense." Her voice failed her. She turned from the camera in obvious anguish.

The reporter turned to the camera. "Mrs. Anne Stoker, wife of the victim is getting no answers from the police. As crime continues to grow..." The story line moved off to generalities, leaving Grady stunned.

"Could it be the same guy?" Grady was thinking rapidly. "Coincidence, Robert had said... He thought he was followed, and now I thought I was. What are the odds?" Grady stood up, mulling it over in his head. He turned away toward the kitchen to get another beer.

The moment he entered the brightly lit room the backdoor smashed open, propelling broken glass through the air.

"Hey!" Grady yelled as a man rushed in slamming him against the refrigerator, sending little magnets bouncing off onto the counter and across the floor.

Grady swung his arm, pushing the intruder back, then hitting him with his fist. Grady reeled under a heavy blow as he was struck suddenly from behind. Another man's hammer-like forearm pounded him repeatedly at the base of his neck, knocking him forward and down, the blows snapping his head back, and finally sending him to the floor.

"Unhhh!" The air blasted from Grady's lungs as he felt a shoe kick deep into his stomach. The kick sent him rolling over against the pantry. Two huge hands grabbed him by the collar and flung him sideways into the living room.

Grady fell over the couch, coming to rest half on the coffee table, half on the floor.

"You like that?" Grady could not see through the man's mask, but the grin showed, as the man stomped viciously on his chest. The heavy foot would have completely crushed Grady's chest, but the coffee table broke in half, absorbing some of the impact.

"Hey, man, take it easy!" The other assailant placed a hand on his partner's shoulder.

"Back off!" The man told him, swinging his left shoulder back to push his partner away. "I got this."

Grady lay there coughing, clutching his ribs as a trickle of blood flowed from his mouth, down his cheek. His vision was blurred and his head was spinning.

"What do..." he sputtered feebly and was cut short as he was grabbed by the shirt and lifted.

"Maybe that will put you in the mood to talk to us." The gruff-voiced man heaved him up and threw him onto the couch, causing pain to shoot through his damaged ribs.

"What do you know about Chris Stoker, Asshole?" The man growled.

"I don't know what you're talking about," Grady answered. His tongue licked his rapidly swelling lip. Grady could see the glint in the assailant's eyes as he felt the back of the man's hand snap across his cheek, jerking his head around and spraying blood onto the couch. A shooting pain ripped through his head.

"Try again!" The gruff voice ordered.

"Tell me what you want. I don't know..."

The man's left fist smashed into the side of Grady's gut. His body was thrown to the side of the couch, shuddering as the air in his chest burst out of his mouth.

"Unnnfhhh!" Grady sagged against the couch, his arms flung across the low-end table.

"Once more." The man pulled his gun from the shoulder holster under his right arm.

"Hey!" the second man yelled.

"Shut up!" The man told him. He pressed the gun into the side of Grady's jaw as he slowly began pulling him back upright. "By the numbers now. Who did you talk to at the NSA?"

Grady's voice came out strained and guttural as his hand clenched around the base of the brass lamp. "Oprah; who do you think, Asshole!" He jerked his arm around, the sharp upper corner of the heavy lamp bashing into the man's forehead as the base rammed into his arm. The man's gun was knocked aside, clattering across the room.

Blood gushed from the deep head wound as the man crumpled to the floor. The second man pulled back, his hands going up defensively. Grady's movement had brought the lamp far to one side. Holding it like a cocked bat he swung at the retreating man. The lampshade flew off, shattering the bulb, darkening the room. Only the television's glow and the light from the kitchen remained.

The second swing yanked out the cord, and caught the attacker in the shoulder, knocking him against the shelves and his hand away from his holstered gun. An avalanche of heavy books fell on the man's head. Bringing up his arms for protection, the assailant felt the lamp plunge into his stomach.

"You like that?" Grady spit out mockingly as he yanked the lamp over his shoulder and swung it into the assailant's chest. The man's fall into the shelves brought them down collapsing onto him. His knees buckled as he fell under the weight. The back of his head made a sickening crunch as Grady swung the lamp around and into it, cracking the bone, and spraying blood across the carpet.

The impact knocked Grady off balance. He fell backward into the wall where he slumped to the floor, gasping for breath. His arms clutched his chest. Lying on the ground next to him, the lamp rocked back and forth in an expanding pool of blood. Sharp pains in his lungs made him grimace as he watched the blood from the silent man's head spread along the baseboard. Grady couldn't catch his breath, but he still tried to force himself up on one arm. The movement sent more pain arching across his body. Shards of stabbing pain raged through his spine, drawing his head back in agony. "Ahhhhh!" Grady's voice died off as quickly as it had risen. Blackness swept over his vision. He slumped to the floor unconscious.

The other man lay in a heap below the couch, the sticky red stain spreading across his face and the fabric. His moan was almost imperceptible as he drew his arm in to push himself up. His partner lay lifeless under the collapsed bookcase. Grady lay before him in the bloody puddle. The man's head was aching vilely, but he realized what a mess he was in. This was not what Blair had in mind.

"Shit! He's going to have my ass." Thinking quickly, he knew he needed to destroy all the evidence of having been there. "Leave no trace," were always his implied orders. The whole thing was fucked up, and it was his fault.

Stumbling out of the house, he made his way to his sedan. He got in and drove quietly to the back of the house. Using no lights, he backed the car over the grass up close to the back doorway. He got out, leaving the engine running, and opened the unlit trunk.

Back inside the house, he pulled Grady away from the bookcase. Then he pushed the heavy shelves and books off his partner, and dragged him from the house and into the waiting trunk. Closing the trunk firmly, he stepped around the side of the car. He opened the rear door and pulled out a large can of mixed nuts from a gym bag. Stepping up to the house door, he pulled the lid off the can. Inside was a gray canister shaped like a can of shaving cream. It had a handle and ring on top. He removed the canister from the nut can, then tossed the empty nut container and lid into the house. The purple markings on the canister read AN-M14 INCEN TH. Clamping his hand around the handle, he put his finger in the ring and pulled it. Suddenly he hesitated. Without throwing the grenade, he patted his jacket where his gun should be. The holster was empty. Growling to himself, he walked back through the smashed back door into the kitchen, and crossed into the dimly lit den. In the moment that he realized Grady's body was missing, the brass lamp came hurtling down onto his head.

Grady, standing on top of the couch behind the threshold, had barely regained his feet and gotten into position. The force of the blow crushed the assailant to the floor as the gray Thermate grenade pitched forward from his hand. His body fell in an unconscious heap. Released from the assailant's grip, the grenade handle sprang open as the grenade bounced across the floor. The ping of the spring-loaded handle popping off the grenade was followed by a hiss, and a thin trail of smoke from the fuse as the weapon began its countdown.

Grady heard the ping and hiss. Running with everything left in his body, he threw himself out the back door. The idling car with the driver's door open sat in front of him. He jumped into the driver's seat, slammed the car into drive, and accelerated through the middle of his yard.

The house erupted in gas, smoke, and brilliant white flames. The ignited Thermate, burning at four thousand degrees Fahrenheit, blazed through everything it touched. Wood and fabric ignited instantly. Molten metal and superheated chemicals splattered everywhere. Particles falling on the assailant's body passed through it rapidly, leaving steaming holes. Metal propane gas pipes melted on contact, adding gas to the conflagration. The explosion opened the wall to the garage, throwing Thermate pieces into Grady's jeep and its gas tank. The explosion of the truck's fuel launched it into the garage roof, shattering the timbers as they were set ablaze.

Grady stomped on the gas pedal, sliding the car from the grass and sidewalk into the road. When the jeep exploded, he saw the pine tree next to the house ignite like a match as the house became fully engulfed. Everything would be gone in a few minutes.

Grady would be gone, too.

Chapter 26

Grady sat in a motel room, daubing his split swollen lip with a washcloth as he watched television. Occasionally turning the cloth to a less bloodied section, or tapping the remote button with his left thumb, he surfed across the channels, scanning for news. His bloody right hand ached as he soaked it in an ice and water-filled bucket. His forehead, wrapped in a towel soaked in the ice water, throbbed painfully. The bruises and swelling gave him a hideous, almost ghoulish appearance. The late hour and pitiful condition of the motel and this room explained the night clerk's willingness to give him a room without any questions. The clerk wouldn't accept a credit card, insisting on cash. Grady's habits of carrying cash and not emptying his pockets until bedtime were proving beneficial. It was sheer luck that he had not changed into exercise clothes. Everything not on his body had gone up in flames.

He had a headache the size of a basketball, but his mind was sharp. What had Robert gotten him into? The two men were obviously not robbers. The phosphorous grenade labeled them as professionals, with access to military-grade equipment. He *had* been followed, and he had been attacked with intent. There wasn't anything subtle about any part of that.

It now seemed unlikely that Chris Stoker's death was accidental, and it was doubtful that the local police would be of any value in keeping away whoever was trying to kill Grady. It was certain that calling the police would trap him for days where "they" would know how to find him. The Pentagon wouldn't be of much use either, since this investigation was "unofficial." They'd take weeks just sorting out what he'd been doing, why Robert had contacted him, and what was in the ashen rubble at what used to be his home. Right now, Grady was a target. Robert must be as well, he reflected.

Grady needed time to figure out how to deal with this situation. Getting out of town made sense, but what would the police say when they finally did get involved? Grady kept going back and forth, arguing with himself over possibilities. He realized he was sitting on his phone. He pulled it out of his pocket. There was a message notification on the screen with Robert's name.

Chapter 27

The telephone went off like an alarm in the dark silent room. Robert jerked up, knocking his half-full water glass off the nightstand while trying to find the phone.

"Damn it!" He cursed.

"Is that the phone?" Tracie asked sleepily.

"Yeah, I've got it." Robert searched for the phone then realized it was in his hand. He slid the screen, punched in his password, saw Grady's name, and hit the answer button. "Grady?"

"Robert?" Grady responded.

"What time it is?" Robert's head felt fuzzy, and the alarm clock was missing. He must have knocked it off the table along with the glass.

"Two-thirty," Grady answered. He seemed to be waiting for Robert to fully awaken before he dispensed any information.

"Grady? What are you calling about? No, wait; did you get my message?" Robert was feeling completely out of it, but waking up fast.

"Can you talk?" Grady's voice didn't have its normal tone. It sounded husky and muffled.

"Hang on. I'm switching rooms." He grabbed for his robe, fumbling with the tie.

"Okay, Hon." Tracie's voice was barely audible through the heavy comforter.

Robert kicked his shirt over onto the spilled water, stomping it twice with his foot to soak it up. Tracie was asleep before Robert got to the hallway, and headed down the hall to the stairs.

"Okay," Robert said, creeping quietly down the stairs as he talked. He sounded as groggy as he felt. He rubbed his eyes with his free hand. As he closed the office door softly behind him, he remembered that the kids were at Alicia's.

Grady didn't sound much better than Robert. He was fully awake, but his cut lip muddied his voice. "Listen Robert, I was attacked at my place after you and I met."

"You were attacked?" Robert asked sharply. He was fully awake now. "What do you mean, 'you were attacked?'"

"Don't ask lawyer questions, Robert—and yeah I got your message. Twice! Once from you, and once from the guys who tried to kill me!" Grady sounded as angry as he felt. "No, I'm not joking. They kicked the shit out of me. And before you ask, these guys were not muggers, or thieves. They were sent to get information the fastest way possible, and then get rid of me. I heard the report on the news about Stoker, and the next thing I knew these guys broke down the backdoor. Now my house is burned to the ground, the two of them are dead, and I'm lucky to be alive. For all I know, more of them will show up at the door here any second." Grady told him.

"Now, just listen to me before you try to rationalize this: nothing else I'm working on made this happen. They specifically asked about Stoker. Whatever you've gotten us into is damned serious. I got lucky. I'm still alive. They aren't." Grady finished.

Robert was stunned. Even as he wondered how any of this could be possible, his mind flashed to Chris. Grady's words sunk into his mind. He knew this confirmed that Chris' death was a deliberate murder. He looked up at the alarm controller to make sure the light was green, showing the alarm system was on and locked. It was.

"Where are you?" Robert was trying to remain calm, and figure out the next move. "Are the police there?"

"We're way past that, Buddy," Grady answered. "Jesus, Robert! I know you weren't military, but don't you watch any action movies? Here's the deal. I'll contact you again at nine. You figure out where I can call you again at ten that will be safe. Not at your house, not at your office, and not on your cell phone. Make it a number I can figure out without you telling me what it is. You need to understand that these guys were *sent*. That means this isn't over. Whoever wants me gone, *still wants me gone*." Grady deliberately emphasized the words. He knew he had to get Robert's brain working on this.

"Okay, I'll figure something out." Robert was thinking fast now. "I wasn't sure about what happened to Chris until now. I thought it might have been an accident—a carjacking, mugging, something that wasn't related to what he was doing. But after this, it's pretty clear that his death is connected to your situation."

"You figured that out, did you? Robert, you're going to have to step up the pace. What the hell have you gotten us into?" Grady responded grimly. "I'm not sticking around here. I've got to go. I'll call you—your office at nine. Watch yourself." He abruptly hung up.

Robert went slowly back to his bed after triple-checking the house alarm and all the locks. Everything was locked up tight, with all the doors and windows wired to the security system. He took out his Smith & Wesson thirty-eight, and removed the trigger lock. It was loaded. He went back into the bedroom and tucked the gun just under the edge of the bed. He still couldn't believe that this was happening. Chris was dead, and now Grady was on the run. Why was this happening? Who the hell was behind it? Robert's eyes stared at the dark ceiling, trying to come up with answers. There was no point in closing them; he wouldn't sleep. Tracie's breathing seemed to grow louder every second. His ears echoed with the drone of her sighing until he thought he might scream. The clock's dim light shining up from where it lay on the floor was hard to read, but he made out "3 a.m." Lifting the covers away, he got up, checked the alarm system again, and then went into the bathroom. He pushed the door quietly closed, locked it, and turned on the shower. The gun rested on the toilet seat.

Chapter 28

Grady sat in another dirty motel; this time in Vienna, Virginia. The small town was quiet. Even the main road just outside his room was quiet. He'd been given the key to a room that had been last remodeled in the early nineteen-seventies, with avocado green as its design focus. It didn't appear to have been cleaned much since then, either. It stank of smoke. The previous resident had left a stale, dirty ashtray sitting next to a non-smoking sign. He didn't look at the sheets. He wouldn't be using the bed anyway. This motel was a good distance from his house, and in an area he never frequented. He had driven several extra miles, and circled a dozen blocks to make sure he wasn't followed.

He'd wedged a chair under the doorknob, and the brown car was parked well away from his room. Grady knew he might have a concussion, and that he shouldn't sleep for at least eight hours. It didn't matter. Sleep wouldn't be coming tonight anyway. M.A.S.H. reruns were playing on the room's old television, which apparently had no volume control along with its snowy screen. A paper cup half-full of burned coffee from the motel office sat on the table next to the bed by a bag of cookies, a box of donuts, and a large can of mixed nuts. Grady had found the food behind the seat of the car, along with an overcoat. He absently reached for the can of nuts as he stared mindlessly at the grainy TV.

Chapter 29

Marty lay across his bed. The LEDs on his computer glowed, adding a garish green light to the room. The color washed across his daughter's picture. He was trying desperately to sort out what was happening, and find some way out of this mess. Christen was trapped, held somewhere, and he couldn't call anyone about it. He had already checked out the web site image they wanted him to use. He had downloaded the software he needed, and learned how to read the watermark on the JPG picture file. He was right, it was a huge, non-repeating polynomial; an equation designed to take in a single variable and return a new number. That number would then be added to the equation, causing an update each time it was accessed. It was a self-contained security system, allowing the user to do whatever they wanted without being detected. These guys were sharp.

Rolling over, he hit the light on his alarm clock. The bright blue electro-luminescent back panel lit up the time. Five-fifteen. He decided to get up, and trudged into the bathroom. He would be dressed and out of the house in less than thirty minutes.

Marty had taken only twenty minutes to get up and out. A short drive later he had waited more than fifteen minutes for a donut shop to open. Marty didn't like coffee, but he sat staring at his third cup, and last bit of his third glazed donut. It was now six-thirty, and he had nowhere to go. Home wasn't home anymore; it belonged to them. He belonged to them.

There was no point in going to the office either. Arriving early would look suspicious. Security frowned on sudden behavior changes. That was assuming they would let him in at all. He had to wait. The waitress was nice enough. He gave her a smile, as she looked his way.

"Would you like anything else?" She was young, and the other two waitresses looked even younger. About Christen's age, he thought, although they could be high school kids.

The acidic coffee was tearing up his stomach, making him tense and burning his throat. "Could I have a milk?"

"Sure," she responded, and headed for the refrigerator cabinet.

He was going to sit there until a few minutes before seven. The pancake house would open then. Breakfast would kill some more time.

The waitress came over with a tiny carton of milk and a glass. "Can I get something else for you?"

"No, thanks." Marty could tell she had seen guys like him before. Lonely and lost. The sign over the counter said, "No tipping." He would tip her anyway.

<u>Chapter 30</u>

Robert dressed and left the bedroom after kissing Tracie's outstretched hand. His mind was still filled with questions about Grady's attack, and concerns for his own safety. Despite this, he noted that Tracie seeing him off to work was quickly becoming ancient history. He pulled up the collar on his overcoat in futile defiance of the cold, and cautiously opened the front door, checking for strange individuals, or cars in the street. Seeing none, he made a dash to get the newspapers. Bolting back to the house he locked the door, and reset the alarm. The slight panting of his breath abated as he collected his briefcase and went to the garage. After twice checking that the house alarm was properly set, he got into his car, and started the engine. Making sure the vehicle's doors had locked he opened the garage door. The street seemed quiet. He backed out and watched the door slowly close.

Driving a little slower than he normally did, Robert made several unnecessary turns, watching to see if he was followed. His hand frequently verified that his cell phone was in the cup holder, while his eyes scanned the mirrors, inspecting the occupants of cars passing by. Once Robert got to the freeway he calmed down a little. Traffic was light, and the sun rising made the cars easier to watch.

He caught himself wondering if he was overreacting, but it only took a minute to remember that Chris's death was very real, and significant—especially now that Grady had been attacked. Robert was fully aware that he could also be a target. Then he realized Tracie was home alone, and unaware of any of this.

Robert had a home alarm, car alarms, a gun...everything but an attack dog. Still, he'd never actually expected to be assaulted. A home invasion or street attack in the places he frequented would be unusual. Sure, everyone worried about it, particularly in big cities, but the odds were pretty low. There was no ignoring that Robert's risk had just risen to a higher level. Chris's death and Grady's attack could not be coincidental. Was he actually in danger? Was Tracie? And what about the boys and Alicia?

Robert needed to focus. He did his clearest thinking in the morning, and the more he thought about this, the more pieces of the puzzle began to fall into place.

Chris's words flashed through his mind. "Someone is going to take control of the OPOV system," Chris had said. Not *trying* to take control; "going to take control." Robert realized that his approach to the investigation had assumed that the effort to take over OPOV was preventable. Now he wondered if a system was already in place, and how big the corruption might be.

Robert felt his frustration building. Questions heavily outweighed any answers he got. Damn it! He felt blocked at every turn. Robert had to find some path to controlling this investigation.

Control, he thought. This was all about control. Control the voting system and you control the power. You'd have to control it nationwide, or the differences in vote counts between states and the final tally would be too obvious. Having that control, not through arms or violence, but through hidden influence, would be incredibly powerful. Even politicians being manipulated would have to endorse the validity of a system designed by the best computer minds in the world, and monitored by so much security. Any effort to publicly deride the system would be viewed as trying to crush public opinion. They'd be called 'un-American', "unpatriotic," or even totalitarian. The more Robert thought about it, the more he realized how brilliant the plan to control OPOV was in its conception. But with every agency in the government watching the system operate, how could someone gain control? Robert had to find the flaw, the fatal security error that would allow control of the system without anyone knowing. The flaw that could change voting results over and over again.

Grady must have gotten closer to the answers than he'd realized, Robert thought. But was it something Grady had found, or someone he'd talked to? That must be it, Robert thought. Grady triggered something, and that was why he was targeted.

So, Robert theorized, he and his family weren't in danger at this point.

Robert pulled into his building's parking area. He acknowledged the security guard, and headed to his office to wait.

Chapter 31

Marty pulled into the NSA parking lot. It was still very early. His tires made fresh tracks across the lightly drifted snow, blown down from the nearby trees. Marty paid no attention to these things, but he did feel the cold as he zipped up his leather jacket. Thrusting his hands into his pockets, he forged ahead to the lobby.

Over breakfast, he had watched the clock tick so slowly that it seemed to count backwards. He tried to kill time with a second stack of pancakes, but they sloshed in his upset stomach. He had wasted enough time over breakfast to not look suspiciously early when he showed up at work. The security guard checked his badge, and Marty moved through to the lockers to unload his pockets. Approaching the airlock, he put his hand to the scan plate. His blood pressure climbed as the thin red line scrolled across his palm. Inside the airlock his anxiety rose further, until his tongue seemed too big for his throat. He had never noticed how loud the scanning equipment hum was. Every muscle tightened. It all seemed to take much longer than usual. He could hardly stand still, waiting for the scan to be completed. When it finally stopped, and the inner lock opened, he almost ran out. He stopped, reminding himself to act as normal as possible. His head was spinning. What did he usually do? He went toward the coffee stand. God, I need more coffee like a hole in the head, he thought. He already had drunk five cups. Instead he went into the bathroom and locked himself in one of the stalls. Sausage was doing flip-flops in his stomach. He sat in the stall with his elbows on his knees, his head propped in his hands.

Terri came driving in just before eight. She had been sitting at her desk wondering where Marty was when he finally showed up at his cubicle. It was eight-fifteen.

"Where have you been? Out partying late?" Terri chided him as he quietly slunk into his cubicle.

"Actually, I came in early. Is that all right with you?" He asked tartly.

"Whoa! Sorry I asked." She responded, looking offended.

"Sorry, Terri," Marty felt irritated and remorseful, all at once. He tried to cover his annoyance, and respond normally. "I don't feel too good, and I didn't sleep well. My stomach is upset. I got up early, ate too much, and drank too much coffee. That's all." Marty thought he was talking too much, and had better shut up.

"Did you eat something different than usual? How come you got up early?" Terri was making idle chatter as she usually did in the morning.

"I just woke up and felt like having a big breakfast. No mystery; no big deal." His curt tone and sleep deprived eyes indicated that he was annoyed.

"OK, I'll catch you later." Terri managed a hasty retreat and turned to her computer screen. "Man, what a grouch," she mumbled not quite under her breath.

Marty felt like a spotlight was burning into the back of his neck. He felt exposed. The cubicle opening was at his back, and his computer monitor was crammed into the corner. Anyone could walk up behind him and look over his shoulder. He pulled off the glare-reducing screen overlay, and set it to one side. The harsh fluorescent lights gave just enough light to make reflections. This way he would notice someone standing behind him.

He worked deliberately, pulling up a complex spreadsheet before he signed onto the net, and accessed the file transfer protocol site. He also downloaded the image program and graphics plug-in he needed to pull the watermark out of the picture.

While it downloaded, he hit the ALT TAB keys to switch to the inconspicuous spreadsheet screen filled with numbers. He acted busy as the computer calmly worked in the background. It only took a minute or two before the virus scan cleared the new files and his security code authorized the file save. He added the plug-in to his graphics package, and pulled out the watermark. No one would notice this activity. Some people played solitaire, pinball, or shoot-everything-in-sight games on their computers. Others surfed the net, or played network chess with fellow employees. IT had approved the sites, with pre-checks, no cookies, no flash, java, mocha, etc., and required personal verification before anyone could access them. Most people were surprised that the boss didn't object, but the long hours of programming were marked with only occasional sparks of intuition and brilliance. These periodic non-businesslike breaks in the monotony actually helped productivity, and went unchecked. There were Foosball and Ping-Pong tables in the break room for the same purpose. Once in a while Marty would mess around with a three-dimensional graphics package he had, or clean up photographs he had downloaded from his digital camera. Those guys that came to his house probably knew about that. Hell, they must have known. They knew everything else.

Once he had the image work done, his security clearance allowed him to access the OPOV control file and add the HEX code polynomial in a remark line. Marty noted how the combination of characters looked almost like a mnemonic he might actually use as a comment.

"These guys are good," Marty thought again. He knew someone would eventually catch the adjustment. When they found it, they would come to him. Then what would happen to Christen?

He saved the file. The automatic log system noted his code as the last person to edit the file, and the screen closed. Done, he thought. Now what? How could he go on with business as usual?

Terri looked over the wall. "Hey, you ready?"

"What?" Marty jumped, panicked for a split second. He checked quickly to make sure nothing incriminating was on his monitor.

"Are you ready for the meeting? You know, the staff meeting? They talk; you listen?" Terri laughed.

Marty generally hated meetings, but this one he welcomed. Today he needed the distraction. "Sure, let's go."

"Are you okay?" Terri asked as they walked down the hall.

"Oh, I'm just tired." Marty forgot that he'd already said that.

"Yeah, so you said. You look like hell, but I figure that's old age setting in." Terri teased him.

"Nice...remind me to bake your next birthday cake. Black icing, licorice flavored—maybe with razor blades." Marty tried to respond in kind.

Terri pushed lightly on his shoulder. "What, no arsenic?"

"How about chocolate Ex-Lax; you're getting older, too."

"Thanks, a lot." Terri pushed his shoulder a little harder for that one.

They went into the meeting and Marty gratefully let his mind lapse into focusing on his boss' presentation. He was sedated into safe oblivion, if only for a short while.

Chapter 32

Robert sat in his office. He'd arrived before Lorraine, probably for the first time since he'd worked in the office. The coffee he'd made sat lukewarm in the cup. It was awful. Pale and bitter. Maybe it was supposed to be eight scoops, not four, he thought.

He was still reaching for answers on how to handle the OPOV problem, but he had come up empty handed. His lawyer's mind went through his trained steps one more time. Motive: everyone in Washington wanted power, money, and votes. So motive was easy to come by, and useless to consider. Opportunity: difficult; the whole OPOV system was under multiple microscopes. Unless you were an insider, or controlled an insider, it would be tough to break in. Even then, the manipulation would have to be hidden. Anything noticeable would be investigated. Means: in this case, how was that different from opportunity? It would have to be someone with access and knowledge about how the system worked.

What Robert had none of, and needed the most, was evidence. Chris's death and Grady's attack weren't evidence, even if they could be linked. The events weren't proof of anything, except that evidence was going to be hard to get, and that staying alive could be a problem.

Robert's chin rested on the heels of his two hands. His elbows pressed into the desk as his middle fingers rubbed his temples. The effort had no beneficial effect, and he found that he was making his temples sore.

Could terrorists be the culprits? They never needed much motivation, just a cause. Their attacks and goals often seemed unrelated, but generally were designed to create chaos. Was there significance to this time and place? The upcoming vote was minor and influenced no election, no foreign policy, and not even much money. Perhaps this was a preamble; a test in preparation for something bigger. But wouldn't that risk showing the hand that wielded the power? That would be a bad idea if they intended to remain a hidden force, or use the system multiple times.

Whoever was to blame, a hidden timetable seemed to be pushing them into action. That would explain why Chris was dead, and why Grady was lucky to be alive. Chris and Grady had threatened that timetable somehow.

The phone's electronic ring jerked his brain back into the office. Thinking that Lorraine probably wasn't in the office yet, he grabbed the receiver.

"Yes?" His curt greeting was out of character, but then, so was answering his own phone. He felt disoriented.

"Mr. Carlton?" A girl with a Texas accent was on the line.

"Yes, who's calling?" Robert tried to regain his composure.

"I'm calling for Mr. Hunt. He was hoping to arrange a meeting."

"I'm sorry," Robert answered automatically, "my schedule is very full. My secretary will be glad to..."

"Sir." Her tone changed. The friendly lilt left her voice, and a tight-jawed hardness replaced it. "Mr. Hunt will be taking pictures of the Washington Monument at eight-thirty, on the hill above the stone tourist kiosk, east of the monument. He suggests you be there." She placed emphasis on the word "suggests," as though politeness was thinly disguising an order.

"What's this about?" Robert demanded. Hunt's name had kicked Robert's brain into gear. He didn't like this guy calling the shots. He wanted some answers.

"Mr. Hunt said you haven't returned his calls," the girl answered, sounding as though she was admonishing a small schoolboy. She continued, "Mr. Hunt said that it's time to 'stoke some barley.' He said you'd understand." Her light tone returned. "May I tell him you're coming?"

Robert felt jolted. It seemed absurd, but the girl was clearly referring to Chris Stoker and Grady Barlow with her juvenile play on words. So Hunt was part of this mess? What the hell was going on?

Robert began, "I'll be there, but you tell Hunt that…"

"Eight-thirty." The girl interrupted, confirming the time as if he hadn't spoken. "Thank you, Sir. Have a nice day." She hung up before he could say anything more. Furiously he checked and found that the Caller ID had been blocked. He would have been shocked if it hadn't been, but it was still frustrating.

"Have a nice day yourself." Robert punched the button for security. After Chris's death and Grady's attack there was no way he was meeting this guy alone. "Get me the JPSO, immediately." He hung up and hit the intercom. "Lorraine, are you there?"

"Yes, Sir. Good m…"

Robert cut her off. "Lorraine, get me Phil Davidson at the Treasury Department."

"Yes, Sir." Lorraine was on the phone with Phil as Agent Carey came briskly through the main door. He did not wait for Lorraine's approval, or acknowledgment, moving straight into Robert's office.

Robert was a little stunned by the fast response. He recognized the agent immediately, and was surprised. "Thank you for getting here so quickly, Agent Carey." Robert had met Carey when he'd been assigned to Ed Bradley. It wasn't commonplace for the Secret Service to respond to Justice Protective Service Officer calls. Robert processed this, and assumed that Carey had been setting up Jack's security with the JPSO, now that he was confirmed as AG. They must have decided to send him to see what Robert was calling about. It seemed a little unusual to Robert, but thinking about it, he figured that the Secret Service might have the equipment necessary for monitoring this meeting.

"Sir. What can I do for you?" Carey responded, getting straight to the point.

Robert reached for the intercom button but it chimed before he hit it. "Mr. Davidson is on line one." Lorraine told him.

Robert hit the speakerphone button. "Phil?"

"Mr. Carlton, nice to hear..."

"No time for that." Robert cut him off. "Phil Davidson, Treasury Department, meet Agent Carey, Secret Service. I am having a meeting on the mall at eight-thirty. I need surveillance. I need it recorded and I want two points of reception and documentation. Can you do it, Phil?"

"Of course, but Agent Carey has everything..." Phil started.

"Can you do it? Yes, or no?" Robert was demanding and short. His mind was too full of problems to beat around the bush.

"Yes...Agent Carey, do you have everything you need?" Phil answered hesitantly. This kind of thing was really the Secret Service's turf, and he knew they'd prefer to keep it that way.

"Yes." Carey was strictly business.

Robert took over the conversation again. "My rendezvous is at the tourist kiosk by the Washington Monument at 8:30. Which of you can cover that best?"

"I can." Agent Carey said. "My partner is still here from the early shift."

"Excellent." Phil sounded relieved. "We don't have much time. I'd better go get the lab set up."

Carey spoke next. "I'll be back in fifteen minutes. I'll send over the frequencies, and I'll need to get under your shirt and belt Mr. Carlton."

"I'll be ready." Robert acknowledged as he hung up the phone. Robert watched as the agent left his office. He would be back in moments with at least one radio microphone 'wire', and probably two. An engineer would be waiting to listen in on a remote receiver. Carey and his partner would have earphones, and possibly more agents listening in. Phil, on the other hand, would be rushing downstairs to the "lab." It was a euphemistic term for a sophisticated listening and decoding system in the Treasury Building. From there everything could be monitored.

Agent Carey was back in seven minutes with two systems.

"We'll use a redundant set on you to ensure transmission. We have more sophisticated equipment, like bone mics, that we prefer to use indoors these days," he explained while he worked "but in these outdoor situations, we get a better signal and recording this way. Also, the receiving dishes for the other choices could be visible if there's not much cover, which there won't be in that location. These are the on/off switches." He pointed to the tops of the two transmitters. In moments, Robert had two microphones and transmitters attached to him with lots of tape. He felt like a Christmas tree with lights strung around it, but somehow better and safer.

"How many people are you expecting, and do you have an expectation of violence?" Carey inquired, still checking his equipment.

"I don't know how many may be in the background, but I suspect I'll only be meeting with one. Violence is a possibility, but unlikely." Robert figured that if Hunt was behind any of this, and wanted to hurt him, he'd never have made it to work in one piece.

"Yes, Sir." Carey was checking the signal and volume from Robert's microphones. "Sir, it will take you under twenty minutes to get there on foot from here; that may be faster than getting to the car. I suggest we get started."

Lorraine was clearly bewildered as Robert and Agent Carey swept past her desk. She seemed uncharacteristically upset by the activity. "Mr. Carlton, I..." she began.

"Not now, Lorraine." Robert and Carey pressed on down the hall. Carey's partner joined them at the top of the stairs. After quick introductions while walking, they parted, using different exits.

Robert set a terrific pace. Carey was right, there was no point in using a car. Looking for a parking spot this time of day was out of the question. The only places possible would be to illegally park in one of the mall turnouts. Plus traffic and lights on the way were unpredictable. They could slow him down.

Robert wondered about Hunt's choice of location for their meeting. Just a few days before he'd met with Chris not far from the same spot. He looked around the area as he headed toward the kiosk. Both sides of the street were rimmed with government buildings, including the Smithsonian Institute. Even in cold weather a few tourists could be seen snapping pictures. The Washington Monument opened at nine, and a line was already forming.

Robert was not feeling the cold anymore. The brisk walk was making him sweat under his overcoat. As he covered the distance he lost his footing on the slippery sidewalk, skating once or twice over the ice.

He heard a tourist ask another why they called this area "The Mall." Robert was thinking he could have told them. "Mall" was defined as a "pedestrian promenade." Maybe that was why Hunt had chosen this location. Lots of people were milling around, despite the weather.

Robert knew he was flooded with adrenaline, and tried to pull his thoughts back to Hunt. Hunt, he realized, had given him little time to get to this meeting. Hunt probably assumed that Robert wouldn't have the resources at hand to set up surveillance on such short notice. Robert was betting that his quick action gave him the upper hand.

It was three minutes after eight-thirty when Robert arrived at the stone building kiosk. The barren surroundings offered little weather protection. The wind whistled past in repeated gusts. Between the wind and Robert's own panting breaths, he had trouble hearing anything around him except the traffic. He stayed away from the protection of the building. It would obstruct his view and that of the two agents.

Robert was looking for the stocky man in his late fifties that he'd met at The White House. He scanned silver-haired passersby. Casually strolling down the hill from the Washington Monument, with a dark hat hiding his silver hair and an overcoat streamlining his frame, Hunt was at his side before Robert recognized him.

"Hello, Mr. Carlton." Hunt sounded almost cheerful.

"Hunt, what's this all about?" Robert cut to the chase, angry with the man for his comfortable greeting.

Hunt seemed to ignore Robert as he held up his hand. In it was a digital camera with a picture of the Washington Monument on it. With a button push it switched images to a picture of a message. It said, "You're wearing a microphone. Turn it off." Hunt smiled meaningfully at Robert.

"I don't know what you're talking about." Robert asserted defiantly.

Hunt grinned. He pressed another button and the display showed a graphic meter. The red bar moved up and down, but stayed high, and red.

Robert reached under his coat to one of the transmitters. Pulling it forward he said, "All right, I'll turn it off." He looked at Hunt who relaxed his arm to a hanging position with the camera by his side. Robert flipped off the switch to the first radio.

"What do you want, Hunt?" He began. "I got your hint about..."

Hunt cut him off with an upheld hand. He held up the camera as if to take a picture. The bar was still high and red.

Robert reached behind his back and turned off the second transmitter. The bar dropped down and the color changed to green.

"Much better. I'd love to talk with you, but it's just too damn cold out here, and you don't have as much time as you thought."

Hunt drawled. "So let me help you out a little. Here's someone you should talk to."

He held up the camera once again. The display read, "NSA – Karlovich."

"But you didn't hear it from me." Hunt flashed a grin at Robert again.

"Why are you telling me this?" Robert said irritably. "Why not just tell me what you know?"

Hunt hit the "delete all" key on the camera, and tucked it away in his pocket. "Mr. Carlton," he said, shaking his head. "Where would the fun be in that? Besides, I'll bet a bright lawyer like you would add me to some list, and I don't cotton to people investigating me. I don't have all the answers, and I don't know what you will find out, but I do know that you should talk to that guy. In fact, I think you should go to his office to talk. That would probably get you the best results."

Robert looked puzzled and was about to ask a question, but Hunt looked away, and continued, "You're absolutely right. The best picture would be from the other side on a nice bright day." He turned away from the monument. In a few dozen steps Hunt was on the curb, and getting into a car that had driven up, unnoticed by Robert. It pulled quickly away. Robert stood silently, the cold breeze chilling him.

Robert was stunned. Hunt had known every step Robert would make. First, he'd killed the radios. Then he'd said nothing important, nothing implicating, making a lip reader or video valueless. He'd held the camera message so close to Robert that no one else could have read it. Furthermore, instead of an expected threat, Robert had received a lead. So, who was Karlovich? Robert repeated the name in his mind as he walked back toward the office.

Chapter 33

Joined by the two Secret Service agents as he neared his office building, Robert told them what had transpired. Agent Carey took notes. Robert withheld the contents of Hunt's phone message. Carey gave Robert an appraising glance, but being used to handling issues on a "need to know" basis, the agents quickly moved on. Robert learned that they had managed to get a few discreet pictures of Hunt, and his departure vehicle. They planned to run the photos by several agencies to see if there was a match for the man. They already had the origin of the car, which apparently came from an executive limo service. They would track the renter, but they advised Robert that it would not be likely to lead them to anything. In all probability, "Hunt" had rented the limo from a hotel lobby, using cash.

Carey asked if Robert needed a security detail. Robert had been thinking about that on the walk back. Given Grady's remarks, and his own reaction to Hunt's meeting, he admitted that he did. He told Carey that he also required one for his family. It had dawned on him, again, that he had neglected to consider Tracie and the kids after hearing from Grady. He'd rationalized that he wasn't a target, so she had no idea that they could be in a very dangerous situation.

Carey left for the building's security room. The other agent followed Robert to his office, planting himself near Lorraine's desk. She had lost her cool demeanor and was noticeably nervous. Neither Robert nor the agent provided any information to her. The agent sat on a chair by Robert's office door, silently watching down the length of the hallway. He left the main door open to obtain the greatest field of view possible. The draft from the hallway chilled the outer office.

Robert called home, and had Alicia put Tracie on the phone. "Tracie, it's me. Nothing's wrong, but I want you..."

"What's going on, Robert? Is it the boys? Did the school call?" Tracie's rapid-fire questions assailed Robert. He never called her in the middle of the day, so he should have known that she would instantly assume there was trouble.

"I said, 'nothing's wrong,' Tracie. Just wait a moment, and let me tell you what the situation is here." Robert cleared his throat.

"Situation?" Tracie began pacing back and forth in the kitchen. Robert could hear her footsteps. Good thing the phone was cordless, he thought. Back in the old days she would have had the cord tied in knots.

"I've asked the security team here to send someone over to stay with you and the kids." Robert stated, wondering how he'd explain this to her. He knew that whatever he told her, it wouldn't be enough.

"What? What's happened? Are you all right?" She was panicking. Tracie had a tendency to react first, and think later. Calm, level-headed behavior had never been her strong suit in crisis situations.

"Calm down, Tracie," Robert said firmly, hoping to interrupt her building anxiety. "Everything is fine. This is simply a precaution." He knew that wouldn't fly, and paused, wondering what to tell her.

"Will you just tell me what's going on?" Tracie sounded frantic. She was rapidly working herself into a frenzy.

"As I said, this is a precaution," Robert reiterated. He decided to give her a list of action items. That usually had the effect of distracting her hysteria. "Tracie, put these instructions on your iPad, so that you won't forget anything." He heard her scrambling through her large designer carryall. When he thought she'd found it, he continued, "When the security team arrives, don't open the door. They will expect you to ask for their names and ID numbers. Then call here before you allow them in the house. We'll verify that they are who they say they are, and they will use a code word that we'll give you. After they give you that code word, you can open the door. Have you got that?" Robert was trying to sound in control, businesslike, and commanding.

"Security Team? Robert, what is this about? Why..." Tracie sounded breathless.

"Don't worry," Robert interrupted. "This is only a safety measure. We are following normal procedure for Homeland Security threats." He was doing his best to sound soothing. "I swear I'm fine, and nothing has happened. The government's being a little over-protective; all right?" He wasn't sure she'd buy it, but he thought that deferring to higher authority might make her see the situation as some standard reaction to a terrorist threat.

"You'd better keep calling me." She demanded. He figured it was an improvement that she was starting to sound angry, rather than worried. "You're scaring the hell out of me, and you know it." She continued, "I'm going to get the boys as soon as the agents get here, and are cleared."

"That's fine." He said, hoping agreeing with her would help.

"And I'm calling Mother," she intoned, making the act sound like a threat.

"Fine. I don't see any problem with that." He answered.

"Call me soon. I expect to hear what this is all about, and you damned well better be prepared to tell me. I don't want any of this, 'it's classified' nonsense, and you'd better not dodge my calls." His technique seemed to be working. Tracie's fear was settling down to some degree, and being replaced by assertive anger.

"I'll call, I promise, Tracie. I have to go. I'll talk to you later." Robert said, and hung up.

It had only been minutes, but it seemed like hours had passed. Robert sat staring at a piece of paper on which he had written the message that Hunt had given him: "NSA – Karlovich."

For the moment Robert decided to assume that Hunt was on his side, or at least working against somebody else. He still had no idea what Hunt had been trying to tell him in their first meeting, but Hunt had now shown his hand. It was clear that he was another puppet master, pulling Robert's strings.

Robert was stuck in an increasingly difficult political position. If Hunt had not been connected to Senator Gregg, he would be having Hunt hauled in for questioning on the basis of Homeland Security—assuming he could find the guy. Gregg made that a political problem. Robert knew that Hunt was not who he claimed to be, but the more he thought about it, the more he realized that it was now Agent Carey's job, or the JPSO's to work on that issue. That freed up Robert to worry about his other problems, and gave him a nice political distance from the Hunt situation.

Robert looked up Karlovich. There were several in the government listings, but one stood out: NSA Division Director, Bill Karlovich.

"Well, that's bigger than I expected," Robert said to himself. He had anticipated finding the name, but not that title. In fact, few titles were listed for NSA employees, and often their names were classified. This guy was a conduit for the administration. He was an official mouthpiece with the skills to handle being visible, and someone who could answer questions without giving too much away. His title meant he'd been involved in the OPOV project from the beginning.

This whole thing felt too pat, Robert thought. This direction to Karlovich was coming too easily. Every finger of the investigation was pointing directly at the NSA. Something didn't feel right about that.

He ignored the phone ringing. He had given Lorraine a short list of whom he wanted to talk with that afternoon. Everyone else would have to wait.

The intercom chimed.

"Colonel Barlow on line one," Lorraine said tensely. She sounded as though she was clenching her teeth together.

Robert had completely forgotten about his call with Grady. He grabbed the phone. "Sorry, Grady," he began, "I had an odd morning..."

"I can't talk long, so just listen." Grady interrupted. He sounded very calm and much clearer this morning, but he wasn't wasting time on pleasantries. "Go to your car and head down Constitution. Go over the river. I'll call you on your cell phone. Got it?"

"Cell phone? I thought you said..." Robert was trying to figure out why Grady wanted to use his cell phone.

"Just do it," Grady said and hung up.

Robert placed the receiver in its cradle. Looking up he saw that the agent had come into the room. "I need to go somewhere. Agent..." he started, then stopped, realizing he'd forgotten the man's name.

"Long, Sir." The Agent answered.

"Right. Sorry." Robert apologized. "Agent Long, I need to leave the office right away. I have to meet an associate outside the downtown area."

"I'll notify Agent Carey. We'll be ready in five minutes." He spun around and left the room with his wrist microphone up to his mouth. By the time Robert had his coat, Agent Carey was coming down the hall. In short order, the three men were in the parking area. Robert told them they were meeting Colonel Barlow. He explained that the Colonel was trying to stay out of sight. Beyond that, he described as little of the situation as possible.

Robert got into his car with Agent Long driving. Agent Carey followed in a plain, dark blue staff car, parked near Robert's car. Agent Long informed Robert that his BMW had been wired for video, audio, and two way GPS tracking. Robert reflected that their efficiency was striking. He also worried that the car was now damaged with wires and cut upholstery. He wondered how they'd gotten his key, but didn't ask. Looking around quickly, he saw that there were no visible or accessible controls for the newly installed features. He did spot a camera lens in the upper corner of the windshield. If he hadn't been told about the changes, he might not have noticed it. Obviously the additions were for covert monitoring by other agents. Robert briefly wondered how many agents were assigned to this case.

He also wondered how they had had time to wire his car. He noticed the security guard in the parking area as they pulled out. Robert thought he might be a different man—he seemed more attentive than the usual guard.

They rolled steadily down Constitution toward Arlington, stopping for the usual traffic and lights.

Robert's pulse throbbed, vibrating more than the engine. Agent Long looked over with a smile, saying, "Don't worry, Sir. We've done this before. The Colonel will probably be watching the bridge. As soon as he sees us crossing it, he'll give you directions to your meeting location. I assume he will call your cell phone? You might want to get it out of your pocket."

Robert looked over at Long with a shocked stare. "If it's that standard, won't anyone watching know what we're doing?" It was uncomfortable having someone else drive his car. Robert tried to ignore the feeling. It seemed trivial given the circumstances.

Long looked surprised. "Well, now that you mention it...yes. Anyone watching would be aware of the situation. Sometimes that is the point."

"That's just great," Robert said sarcastically. He sat fiddling with the phone as the bridge came closer.

They had reached the bridge. About halfway across, Robert looked at Agent Long and said, "I thought you said..."

The phone rang.

Robert jerked the phone up. "Yes," Robert answered.

"Take the next right onto George Washington."

"Take the next right onto George Washington," Robert repeated.

Agent Long switched lanes quickly to make the exit, just at the end of the bridge.

"Take the exit to the Roosevelt Island parking lot, and park at the end. Meet me on the bridge." Grady added.

"Park in the Roosevelt parking lot, at the end," Robert told Long.

Long pulled his wrist microphone up to his mouth. "We're taking the turn-off to the Roosevelt Island parking lot." Long's matter of fact tone was somehow not comforting, Robert thought. He felt on edge—why were the agents so calm?

Long turned to Robert, "It's a reasonably good spot," he commented. "There will be some people, but lots of space for talking." Long frowned as he mentioned, "There's limited access."

Clearly this was not Long's first time in this situation, or in this parking lot, Robert reflected. He felt his nerves tightening across his neck and back. As they reached the parking lot, he saw that it could only be accessed from a single entrance on the northbound side of the George Washington Parkway. That one-way flow of controlled traffic probably had been just what Grady wanted, Robert realized. He hoped Grady had considered that he and Agent Long might have been followed.

As they pulled into the parking lot near the bridge, Robert spotted Grady easily, standing midway on the bridge to the island, wearing an overcoat and gym shoes.

"There he is, on the island bridge. That's Colonel Barlow." He told Long.

Getting out of the car, Agent Long told Robert to wait while Carey went out on the bridge first. Before Carey stepped onto the bridge to begin walking toward Grady, Robert's phone rang again.

"Yes?" he answered.

"Just you," Grady said.

Robert relayed the message, telling Long that Grady wasn't a threat, but that someone following them could be. Long radioed Carey, who came to a halt, then returned to the stairs at the head of the bridge.

Robert walked out to see Grady alone.

Grady stood in the middle of the bridge with his back to the Secret Service Agents. He rested his arms on the railing, motioning Robert over to join him. Carey and Long stood on the shore, scanning the area.

"Jesus, you look like hell." Robert looked at Grady's face and felt disoriented. This clandestine behavior was making him edgy. At the same time he was relieved to see Grady. "Why the cloak and dagger?"

"Cloak and dagger?" Grady removed his sunglasses to give Robert the full effect of his swollen, damaged face. "Have you forgotten about my call last night? Maybe if your face looked like mine you'd be careful, too. You seem to have some awareness of the situation," he added, nodding toward Carey and Long. "Those two guys with you aren't dates, are they?"

"You're right, Grady. My apologies," Robert answered, suddenly realizing how confused he'd become by the morning's events. "I've been out of my element since you called. I've never been involved in something like this, and the whole thing keeps getting more complicated. Every time I turn around there's some new angle, but I can't get any answers to what's happening. I'm trying to feel my way through it, but I'm not getting very far." Robert looked at Grady. "And I've planted you right in the middle of whatever this is. What are you planning to do now? Do you want some protection?"

Grady shrugged off his irritation at Robert's initial comments, and sighed. "It's already been a long day for me. I had to be sure that we'd notice if either of us was followed. I've been here long enough to check out everyone that has crossed, or not crossed this bridge. Any followers would look pretty obvious right now, don't you think?" He didn't wait for Robert's answer before he continued, "No, the kind of protection you can offer won't work for me now. I'm leaving—disappearing."

"What do you mean, 'leaving'?" Robert asked automatically. "Where are you going?"

Grady tried to lift an eyebrow, but his face hurt too much. "If I told you where I was going, Robert," he said with some asperity, "it wouldn't do much good to disappear, would it? You're still not getting this. These guys were trying to get rid of me—permanently. I won't be worth much to you dead, and frankly, I'm not quite ready to be put out of my misery."

Robert didn't know how to answer that statement. He looked down the length of the bridge, and across the water at the two agents.

Robert noticed that the agents were strolling back and forth somewhat casually, but they also seemed agitated. The chilly air and strong breezes made business attire feel thin, but this didn't seem to be about temperature—they weren't huddled into their coats trying to keep warm. He was sure they didn't like the conditions of the meeting. Grady was an unpredictable factor in an unprepared-for day, and it was unsettling for the agents. At least that made sense in this crazy morning.

In the distance, a few people were walking back across the bridge from the park, wearing thick coats and taking pictures. Robert realized that he needed to wrap up this meeting. He looked back at Grady, surveying his bruised face.

"Sorry, Counselor, but I'm not sure you have felt the full impact of what you've gotten us into." Grady was saying. "On the other hand, I have." He stood favoring one leg, his lip was four times larger on one side, and his eye was almost swollen shut. Even through his dark complexion his forehead had turned terrible shades of sickly colors.

Robert grimaced. "Hurt much? Have you seen a doctor?"

Grady looked at him disparagingly. "Sure, Robert. I just strolled in, and said, 'Doctor, I can explain everything. It was just a little misunderstanding. Ran into a door four hundred times.' I'm sure my military ID and a bar room fight would explain it all."

"I see what you mean." Robert sighed. "Grady, I think we can safely say there's a connection between what you've been working on for me, and your attack."

"D'ya think? Christ, Robert; how long did it take you to figure that out?" Grady flared at him. "Your informant, Chris Stoker started it; now he's dead. You put me on this, and I should be dead." He saw Robert flash a questioning look at him, and said. "Do you understand how lucky I am to be alive? My house is gone; burned to the ground. My Jeep, my bike, pictures—everything I owned has been blown to pieces. I'm on the run. I feel broken all over. And brilliant lawyer that you are, you've decided there's a 'connection' between my situation and your investigation. Excellent deduction, Mr. Associate Attorney General! Well done." Grady shook his head, and dropped his sarcastic tone. "Robert, we're in deep shit here! You've gotten us into something that's big. It's way beyond any 'unofficial investigation.' Somebody doesn't like where your research is going, and they think we all know too much. I suggest you get your department mobilized, and armed. You don't have any choice now. This thing had better become official. It's either that, or you drop the whole investigation, and drop it loud enough so that whoever's behind this hears you drop it from a mile away."

"I can't drop it," Robert said firmly.

"Then you have a problem, and so do I," Grady told him, looking him straight in the eye.

"I still need your help," Robert said. "I'm stuck, Grady. The only direction I can move is forward, and I can't do it alone."

Grady was angry. "I'm in whether I like it or not—and by the way, I don't! Robert, do you understand that as long as you won't let go, I'm a moving target? I think I'm entitled to know why you still think I should help you."

Robert had done some thinking while Grady vented. He knew he was about to make himself sound even more callous. He fiddled with the railing, took a deep breath, then turned to look at Grady again, but stopped talking as the tourists walked past. After holding his breath until they got by, he spoke. "Look, Grady, I'm sorry this has happened, but neither of us have much choice in the matter. I can't stop this investigation, so whoever is after you isn't going to stop trying to kill you. I can't elevate this investigation without direct evidence linking you, Chris, the violence, and OPOV—which I don't have. I'll figure it out, but in the meantime, you have two choices: you can either go on the run, and hope I figure this mess out before the killers find you again, or you can help me bring them down. If these guys come after me before I get them, you won't ever be able to stop running. Frankly, I don't think I'd manage as well as you did last night. If they come for me, I'm a goner. Plus, I've got a wife and two kids they'll use to take me down. Either way, you're toast. If they don't get me, the politics will. My career will be in shreds."

Grady looked away from Robert. He wanted to knock him off the bridge. He'd turned the whole thing over and over in his mind, and he knew what Robert was saying was true. It wasn't any easier to accept than it had been at 3 a.m. He'd hoped that Robert could pull some rabbit out of his hat.

"That was way too melodramatic." Grady almost smiled but it hurt his lip. "Look, you have position and security, and I can disappear. But I can also keep digging into this from a distance. So, what do you want me to do?" Grady asked, feeling clearer. It was amazing how Robert's outburst had refocused his thoughts.

"The crypto guys at the Pentagon. I need you to get whatever they find." Robert said. "They won't talk to me, and they'll know something is up if I contact them. I need you to keep them on this, but it still has to look like a research project to them. I also need to know why your visit to them triggered the attack on you. I have no idea how to figure that out, but if you see a connection..."

"Research." Grady tried laughing sardonically, but ended up coughing. Recovering, he looked at Robert again. "So I have to hide, and find a way to communicate with you and Crypto, and do some research. You don't ask for much, do you?" They both stood silently for a moment. Grady spoke first. "'Never volunteer' we say, but I'm always sticking my neck out, waiting for the axe to fall." He managed a strangled chuckle. "I guess I'm in this with you as deep as I can wade, Robert. I don't know how I'm going to be able to talk to those guys again. Hell, I don't even have a uniform! They're all in ashes. I don't suppose that would make much difference to them. One look at my face and they would all act like they never met me." His voice rose. "Don't try to call or find me, Robert. If I'm doing this, I'm doing it my way. Take it, or leave it."

"Of course. You'll initiate all calls, but if something comes up..." Robert began.

"Forget it," Grady interrupted. "You're not going to know where I am. And don't put any of your security boys, or investigators on finding me. I'm not going to discriminate when it comes to defending myself against anyone who seems a little too interested."

Robert held up his hand defensively. "No, I don't want to know where you are. But if something comes up I'll use this." Robert pulled his secure text pager from his belt. "Works anywhere on the planet. I'll put in thirteen, then the number. If you can't call, hit reply and you can type in a message, then send. I'll get it like a text, but securely."

"Thirteen, perfect." Grady took the device. "No one in their right mind would use that number first. I assume this is monitored?"

"Yes, everything is these days. It's just to initiate contact. I'll use phones I've never used before, and I'll wait only fifteen minutes, then move to a new one. You'll know it's me." Robert offered his hand. "You better get a pay-as-you-go cell phone."

Grady accepted his handshake. "I plan to, but not around here. You better get us out of this, Robert."

"We'll get out of this, Grady. I promise."

"Spoken like a real politician." Grady stepped away from the railing. "Do me a favor." Robert nodded his acceptance. "Stay here for five minutes so that neither of your two guards tries to follow me."

"You're worried about the Secret Service?" Robert looked surprised.

"Secret Service?" Grady paused. "You bet. I'm worried about everybody." Grady started walking back to his car with a noticeable limp. "Forgive me if I don't trust anyone right now."

Robert kept his position on the bridge. As Grady reached the halfway point to land, Robert motioned for Long and Carey to stand well back, and let Grady go. The agents watched Grady walk past them. Their eyes locked with his, but no word was exchanged. Robert saw Grady get into a brown sedan, and pull out of the parking lot.

Robert walked to shore and stood next to Agent Carey.

"Well, Sir?" Carey asked as they watched Grady's taillights disappear around some trees.

"I'm not sure." Robert mused as he watched Grady leave. "We have a lot of problems, and very few answers."

"We need to report in on our situation, Sir."

Robert watched as Grady's car went down the main road passing behind the trees. Robert turned back toward Carey. "I want to make sure the team is on their way to cover my family."

"Yes, Sir. I'll make the call." Carey reached into his pocket for his cell phone.

The three of them waited patiently for Carey to get a check-in from the other agents, who responded that they were loading up, and would be on their way to Robert's house momentarily. The Agents and Robert began walking to the cars.

An explosion from the far side of the trees down near Key Bridge ripped through the air. The force of the blast could be felt throughout the parking area. Robert could feel the heat. Looking up, he saw a huge plume of gray smoke billow into the air, followed by bright yellow flames, and brilliant white trails that arched like fireworks through the sky. The sound of squealing tires and a crunch of metal from cars on top of the bridge followed as a second explosion sent red flames rushing up one side of the gray smoke column. Disgorging a black cloud into the first explosion's smoke, they rose higher in a mushroom shaped cloud.

"Stay here!" Carey yelled at Robert, running to his car. Long fired up the engine on the BMW, and positioned the car to leave. Robert got into the passenger side.

Spinning his tires as he drove, Carey reached the main road quickly and saw in front of him a conflagration of flames and smoke. They were coming from the incinerated remains of a four-door sedan, cocked at an angle partway on the grass and curb. The engine, interior, and tires all burned violently. No glass or paint remained, but he could tell it was the same kind of car Colonel Barlow had been driving. Several cars had collided, and were stopped short of the explosion. The car was a crematorium for anything, or anybody left inside.

"Long." He yelled into his microphone. "Leave now! I'll take point from the ramp." Carey's words launched Agent Long into action. He said nothing to Robert. Dropping the car into gear the tires squealed as he raced for the exit.

"Get down!" Long pushed Robert's head toward the seat. Robert was too disoriented to understand what Long was telling him and bobbed back up, looking out the window.

Carey put his car in reverse and backed his way toward the parking area exit, blocking the first lane of the main road. Just as Long arrived, he accelerated, taking up position in front as both cars sped across traffic, over the grassy median and onto the southbound lanes of the roadway.

"What's going on? What's happening?" Robert yelled at Long, as he struggled to stay seated in the bouncing car. Long's focus was on his driving. He didn't answer.

Robert's face had blanched when they'd driven past the burning car. He knew it was the car Grady had been driving.

Chapter 34

Robert sat in his office...just sat. He didn't notice the clock ticking. The coffee on his desk was cold. His computer sat in his briefcase. His overcoat had been hung up by Lorraine. He wasn't in shock. That would be too physical; too tangible. He was staggered. He had been jolted into silent limbo. He had not spoken since his eyes had filled with the flames and smoke of Grady's burning car. The gutted hulk continued to burn in his mind. The flames leaped in Robert's brain without diminishing. The car blazed without being consumed.

They had driven straight back to the office. The secure parking and building made sense. Robert had not noticed whether Long spoke, either to him, or to Carey on the radio. All he could hear and see were flames and smoke. In the elevator the silence continued as the door opened on a lower floor. Carey got out to go to security. Long continued up with Robert and took his station outside the door.

Blaring into the silence of his office, the ringing phone jerked Robert's mind back into his body. He grabbed at the phone. Lorraine was on the line, but Robert only heard Tracie's voice.

"Tracie? What's wrong?" He asked her, wondering why his voice sounded so strange in his ears.

"You didn't call!" She was distraught. Robert could hear the boys arguing in the background. Relief crept over him.

"I'm sorry. It's been...we've been very busy here." His response was wooden, canned sounding. He was not fully coherent, his stunned nerves still overwhelmed.

"You promised!" Tracie's shout silenced the boys. Her fear had set them at each other earlier, now the fear was compelling them to silence as they mutely watched her. "You said you'd call, and once again, you didn't call! This is so typical of you, Robert! You put me on edge, and then forget all about me. You didn't even think about me and the boys!"

"I really am sorry, Tracie," Robert answered, trying to respond. "Look, there's nothing to be worried about. You need to stay with your routine, and wait for the agents to get there."

"Why aren't they here, yet? You're not telling me what's happened, or why the agents are coming. It's scaring the boys. I can't do this! You can't do this to me, Robert!" He knew that Tracie's fingers were clenched on the phone, her knuckles white from the pressure.

"I can't tell you more, Tracie because there's nothing to tell." Robert wracked his brain for a plausible reason, some kind of story she would accept. "There was a bomb threat." He couldn't believe he had said that. She would never buy it.

"A bomb threat? Where?" Tracie sounded shocked.

"Our offices. We're just taking precautions." Robert answered. He knew he kept using the same phrases over and over with her, but he couldn't make his mind come up with anything else.

"Your building? Then why are you there?" Tracie asked, now sounding suspicious.

"It's the other wing." Robert was trapped now. He knew it the minute the words came out of his mouth. He was backed into his own corner.

Tracie's fear was rapidly becoming anger. "A bomb in the other wing?" She over enunciated each word. Her voice was carrying acidic fumes over the phone line, burning into Robert's ear.

"Look, Tracie, I genuinely can't talk right now. There's absolutely no reason you should be worried, since they haven't found any evidence that there actually is a bomb. Okay? I'll explain when I get home."

"You'd better, Robert. Don't leave me hanging like that again!" Tracie slammed the phone down, then hit the off button and slammed it down again.

Robert set his phone slowly down on the cradle. That had not gone well. The exchange had caught him flat-footed, but now he was awake. He knew he had to take action.

He could feel the presence of Agent Long outside his door. He could hear Lorraine talking to a caller, her voice unnaturally high. The stress was building, spreading to everyone like an infection. He needed time to think, and to decide what to do, and where to start.

Robert thought his mind had cleared, but he found he still couldn't clear the image of Grady's burning car. Grady's battered appearance was silhouetted in his mind against a background of the explosion that had killed him.

Robert stared at three names scribbled on a legal pad: Hunt, Karlovich, and Gregg. He kept repeating the names silently. Was Hunt a threat as he'd first assumed, or an ally? Karlovich; was he the source of the problem, or another piece in this expanding puzzle? Senator Gregg was a significant question mark. Why was he connected, interested, or even involved?

Then there was the President. Robert would normally have assumed that the President's concerns would be part of a pre-vote checklist. At least that's what he'd have thought if Gregg hadn't entered the picture.

Robert knew he was going to be handicapped without Grady's help. Did that even matter now? Wasn't this the FBI's problem?

He mulled that over for a moment. He still had no choice but to continue his investigation. Nothing directly linked Grady's attack, death, or Chris's death to his investigation. Grady had mentioned the idea of dropping the investigation, but Robert knew that he'd be outmaneuvered by Senator Gregg, and his boss on that one. They'd already made it clear that wasn't an option. If OPOV fell apart, and he hadn't discovered why and how it happened, his career would be over. They'd deliberately placed him in that position as the scapegoat.

For the investigation to move forward, he figured he'd better find out more about Karlovich. Whether Hunt had handed him Karlovich, or he was simply a logical beginning in finding any security problem with OPOV and The NSA didn't matter. He had, indirectly, been Chris' boss, and had too much to lose if the NSA's security around OPOV failed. If he wasn't a perpetrator in this mess, he should be open to a meeting.

Spinning his chair around to his briefcase, Robert yanked out his computer and snapped it into the docking station. Punching the ON button, he intoned, "Come on…come on," impatiently tapping on the machine as it slowly booted. He could have asked Lorraine to look up Karlovich's number, but he didn't want her or anyone else to know what he was doing. Finally the computer desktop screen came up, and he signed into the directory listing for the NSA. Karlovich's name, phone number, and NSA building code were at the top of the page. Robert yanked the phone closer to him and dialed the number.

"Systems Group. This is Francis. May I direct your call?" The receptionist answered.

"Yes, Bill Karlovich, please," Robert responded.

"May I tell him who's calling?" Francis asked mechanically.

"Robert Carlton, US Associate Attorney General," Robert answered. He'd figured he'd better make formal use of the title to get Karlovich's attention.

"Thank you, I'll see if he's available. One moment."

Robert could hear the line clicking several times as he was put on hold, and then forwarded.

"Mr. Carlton, this is Bill Karlovich. How can I help you?" The man sounded confident, polished, and at ease.

"I don't believe we've met, I'm…" Robert began.

"Actually, we met at the spring gala last year," Karlovich cut him off mid-sentence.

Robert thought for a moment. Karlovich should know who he was, as would most of Washington, but he couldn't remember ever having met him. It was entirely possible that they had met briefly at some event, but Robert thought he would have remembered meeting an NSA Director.

"Yes, of course," Robert covered. "I appreciate your remembering. I need to get together with you."

"You have some questions about the implementation of the OPOV system, I assume," Karlovich said, more as a statement than a question.

Robert was taken aback by this insight, then realized that Karlovich, while being in charge of many projects, had only one major public program; OPOV. "Yes, precisely," he answered, hiding his surprise. "I'm checking on a few final security issues, and need to meet with you to discuss them. I would prefer to meet today."

"I'm at your disposal, Mr. Carlton. Would one o'clock be acceptable? I can have a conference room made available. I could perhaps arrange a briefing, and a tour."

"Thank you, no," Robert answered firmly. "I don't need a briefing, or tour."

"Perhaps you would prefer your offices?" Karlovich responded. "We'd have to meet later, but I'd be happy to come over to you."

"No, your office will be fine. I have some items I need to clarify, and I think you can help." Robert felt that Karlovich was being somehow a little too hospitable and deferential. The quick timing worked for his agenda, though, and being out of the office sounded good.

"One o'clock then. Do you need directions?" Karlovich inquired.

"No, I know the way to your building. I'll see you at one." Robert confirmed.

"Good. I'll meet you in the main lobby by the security desk. I'll have everything arranged." Karlovich responded.

"Thank you." Robert hung up. Either Bill Karlovich was the smoothest director he had ever heard of, or he had expected his call. It felt like a set-up. Hitting the intercom button he asked Lorraine to come in.

"Yes, Sir?" Lorraine asked as she came into the room, notepad in hand.

"Get hold of Jerry, and have him come over. Then arrange for Agent Carey and Phil Davidson to meet me here...in a half-hour, if possible. Also, check the schedule and assignments for Singer and Nelson."

"Yes, Sir." Lorraine rapidly jotted down the action items, and left the room, closing the door behind her.

Gerald Turner, or Jerry as everyone knew him, was the head of the Office of Intergovernmental and Public Liaisons.

Jerry came through the door into Robert's office fifteen minutes later. "Hello, Robert; what can I do for you?"

Jerry was older than Robert, and more experienced. He had been in the Justice Department for years. He was senior to Robert in every way, except in title and connections. His salt and pepper smoothly combed hair and tailored suits screamed political ambition. Though Jerry had been passed over by Robert, there was no particular animosity between the two. Jerry had seen four Attorney Generals come and go, along with their Deputies and Associates, and in his opinion Robert was the next ex-Associate Attorney General. Robert preferred to leave Jerry to his own duties most of the time, since he had a heavy backlog, and did his job well. Generally, they kept out of each other's way, meeting only during department staff meetings.

"Jerry, I'm going to need you to drop what you're doing, and help me on something." Robert told him without any preamble. "How fast can you be available?"

Jerry winced noticeably. Pulling out his cell phone from his pocket, he scanned his priority list and calendar. "I have the justices for two sessions this week, a piece for Harvard Business Review, and the usual assortment of meetings."

Robert looked straight at him. "You'll have to keep the Supreme Court commitments. Put off HBR, and your other work. Don't take commitments for the next week unless you have to."

Jerry sat down, raising one eyebrow and crossing his legs comfortably. "What's up?"

"I need you to manage a team to dig into the One Person, One Vote system. This will require you to review how the different department jurisdictions apply, who controls which elements, how the states interact; the whole ball of wax."

"What, more bureaucratic rehashing? Isn't that the same thing we did two years ago?" Jerry responded, sighing. He looked annoyed, and prepared to fight Robert's request.

"There will be some rehashing, Jerry, but the report needs to be refreshed." Robert answered. "A lot changes in two years, even with the strict guidelines surrounding OPOV. This upcoming test has become more crucial than we realized, and the spotlight is on the program again."

Robert shifted in his seat, and leaned toward Jerry before continuing. "You know the committee never decided on a single control point, and that's leaving room for jurisdictional confusion. That's landed this thing back in our laps. The President and the Senate Rules Committee have asked us to make some discreet inquiries into who's in charge of what section. I want to be sure there will be no obvious security process problems. Some may have cropped up with this dotted-line responsibility going in several directions. I need to know the complete chain of responsibility and authority through each branch, and how the communication flow is handled—right down to the collection of the votes. The President wants this test to go smoothly, and I want you to coordinate whatever it takes to cover all the bases."

"Look for anything that could be considered a flaw," he continued. "For example, there may be a security point that everyone assumes is covered by another group. I would like to hear that two agencies are covering every critical spot, if not, changes might be required. You'll find all you need to get started in the original reports, but take nothing at face value. Re-check everything. I want to be sure we didn't overlook anything, and that no procedures have been changed. Break up the sections, and spread the load across the team. Lorraine can get you copies of whatever you need."

Jerry was a veteran of political investigations. He knew Robert was looking for something specific. "Do you know who's dropping the ball?" He asked directly.

"I'm not saying that's happening," Robert stated firmly. One thing he didn't need right now was a rumor flying around government offices. That could make things worse, or send whoever was behind this into hiding. "I'm verifying security. I have reason to believe that NSA is the most likely place for any problems to occur, based on the amount of responsibility they are shouldering."

Jerry looked unconvinced. Robert knew that he was assessing whether this could be a career making opportunity, or if it was Robert's attempt to cover his ass in case anything went wrong.

"Any questions?" Robert pushed.

"Whose team do I use?" Jerry sounded irritated.

Robert hit the intercom button. "Lorraine?"

"Yes, sir?"

"Did you find out what Singer and Nelson are doing?"

"They are both available. Ms. Singer says her staff is tied up on the U.N. Trade Embargo issues, but could fit in a special project. In other words, they'd be glad to have a diversion. Mr. Nelson says his staff can request postponements, but he would have to verify with Mr. Turner, of course."

"Thank you, Lorraine. Send them notification that they are assigned to Jerry for two weeks." Robert released the intercom button. "Well, Jerry, there are your team leaders."

Jerry narrowed his eyes. Robert had just assigned two of the best investigators the department had to him. "This must be more important than you've let on." Jerry said, running his hand along the arm of the chair casually.

"It is," Robert admitted, "but that can't leave the room for now."

"Understood," Jerry seemed slightly mollified. The fact that this was clearly a significant duty was gratifying. His name would be in any report that was generated. He rose and headed for the door. "What's your timeline?"

"I need a list of who's who in the authority flow for each major process step by tomorrow. The day after, at the latest. After that, I'll need a daily update on your progress and any findings. If feasible, start from the end point, or from the top of the pyramid, and work down to the county level."

Jerry sighed, but left without further conversation. Robert knew he would do a good job—probably better than Robert would have done. He also knew that Jerry was not his friend, or a partner. Jerry was looking for an opportunity to show off his experience level. In a strange way that made him even more valuable and trustworthy.

As soon as Jerry left, Lorraine came into the office. "Would you like to see Agent Carey and Mr. Davidson now?"

"Yes, have them come in." Robert was surprised that they had already arrived.

The door swung open, with Long pushing it wide. "I'll take a break and grab a sandwich, if that's convenient," Long spoke to both Robert and Carey through the open door.

"Yes, of course. Thank you, Agent Long." Robert acknowledged.

Almost immediately Carey was standing stiffly by Robert's desk. Davidson, next to him, looked smaller, older, and out of shape. Phil certainly didn't present the appearance of someone so capable in his work.

"I appreciate you both understanding the urgency here." Robert smiled at Phil.

"I was comparing notes with Agent Carey on your little morning meeting when your call came," Phil responded. In spite of his dour expression, Phil seemed to be glad to be involved in the field work. His expression reflected his recognition of what had happened, and the gravity of Grady's death, but he also seemed excited to be part of this team.

"Gentlemen, please take a seat." Robert gestured to two of his guest chairs. "There have been two incidents that I need you to check into." Robert was on unfamiliar and delicate turf—he wondered how to approach this. The Secret Service had virtually unlimited power in certain circumstances, but the President and their own management decided when and where that power would be used. This investigation might well be outside their interests, or jurisdiction. "I believe these events are related. The first incident is the death of Chris Stoker."

Carey was taking notes on a small paper spiral pad.

"That's Chris with a C and Stoker, s-t-o-k-e-r, male," Robert added.

"Caucasian?" asked Carey.

"Yes. Non-military. He was working for the NSA. He was shot in his car leaving DC last Friday. The second is an assault against

Lt. Colonel Grady Barlow that occurred at his home in Virginia last night. To my knowledge, Colonel Barlow did not report the event to the police. A fire occurred, so the fire department should have responded. You might check with them. Phil, I'm sure Carey has already mentioned Barlow's car exploding."

"Yes, he filled me in." Phil glanced over at Carey.

"Good. Obviously, you have become part of this investigation, but let's limit involving others on a 'need to know' basis." Robert sized up Carey. "Let's make it official. I believe there is a link between Stoker, Barlow, and Hunt. Hunt used both Stoker's and Barlow's names to get me to that meeting. He used the phrase 'It's time to Stoke some Barley' to get my attention. Given the situation, those words sound somewhat threatening. I don't know what his connection to them is. That's all I can tell you. Now, do you have anything to fill me in on?"

"I made some inquiries into the explosion of the vehicle Colonel Barlow was driving." Carey began. "A body was found in the car; likely male. It was found curled up in the floorboard of the burned car, and burned beyond recognition. At this time, a positive identification has not been made. There were two explosions; the first and primary was from an explosive device, and the secondary was the fuel tank."

"Phil," Robert said, "I need you two to find out what the police know about both of these incidents, whether any other government agencies are investigating, or are involved in any way, and what they might know."

Carey noted this on his pad.

Phil's hand lifted slightly as if asking to speak.

"Phil, I need to you catch up here, and you don't have to ask my permission to speak." Robert said impatiently.

"No, no. I'm with you now." Phil answered. "You know that the Secret Service and Treasury Department have very specific rules, and their jurisdiction is almost non-existent outside those guidelines." Phil glanced at Agent Carey as he spoke.

"Yes, I know." Robert decided to establish some turf of his own. "I also know that computer fraud and falsified identity crimes are in your jurisdiction."

"Clearly. We've discussed that before, and you know I feel the Secret Service should be..." Phil began.

"Exactly." Robert cut off Phil's approaching oratory. "That's why I've asked you both here." He paused for a moment before continuing. "I have reason to believe these two incidents and these three people are directly related to an attempt to compromise the OPOV system. This is, of course, for your ears only at this time."

Carey and Davidson both frowned, and looked slightly perplexed. They waited for Robert to explain. He didn't.

"Has an investigation been opened?" Carey finally asked, breaking the silence of the room.

"I'm not at liberty to disclose that at this time," Robert parried. He was hoping that response would shut down any more questions.

"Officially unofficial. Check. But who..." Phil began asking, then cut himself off. After a short pause, he questioned, "All right; any suggestions about where we should begin?"

"Phil, I don't know who you need to contact," responded Robert, "but I need to know everything about Stoker, Barlow and Hunt. I'm betting your team and connections can move faster than I can, using the public channels. I assume the police departments would be the place to start. I don't really care how you do it; I just need everything you can get. I'm sure agent Carey has already learned something about Hunt. Can you two coordinate with each other and handle this?"

Agent Carey had regained his stoic composure. "That shouldn't be a problem. We should be able to access all information related to the incidents, public or otherwise. We'll investigate any avenues that haven't been covered, and stay as much under everyone's radar as possible. The President authorized any such discretionary decisions when he assigned us to your offices."

"Wait a minute," Robert stopped him, wondering if he'd heard that correctly. He leaned forward. "What do you mean, 'the President assigned you to my offices?' Aren't you assigned to the building?"

Carey's face was unwavering. "Beyond the President, Vice President and their families, the Secret Service's mission includes security at The White House, The Treasury Building, The Treasury Annex, counterfeit currency, financial systems, buildings which house presidential offices, the Vice President's residence, a few foreign diplomatic missions in Washington, former Presidents, and other areas as designated by the President. He specified The Office of the Attorney General, Deputy Attorney General, and the Associate Attorney General, following Attorney General Bradley's accident."

"Your offices would only be covered at The President's request." Phil acknowledged to Robert. "Normally no security outside the JPSO would be associated with your offices. I didn't think about that until now. Why would extra security be assigned?" Phil asked the question out loud, but more to himself than to anyone.

Robert was also wondering about the implications of what had just been said. Regrouping, he ignored Phil's question, and commented, "Then I can expect significant assistance."

"Yes, as it relates to your protection," Carey answered.

Robert looked directly at Phil, sending him the message that he needed to take the lead.

Phil looked at Carey. "I need all the details on your assignment." Then he looked back at Robert. "I can keep the team small by using the same agents that manned the listening post when you had your meeting on The Mall."

"We'll debrief after I talk to my section leader." Carey was going by the book.

Robert rose from his chair. "I want to be clear about this: I think there is a definite connection between OPOV, Stoker's, and Barlow's deaths, and this man 'Hunt,' also. We don't have time to wait around for the answers to become evident. This thing has become urgent."

Davidson and Carey got ready to leave. "If that's all you needed, we have some work to do," Phil said.

Robert nodded, and watched as the two men left.

"So..." Robert thought to himself, "The President assigned Secret Service to me, but didn't mention it. Why didn't he say something?"

Robert thought about that. "Good God," he realized. "Chris was right. Bradley's death wasn't a fishing accident, and the President knows it."

Chapter 35

Blair gripped the armrest of his car. His fingertips sunk into the stiff leather, while his jaw muscles flexed with a slight clicking of the tendons.

"So...they haven't checked in. Barlow's home was burned to the ground last night. Barlow contacts Carlton, and then blows up in his car when he tries to leave. That's what you are telling me?"

"Yes, Sir." The man on the phone answered.

"You waited to tell me this until now? You're telling me NOW? Could you have possibly screwed up any worse than this?" Blair was furious.

"Sir, I..."

"Shut UP!" Blair's fingernails threatened to penetrate the leather and tear the cover off. "I need to think."

"But, they..." The man began saying.

"Don't speak! It's not 'they;' it's you!" His voice carried a noticeable growl. "*They* are dead. And if not, '*they*' are dead to me. Understand? And that leaves *you*. Got it? *You*."

Silence came from the other end. Updating Blair on bad news was the last thing the man had wanted to do. The fewer words spoken about this, the better, he decided. In the history of botched jobs, the Barlow FUBAR was one of the biggest messes possible.

The two operatives had royally screwed this job. If they weren't dead already, they were going to wish they were. Barlow was to have been visited for the sole purpose of getting him and Carlton worked up over the OPOV infiltration. That was it. The orders had been to make them paranoid, tense—call it what you like, but the idea was to get them moving faster. That had been the job. Rough Barlow up, ask questions, make a threat that he should drop the investigation, then bail. It had been a simple assignment that had gotten totally out of control.

"Burned to the ground. That's the last resort in covering up mistakes." Blair stated.

"Yes, Sir."

"Don't interrupt. So, now a scorched crater marks the spot. What could be worse? Oh, wait! Barlow gets loose, and then is blown up in fire and smoke in broad daylight on a freeway."

"Yes, Sir."

"Shut up! Fire and smoke. Sound familiar? Can I assume our guys did both firebombs? Did they seriously kill him in broad daylight, with a hundred or so witnesses?"

Silence issued from the phone.

"Well?" Blair insisted.

"I don't know, Sir."

"Of course you don't know." Blair wasn't letting go of his anger. "How could I expect anyone so remiss in their supervisory duties to know what the hell happened with two of his operatives? Find them! I want answers, and I want them now. I want their asses in a sling. I want them locked in a room with no doors or windows until I decide what to do. Got that? Then I want you to find out what the authorities, any authorities, know about both fires. Bodies. I need to know how many they found, and what names they've put with them. I'll get more people in."

"Yes, Sir." The man repeated, "Find them. Lock them up. Find out how many bodies they found, and their names."

"Update me on each step. If you stop to shit, I want a detailed report of it." Blair ended the call and immediately dialed another number. A woman answered.

"Yes?" She answered promptly.

"Are you available?" Blair questioned.

"Yes." She answered.

"D.C. location 3." He told her.

"5 PM." She responded.

"Good." Blair hit the end button again. "Idiots." Firing up the engine of his faded gray sedan, Blair headed back toward Washington.

Chapter 36

"Hey, are you alive?" Terri's sprightly voice popped up over the cubicle wall toward Marty. She stood up on her tiptoes, and looked as far over the fabric-covered panel as she could. "I've been waiting all morning for you to ask me to lunch, and nothing. Not a word. Well, it's almost twelve-thirty, and I'm not waiting anymore. So, are you hungry, or what?"

"What?" Marty seemed not to have heard a word Terri had just said.

Terri sighed in exasperation. "I said, 'Are you hungry?' Boy, you're such a grouch today!"

"I'm not. You're just a pest." Marty shoved his chair back as he logged off from his computer. "Let's go."

"Well, that's certainly decisive. I should have asked earlier." Terri answered, ignoring his gibe. She grabbed her coat and catching up to Marty, headed for the airlock. It was late for the lunch rush, so there was no line. Terri pressed her hand to the scanner and stepped into the airlock. When Marty emerged on the other side, she was waiting with his wallet and keys from the locker.

"So, where are you taking us today?" she inquired.

"I'd like a burger," Marty answered.

"Whoa, you are aggressive today! I like it. Predictable, Mr. Burger, but I like it." She put on a cute grin. "I admire that in a man. It's almost as fun as being scanned all over by the airlock." She turned and they headed out the door. The guard was setting out the welcome sign.

"I wonder which VIP is coming." She didn't bother to read the name.

Marty shrugged. He couldn't care less, unable to think about anything except what he had been doing. They headed off to the car in silence.

Robert arrived shortly after Marty and Terri left the parking lot. Robert walked up to the security desk with Agent Carey on his right, and Agent Long on his left.

Agent Carey spoke. "Associate Attorney General Carlton to see Director Karlovich." Carey nodded his head toward Robert.

"Yes, Gentlemen. You are expected," the guard responded. "The Director is in security now. May I see your identification?"

They handed the guard their IDs. While the guard closely examined the cards, Robert scanned the lobby. He was unhappily surprised to see his name on the welcome board right by the doorway. It said, "Deputy Attorney General Carlton." The only thing good about that was the promotion it gave him.

"Here are your IDs and badges. The Director will be here shortly." The guard did not smile.

"Could you take down the sign, please?" Robert pointed to the welcome sign.

"Yes, Sir. Not a problem." The guard immediately moved from behind the desk and placed the sign back behind it, facing the wall.

Karlovich stepped out of the airlock and came briskly over to introduce himself.

"Bill Karlovich, it's a pleasure to see you again." He shook hands with Robert. He acknowledged Carey with a nod of his head. "Agent Carey. Well, shall we go to the conference room and get started?" He moved past them to lead the way. Agent Long planted himself in the lobby, near the desk.

Karlovich looked at the sign behind the desk as he passed by, and then at the guard who shrugged slightly while nodding toward Robert.

Karlovich led the way to a conference room off the lobby, where they all settled into seats around a table. Although Robert had declined a formal presentation, Karlovich seemed to feel it was essential. Two of Karlovich's assistants took over, using formal slides on a large flat panel HDTV display mounted to the wall.

Even though Robert had been in on the program since its inception, he couldn't help feeling that OPOV was an impressive system. The security had definitely been crafted by some of the most brilliant minds in the field. A full staff of Internet experts handled interfacing and server issues, and a group of cryptologists handled security.

The technology was complex, driven by a simple and elegant concept. Within the NSA building was a master server. This computer maintained all the software and incoming vote totals. It had several layers of protection and firewalls, and both hardware and software were positioned between it and the outside world where it connected to the external government controlled Internet. Three massive, secure broadband connections held the capability of handling more phone lines than a large city would need. Two server farms, filled with computers running beside the master server mirrored the main system, creating massive redundancy. The first mirroring computer stayed ten commands behind the master computer, halting both systems at the first sign of trouble. This would give the operators a chance to see what had gone wrong, and make corrections while another computer buffered the system. If the problem could be corrected, the system could resume from the buffer with no lost data. If not, the system would drop the master computer, and restart from the point at which the first mirroring computer had encountered the trouble spot.

The second mirror system ran one thousand operations behind the first, providing a fallback position if an error was catastrophic, or if it affected the first mirror. Neither of the mirrors attached directly to the Internet, and each had safety buffers between them for added security. Multiple equipment manufacturers provided the equipment, and multiple operating systems ran autonomously. All of this was designed to thwart any combination of virus, worm, malware, embedded code or whatever creative terrorist attack could be attempted. It was a startling array of technology.

The next step was to put protection into the communications that ran back and forth on the Internet. Here they were using an advanced 'certificate' system, a full generation beyond VPN styled systems. The technical process surpassed Robert's knowledge base, but he got the gist of it as the slides were presented. Essentially, each person in the United States was assigned a certificate number that identified him or her uniquely. The numbers came from retina scans, or thumbprints if a voter didn't agree to retinal scanning. The thumbprint approach required additional photo ID. Next, an algorithm was generated using the certificate number combined with a Social Security Number, and a randomly generated numeric code. The end result was a certificate that each voter was assigned and issued, in the form of an RFID tag embedded in their driver's license, or government issued identification. It contained an individual algorithm that the voter would use, either on his or her own computer, or on a voting center computer. A corresponding set sat on the main system at the NSA. The algorithms and codes changed based on date and time, leaving information available for no more than a few seconds at any time.

Robert found his head swimming, since this was only the beginning. A brief history of cryptography followed. The team of cryptanalysts had all been spawned from the days of William Friedman and Yardley, studying systems like the Japanese "Purple" and "The Black Room." If it had been a British presentation names like Tommy Flowers and Alan Turing would have been named. The discussion moved quickly to examples of what they were now doing to protect the system. Their resulting convoluted contortions of letters and numbers were dazzling. Although Robert had been briefed on all this before, the explanations were as confusing as the cryptography. These discussions were presented only in metaphors, not as current solution techniques to protect secrecy. Robert tried to appear as though he understood everything to keep the presentation moving, but he felt dazed.

Robert tuned back into the conversation as one of the assistants related that the algorithm would change every time it was used, and only the sending and receiving ends would know what change was requested. A machine "listening in" on the Internet would have to see every transaction, without error, for thousands of exchanges before it could possibly spot the algorithmic root. This made it practically impossible to break. Banks, brokerages, and information services had been using similar, but less elaborate certificate systems since "The Great Recession," and its following "Lost Decade," with exceptional security performance results. This system was much more extreme.

Using several techniques developed for military installations, OPOV's security continued with special modulate/demodulate systems installed between all the subtotal stations. These were the decentralized computers where votes were tallied, usually in large cities and heavily populated counties, and then for each state. From there, only the subtotal was passed on. Each of these machines was on a protected secure line. The modems monitored any fluctuation in modulation. Even electromagnetic changes could be detected, since they would cause tiny delays, or phase shifts. Of course this was for copper transmission. It was slightly different for optical fiber.

All of this modulation monitoring was overkill, the presenters explained, since the data could be read, but not modified. The new IDs would effectively obsolete social security numbers, they added, since the new ID could be verified by the person's physiology with ninety-nine point nine plus percent accuracy every time it was scanned, a side benefit that would end ID theft. The implications were staggering. Robert wondered again whether this introduction would make personal lives more private, and safer, or more public, and increasingly controlled by outsiders.

One of the presenters was wrapping up the lecture. He told Robert that the concepts were founded on established principles of Quantum Cryptography with Coherent States. "So," he continued, "without going into excruciating detail, that is our system. Any questions, Sir?"

"Very impressive." Robert acknowledged. "But for this layman, you're a little late on leaving out the excruciating detail."

Turning toward Karlovich, he said, "Bill, I have an understanding of why you think the system will work. I'm comfortable with that. What I'm looking for is where it might fail. There have been flaws in every technological breakthrough of every era, and they have been successfully exploited. Plus, there is the human element." Robert stopped, allowing silence to fill the room. Karlovich didn't seem to be picking up the ball. "Don't hold back," he urged. "You're not the only agency on this project. There's always a weak spot, and I need to know what you think we're up against."

Karlovich reflected quietly for a moment, then said, "For that discussion, I think we should move into the secure facility, and I'll show you what we're working on there." Bill stood and indicated they should leave the conference room. "I should warn you that your first time through the airlock will take several minutes while it analyzes you, and sets up a file. Try not to move, since that will slow down the process. You'll have to leave wallets, keys, and anything magnetic or metallic here. Do you have any medical implants?"

"No." Robert shook his head.

Upon returning to the lobby, Karlovich indicated that they should leave their belongings in the locker area, past the guard's desk. Carey looked uncomfortable leaving his gun, but unloaded it, and placed the weapon in the gun box provided without comment. The lockers had user assignable locking codes, so Robert was not concerned leaving his wallet. They stepped up to the scanner. The Director placed his hand on top. It only took one pass to verify him. The door opened. "Don't worry, it will recognize you as being new to the facility, and give you verbal instructions if needed." He stepped inside and the door closed.

In little more than a minute the indicator panel flashed, "Ready." Robert placed his hand against the panel. It ran three scans before opening the door. He stepped in, and in about three minutes, he arrived in the operations area.

"Not too bad, I hope?" Karlovich smiled.

"I'd hate to go through there if I was claustrophobic."

"That would be a problem. I should have asked, but there's not much choice. You can see that we are quite serious about security."

Agent Carey stepped from the airlock. Robert thought it had taken him significantly less time to be cleared.

Karlovich gestured in a circle around the room. "This is the center of our OPOV software management operation. As you can see, we have a small team. They are extremely select individuals." He began walking toward his office. "We work on the highly secret portions of code here, and we control how all of the code is implemented, placed on the system, and monitored. All the security changes occur here, and never leave the room. The computers themselves are behind that wall on your left, except of course for the third system, and second backup, which are in a different secure facility not near this location. "

They went into Karlovich's office. With the door closed he proceeded to layout the elaborate software system with all its security bells and whistles. Robert glazed over quickly, and began to feel sleepy. He tried to keep alert, and realized that he was being given another explanation of why the system would work, not how it could be infiltrated. He began to wonder if by coming here as he had, he'd set himself up for a public relations tour. He began to feel that the trip had been a mistake.

Chapter 37

Terri hopped into Marty's car. "Not bad! That double chili-cheese burger hit the spot."

"I can't believe you ate that thing. How can you stay in such great shape eating like that? It gave me gas just looking at it."

"You get gas eating scrambled eggs."

"And what of it?" Marty snapped. "Eggs affect a lot of people that way."

"Hey, I was only kidding. And it was your idea to get a burger, anyway. You been getting much sleep lately?" Marty ignored Terri's gibe, and instead focused on the fact that she had not put her seatbelt on. She never wore her seatbelt in his car, and it bugged the hell out of him.

"That was a gut bomb you ate, not a burger, and you know, there is a seatbelt law here," he reminded her for the hundredth time.

"Yeah, yeah. I just don't want to get trapped in your car after you wreck it. You like seat belt cleavage, but not all of us are into it." She grabbed the belt and snapped it in place. The shoulder harness snuggled nicely between her breasts. "Happy? Now tell me: sleep? Yes, or no?"

"It's not really a problem. I just can't stand my cooking, that's all." Marty dodged.

"Swanson, or Stouffers? I'm sure you're a regular Chef Prudhomme. How's Christen? Everything okay there?" Terri looked intently at Marty.

"Of course! She's fine. What made you ask that?" Marty was clearly agitated by the question.

"Hey, just asking. Don't bite my head off." She pushed against the back of her seat, crossing her arms defiantly. "You need to cut back on the caffeine."

"Sorry, I'm just on edge. You're right; too much coffee. Christen is fine, but I don't hear from her much." It was easier for Marty to lie when it contained a little truth.

They didn't speak again until they reached the lockers, and then they only had the usual exchange with security.

As they walked toward their cubicles, Robert, Carey, and the Director came out of Karlovich's office and walked toward the airlock, heading straight at them. Terri smiled toward Robert. Robert smiled back automatically.

"Hello," Terri said as they passed directly in front of Chris Stoker's cubicle. Marty nodded with a barely noticeable smile.

"Hello," Robert responded automatically. Suddenly struck with surprise, he had to resist commenting when he saw Chris's name tag next to the cubicle entrance. He tried to keep the muscles in his face neutral as they passed.

Carey made eye contact with Terri who coquettishly tipped her head to the side and looked up, saying slowly. "Hi...taking a tour?" Her smile was infectious, and captivating.

"Yes, we did." Carey smiled as he spoke. Robert was surprised at Carey's response. She was very attractive, and clearly liked Carey's appearance, but he would have thought Carey was too controlled to respond.

Carey pointed toward the airlock. "Here we are, Sir." His bodyguard demeanor returned instantly.

Robert had walked past Chris' name tag on the wall without mentioning it, concerned that he might reveal something. To say nothing might give him leverage. To ask anything about Chris might give away his interest, and wasn't likely to further his knowledge. Still...

"Oh, yes, thank you." Robert moved to the airlock and began to place his palm on the hand scanner, but instead stopped, and turned to Karlovich.

"I noticed a name back there. Chris Stoker. It's very familiar."

"Oh? He is on vacation right now, or I would introduce you." Bill responded.

Carey added flatly. "A Chris Stoker was recently reported killed. Wife Anne. Is this the same Stoker?"

Bill Karlovich was visibly stunned. His voice had a stilted, almost stuttering undercurrent as he answered. "I...I had no idea. Yes, Anne. Anne, that's his wife's name. What happened?"

Robert was glaring at Carey. So much for the legendary stoicism of the Secret Service, he thought, clenching his teeth. Carey noticed his look, and attempted a recovery.

"I'm sorry. I'm sure it is a coincidence. We scan what is happening in the area, and I just happened to recall a news feed. Perhaps I was mistaken."

"I don't think so." Karlovich had recovered, stiffening with chilly composure. "I'll have this checked out immediately."

There was an awkward pause before Robert spoke. "I think perhaps we can help each other out here, Bill. Agent Carey, since you mentioned it, could you do a little research on what you remember? Perhaps you could locate the source of the information, and discover the details? That might be of some assistance to Director Karlovich."

"Yes, of course," Carey answered, returning to his robotic style of speaking.

"I'd appreciate it," Karlovich said rigidly.

Marty's eyes had not been on Robert as they passed. He was staring at Carey, who had looked directly at him with what seemed to be a smirk at the corner of his mouth. He had watched and listened as Carey spoke to Terri. Now he could hear clearly what was being said while the group stood next to the airlock.

Terri came up behind Marty and spoke quietly into his ear. "Did you hear what I just heard?"

"Yes," Marty answered woodenly.

"Chris is dead?" Terri waited for a response. She moved to Marty's side, trying to get his attention, and stop him from staring. "That guy—the tall buff looking one—do you know him?"

"Who?" Marty was standing very still.

"The tall guy who looks like some kind of bodyguard, that's who," Terri replied indignantly.

"No, never saw him before." Marty went quickly back to his computer, and started typing.

Terri came up behind him. "Try the Post. They must have something on it."

"What?" Marty asked, distractedly.

"Chris! Whatever it was that happened to Chris." Terri said.

"Right. Yeah, I'm looking it up." Marty responded, still typing.

"I'll check, too." Terri looked slightly skeptical as she scooted over to her cube. "'Right' my ass," she said under her breath.

Robert and Carey left through the airlock. Karlovich had disappeared from sight.

Chapter 38

Walking to the car, Robert and the two agents were silent. No words were exchanged until Long asked: "Where to?"

"The office." Robert's stoic voice was colder than the parking lot. "So what was that all about?" His teeth ground together.

"Sir?" Long answered, seeming bewildered.

"Agent Carey." Robert redirected his gaze. "Why did you blurt out the information about Stoker?"

There was almost no delay in Carey's response. "I thought since you brought it up, you wished to explore the subject. The Director appeared unaware of the situation."

"I asked you and Phil to keep this investigation internal, but you decided to share information with the NSA. The fact he was unaware is interesting, but..." Robert stopped lecturing for a moment. "Never mind." He paused again. "Let's keep this quiet, going forward." Robert resolved to have Carey and Long outside of his meetings.

"Yes, Sir." Both responded.

Robert added this odd Secret Service behavior to the list of data milling around his head. He went back to reviewing the meeting with Karlovich. Despite being extraordinarily cautious, had the Director really been unaware that a key security level employee had been shot? "That makes no sense," he thought. "There's no way Karlovich didn't know. So, if he knew, he lied."

Had Karlovich known of Stoker's connection to Robert? If he hadn't before, Robert would bet that he did now. Did anyone else at the NSA know Chris was dead? Was there any way to prove that Karlovich had known?

"Turn around." Robert suddenly said forcefully. "We're going back."

"Pull up by the front entrance. I'll only be a minute." Robert told the Agents. "You can wait here." Hopping out of the car, he left Long and Carey behind and went in directly to the guard.

"May I help you?" the guard asked as Robert approached.

"Yes, I can't seem to find my sunglasses. Can you check the lockers to see if I left them there?" He asked the guard.

"Certainly." The guard turned off his video monitors, tapped the off-station button and went to check the various unlocked spaces and visitor lockers. He came back empty-handed.

"I'm sorry Sir, I don't see them here." He sat again, simultaneously reactivating his surveillance gear, and entering data in his log.

"Thanks, they must be in the car somewhere. I'll look again." Robert turned as if to leave, then turned back. "Oh, I forgot to pass on my condolences for Chris Stoker's murder to Bill. Could you give him that message?" Robert knew they had not discussed Chris outside the secure area. He waited for the guard's reaction.

"Yes, Sir," came the response. The guard didn't miss a beat in his typing.

"Thank you." Robert turned and took a step. "Hang on—can I scribble a note for Bill to give Chris' wife? In fact, I'll just write a quick condolence to Bill, too, if I can use a pen and paper."

"Yes, Sir." The guard was expressionless as he handed over the materials.

"Not even a blink or pause at the word 'murder.'" Robert thought as he wrote two short notes, and handed them back to the guard. "Do you know if there's a memorial fund set up, or donations are being taken for the wife?" he asked.

"I don't know, Sir. I can ask the Director. Mrs. Stoker was here this morning to collect a few things left in Mr. Stoker's outside locker."

"Thanks—don't worry about it. I'll call Bill later." Robert turned and headed out the door.

"Did you get what you needed, Sir?" Carey asked from the front seat.

"Yes, I did." Robert had indeed learned something. He had his first solid lead. Karlovich had lied to him. "My first suspect," Robert thought, as he sat back in the seat.

Chapter 39

Sitting on the exercise bike Christen had just peddled past the one hundred-mile mark. Riding the bike was already getting old. The TV wasn't much help. No cable; just an antenna. The selection was extremely limited. The nights were slow and lonely, but the days were like living in hell.

Mary had been right about everything. They were in the middle of nowhere. Without TV, the silence was deafening. A vacationer might have found it restful, but as a captive it was depressing and terrifying. Christen was cut off from everything that was familiar to her. The digital world she'd attached herself to had been amputated from her body and mind. She found herself constantly fighting back tears of depression and fear.

Taking her freedom and social world hadn't been enough. They had taken her dignity, too. She had no bathroom door to close for privacy. It had been removed, so when she sat on the toilet she could be seen from anywhere in the living room. Christen tried hiding behind a towel or resting it across her lap. That helped a little, but even the semi-public dorm life hadn't prepared her for this feeling of violation. She hadn't showered. She couldn't imagine it. The curtain was clear plastic. She was terrified at the thought of being more vulnerable than she already was, and being naked seemed the ultimate in susceptibility. She was losing trust in her own thoughts. Her own conscious and subconscious were teaming up to drive her mad.

Her only solace was the way Mary totally ignored her. The only time she even noticed her was when she brought the food. That happened three times a day, like clockwork. The food was always vacuum-sealed, microwaved, and came with a glass of water. Tough, flavorless pancakes and water at eight, Salisbury steak and water at eleven-thirty, and turkey dinner with water at six. Then, without a word, Mary would turn off the TV and lights at ten.

Christen had listened longingly to the sound of a soda can popping open with its characteristic fizzing from the other room. She hadn't been offered any, and she was afraid to ask. Mary stayed in the other half of the cabin. There was no radio or TV over there, at least as far as Christen could tell. Mary must have been reading a book, or maybe she had headphones for music or TV, Christen thought. Maybe Mary didn't need distractions, instead just sitting inhumanly silent all day. Occasionally Mary would go into the other bathroom, leaving the door cracked enough so that she could hear sounds. When she came out she would go back into the kitchen, out of sight again. It was driving Christen insane.

She heard the microwave door snap open and then close loudly. A few beeps and the smell of Salisbury steak crept into the room. Christen knew the drill and quickly slid the coffee table over so she could set up the TV tray. She worked quickly to straighten the room. Mary would notice if anything was out of place, and would stand there silently with the food. She would remain expressionless, waiting for Christen to fix the problem before she would leave the meal. Taking her place on the sofa, Christen placed her hands on her lap, sat up straight, and waited behind the empty tray.

The moment the eleven-thirty commercials came on Christen's TV, Mary marched into the room with the heated plastic food dish in her gloved left hand. Her right held a fast food packet containing a napkin and a plastic fork, and a plastic glass of water. She wore black sweats and gray running shoes. Her closely cropped jet-black hair looked oily and matted, her pale skin made her dark eyes and thick eyebrows more glaring. She said nothing, just placed the food onto the TV tray, set down the water, and turned to leave.

"May I have a soda?" Christen's pathetic sounding words quivered with fear. Christen cringed slightly at the sound of her own voice. She wanted to take the request back the second she heard it move past her lips. Mary stood silently, her back to Christen. She didn't move. Christen began to shrink back as the soundless moment seemed to stretch on.

Finally, Mary walked away into the kitchen. Christen felt herself breathe again, but she was afraid to think. She just stared at the dull brown gravy, half covering the dead, brown-grey colored meat steaming in the dish. Christen was stunned to see Mary return with a Coke in her hand.

Christen broke into a half-smile, and tried to appear grateful. "Thank you," she said.

Mary's face had no expression, which on her, looked like a frown as she turned and walked away.

Christen picked up the remote and turned up the TV volume a little. It was a rerun of "Friends" and at that moment one of the young female actresses giggled.

Mary burst around the corner. Her face was stretched across her head with anger. In three strides she covered the room and grabbed the Coke can, her face low to the tray and glaring at Christen.

"You think this is funny?" Mary raised the can.

Christen turned quickly, jerking up her arms to protect her face. The handcuff on her wrist yanked at the chain. The heavy links caught the tray and spun it toward Mary's leg. It fell short of hitting Mary, glancing off the coffee table and crashing to the floor.

Mary's reflexes were so fast that Christen couldn't even see what was happening. Mary's right hand swung down and around. The force of her body turned with the hand, crushing the Coke can against Christen's cowering head. The thick top edge of the can sliced into her scalp.

Christen plunged back into the couch, her leg jutting out in the movement, kicking the fallen TV tray into Mary. With her left hand, Mary thrust the tray off to the side as she swung her right hand backward across Christen's face with the mangled Coke can. Christen lay flat out on the couch, unconscious.

"Think this is a God damned game?" Mary slapped the tray away as its spindly legs got in her way. She marched into the kitchen, returning moments later with a glass of water and a first aid kit. She threw the water into Christen's face. Christen jerked up, sputtering, as water mixed with blood streamed into her eyes.

"Clean yourself up." Mary tossed the first aid kit onto Christen's stomach and left the room. "And straighten that room up!" She yelled from the kitchen.

Christen clutched the bright red and white kit and fought her sobs, trying to keep quiet. She was still on the couch with her knees pulled up, rocking slightly when Mary came back with a commando knife gripped in her right hand.

"Don't move!" Her voice demanded compliance.

Christen stared at the knife. Its six-inch blade had a mirror finish edge, the tip rising in an arch to an unbelievably sharp point. The knife came closer as Mary reached forward and grabbed Christen's shirttail, yanking it out of her pants.

Christen's mouth opened but she choked back the scream.

Mary thrust the blade under Christen's blood stained shirt and pulled at the knife. The finely honed edge sliced through her shirt halfway up. Again, Mary thrust the knife under Christen's shirt up to her shoulder and pulled it back, cutting the shirt open to the arm. Christen felt the cold steel against her skin, the edge threatening to slice her open. A third time the flashing blade came at her, going up the shirt sleeve and slicing it away. Mary pulled Christen's shirt to the side and grabbed the shoulder strap of her bra. Tugging it toward her, Mary pulled the bra strap, jerking Christen up with it, and cut through the elastic with a swipe.

She pushed Christen back into the couch. Mary's voice was filled with malice. "Now get rid of those clothes and take a bath. You smell."

Christen pulled vainly at her blouse trying to cover herself as the sobs burst out. Mary had moved away around the corner, tossing a sweat-shirt and sweatpants into the room.

"Wear these. Take off your clothes and get cleaned up...now!"

Mary's yell snapped Christen's eyes open. She knew she had to obey and started sitting up. Mary's look told her to move faster. She undid her pants, pulling them down to her shoes. She untied her shoes and pulled them off, placing them by the couch and taking off her socks, placed them in the shoes. One leg at a time, she pulled her pants off.

"Toss them over there." Mary pointed at the wall with her knife.

Christen could not fight back the tears, but she managed to hold back the sobs with only halting breaths choked back. Mary had cut the shirt and bra so that they would come off around the handcuff and chain. Christen pulled the shredded shirt over her head, the collar catching on the cut in her cheek and making her wince. She was alarmed at the amount of blood, her blood, on the shirt as she tossed it over. The bra was covered in blood, too. Christen looked up pitifully.

"All of it. You're filthy." Mary's face held only anger.

Christen reached back and undid her bra. The remaining strap fell off her shoulder as she pulled it off and tossed it onto the pile. Bending down she pulled her panties down past her knees and then off. The blood had washed down her stomach to stain the lace edge around the top of her satin finish underwear. The water and blood mixed to spread the pink-red stain everywhere. She tossed them onto the pile and stood awkwardly naked before Mary. Her hands moved to try and cover herself as she hunched forward.

"Well?" Mary looked mad as ever. "Take the clean clothes and the kit. Get in the shower and get cleaned up."

Christen collected the sweats and first aid kit and very slowly walked to the bathroom. She stumbled as the handcuff pulled at her wrist. The chain was tangled in the legs of the TV tray and she bent down to clear it. As soon as she entered the bathroom, Mary bent over and with one hand, snatched up Christen's blood stained clothes and disappeared into the kitchen.

In the door-less bathroom, Christen looked into the mirror with tears flowing down her face. The cut across her cheek had slowed its bleeding. It was about an inch long and just below the cheekbone. The cut on her head was just outside the hairline and the blood was still oozing out. It made a tiny stream that ran down her temple, just in front of her ear, and down her neck. Reaching the smooth curve of her collarbone the blood pooled in the line above it. The splashed Coke and water made it all look worse. Her young, beautiful face looked like she had been thrown through a window. A dark bruise was already forming under her right eye. Turning on the water in the sink, she tried to splash some water on her face. The pain shot through her head. She collapsed forward onto her elbows and cried uncontrollably into the sink.

Chapter 40

Marty just sat at his computer. He hadn't moved and he wasn't doing anything. His screen was blank except for the time-out notice, and the request to re-enter his password. Once his phone rang. He didn't answer it. He just let it roll over to voice mail.

Marty had seen Carey before. Carey had been at one of the early OPOV committee meetings, but that wasn't what tugged at him or jumped his pulse. It was his voice that Marty had heard during the conversation at the airlock. It was the same voice he heard at his house. The same voice that said it would come back if he failed. The more he thought about it, the more he knew. He could hardly believe it. He turned it over and over in his mind. Finally, he stopped denying it. Carey had been one of the two men that had attacked him at home.

His stature, his walk, even his trousers looked the same as the guy in the non-pinstriped pants. He had only really seen the guy's eyes, and it had been dark. Maybe too dark, Marty thought, and tried to shake off the idea. Men's pants all looked alike, didn't they? He was grasping at straws, paranoid, and recoiling from shadows. He understood he was becoming desperate, but those eyes he had seen were the same. He became more and more sure. Carey had looked at him in the same way that night—like he was less than human, or a bug that could be squashed.

Over and over again Marty considered the possibilities. What had Carey been doing at the NSA, and who was the VIP who had been with him? How could Carey be one of the men who had his daughter? His mind was reeling and he couldn't think. He had to get out of his cubicle for a few minutes. He grabbed his coffee cup and left, moving toward the snack room.

Out of the corner of her eye, Terri watched him go. She headed the same way, looking casual, and following some distance behind him.

Marty was standing at the coffee pot when Terri walked in.

"Hey, whatcha workin' on?" She tried to let her usual carefree humor come through her voice.

"Nothing," Marty answered her sourly, barely acknowledging her presence.

"Well, I'm a sucker for scintillating conversation, and yours certainly is unique today, but I really must get back." She retorted stiffly. She grabbed a Styrofoam cup and poured herself some decaf. Acrid steam from the long overheated coffee filled her nose.

Marty guiltily realized what a jerk he'd been. He wondered what he could say without giving away his total lack of composure. He needed to act normal. If he gave himself away it would get Christen killed.

"Sorry, I'm just..." he began.

"Crabby." Terri shot back. "Boy, you're going to have to snap out of it. If you need sleep that much, you'd better take some time off, and get it. Relax."

"Sorry, Terri." Marty apologized again. "So, any idea who the VIP was?" Marty tried to sideline her, and at the same time change the subject to something he wanted to ask anyway.

"How should I know? Why don't you check the department schedule?" Terri sounded like she was still offended. She dumped some sweetener and powdered creamer into her cup, stirring it with a plastic stick.

"Just wondering. You seemed interested." Of course, why hadn't he thought of the schedule? Marty started back to his cube with Terri following.

Terri's face brightened. "I have an idea. You want to go have a drink after work tonight? Maybe watch the game? Relax a little?" She had never really socialized much after work with Marty, but her naturally outgoing personality blended with the invitation.

"No, thanks. I have some stuff to do tonight." Marty responded robotically, distracted by his thoughts.

"Like what? Microwave dinner, get the mail, and maybe do some laundry?" Terri realized she was pushing a little hard, and decided she would stop if he turned her down again.

"No, I have something important to take care of. I'll take a rain check if that's okay?" Marty knew he was sounding obnoxious, considering that Terri was just trying to be nice. He didn't want to upset her, but he was headed into a nasty funk, and couldn't pull himself out.

"Sure, anytime." Terri gave up. Going into her cube, she sat down at her computer.

Marty did the same. He signed on, and pulled up the department meeting schedule. It was there. Lobby conference room, two p.m. to three, Bill Karlovich, Larry Felder and Frank Shell, plus two guest badges for Deputy Attorney General Robert Carlton and Agent Paul Carey. Marty wondered what the Deputy Attorney General would be doing at the NSA with an agent in tow. He had heard of Carlton. Marty kept up with D.C. politics through C-Span, but it was the death of the Attorney General headline that had put Carlton's name in the public eye. Otherwise Marty would never have heard of Robert.

What about "Agent" Carey? Was he FBI? Marty tried to remember what Carey's title had been at the time of the OPOV Committee meetings. He felt ridiculous for his suspicions. How could the FBI, or any federal agent for that matter, be abducting his daughter? But there was something about Carey that was giving him a bad feeling. The more he thought about it, the more convinced he became that Carey had been in his house last night.

Chapter 41

Robert had been silent during the drive to his office. Had Hunt expected Robert to ferret out Karlovich as a suspect? Had Karlovich killed Chris? Was he trying to cover up infiltration and control of OPOV? Why would he want control? There were too many pieces of the puzzle still missing for Robert to make any sense of this mess.

Something else was bugging him. Robert found himself thinking about Agent Carey. Obviously Carey had been to the NSA in advance of their visit that day. He must have been through the airlock in the past, since it let him through so quickly. Additionally, Karlovich and the security guard had both known Carey's name on sight. They didn't bat an eye when he joined them on the tour, or in the meetings. But Agent Long had been left outside without a second thought.

"Am I jumping at shadows now?" Robert wondered. He walked through the sequence in his mind. He decided to pose a question to Carey.

"Agent Carey," Robert asked slowly.

"Yes, Sir?" He answered from the front seat of the car without turning around.

"You've been to that division of the NSA before." Robert voiced it as a statement.

"Yes, Sir." There was no inflection in his voice. Then he volunteered, "I was in a meeting there during the initial security support committee session." Carey answered matter-of-factly.

That was logical, Robert thought, but did it follow that both the guard and Karlovich would have known Carey by name? He was beginning to wonder whose side Carey was on. Robert asked no more questions, deciding to wait until his lawyer's brain could come up with more evidence to support the direction his mind was going.

Then it occurred to him that the guard had prepared two badges: one for Carey, and one for Robert.

"But I didn't tell Karlovich that Carey was coming," he thought.

Sitting in his office Robert continued thinking about Agent Carey. He was convinced now that Carey was hiding something from him. The whole visit with the NSA had rubbed him the wrong way. Had Hunt expected Robert to stumble on Carey's familiarity there? Robert shook his head. There was more. There had to be. He simply couldn't see it yet.

Robert felt exhausted. He was tired of coming up against impossible questions, with unimaginable answers. What he needed were results. At this point he didn't see much hope of getting any. In the last week his life had spun out of control, and in the process he'd lost two friends. He needed help, but from whom?

Picking up the phone slowly, he hesitated. The phone rang in his hand, making him jump slightly. Lorraine's voice came over the intercom.

"Mr. Carlton, it's your wife."

Robert hit the button. "Tracie, what's up?" He asked curtly, his mind still flooded with questions.

"Robert, there are two men finally at the door, claiming they are with the Secret Service." She sounded upset. "You told me to call."

Robert glanced at the clock, feeling disoriented. Why had the Secret Service taken so long to get to his house? He'd assumed that they would have arrived while he'd been at the NSA. Quickly coming back to the present, he tried his best to sound reassuring.

"That's great, Honey. Hang on a second." Robert set the phone down on his desk, and went to see Agent Long outside his door.

"Robert?" Tracie was saying, not realizing that he'd walked away from the phone. "Robert? Robert?" Her tone was rising, and her voice getting more stressed. By the time he was back, she was on the verge of hysteria.

Robert hit the speaker button. "Tracie, I'm back."

"Where did you go? Did you hear a word I said?" Tracie was almost shrieking in her anxiety.

"Sorry, Honey. I went to get Agent Long. He is here with me." Robert answered soothingly.

"Mrs. Carlton, this is Agent Long. I'm here to make sure you are set up securely with the agents we've sent to be with you and your family." Long sounded calm and controlled. "Could you tell me the ID numbers, names, and verbal codes of each agent please?"

Tracie had the information written down in front of her, and repeated the data to Long, sounding calmer.

"Very good, Mrs. Carlton. Next, can you tell me the distinguishing visible physical characteristic of each man?" Long continued.

"The taller man has a light brown mole on his left eyelid, and the shorter man has a 'V' shaped scar on his left thumb. They pointed these out so I could see them through the peep hole." Tracie told him.

"Very good, Mrs. Carlton. I can confirm for you that those men are our agents, and they have been assigned to you, and to your household. Please let them in, and they will instruct you regarding their procedures. They will let you know what they are doing at each step as they secure your home. If you must leave the house, one agent will be with you at all times. We would rather you not leave, and that you not split up the family. If an errand needs to be run, let one of the agents know, and he will instruct you in the proper procedure. Do you understand, and are you comfortable with this information, Mrs. Carlton?" Agent Long seemed experienced at handling distressed clients. Under his professional management it was clear that Tracie was becoming less scared, and regaining more common irritation.

"Yes, I do understand what you said, and no; I definitely am not comfortable! How in the world do you think any of this could be 'comfortable'?" Tracie was actually building some anger, now that her anxiety was wearing off.

"I understand, Ma'am. This is a very stressful situation for you, but the agents are there for your family's safety and security. Let me get you back to Mr. Carlton. Thank you, again, for your cooperation."

Long indicated he was done, and Robert picked up the handset. "Tracie, I'm back on."

"Robert, what's happening? I think you'd better start giving me some straight answers—and I don't want any of this 'national security nonsense.' I'm not an idiot. I know when something's gone wrong, and if our family has to be protected I have a right to know what's happening." Her anger was growing stronger, but Robert heard an edge of fear lingering in her voice.

"Tracie, you're right; you do have a right to know. I can't talk about this over the phone, but I'll explain everything when I get home. In the meantime, Let the agents in, follow their instructions, and try not to worry. I have a few things left to do here, and I'll be on my way."

"You'd better hurry, Robert. I don't like this, and I don't like not knowing what's going on. You know how I hate..."

"I understand." Robert cut her off. "I'll do my best to explain when I get home," Robert repeated, and then hung up. "Thanks, Agent Long."

"Our pleasure," Long answered. He left the room and closed the door.

Robert knew he was in for it when he got home, but he felt better about Tracie and the kids now. He honestly had forgotten all about them, again.

Robert knew what he had to do, He hated resorting to it, but he'd run out of options. He took a deep breath, and then called his father.

His father's private secretary answered, and asked him to hold while she connected him.

Waiting, Robert hoped that he wasn't making a mistake.

Besides being a top executive at one of the largest oil companies in the United States, Robert's father had become increasingly politically powerful over the years. With that power had come more wealth, which had bought more influence. Vacation homes, yachts, lavish parties, and VIPs were everywhere in his life. He was one of the men who ran the country from behind the scenes. His position at his company seemed almost a disguise for his Washington D.C. lobbying. No, actually, Robert thought, it *was* a disguise.

Robert and his father weren't close. His father had never spent much time displaying affection. Love was an uncontrollable emotion, and Robert's father was all about control. Their relationship was held together with the glue of achievement and public recognition. His father's unrelenting desire for power made Robert feel permanently subordinate. There was no comfort in the relationship, but Robert knew that if there was something brewing in DC, his father either had a hand in it, or was familiar with the details.

"Robbie, good to hear from you." His father's voice boomed over the line, interrupting his thinking.

"Hello, Father." He clenched his teeth, thinking about how his father refused to use his adult name, Robert.

"How's the work?"

"Fine." Robert felt uncomfortable talking to his father about his work, even though that's exactly what he had intended to do. He decided to cut to the chase. "I called to ask you a question. Do you have a few minutes?"

"Certainly; everything going well?" His father made that sound like more of a remonstrative remark than a concern.

"Yes. Fine. I need to know..." he began, struggling with his words. He started over. "Did you know the President assigned the Secret Service to cover my office after Bradley's accident?"

The phone remained silent for an uncomfortably long time.

"Yes." The answer finally came back. "Tom and I discussed it."

Even though he had been expecting the answer, Robert was taken aback, disappointed, and stunned all at once. His father had discussed a situation regarding his safety with the President, but neither had mentioned it to him. Robert was the acting Deputy Attorney General of the United States of America, but the President discussed issues of national security with his father, not with him. *National security*! Not simply his personal safety.

His father continued. "We were concerned. You never know whether some things are a coincidence, or if there might be more to the situation. It seemed a prudent decision."

"Was it your idea, or the President's?" Robert felt unusually bold. Usually his father asked the questions. Robert's job had always been to listen. Another silence made him very uneasy.

"It was my request." His father had thought about that simple statement a long time. He was either deliberately excluding, or shielding the President from the decision that had been made. Why?

Robert tried to think quickly. "You know that I am actively using the Secret Service on my current investigation?"

"Yes, I think that's wise."

Damn it! How the hell did he know that? Had Carey reported that information to the President? What shocked Robert was not that the President had been informed, but that the information had already been disseminated to his father.

"Why would you say that?" Robert asked, hoping for a clue to what else his father might know.

"It's obviously in your best interest to use whatever resources are available," his father answered smoothly.

An evasive answer, Robert thought. Robert's question had not been well defined, but it was clear that his father didn't want to address it in depth. Robert decided to be as direct as possible. He had little to lose, and he needed to get his bearings. "Father, do you have any specific knowledge that my investigation and the situation with OPOV are related to Bradley's accident?"

His father easily detected the cross-examination technique, and quickly diverted the conversation. His tone shifted to sounding parental and indignant. "I don't know why you think that I'd know anything about that. I'm simply trying to help you, and make sure that you and your family are safe. Instead of hearing that he's grateful for my concern, my son wants to put me on the stand, and question me! I think you need to work on your attitude. You have an important position, you have a problem on your hands, and the President is asking you for answers. Yet, you seem to have nothing better to do than to call me, and question my interest and involvement? I hope you're smarter than this in your interactions with Tom, Robbie."

Robert immediately felt defensive. He fought the urge to respond to his father as he would have when he was younger. He felt angry, resentful, and childish, as his father meant him to feel. He forced down his emotions, and stumbled into a response. "I'm sorry, Father. I know you are concerned, and I appreciate that. I was simply attempting..." Robert stumbled, not knowing where to go with the statement. Grimacing, he silently cursed himself for letting his father sidetrack him once again. He'd irrevocably lost the line of questioning.

"You need to concentrate on the issue at hand, Son, and stop focusing on these extraneous incidentals." His father was continuing in a commanding tone. He finished with, "I have some important calls to make before my next meeting."

"Yes, of course. Thank you for your time." Robert answered mechanically.

"I'm glad everything's going well. Keep up the good work." His father hung up.

Robert wondered why he'd made the call. He should have known that if his father wanted to tell him anything, it would be because he had an agenda—not because Robert needed information. It was typical for his father to wrap up the conversation on a controlled, seemingly positive note. His father never accepted or acknowledged a lack of mutual understanding.

He also never accepted a question he didn't want to answer. Robert had always joked that his father was "the king of diversion; Teflon Man." Anything he didn't want to take the hit for slid away in a sea of distraction. Like all guys made of Teflon, nothing bad ever stuck.

Robert slumped back into his chair. His waning energy was now gone; sucked out completely. He regretted calling his father for information, but he had learned a few things.

He had confirmed that the President and his father were in close communication about Robert, and about OPOV. They had known that something was very wrong when Bradley died, or at least they suspected that was the case. Had Jack been told? Why hadn't Robert been informed? And why was he being plunged into a dangerous investigation with limited official assistance?

Robert realized that there was another question he should be asking. Who, or what had tipped them off that Bradley's death wasn't an accident?

Chapter 42

Marty had been staring at his computer for hours now, and he hadn't touched a key or the mouse. He was reviewing over and over again the break-in at his house. Every time he re-played it the image of the man's eyes became more accentuated, his voice more pronounced. The recollection became bigger, brighter—almost a caricature of what he had actually experienced. The memory was sharper than anything he could possibly have seen or heard that night—but Marty was sure now that one of the men had been Carey. Marty sat thinking, unaware that his behavior was being observed.

Agent Paul Carey was seated in the basement of the Justice Building. No one else was in the secured room. Long was upstairs, sitting outside Carlton's office. Several optical disk recorders were quietly running. Their level meters indicated conversations were being actively recorded. Racks of sensor indicators on the wall were set to monitor secure lines, and some cameras were recording digital video in various offices. Carey watched one of the banks as he picked up a phone receiver. Several red lights came on, flickered, and turned green. One of the video screens was drawing his eye. He dialed a number and waited.

"Yes?" A voice answered.

"Have you had time to review that data?" Carey knew the sound of the voice he had called. Carey's voice was also easily identified to the man on the other end of the phone.

"We may have a problem." The voice came back.

"You'll let me know if it needs addressing." Carey responded.

"Yes. Stay with what you're doing."

"Right." Carey hung up.

Bill Karlovich came out of his office and strolled casually down the row of cubicles. The staff was accustomed to his end of the day, bed-check behavior. It was his way of showing "management support" to his underlings. He'd once gone to a seminar that touted the virtues of "Management by Walking Around," and the title had stuck with him. He'd never really understood the actual working concept, but he walked around anyway. His management liked to know he was in touch with his employees, and the habit made him feel as though he was. His routine was to slow down at each cubicle opening, and if the occupant made eye contact, or had a question to ask, he'd exchange a few words with them. Most of the conversations started with, "How are things going?" Or, "How's the family?"

When he reached Marty's cube, Marty did not look up. Bill stopped anyway.

"So, how's the project going?" Bill asked.

"Fine, Sir. No problems." Marty still did not turn around, concentrating on his monitors.

"Good, I'm glad to hear it. No deadline problems? No bugs?" Karlovich persisted.

"No, just the usual; everything is going fine." Marty was attempting to hide his irritation and nervousness.

"Good. Good." Bill continued his stroll.

"Terri! Life treating you well?" He smiled.

Terri swung around in her chair, flashing some leg at him as her skirt rode up her thigh. "It's terrible, my car wouldn't start, and my dog died. I desperately need to talk to someone," she said conversationally, smiling.

"Well, just let me know if there's anything I can help with." Karlovich's eyes never got higher than her thigh.

As soon as Bill was out of earshot, Terri crept over into Marty's cube. "I love doing that to him. He can't hear a word I'm saying if my skirt's more than an inch above my knee."

Marty didn't hear a word she was saying, either. His mind was spinning with implications and paranoia. His imagination had been building outlandish scenarios for hours. He couldn't believe they hadn't spotted the file change he had made. It was glaring to him. They had to know. How could the NSA's internal security miss it? He knew they were setting him up; that it was all a plot. They'd find the connection, nail him, and they wouldn't care if Christen was murdered in the process. He'd go to prison forever.

"Hey, are you listening to me?" Terri smacked him lightly on the shoulder.

"What? No—I mean, yes. I'm sorry, what were you saying?" Marty tried to come out of his stupor.

"Forget it. It's almost five. Let's get out of here." She went back to her chair and grabbed her coat. Returning to his cube, she pulled his coat off the hook, and tossed it into his lap. "You, too. Time to leave. The boss just finished his bed check."

Marty mechanically got up, and put on his coat.

"That's a good boy." Terri playfully gave him a little shove to get him walking. Then, mimicking his voice she intoned, "Why don't I buy you a drink?" Recovering her own voice she answered with a smile; "Why yes, that would be nice. Thank you." Tracie pushed Marty into the airlock.

"Okay." Marty gave in on the other side of the airlock. He had forgotten his earlier rejection of her invitation. The airlock had given him time to think about going home, and he knew he didn't want to do that. Not there. Anywhere but there. Getting a drink sounded like a good idea.

Karlovich sat in his office watching Terri and Marty on the parking area security camera. When they reached her car, he picked up the phone.

Chapter 43

Lorraine chimed in on the intercom, "Mr. Turner is here to see you."

"Send him in." Robert had been expecting Jerry to arrive with his first report.

Jerry came through the door. He brusquely handed over a packet of twenty or so pages. "Here's the report. We've only had time to document an outline of the analysis of the original work. You'll find the section assignments, individual owners, deadlines, and their preliminary reviews in this batch."

Robert accepted the document. "I appreciate your promptness, Jerry." He scanned it enough to see that each section was done in a different writing style. These were indeed individual reports compiled together. That would make it fresh and unbiased, which was exactly what he wanted.

"This will do just fine. It looks very thorough." He commented.

"If there's nothing else, I have a lot to do." Turner was moving toward the door before he finished his sentence.

"No, that's it." Robert said. Jerry appeared to have re-acquired the chip on his shoulder. Robert figured this meant that his team wasn't finding any significant problems, and that Jerry saw the exercise as a waste of time.

"Lorraine," Robert called through the closing door.

"Yes, sir." Lorraine entered the office.

"Arrange for a courier at five. I'll want copies of this confidential document delivered to The President, and to Senator Gregg's office. Start a standard daily update report cover letter. Title it: OPOV Update, Office of, etc.."

"Attorney General Letterhead, and standard office folio covers?"

"Yes, the black ones," Robert said absently.

"Yes, Sir. By the way, it's five now." She went back to her desk.

Robert began quickly scanning through the material, making sure there was nothing in it he wouldn't want sent forward. It contained assignments, timelines, repeats of information already documented, and political jargon. It was thorough, and was full of the kind of stuff that would keep everybody off his back for a day or two. Jerry was good at that kind of report, and this document was no exception.

Robert finished his reading. Reaching toward the phone, he tapped the intercom button once.

Lorraine popped her head in the office. "The courier will be here in five minutes." Her years of experience and a computer full of templates made this kind of letter quick and easy. Handing him three identical cover letters, she watched as he quickly read the first, then signed each one.

He handed all the documents to her. "Don't file the original, yet. I need it back. Just put it on my desk."

Lorraine took the papers and left without a word. Underneath her professional demeanor, Robert clearly felt something amiss. What was it? Annoyance? Stress? He knew she was wondering why he had security, but he thought it would be better for her not to know.

He punched the intercom button, again.

"Yes, Sir?" Lorraine answered promptly.

"No word from Agent Carey?" He queried.

Agent Long leaned toward Lorraine's desk and answered. "No, Sir. At last call he was running some checks with Mr. Davidson. I don't believe they will be done until much later."

"If you hear from either of them I want an update. I'll be ready to leave in a few minutes." Robert let go of the button.

Turning to his computer he started the shutdown process and began loading some papers in his briefcase. Lorraine came in with the original report from Jerry set in a black cover. Robert added it to the contents of the briefcase.

"Thanks, Lorraine. I'm going to head for the house. You can call it a day whenever you're ready." Robert didn't pause to consider that her day should already have been over.

"Thank you, Mr. Carlton." She said automatically as she headed for her desk.

Robert went to the closet and got his coat. As he walked out the door Long met him, ready to go.

As he and Agent Long exited the office, Lorraine picked up a call.

"Associate Attorney General's office, Lorraine speaking, how may I help you?"

Robert ignored the activity, and with Long in tow started down the hall.

"Mr. Carlton!" Lorraine called out from the office and down the hall. "I have a call for you, he says it's urgent!"

Robert stopped abruptly. Normally Lorraine wouldn't have bothered him with any call, and she would have messaged him with anything considered vital information.

"Who is it?" He called back.

"All he said was, 'It's thirteen and it's urgent!' I thought you'd want to know."

Robert ran back to the office. "Put it through." He blurted out as he ran past Lorraine's desk, slamming the door behind him.

He couldn't believe it. There was no way this call could be happening. Grady was alive!

Chapter 44

From the moment Grady pulled the top off the can of mixed nuts, his path to invisibility unfolded like a roadmap with only one direction.

Instead of nuts inside, he'd found a gray canister shaped like a spray paint can, with a lever handle and ring on top. The purple markings read AN-M14 INCEN TH. After a few shocked seconds, Grady realized he was looking at an incendiary grenade.

Sitting on the bed, he stared at the grenade, gently pulling it from the can. He felt its heft as he held it in his hand. He knew it was the same thing that had been used on his house. He knew what it could do.

A plan began to gel in his aching head. Deciding to see what else might be in the car, Grady pulled his shoes on and headed out across the parking area to where he'd left the brown vehicle.

Opening the doors he found nothing of use except a map of DC, and one for the Alexandria, Virginia area. He thought that was a little unusual, in this era of GPS. Maybe these guys hadn't trusted GPS and cell phone location technology to be one-way data. He decided that maybe they'd been smarter than they had appeared.

The glove box didn't have any registration information. Grady tried the under-dash trunk release, but found it didn't work. There was a second key on the ring, which he assumed opened the trunk. He put the key into the trunk latch and turned it. Pulling out the key, he let the lid rise. When it opened, he dropped the keys on the ground.

"Jesus!" Grady jumped back from the car.

With eyes wide open, the dead man in the trunk stared up at Grady. Dried blood from a gaping head wound matted the man's hair, and was smeared over his face. Grady's stomach rose into his throat as he tried to look away from the grizzly sight. He edged forward, reaching up to pull down the trunk lid. He barely managed to catch it as it fell, keeping the lid from slamming shut. Panicked, he looked around, but quickly remembered there'd been no sign of life in this mostly empty parking lot when he'd entered it. The dim early morning hour was in his favor, too. It was doubtful that anyone would have been able to see anything in the trunk. He slowly raised the lid again. His heart pounded and his hands shook a little. He reached in and patted the man down. There was no wallet, but he found an empty gun holster with a spare magazine attached to it. There was also a money clip with several hundred-dollar bills, a few twenties, a license, and a credit card. The guy had been sloppy. Grady knew that assassins didn't usually carry anything that could identify them. Despite his revulsion, Grady stuffed the money, license, and credit card into his pocket. He had a feeling they'd come in handy.

Behind the dead body, in the recesses of the trunk, was a black gym bag. With some difficulty, Grady pulled it past the dead man's shoulder, and out of the trunk. He closed the lid as quietly as he could. Picking up the keys, he headed back to the room. It was hard to walk without constantly glancing back at the car or staring at each room window to see if peering eyes were watching him.

In the room, his plan gained depth and clarity. He'd been lucky. The gym bag contained a sweat-shirt and pants, along with a pair of gym socks and sneakers. Everything was too big, but it would do to replace his stained clothing and dress shoes.

The steps became clearer in Grady's mind after he dressed, and cleaned all evidence of his stay from the room. He tossed everything, even the garbage from his room into the gym bag, and took it out to the car. He made a quick drugstore trip, then got back into the car and drove to the airport. Grady left the brown sedan in the close-in parking, and took the shuttle bus to rent a nondescript economy car, using the dead man's card and license. The rental car clerk was distracted and hardly gave the license picture more than a glance. Grady had doctored the license using a picture from one of his own cards, with the help of a cheap razor and some Super Glue.

It wasn't perfect, but it was passable. Grady was thankful that the dead guy didn't have one of the new, harder to fake licenses.

Consulting the map, he decided that Roosevelt Island was a good location for carrying out his plan. He drove to the parking lot there, parked the rental, and using his newly acquired pay-as-you-go cell phone, called a cab. He had it drive him back to the airport.

Grady had parked the brown sedan in a dark section of the garage surrounded by cars. No one seemed interested as he drove out of the airport, or as he continued behind a rundown, empty shopping strip. It was still early, so he figured that the chances of a passerby spotting him were slim. He saw nothing resembling a camera in the area. A ten-foot wall hid him from the houses behind the strip. He pulled the car next to a dumpster.

It was easier than he'd thought to drag the dead man out of the trunk and into the floorboard of the car, on the front passenger side. Grady's adrenaline was flowing, but knowing that scraping the body on the ground didn't matter helped him accomplish the task. The dead man ended up in a crumpled position with his knees on the floor and his chest and head face down in the seat. His head was cocked at a grotesque angle against the bottom back of the chair. Grady had to move the seat all the way back to make the body fit. After he pulled the blanket from his hotel bed over the corpse, and stuffed the two pillows on either side, all he needed was some trash to complete the disguise. The dumpster provided plenty of fast food bags, Kleenex, candy wrappers, paper cups, and plastic bags, which he liberally distributed around the car. He made sure some of the garbage was on the dashboard, as well. The car quickly became a pigsty. No one would want to look under the lumpy blanket. The grenade was tucked under the blanket, behind a pillow and against the man's face.

Grady's plan was simple. Get Robert to meet him at the tourist parking lot. Say what he had to say, then leave first, and fast.

It had all been less difficult to achieve than he'd thought. Once he'd driven the brown car back to the Roosevelt Island parking lot, Grady re-parked the rental car in the emergency lane outside the exit, far enough down the road so the trees blocked the view. With the flashers on, it might get tagged, but it would take hours for a tow truck to arrive.

When he'd left Robert on the bridge and started the brown sedan's engine, Grady had set his plan in motion. After leaving the parking lot, he'd pulled the sedan partially into the grass at an angle behind the rental car, jumped out, and started the rental's engine. Leaving the door open, he ran back to the brown car and reached in through the window for the grenade. He took a quick look at the parking area exit, and seeing no one, pulled the pin. As the grenade fell into the floorboard under the pedals, Grady ran to the white rental car and sped away.

The explosion filled his rear view mirror. The power of the blast seemed to push him forward faster. Grady made several road changes, immediately heading north, and glancing back constantly. He made one stop for coffee and a muffin, paying cash. Scanning the parking lot for suspicious cars, he made a complete circle around the shops before leaving and driving to Baltimore, then traveled up Eighty-three to Harrisburg. Switching to eighty-one, he headed toward Scranton. Pennsylvania was cold and grey. Two days had passed since the last snowstorm, so the roads were clear except for annoying patches of sand and dirty salt.

Low clouds rushed by overhead, while passing trucks threw salt crystals and sand into his windshield. He worried about being tailed. While crossing a bridge he threw Robert's beeper and his old cell phone into the river. If a homing device or 911 GPS tracker had been placed in either one, they'd become worthless in the icy water. He drove at the speed limit, watching his mirrors continuously.

Reaching for his travel mug, he found only a trace of stone cold coffee left in the bottom. He decided he could use a good espresso, but the desire to put some distance behind him outweighed that need.

When he found himself almost nodding off, he followed the signs for Scranton, and pulled off in search of fresh java. Spotting a small café with an Espresso sign he drove into the parking lot. After ordering up a quad shot Grande Mocha, and adding a huge turkey and provolone hoagie, he headed to a quiet table in the back, near the bathrooms.

He finally let himself take a deep, long breath. The ensuing exhale allowed some of his stress to escape. He had made a lot of stops that morning, withdrawing a large amount of cash from several ATMs back in Arlington, and pausing to take cash from his credit card—every last bit he could get before it gave him a 'locked' message. He knew he had to cease using the card anyway. He also had to make phone calls without being traced, so he'd gone to a convenience store and paid cash for a second pay-as-you-go phone.

Grady also had taken the time to call a business that offered secretarial services, including a receptionist and answering service. A friend of his had used it when he'd set up his own business, to make himself sound as though he had an office. They were open 24 hours. Grady set up an account. The deal included use of any of their services, including call transferring. Now all he had to do was run calls through them, and his calls couldn't be traced. He paid for two months in advance with the dead man's card. It was still working.

After he'd finished about half of his coffee and sandwich, Grady pulled out a slip of hotel paper with four numbers on it. He picked up his new cell phone and called the first number.

"Reception Services, how may I help you?" a woman's voice intoned.

"This is account D17948, could you transfer me to this number?" He gave the receptionist the number on the key chain John McGarrity had given him, and waited through the clicking and ringing sounds of the transfer. He heard it connect with the corresponding beep. He quickly input the six-digit code now showing on the key chain, and it clicked again. It was working.

"Brilliant," Grady was thinking to himself as the connection went through.

"John McGarrity."

"John, Colonel Grady Barlow here. I know it's a little soon, but have you come up with anything?"

"Much too soon for anything definitive, Colonel, but we have made some headway." John's voice was casual and unhurried. "We've examined much of the system structure, and think the most likely approach to breaking in would be in the first file outside the firewall that addresses the roll-up centers. I could tell you more, but we normally wouldn't discuss that over a phone."

"I understand," Grady answered. "I think I have a picture of what you're talking about. Who would have access to that file?"

"Everyone on the web," John responded, "but it would be extremely hard to find the file, even if you knew what you were looking for. To prevent that, the organization has only a couple of people who can access or track that type of file, and they move it regularly to keep it hidden. They give it different IP addresses, and so forth. It's protected by a kind of virus scanner that detects unauthorized changes, rejects them, and actively notifies the owner. It also initiates the first cycle of the spider web, if you recall our briefing. That's the weakest spot we've found at this point. Right now Pat is trying to hack into it, to see if she can find one of those files and modify it. That's it, so far."

"That's great John, when do you think you'll know if you can break in?" Grady asked.

"There's no way to tell. Two days, perhaps. Maybe more." John told him.

"I'll check back. Anything else?" Grady was ready to wind up the call.

"Nope, not yet," John answered.

"Thanks, I'll call you later." Grady hung up. With a satisfied look at the key chain, he put it back in his pocket. Finishing off the sandwich and most of the chips that had come with it, he proceeded to gulp down the remaining coffee. Wiping his mouth with a thin paper napkin, he got up and headed toward the cashier. He handed the clerk his travel mug, saying, "same again." The guy behind the counter complied, handing him back his filled travel mug within a few minutes. Grady paid with a twenty-dollar bill, and left a tip in the jar.

"Thanks for coming in." The counter guy said pleasantly.

"Thanks. See you next time." Grady called back over his shoulder. "Oh," Grady spun around, asking, "What's the best way to eighty-four from here?"

"Just get on Eighty-one North, and catch the Three-eighty South. That will take you straight to Eighty-four." The guy told him.

"Thanks." Grady turned and pulled the door open, heading out to his rental.

He had only driven a short distance when, despite all the coffee, he was starting to nod again. He realized he wasn't holding his lane. He was exhausted, and the heavy sandwich was putting him under.

"Turkey and Tryptophan..." he said to himself, "should have considered that." Even that thought processed sluggishly through his brain.

By the time he reached the edge of the next town he was forced to find a place to sleep. He exited off the road near two old, run-down, roadside inns. Since it was still very early in the day they were almost empty. Each had only one car in the parking lot, probably belonging to the desk clerks. He picked the least disgusting looking place, and pulled in.

The clerk seemed a little wary of Grady, taking several long looks at his face and at his car. Grady thought the guy was probably wondering if there was a girl out in the rental car. An assignation was the last thing on Grady's mind. He ignored the clerk and took the key. Once inside the room, he hit the bed face first, and passed out.

Bang! Grady jerked upright as the door from the next room slammed shut.

He ran his hands over his face and hair, and looked at the clock. It was a few minutes after five o'clock. He'd really been conked out. He was so groggy he could hardly focus. Stumbling to the door, he opened it and put the "Do Not Disturb'" sign out. He closed the door, threw the latch shut, and slid the chain on, propping a chair under the handle. His mouth tasted like old combat boots and his breath was worse. Sitting on the edge of the bed he pulled out his list of phone numbers, grabbed his cell phone and called the answering service.

"Reception Services, how may I help you?" A woman's voice answered.

"This is account D17948, could you transfer me?" He gave the number for Robert Carlton. The call went through quickly.

"Attorney General's office, Lorraine speaking; how may I help you?"

"Is he in?" Grady sounded a little groggy but anxious.

"I'm sorry, Mr. Carlton has left for the day. May I tell him who called, and take a message?" Lorraine was dismissive sounding, but courteously efficient as always.

Grady figured she was running interference for Robert, but that he was still there. "Tell him it's thirteen, and it's urgent. He'll understand." Grady's voice carried a tone of command.

Lorraine didn't like the sound of a message with no name. Her day and her desk had become disordered, and out of control. Normally she would have informed the caller that she would attempt to pass on the message, but that Mr. Carlton had, indeed, left the office. Today wasn't a normal day, and Grady's tone had its desired effect.

"Could you hold for a moment?" Lorraine hit the hold button and uncharacteristically called out to Robert, as he and Agent Long headed down the hall.

"Mr. Carlton!" Lorraine was as close to shouting as her voice ever got, "I have a call for you. He says it's urgent!"

Robert stopped abruptly. Lorraine generally didn't raise her voice, and she never called him back into the office unless there was an emergency.

"Who is it?" He called back.

"All he said was, 'it's thirteen and it's urgent!'"

Chapter 45

Robert sat panting lightly at his desk. He'd ripped the receiver off its rest when the call transfer rang in. The room still echoed from the slamming door behind him. "You're alive!" He almost shouted, but choked down the volume thinking about Agent Long outside the door. "Where are you?"

Grady's voice was rough and abnormally low. "That clears up my first question. I was going to ask if I've been placed on the deceased list." There was a pause as he recalculated. "You shouldn't have given yourself away when you answered, Robert. For all you knew...never mind. Forget it. Look I don't have a lot of time, so just listen: first, as far as everyone else is concerned, I'm still dead. Got that?"

Robert thought for a moment. It finally flashed through his mind that maybe Grady hadn't escaped death, maybe he'd planned to escape; planned the death. "Yes; I get it." He answered.

"Good." Grady was glad that Robert seemed to be catching on. "I talked to our crypto guys, and they think they're making progress. I'm going to keep in touch with them, but I'm going to be moving around."

"What about the explosion? Are you all right?" Robert couldn't help asking.

"I hope your calls aren't monitored, Robert. I can't afford any extra ears listening in—we both need to be careful about what we say. That explosion killed me, Robert. Don't think any thought besides that one. I'll tell you more when I think it's safe. Until then, I don't trust anyone. You shouldn't either. I'll be keeping these calls short. Don't try to find me; it'll be a waste of your time. You can leave a message at this number." He gave Robert a number for the message service. "Get yourself a disposable phone and leave a message for 'Thirteen' with the new number. That's it for now. I'll call you tomorrow."

"Don't you want to hear what we're working on here?" Robert was still reeling from hearing Grady's voice. He hadn't quite grasped that Grady was on the run.

"No. I'll ask when I want to know something. Remember...I'm dead." Grady hung up.

Robert sat staring at the phone. Grady had staged his own death, and Robert was the only one who knew. Robert sat, questioning what he should do next.

He suddenly realized that Lorraine and Long now knew there was someone with a code name of "Thirteen." There wasn't much he could do about that, but he'd have to be more careful.

Grady sat on the bed worrying about his actions. Had he covered his tracks well enough? Was there a flaw in his logic? He thought about brushing his teeth and remembered he had no toothbrush, and no fresh clothes. What he had on was the sum total of his belongings. He ripped back the bed covers, kicked off his shoes, and pulled off his shirt and pants. He took a quick look in the mirror. Dark bruises had formed on his side and shoulder. If he hadn't been in such good shape it would have been worse. He pressed a bruise covering several ribs and grimaced. With that he turned off the light, and piled into bed. In moments he was snoring loudly.

Robert said nothing to Lorraine or Agent Long when he left his office. Initially, his thoughts were too jumbled. He couldn't bring himself to make idle chitchat with Long on the drive home, either. The silence made him progressively more jittery and uncomfortable, but the longer he waited to start a conversation, the harder it became. He finally gave up trying.

One of the agents attending Tracie and the kids opened the front door as Long drove up to the house. Looking left and right, the agent nodded. Robert and Long got out of the car and went inside. Tracie was sitting in the living room with another agent. A long row of suitcases sat by the front door.

"Tracie?" Robert looked at the suitcases, and then at her inquiringly.

"We're leaving." She stated flatly, looking angry and worn out. Her fingers dug deeply into the upholstery of her chair.

Robert had dismissed Tracie and the kids to the back of his mind. Once he'd known the Agents were in residence, he'd forgotten them. Tracie had apparently not been mollified by the Agents' presence. The suitcases made a clear statement. She didn't feel safe, and she wasn't happy that he'd been too tied up to call her.

"I called Mom, and I'm taking the kids to see her." Tracie continued in her flat, aggressive tone.

Robert looked at the agent and said, "Could you excuse us?" The agent nodded and left the room.

"Don and Peter have been great," Tracie said defensively, referring to the Agents in the house. "They've taken care of everything." She got quiet for a second. Her eyes shifted away from Robert's. She blurted out, "I called your father. He took care of..."

"You called my father?" Robert interrupted. He could feel his blood pressure rise, again.

"You haven't told me what's going on. I haven't heard anything from you about what's happening. Not one word!" Tracie snapped accusingly. Her voice rose in pitch and volume. "Something's really wrong. You're scared. I can tell, and you haven't told me anything. All I've known all day is that there's some threat that's bad enough for us to have the Secret Service in our home. Your father knows more than I do!"

"What did he tell you?" Robert's voice rose to match her volume.

Tracie yelled at him. "That doesn't matter! You're not listening!" Her comments were punctuated by increasing emphasis.

"I can't take this, and I shouldn't have to, Robert! You're incredibly inconsiderate when you get wrapped up in your own little world. Did you stop for a moment to think about what would be going through my mind?"

Robert tried to calm his voice, but it didn't work. "Tell me what Father said. I need to know what he told you." Robert stood facing her.

Tracie jumped up from her chair. "Listen to yourself! You don't even care that I'm terrified. You should be talking to me, but you're more worried about what people are saying than what I'm going through. I'm taking the boys, and leaving now. If you can bring yourself to have a real conversation with me, call. James! Andrew!" She called out, turning away from Robert.

"Coming, Mom!" They each answered.

"Alicia! We're going!" Tracie yelled.

"Tracie, you know there are things I can't tell you about in this job. Look, you need to stay here, in this house. It's safer. Turn around, please, and listen to me! I'll tell you what I can, but I need to have you look at me." Robert didn't know what to do. He trailed behind her with his hands outstretched.

"You'll 'tell me what you can'?" Tracie repeated sarcastically. "I'm your wife, Robert. I shouldn't be the last person on your mind. The kids and I should be your first priority. I'm not going to listen to another fabrication designed to keep me in the dark, and sitting here knitting, or something. Besides, anything you tell me now would be too little, and too late. You should have thought of that earlier."

"Tracie, I couldn't talk to you earlier, but I am talking to you now." Robert felt like he was arguing with a rhinoceros—an angry rhinoceros.

Tracie turned momentarily to face him. "Can you actually tell me what's going on? Can you promise to keep me informed, and actually call me occasionally during the day?"

Robert stared blankly at her, trying to think of something he could say that would satisfy her. He knew that what he was going to say wouldn't justify the need for agents in their home. His delayed answer was too slow for Tracie.

"Forget it, Robert." Tracie turned and stomped toward the door, talking as she went. "Don is going with us, as well as Alicia. Peter will stay with you. Don says another agent will join us on the way." The boys showed up, and Tracie started pushing them toward the door. "I'm sorry, Robert," she continued almost in a whisper, "but whatever this is about, I can't risk my children. I'm taking the gun, but I'm not going to hide in this house from some mysterious threat. It's pretty annoying that you can't seem to tell me anything, but that your father seems to be able to do so. It seems as though you just don't *want* to tell me anything."

Robert gave it one last try. "Tracie, if you'd just tell me what my father said, I might be able to fill in some blanks. I don't know what he thinks he knows, but..."

"Robert, the point is that you should have called. You should have wanted to call me. You should have been worried sick about us." Tracie closed the conversation with her glare. She and the boys grabbed their bags, and headed out the door.

Tracie slowed down just outside the door, and turned to look at him. Her face suddenly softened slightly. "Take care of yourself, Robert. I, at least, care about what happens to you," she said. She touched his face with her hand. Her eyes were red and tears were pooling in them. She reached up and kissed him lightly, then turned away. "Come on boys. Say goodbye to your father." The deep freeze was instantly back.

"'Bye, Dad." Andrew called out without looking back. James didn't say anything.

Robert stood in the open front doorway. Agent "Peter" stood behind him as Tracie, the kids, Alicia, and Agent "Don" pulled away in Tracie's Volvo station wagon. Robert waived, but none of them were watching. Turning to go into the house, Robert looked at Peter.

"Agent..." he began, realizing that he didn't know the man's last name.

"Karelonski." Peter replied.

"Uh, huh. Peter, Agent Long, you guys up for some takeout?" Robert slammed the door behind him.

Chapter 46

When Grady finally woke up his thick, dry tongue didn't seem to fit in his mouth. Flipping on the light and gazing around the room, he remembered the cheap, roadside motel. It looked worse now. Glancing at his watch he was shocked to see it was just after eight o'clock.

"Jesus, did I crash, or what?" It didn't really matter, but he'd wanted to get where he was going before dark. It was too late for that now. Reaching for the cell phone he immediately regretted not getting a smartphone with a data plan. It was going to be harder to look up phone numbers and other information he was used to having at his disposal without one. He dialed the service, and had them look up the Great Pines B&B in Henniker, New Hampshire, then transfer him.

"That wasn't such a good idea," he realized. "I just breached my own security plan. Now they know where I'm going."

"Great Pines B&B, this is Sue," a voice broke into his thoughts.

"Sue! Colonel Barlow here," Grady responded.

"Hello, again, Colonel. Coming to visit?" Sue asked immediately.

"Can you squeeze me in tonight?" Grady asked.

"Yes, we'd love to have you. What time will you be arriving?"

Grady gratefully sighed. "Late. Can you put the key under the mat?"

"Certainly, Colonel," Sue told him. "You'll have cottage number three. How long can you stay?"

"About a week. Will that work for you?"

"We might have a conflict the day after tomorrow, but we could have a cancellation. If not, you can have the manager's guest room."

"Thanks, Sue. You're a gem. I'll see you tomorrow morning for breakfast."

"We're having Lingonberry stuffed waffles." She told him.

"My favorite," Grady answered. "Thanks, again."

Grady hung up. Great Pines had been his and Keisha's favorite hideaway. The trees were big and numerous, and the individual cottages felt like honeymoon retreats. Sue was the owner of the B&B, and a wonderful innkeeper. The "guest room" she had offered him was actually in her own house. She, Grady, and Keisha had become fast friends on their first visit. Sue had invited them to dinner at her house each time they'd stayed.

One of the best features about the place was its proximity to Pats Peak, a neat little ski resort that had a slope for every style. Keisha liked the blue runs. She and Grady would ski together until she tired out, or until his need for adventure took him to the double diamond. That run was a cut of trees under the lift. Compared to the Rocky Mountains Grady had skied none of the slopes were steep, but the icy crust made the runs difficult—even treacherous.

Grady felt a catch in his throat, thinking about his and Keisha's getaways to the slopes and the Inn. Even toward the end, when Keisha couldn't walk well, they visited to see the snow. The little cottages held lots of good memories. Good enough to overcome the wave of sadness Grady felt whenever he remembered his wife.

Grady cleared his thoughts. Back to business. He jumped in the shower, dried off, and put on his clothes again. They weren't too bad for not having been cleaned, but that wouldn't last. As he checked out, he asked the clerk for directions to the nearest Walmart or Target. An hour later, his stomach full of pizza, the rental car's tank full of gas, and the rear seat full of jeans, shirts, socks, sweaters, underwear, and personal care items, Grady was on his way again. He had two hundred and fifty miles to go before he would be tucked away in the trees of New Hampshire.

Chapter 47

Blair had been listening to the recording of Robert's voice, talking with the evidently not dead Grady Barlow. The voices reverberated in Blair's ears. His teeth locked together as he drew a mouthful of dark beer from the bottle. Ending the recording for the second time, he set his phone down on the bar.

No word had come from his two men assigned to pressure Barlow. It should have been a simple task: push Barlow back in the direction of Stoker. Get him and Carlton thinking that Stoker and Karlovich were the NSA connections they needed to find, and they'd blow the whole thing wide open. Carlton had gone to the NSA and met with Karlovich. That part seemed to be working. Unless he was an idiot, Carlton had made that connection.

The Barlow incident was another story. It had been a complete failure. The plan had gone entirely wrong. At first he'd thought Barlow had been killed, which was unnecessary, but recoverable. Now he had voice confirmation that Barlow was still alive, and it was likely that Blair's operatives were dead. That was just as well. He'd have had to remove them himself after their inept handling of the affair. Now he had to figure out how much exposure they'd had.

He took another swig of beer, and began punching in a number on his phone. Blair never used speed dial or stored contacts in his phone. The only memory he trusted was the one in his head. He erased all recent call history every night, and sometimes during the day, as well. He insisted others do the same.

Agent Carey's voice came through the phone. "Yes."

"Find Barlow. Just find him, and don't lose track of him." Blair commanded.

"Right." Carey responded.

Blair added, "Any headway on Karlovich?"

"He made the connection. I'm not sure what his next move is, but I'm on top of it." Carey said.

"See that you stay on it, and find Barlow." Blair ended the call. A raucous group of salesmen with hideous ties came through the front door of the bar, prompting Blair to rise from his stool and walk to a booth in the back.

The red and white gingham tablecloth covering the table typified the Italian restaurant. It was a stereotyped place, with fake columns on the walls framing painted grapes and villas on hillsides. Blair had broken his rule, visiting this restaurant five times. He liked it. The food was good, the place was convenient, and the ever-changing servers didn't seem to recognize him. His booth seat allowed him to see arrivals, but the shadows protected him from being viewed.

A menu, bread, and fresh beer arrived quickly. He didn't wait long for the waiter to return and take his order. Veal Picatta suited him tonight. When the waiter left, Blair picked up his phone and punched in another number. It rang several times.

"Yes?" A man's voice answered.

"Is this a good time?" Blair asked.

"Make it quick." The man's voice was strong, but sounded out of breath.

"Barlow is alive. It's confirmed, and Carlton knows it." Blair reported.

"I haven't heard of any NSA activity." It was an inquiry as much as it was a statement.

"There was a meeting." Blair answered, "He's slow on the uptake, but the pieces are coming together."

The phone was silent for a prolonged period. Finally, still slightly out of breath, the man spoke again.

"Locate the other gentlemen."

"I'm already on it," Blair assured him.

"You need to stay on top of this better. No more surprises. This needs to stay on track—our track. Our strategy." There was a pause, but Blair knew better than to interrupt. "I want to deliver a message. I'll have the particulars in an envelope at the office. Send one of your couriers to pick it up at 9 a.m."

"Right," Blair confirmed.

Gregg abruptly ended the call, and placed the cell phone on the nightstand. He turned to the naked woman kneeling on the floor next to the bed. Gregg's large girth rose up from the sheets in a pale mound of bare flesh.

"I'd like you to do something for me." He told her.

"Of course." She smiled suggestively, and leaned toward his legs and stomach.

"Yes, that, too," Gregg confirmed, "but in a moment."

The woman leaned back, her smiled tinged slightly with apprehension.

"You've been frequently visiting Senator Farrell." Gregg continued smoothly. "See him again. Make it tomorrow night. You'll be getting a ride from an associate of mine. He'll pick you up at your favorite restaurant at eight. You'll get instructions from him then. Do whatever he tells you to do, Carol." Gregg's smile seemed more menacing than genial.

The woman tried to hide her surprise and anxiety.

"Yes," Gregg confirmed. "I know all about whom you see, and when you see them. You didn't think your distinguished client list came by mere luck, did you?" Gregg enjoyed his power. He also enjoyed the woman's mixed expression of subservience and fear. He smiled.

"But, I don't call the Senator," Carol stammered. "He calls me."

"That won't be a problem. You just do what I tell you to do, and you'll continue to enjoy all the fine rewards a girl like you should have. Now, I think it's time for you to show a little gratitude for my generosity, don't you?" He grabbed her hair, pressing her head forward, and her face down.

Chapter 48

Terri and Marty sat in a large, noisy bar, open to an equally boisterous restaurant. His beer was half gone; she was on her second.

"Like the wings?" Terri had been making idle conversation for some time, trying to loosen Marty up. Marty had been gradually getting more sociable, responding with the occasional syllable.

"Sure." Still ill at ease, Marty couldn't comfortably make eye contact with Terri, but he was at least trying to sound casual. He felt better being with her than being alone, but his mind was still cluttered and confused. Seeing the chicken wings reminded him of Christen. She and her friends practically lived on them.

"I like the way they add that little bowl of red pepper oil on the side. It really spices it up." Terri was her upbeat self.

Marty drifted off again. He hadn't felt this lost since his divorce. Life had been a disaster for him back then. The last lawyer session followed by his wife's departure had left him in a mood that could only be called suicidal. She'd taken the money, the furniture, the car, and his daughter. She'd even taken custody of his dog. For years, Marty acted as though he was still married, unable to accept his life and move on.

Fortunately, his daughter had shown that she missed him, and still cared for him. They seldom saw each other, but she wrote long emails pretty regularly, texted him, and sometimes there was a phone call.

Now life had brought him a fresh private hell. With Christen's life in the balance, he felt it was more than he could take.

Terri watched, looking for some way to break the mood. "Hey! Are you in there, or should I go pick up some guy in the bar?" She teased.

"Sorry, I drifted for a minute." Marty answered, attempting to rejoin the conversation, but looking decidedly glum.

"What were you thinking about?" Terri asked.

"Nothing, just a billboard story." Marty attempted a smile.

"What's a billboard story?" Terri leaned forward onto her elbows. Her blouse opened just enough to be enticing. Marty didn't seem to notice.

"You know...that's when you see something that spurs a thought, which leads you to something else, then the next thing, and so on. Before you know it, you can't remember how your brain ended up where it is. It's like seeing billboards on a freeway." Marty explained.

"So, again," Terri pressed, "what were you thinking about?"

"Nothing, really." Marty wanted to change the subject.

"Nothing. Well, that makes me feel special." She made a pouting face. "It's not fair! You have to tell me about at least one of the billboards." Terri insisted, sitting back and crossing her arms defiantly.

Marty concentrated for a moment. "I was thinking that she gave away my dog."

"What?" Terri leaned forward again. "Your dog? What dog?"

Marty took a deep draft from his beer. "When my wife divorced me, she insisted on taking the dog." He said quietly. "Two months after our paperwork was final, she gave the dog away. She did it out of spite."

"Now that's depressing," Terri said, shaking her head. "I've heard of things like that. Women take their husband's golf clubs, then sell them. Guys throw their wife's shoes in the garbage."

"Yeah, she did it out of spite," Marty repeated.

"Another one?" Terri asked, gesturing toward the empty bar glasses.

"You buying?" Marty asked automatically.

Terri caught the eye of the bartender and ordered another round. "Well, Marty, that was years ago. What's bugging you this week?"

"Nothing," Marty said, wishing she'd stop talking.

"Try again, Tough Guy." Terri pushed.

"Remember when I said I was short on sleep? I guess I meant it." Marty answered gruffly.

Terri looked hurt. "I thought I was your friend? Friends talk. Friends tell each other what's bugging 'em."

"You are my friend, Terri." Marty gave up the attitude. He felt tired, but he didn't want her to leave. "You're my only friend." He muttered. Marty almost regretted saying that. Then he thought, 'What the hell.'

"No! That's *really* sad. You need to get out more," Terri ribbed him, "but I'm flattered. So, tell me about it."

The bartender came over with two fresh beers. Terri handed him her old one. The bottle wasn't empty, but the bartender didn't care, and Marty didn't notice. Marty picked his up and took a long drink, deciding to tell a partial truth. "Christen is having some trouble at school. It's her first year."

"I know how that goes. You're behind me by a whole beer, by the way. We've got to work on getting you caught up." She raised her hand to the bartender, then turned back to Marty. "Want to talk about it?"

"No, that's enough about me. We both know I have no life." Marty managed a weak smile, and said, "Tell me what you do outside of work. I could use a little vicarious excitement." Maybe it was the beer, the act of smiling, or the company, but with another big gulp, Marty began feeling better. In the back of his mind he was still playing out his nightmare, but it was getting disjointed. It was fragmenting, and growing fainter. He thought that maybe he could put the anxiety aside for a few hours.

Chapter 49

Robert sat in the study. He and the agents had finished a couple of large pizzas and a full liter of Coke. Cinnamon sugared blobs of pizza dough had followed. Peter had gone to pick the food up, after talking Robert out of pizza delivery for security reasons, although Robert had been convinced he would recognize the local delivery guy. Neither agent wanted to take the chance. Robert knew they were right. After eating, Agent Long had left for the night, taking Peter's car. He planned to return in the morning.

Robert now sat in the study. It was quiet, except for the hum of the computer fan, and an occasional pepperoni growl from his stomach. He had fiddled with the phone several times, wanting to talk to someone.

Grady worried him. Was it possible for him to disappear in this day and age, with so much tracking technology available? Robert kept thinking he should have had Grady put into protective custody.

Standing up to stretch, Robert couldn't get his muscles to relax. The image of Grady's car exploding on Roosevelt Island remained vivid. The impact should have lessened, now that he knew Grady hadn't died, but it bothered him. Something else bothered him—a body had been in the car, and Grady had planted it there. Where had it come from? What had Grady done? Maybe Grady was right to leave town and go underground.

Robert couldn't help thinking about how the investigation was going to affect his career, and his promotion. Given the circumstances, he knew he should be focused on other things, but he was well aware of the fragility of his position. He was the guy on the bubble, and it was clear he'd be sacrificed if anything went wrong. This investigation had become very visible, even at the Presidential level, and Robert clearly did not have the situation under control. He didn't need Gregg breathing down his neck, complicating matters, and reminding him of that fact.

Robert's mind kept coming back to Hunt. Hunt clearly wanted to influence the investigation, and he had. Was Hunt a power broker? He didn't seem to wield influence in the usual circles Robert inhabited. Was Senator Gregg one of Hunt's friends, or had he simply granted him the favor of an introduction to Robert? Why was Hunt feeding Robert information? And come to think of it, why hadn't Agent Carey reported anything about Hunt, yet?

Robert was frustrated. The questions kept piling up, and hours were slipping by without any answers. Thinking about Agent Carey, he wondered again about his connection to the NSA. Karlovich had known Carey was coming—or the guard had known. Why? Robert wasn't sure why that was important, but he had the feeling he'd better find out more about it, and how deeply Karlovich was connected. The guy seemed like a sharp bureaucrat. Was he the linchpin, or would he lead to whoever was behind all of this?

Lurking in the background was Robert's father. His father seemed to expect Robert to conjure up an indictment against a still unknown perpetrator of a possible crime. Was he assuming that perpetrators existed, or did he know?

Robert was getting a headache. Leaving the study, he went into the living room to get a snifter from the bar, and some brandy. He found a bottle of Remy Martin XO Cognac that had been given to Tracie by some dignitary. Close enough to brandy, he decided. Tracie would never drink it, so he might as well.

He broke the seal and poured. Concentrating on the cognac's aroma, he held the glass in both hands. Taking a sip, he felt the smooth liquid burn as it slid down his throat. The alcohol carried powerful fragrances and flavors of baked pear, orange marmalade and spices across his tongue and then back through his nostrils as he exhaled. Heat swept through him. The house suddenly felt warmer as the liquor detonated on cue just above his stomach and again deep inside. He added a little more to the glass, thumped the cork back into the bottle, and went back into the study. He noticed

Agent Karelonski sitting in the hall near the front door, reading an electronic book. His gun sat within easy reach on the hall table. Robert figured there was no point in offering a drink to the agent. He closed the door behind him.

Robert settled in at his desk to go over everything that had happened. It had only been five days since he and Chris had talked, he realized with a shock. It seemed like a lifetime. He soon had the desktop covered with notes, diagrams, lines, arrows, and questions.

<u>Chapter 50</u>

Marty and Terri were enjoying themselves, having had too much beer and too little food. Marty was now a full beer ahead of Terri, but didn't notice or care. The conversation had touched on almost every subject possible. They had talked about the news, basketball, exercise machines, motorcycles, leather jackets, and bathing suits. The subjects were born from whatever caught their attention on the televisions generously scattered around the walls. Warm vacation spots and suntan lotion became particularly amusing topics.

"Oh, I liked Hawaii, but the Caribbean is my favorite." Terri had been to Martinique the previous year. "The water is warmer, and the breezes are softer. Plus, I like smaller hotels with fewer people on the beaches."

"What about night life?" Marty had never been to any islands. "Isn't Hawaii more active? And Mexico is always advertising their night clubs."

Terri had an enthusiastic response, remembering the island. "Martinique is great! There's always a bar open with dancing. There are lots of beaches, gorgeous sand, and good snorkeling. I got my best tan ever! It's French, you know, and they are so open about bathing suit options. I picked up a tanning bikini I would be too afraid to wear any place else."

Marty was feeling bold. He leaned forward, and put on his best lady killer smile. "I never pegged you for being shy, Terri." Alcohol had loosened him up. Flirting was not his core competency. Any other girl would have laughed at him.

Terri responded saucily, "My tanning bikini is pretty tiny, and the sun goes right through it. I feel naked in it—and I am shy, sometimes." Terri's smile matched Marty's as she leaned in towards him. "If you hold that suit up to the light you can see right through it. No tan lines. It's amazing. I did feel incredibly free wearing it...and it was a rush being so daring." She stood up, laughing. "I'll leave you with that thought. I've got to go to the ladies room. Don't move. I'll be right back." She grinned as she walked past him toward the bathrooms, her hips moving with a slightly exaggerated sway.

Marty couldn't help but blush. Terri was much younger than he was, and very attractive. She was nicely shaped, and full of energy. Somehow she seemed easy to talk to, and that surprised Marty. He was never very good around women. He would never have met his wife except for some friends having thrown them together in college. Terri was different. Not only could he talk to her, but he could also relax around her. She seemed relaxed around him, too.

What a night. More than once they had laughed at the same commercial. Twice her hand had been on his thigh. Now she was almost talking dirty to him. Marty found himself grinning, and imagining that bikini. He was enjoying her teasing. He didn't really expect anything to come out of it, but he was enjoying thinking like a bad boy for a change.

Sneaking up behind him, Terri rubbed his shoulders a little. "Miss me?"

He didn't jerk outwardly, but his body was responding to her touch. He hadn't felt a woman's hands on him that way in a while, and it made him almost giddy. Marty's eyes dilated. He was melting rapidly. Terri could tell, and her smile broadened. When she sat, he noticed the next button down on her blouse was not quite done, and as she moved and laughed it came completely undone. Several times, Marty saw a lot of her shiny, low-cut bra, and the rounded tops of her breasts. The lively conversation continued to wander. It never came back to the beaches or the bikini, but Marty didn't notice. He was having trouble concentrating.

A last round of beers didn't get finished. The football games were over, and the bar began to empty.

"Well, it's a school night. We'd better get out of here." Terri announced.

"Yes, you're right." Marty agreed as he looked at his watch. He wasn't feeling the least bit tired. He thought he could have stayed all night. "We've got an early morning tomorrow."

They didn't talk much as Terri drove them back to the office. It was a short drive, and Marty was content to daydream. Neither of them wanted to risk adding anything clumsy to a satisfying evening. She pulled up next to his car to drop him off.

"Well, it's been fun." She smiled broadly. The alcohol was continuing to have its effect despite the brisk night air. "I'll see you tomorrow." Her smile warmed Marty all over again.

Marty figured he'd better remember he was a gentleman, and started to get out of the car.

"I really had fun," He said as he put his foot out.

"Me, too." She smiled. "But I really have to go."

Marty was disappointed. Somehow he'd hoped she'd stop him.

"I have to go to the bathroom," she giggled. "I'll use the one in the lobby."

Marty's smile returned. "I'll wait, and make sure you're safe." Marty was continuing his gentlemanly stance.

"No, no." She insisted. "Go home. I'll see you tomorrow. I'll be fine."

He could tell she meant it, so he got out and closed the door. With a wave, he got in his car as she walked quickly towards the building. With all the security around their building, he knew she would be fine, but he was a little deflated at the evening's outcome. He wasn't sure he was ready to get involved with Terri, but somehow he'd hoped for more than this.

Marty cranked the engine, and drove away. He was feeling very relaxed, and sexually charged at the same time. His mind kept wandering back to the beach and Terri's bikini. He almost missed the turn to his neighborhood, and went across the centerline once or twice. His eyes seemed to have trouble focusing, but rolling down the window helped. It was freezing outside. The defroster couldn't get warm enough to melt the ice crystals off his windshield. Fortunately, there weren't many cars on the road.

As he approached his house, his good humor faded. It was dark. The cold was putting a chill on the sunlit sandy beach in his head. Only last night he had been assaulted in his living room. He wanted to go back to the bar and stay out all night, but he knew that wouldn't fix anything. He slipped rapidly back into his negative mindset. By the time he unlocked the door and went inside he felt lonelier than ever. Turning on every light in the house and the TV, he checked for messages on the machine. There were none. He sat in front of the flickering TV screen, not caring what was on it. Marty dreaded the ring of the telephone. He found himself hoping that no one would call, and at the same time, begging the phone to ring. He went in the kitchen and grabbed a beer. Passing out seemed better than spending the night awake.

Chapter 51

Grady's drive had been fairly quick. The roads were so cold that the dry snow blew across them without sticking. His biggest worry about hitting black ice hadn't materialized. He'd forgotten it after driving for a while. He had other things on his mind.

Stopping twice for coffee and bathroom breaks, he was now on small, familiar feeling roads, and was anxious to get to bed. Sleeping in the middle of the day wasn't as satisfying as getting night rest, and he'd had far too little of either. Grady had a theory that sleep between ten and midnight was better than sleep after midnight, regardless of how long you slept. He was looking forward to deep, uninterrupted recuperation. He knew it would take at least another day to recover from his recent emotional experiences. The bruises would be slower to heal.

It was about one-thirty in the morning when he finally spotted the B&B. Pulling into the driveway, he turned off his headlights, and used the parking lights to navigate. He had to pass several cottages on the way to number three, and his lights would have flashed brightly through the windows of the other guest houses. He checked each car as he drove by, looking for any that didn't blend into the scenery. They all looked like rental cars; small, cheap, and white, except one Cadillac with a box of tissue in the rear window. Retired couple, he thought. He didn't feel much safer, but every little bit helped.

The key was under the mat, right where he expected it. After he'd turned on every light and looked in each closet and corner of the cottage, he unloaded the car.

The place was just as he expected—just as he'd seen it the last time he'd been there. It was neat, cheerful, and decidedly feminine. There were lots of frills and lace making everything fluffy and soft. The nightstand had two chocolate covered cherries, mint cordials, and the bath smelled of lilacs. It was wonderfully familiar, comfortable, and full of memories.

Dumping out the plastic Walmart bags on the bed, he separated toiletries from clothes, and put each in their proper place. He stripped the tags and labels off the blue jeans with his new nail clippers, and ironed one shirt. The local television news droned on about weather and high school football while he worked.

The familiar activity was helping him unwind from the drive. Picking up his cold paper coffee cup, he decided to pour it out and toss it in the trash.

Turning down the volume slightly, he chose a boring looking movie from the selection of satellite channels. Stripping down, he got into bed, and turned off the lights. The TV noise kept him from thinking. It was only moments before he was snoring, but surges of smoke and explosions of fire began cascading through his head in nonsensical and badly edited story lines. His closed eyes darted back and forth while his body clenched and moved in his sleep.

Chapter 52

Christen lay in the dark, shaking, half from cold, half from fear. As always, Mary had turned off the TV and lights promptly at ten. The air from outside seeped through cracks in the walls, flowing down from the window over the sofa bed. It reached Christen's head, making her wounds ache more. She spun around so she could lie with her head toward the middle of the room, and her feet near the windowsill.

Christen had scrubbed her cuts while she was in the shower. She scrubbed everything, as much to cleanse her heart as her body. The cuts stung angrily, but she had to get them clean. She cried the whole time. Her sobbing was quiet, so as not to anger Mary, but holding back made her chest cramp with sharp twinges. Fear sent convulsions through her back as she fought back the wailing inside.

She had put on the sweats. There was no bra, but she'd found cotton panties folded up with the pants. The top had been cut to accommodate her handcuffed wrist, and Velcro ironed onto the edges. That made it easier to put on with the handcuff and chain in place.

Even though Mary had used her knife only to cut away Christen's clothes, the fear of that brightly honed blade lingered. Its silver shine remained vivid in her blood-stained memory.

When she'd finished dressing, she'd looked up into the mirror. Tears ran uncontrollably from her eyes at the sight of her cut and bruised face. She was hardly recognizable. The first aid kit had some surgical strips, and she tried her best to pull the cuts tight, so the strips could hold the ragged edges together. An extra set of hands and a good nurse would have helped. Christen hoped she had done a good job and prevented most of the scarring. With antiseptic and bandages in place, she had done her best to tidy up the bathroom and clean up the splattered food.

Once everything was straight and clean, she set the dirty towels in a neatly folded stack where her clothes had been. The food had been all over the floor and the battered coke can had drying blood on its edge, but there was a little soda left inside. Christen had picked off the small bits of dust and debris from the food which remained in the serving dish, and then ate it all. She assumed that not eating would bring worse consequences, and she couldn't face that.

From that time on she had seen nothing of Mary. The empty lunch dish now sat cold and dry on the tray. Dinnertime had come and gone, yet she heard no sound. At ten, Mary had come in and without a word turned off the TV and took the empty food dish and towels away, switching off the lights as she left. Christen had been terrified to move in her presence, or even breathe.

Her forehead and swollen eye throbbed miserably. Tears rolled across her face as Christen cried into her pillow. She hoped her face would heal. She hoped there would be a day left in her life for it to matter. She hoped today would end.

Chapter 53

Jerking his head up from the desk, Robert rocked back suddenly in the rolling chair. The chair glided away from the desk over the smooth hardwood floor, throwing him off-balance. His feet rose off the ground as he scrambled to regain his equilibrium. The doorbell rang again, and he realized what had awakened him.

Looking around the desktop he realized he had no gun, or any suitable defense nearby. He held himself and the chair still with both hands on the desk as he listened to Peter's steps approaching the front door. Robert could hear Peter open the door without any call for identification, or greeting. Robert looked around. The only safety was underneath the desk. He was thinking about that when there was a knock at the study door.

"Mr. Carlton? It's Agent Karelonski. May I come in?"

Robert still felt disoriented. "Who's with you?"

"Agent Brown has come to replace me. I'd like to introduce you."

He sounded relaxed and unemotional. Robert answered with just a touch of apprehension in his voice. "Come in."

The door opened and the two men came in. Peter had straightened his tie and put his charcoal gray jacket back on. Agent Brown was dressed in what looked like an identical suit. If they had been wearing dark sunglasses they could have been characters from a movie.

"This is Agent Brown." Peter gestured toward his partner.

Brown extended his hand toward Robert. "Pleased to meet you, Sir."

"My pleasure," Robert replied. He turned to Peter. "I thought the other agent was your partner."

"We train in several different sized groups. Groups of four to six are most common. We're all partners and work as teams. We are a team of six." Agent Peter responded. "We primarily help out on presidential assignments, or dignitaries' trips. We're one of the advance security teams that arrive before the President."

"Of course." Robert could see the logic in that. "I didn't hear you talk. How did you know who it was? And what time is it?" It was still dark outside.

"It's twelve-thirty, Sir." Then touching his earpiece Agent Peter said, "We use radio communications. We stay in contact with each other."

Robert was beginning to wake up fully, his eyes blinking away the drowsiness.

"Fewer surprises that way." Peter continued, smiling. "Well, it's time for me to get some shut-eye. Mrs. Carlton said we could use the guest room."

"Yes, of course. The bed's always made up in there, and there should be plenty of towels in the guest bathroom. There are guest supplies in the drawers. Toothbrushes, shampoo and so forth." Robert sat back in the chair as the two agents left the room, closing the door. He rubbed his eyes and ran his fingers through his hair. It was badly disheveled. The heat of his right cheek told him it was red from pressing into his desk while he slept. His collar was askew, and in general he knew he must appear to be a wreck. He decided to go upstairs and get a little real sleep in his bed. He wasn't going to achieve anything being groggy and exhausted.

When Robert reached the bedroom, the closet sent another shockwave through his system. Now he could see why Tracie had placed so many suitcases in the hallway. There was nothing casual left in her closet. One full side was empty. There were still dozens of shoes, dresses, and formal outfits, handbags, hats, scarves, and negligees, but there was no doubt that Tracie planned to be gone for some time.

Quickly checking the boy's rooms he found the same half-empty closets and drawers. The car must have already been partially packed with their stuff when he'd arrived. Tracie's half of the bathroom was devoid of most of her makeup, hair accessories, perfume, and jewelry. The boy's pictures were gone, but Robert's picture still sat on the table. It stood alone except for a note leaning against it.

"You should have called."

Tracie

Robert frowned at the reprimand, wadded up the note, and threw it into the corner.

Chapter 54

Marty lay stretched out on the couch as the sun flickered through the trees into his eyes. It was sunrise. He clenched his eyes shut. The frost on the leaves glistened as the weak winter sun shot through them, creating alternating flashes of light and dark on his face. The light flickered and dimmed as the sun rose over the edge of clouds many miles away. Another gray, dreary day began.

Groaning, Marty opened first one eye, then the next. He squinted, raising his hand to block the faint light, but it was already gone. Cold and gray prevailed.

"Unhhhhh," he groaned again, as his head pounded with the movement. His tongue rolled to each side of his pasty mouth, then across his teeth, feeling dry, sticky, swollen, and much too big. As he lifted himself slowly into a sitting position, he knocked over two empty bottles. He almost hit the third bottle as he overbalanced, putting out his hand to steady himself. He let out a low grumbling, "bleh," and dragged himself to the bathroom.

Digging through his medicine cabinet, he knocked over several old prescription containers that clattered into the sink. His head rang with the noise.

"God!" The guttural word was barely audible as his hand moved to the side of his thrumming head. He finally dug out an old, wrinkled packet of effervescing antacid, and dropped the tablets into his water glass. His head jerked away from the glass. The fizzing mixture always smelled bad to him, but it smelled really awful when he had a hangover. His eyes alternated between open and closed as he drank the foul mixture. It tasted worse than he remembered. He thought he would throw it right back up, but he kept it down after two gulps. He didn't think it would help, but he had to try something.

What a night, he thought to himself. Trudging into the kitchen, he recalled how he used to be able to drink three six-packs of beer by himself, and had never felt this bad. He was out of practice, and no longer had the ability to sleep until noon as he had in his twenties. Now he suffered for his excesses.

Marty staggered into the kitchen. Ignoring a burnt smell emanating from the coffee maker, he dropped some fresh coffee grounds on top of the old ones in the filter. He poured two cups of water into the top, and switched on the machine. Leaning heavily on the counter, he grabbed the TV remote and clicked on the early news. He didn't expect to hear anything. He just wanted some sound. The coffee didn't take long as it poured directly into his giant mug. It was too hot to drink, so he carried it toward the bathroom, leaving the last drops to fall, hissing, onto the hot pad. Turning on the shower and stripping off his clothes, he stepped in.

He stood with his head bent forward under the spray for several minutes, not moving. Eventually he washed his hair and soaped down. His eyes began to fully open as he climbed out and dried off. Pulling on his robe, he latched his hands around the coffee mug and took a deep swallow of the harsh, bitter drink.

"Oh, God." The coffee was awful, but it had the desired effect. Grimacing, he set the mug on the counter. By the time he'd shaved and dried his hair, the mug was empty. He got dressed and headed out to the car.

The windshield was covered in frost. He grumbled to himself, as he did every day, about cleaning out the garage so he could park inside. His ice scraper was a heavy one, with an attached simulated sheepskin mitt. He made short work of the windows as the car warmed up, and was soon on his way to work. He would be late, but that no longer mattered. He'd decided what must be done.

Chapter 55

Robert did not feel particularly spry, but he had gotten ready quickly after the alarm jerked him up from bed. The Agents were up and ready to go. It was hard to tell how much sleep either had gotten.

Robert had shown them around the kitchen, and offered the use of the espresso machine earlier. Brown apparently had made lattes before, and set them each up with one to go, after locating cups and lids. Robert accepted his, and decided they would stop for egg and bagel sandwiches along the way at a place he frequented. Drive-up windows were apparently a risk, so one of the agents went in and ordered, returning with the sandwiches and Robert's change.

Robert was discovering that it was handy having a chauffeur. Not only did he eat the sandwich and drink his large coffee without risking his life by driving at the same time, but he also made several calls and texted en-route to the office. He confirmed a meeting with Carey and Davidson, which would take place upon his arrival, and set up a time for Jerry to give his update. He also picked up his messages from Lorraine. Lorraine was in the office early, as usual.

By the time he arrived at his office Carey and Davidson were waiting inside. Agent Long had taken his customary seat, facing the hallway with his back to Robert's office door.

"Good morning, Lorraine...Agent Long." Robert was feeling the coffee buzz.

"Good morning, Mr. Carlton." Lorraine seemed to have recovered from her attack of nerves.

"Good morning, Sir," Long replied.

"Good morning, Gentlemen," Robert said to Carey and Davidson as he walked into his office. Both men started to rise from the guest chairs near Robert's desk. "Please stay seated," he said, motioning to stop them from getting up. "We'll go over everything in just a minute."

Robert opened the closet and hung up his coat. "Can Lorraine get you anything? Coffee?" he asked the men.

"No, thank you." They said, almost in unison.

"She already asked." Phil held up his coffee mug in his right hand, and an onion bagel in the left, with a smile on his face.

"Of course, I should have realized that." Robert smiled, and moved to the backside of his desk. Hitting the intercom button he said, "Lorraine, could you please get me some coffee, and a bagel?"

The words had hardly left his mouth before Lorraine was placing the coffee cup and bagel at Robert's elbow. "Thanks, Lorraine." Lorraine frowned slightly, and waited for a moment, clearly hoping for some enlightenment about the previous day's events, and Robert's need for protection.

Robert ignored her completely, and Lorraine left as he turned his full attention to Carey and Davidson. He still felt a little wired from the espresso. He wondered if it showed. He was feeling a need to get a lot of answers this morning.

"Have you been able to find out anything about any of the items on our list?" He asked the men. Glancing back and forth at each of them, he waited for an answer.

Carey began. "We've checked the police reports for each incident you mentioned. Chris Stoker's death was obviously a homicide. They have turned up no witnesses." Carey was reading the reports, photographed on his smartphone. "The front bumper of his car showed damage from a recent collision. There is no report of an earlier accident, and his estranged wife does not recall him mentioning any previous accident." He swiped the page. "There were traces of gray spray-paint, not automotive, on the grill, and the height of the bumper impact would suggest that the car hit a passenger vehicle. Stoker's head hit the steering wheel, based on a bruise going across his forehead. The police have surmised he hit a car from behind, doing twenty, to twenty-five miles an hour at impact. His airbags did not deploy."

"Not automotive paint?" Robert asked, mystified.

"No, Sir." Carey replied, "Standard hardware store stuff."

"What does that mean?" Robert asked. Hadn't Carey just said that the height of the damage correlated with the bumper of another car?

"It's too early to speculate, Sir. It could be unrelated to the impact, but it is most likely Mr. Stoker hit a car that was cheaply spray painted, or touched-up with spray paint." Carey swiped to another page as Phil shifted in his chair, munching the last of his bagel. Robert continued to listen intently.

"Stoker was shot at extremely close range by a .40 pistol. Based on the ballistic scoring, they think it was a SIG P229. The bullet weight was on the high side at 200 grains, and there was a set of brush scores. This indicates a suppressor may have been used, but they can't be absolutely sure because of damage to the slug from the window, skull, and far door panel."

Robert could feel his stomach churning. "The window?"

Carey continued as if reading a menu. "The shot was fired through the driver's side window."

"A suppressor?" Robert queried.

"Yes. You might call it a silencer." Carey translated.

"A silencer," repeated Robert, thinking that was not the average car-jack or street hoodlum gun.

"Yes," nodded Carey, evidently picking up on Robert's next question. "His wallet, rings, watch, and car were left at the scene. This sounds like a professional hit, not a robbery. There are no suspects." Carey finished reading the report, and looked up. His face showed no expression.

"That's it?" Robert was noticeably discouraged, and sounded it. All that report had given him was more questions.

"That's all they have. I reviewed all the police, paramedic, and preliminary Medical Examiner notes." Carey swiped to a different report. "As to the assault on Lieutenant Colonel Grady Barlow..."

Carey scanned down the page. "His home has been burned down to the foundation. The garage also burned down, but large portions were apparently blown away from the fire by the exploding gasoline, vehicle, and motorcycle. Remains of a body were found near the point of origin—the living room, they think. It was an incendiary explosion. The body can't be identified at this point. There is very little left, but the police assumed it to be Barlow, and have requested his dental records."

"But it wasn't Barlow." Robert interjected.

"We know that, Sir, but I did not advise them of that fact. If you feel it would expedite the investigation, we could tell them, but then there would be inquires as to how we know, and how we are involved with the case." Carey continued unruffled. "The fire department reports that the explosion and fire were most likely arson, caused by a military incendiary-type hand grenade."

"A what?" Robert expected to hear something out of the ordinary, but the idea of a grenade surprised him. "How do they know?"

Carey continued from further in the report. "A fuse mechanism was found in the area of the living room near the kitchen. It was an M201A1 fuse. This would be a match for an AN-M14 TH3 incendiary hand grenade. Apparently there is a former marine on the fire investigation team. When he spotted the fuse, he reported it to the ATF."

"Great." Robert groaned. "Now the ATF is involved. Incendiary—you mean a phosphorous grenade." Robert ventured.

"No, the most common phosphorous grenade would be the M15. It uses an M206A2 fuse. The explosion is different. The grenade used in this case seems to have been a Thermate grenade." Carey seemed confident about his knowledge. "The Thermate material burns very hot—over four-thousand degrees." Carey referenced his report again. "Some molten particles made direct contact with the body and damaged the teeth extensively. Even dental records will take time to confirm. Beyond that, the police reported that it was impossible to determine whether there had been a break-in, or struggle, which, considering the condition of the structure and the extent of the burn, is not surprising. There were fresh tire tracks behind the house and nearby. The police are interviewing the neighbors, hoping for some eyewitness accounts, but it was late and dark enough that the neighbors were all inside. They live a little too far away to see anything specific, anyway."

Carey looked up from his phone. "I would say that the police would not have actively considered the idea of a break-in, assault, or foul play so soon, had it not been for the grenade fuse. That, combined with the human remains, will require a homicide investigation in addition to the arson investigation. With all that in mind, the tire tracks will be considered suspicious. They have made casts."

Robert had been listening intently, numbly. After a long pause, he asked, "Have you any idea who was found burned in the house?"

Carey responded flatly. "None. There are no public records of a second occupant of Barlow's residence, so I assume it is one of the assailants."

"What about the car explosion we witnessed?" Robert asked.

Carey swiped to the next page. "As I told you earlier, they found a body in the kneeling position in the right front floorboard, face pressed down into the seat. The body is burned beyond recognition, just like the one in the house. It is no more than a partial skeleton now. Molten remains of a release handle in the car, and a pin in the roadway near the car were discovered." Carey looked up at Robert. "I would guess it came from the same kind of grenade. The police will figure that out soon. That common factor will pop up on the ATF computer, and the two incidents will be linked. From that point, Homeland Security is likely to get involved, and would take full charge of both investigations." Looking back to the report, he continued. "They have positively identified the body as Barlow's from his dog tag. Apparently he kept one in his wallet, and the metal resisted the high temperatures, thanks in part to the layers of wallet materials, and the body being between it and the explosion."

"Homeland Security," Robert said, then sat back in his chair, silent. Carey and Phil watched quietly as he mulled over the information.

Robert mentally tallied some salient points. First, Phil, Carey, and Long knew that Grady had survived the attack in his home, but Robert alone knew Grady was still alive. Robert knew the man in the car was someone else, but whom? Grady had told Robert that two men had attacked him, but Robert didn't remember telling Carey how many there were, yet he'd used the words, "one of the assailants." How did he know that there had been more than one assailant?

Phil had waited long enough. He turned to Carey, saying, "Dog tag; that's it? That isn't conclusive. Have they checked dental records on the car victim?"

Carey looked at Phil. "That police unit also requested Barlow's dental records, but it will take time to get them. Plus, the grenade destroyed most of the teeth and bone. At some point the report from Barlow's house might be connected with the car explosion. The reports will be compared. When the determination that Barlow was killed in the car explosion comes through, they'll start trying to figure out who died in his house."

Robert still sat quietly thinking. Phil and Carey both turned toward him. Robert felt their eyes fall on him, and he looked up. "What about that car that exploded? I think Grady drove a Jeep Wagoneer, or some kind of smaller SUV. That car didn't look like his choice of vehicle."

Carey quickly surveyed the reports. "There's no specific mention of that type of vehicle, but the Wagoneer may have been the car that blew up in Barlow's garage. The police will check the serial numbers on both vehicles, and determine where they came from."

Robert decided to redirect the line of questioning away from Grady. Grady wanted to be missing, and focusing too much on any aspect of the police investigations might give Carey cause to wonder about Grady's "death."

Robert paused before asking, "What about Hunt? Have you found out anything about him?"

"I ran Hunt's photo through several agencies. They have no record of him." Carey closed his phone app.

"That's it?" Robert asked again. "Nothing else?"

"Yes, Sir. That's all at this time. Of course we are continuing the background check, based on facial recognition."

Robert thought for a minute.

"Then explain how could Hunt could get into the White House without verifiable ID? That doesn't make much sense if there's no documentation on him."

Carey didn't respond to that immediately. He made a show of opening a new app on his phone and typing in some notes. "I'll check with Whitehouse security immediately."

"Wouldn't that be the Secret Service?" Robert asked pointedly.

"No, Sir." Carey responded, not looking up from his phone. "They're connected, but not our personnel. It may take some time, since they tend to protect their information."

Robert thought about that for a moment. He wasn't sure he bought Carey's dodge on that. He deliberately left an uncomfortable silence in the room.

"Unfortunately we have no conclusions at this time." Carey evidently felt the need to break the silence. "There is no obvious link between these incidences from a police point of view, but I think the ATF will make a connection in twenty-four hours, or less.

Our information might accelerate their investigations, but that could compromise your investigation. It's up to you, but I don't think they will be able to help us at this juncture, unless we give them more to work with. We should not withhold information for more than 72 hours, unless we have justifiable cause. It would breach interagency protocols."

"Anything to add, Phil?" Robert asked, hoping that Phil may have discovered something that would give him some direction.

Phil did not make direct eye contact, looking at something between Robert and Carey. "No, that about covers it." He answered.

Robert sat thinking, not looking directly at either man. He was desperate to know more. He had become increasingly suspicious of everyone around him, but he had little to substantiate any definite theory. "Keep checking. It seems likely that we're missing something that is key to this puzzle. Do you need anything else from me?"

Both Carey and Davidson stood up to leave. "That's all, Sir." Carey answered.

"Okay, thanks. I'd like a report back on Hunt as soon as possible." Robert stood, and moved toward the door with them. As Carey went out into the reception area, Robert quickly added. "Oh! Hang on a minute, Phil."

Phil and Carey both turned.

"I almost forgot. I have a question about that jurisdiction problem we tossed around a few months ago on OPOV, Phil. Have you got another minute? If you don't, we can connect later. With everything that's happened, I keep forgetting to ask you about it." Robert said, shaking his head.

Phil answered, "Sure." He began talking as he walked back into Robert's office, letting the door swing closed as he entered. "As we discussed, I am a firm believer that the OPOV falls under our jurisdiction based on..."

As the door clicked shut behind them, Phil was still talking.

"Phil." Robert interrupted quietly. "I get the feeling you think Carey left something out."

"No, not at all. It was a very thorough briefing." Phil shuffled his feet, but didn't seem surprised at Robert's question.

"Perhaps there was some detail that caught your attention, then." Robert cross-examined.

"Yes, there were two small things." Phil hesitated, looking uneasy.

"Phil, I need to know everything, no matter how insignificant it may seem," Robert told him.

Phil still looked uncomfortable, but answered, "Well, it's probably nothing, but the .40 pistol used to kill Stoker is a pistol originally designed to support the FBI. If it *was* a SIG-Sauer P229, that is. That's the same model used by the US Coast Guard now."

Robert thought about that for a moment. "So, it's a commonly available gun, right?"

"Yes, very. I mean, you won't see some low-life criminal buying one in just any store, but it is mass produced and available." Phil edged closer. "It's just...you wondered if there was a connection between the two incidents. Add to that, military grenades, and, well..."

"Are you saying," Robert began asking incredulously, "that it was the FBI or Coast Guard?"

"No," Phil answered, "but this is not a typical criminal situation. And wouldn't a professional hit man use a revolver, not a pistol that ejects the brass?" He paused for a moment, then continued, "Then again, a pistol is quieter, when equipped with a silencer. There's not much point to a suppressor on a revolver." Phil shifted uncomfortably as he argued with himself. "I'm sure Carey thought it was unimportant, but I was surprised he didn't mention any of it. And I wondered why he hadn't asked the White House staff for

Hunt's records, too, but maybe there's some turf war going on over there." He paused. "I'm sure he just didn't want to make connections about the grenades and gun without having more information." He tried to sound comfortable with that assertion, but he clearly thought it was strange that Carey had left out those details.

Robert thought it was odd, too, and he still didn't remember telling Carey there had been more than one assailant. Realizing that Phil was staring at him, Robert straightened up. "Thanks, Phil. I'll let you know more when I can." Robert moved toward the door, signaling that the conversation had ended.

Chapter 56

Arriving a little late, Marty got the usual long look from security. He didn't stop to chat with any of his co-workers. That was normal, but uncharacteristically he didn't grab his typical coffee. He'd decided that the harsh sludge he'd ingested at home was enough to keep him going for a week.

He navigated around Terri's cubical to avoid the chitchat he assumed was coming, and went straight to his computer monitor. First, he pulled up a screen full of statistics. Then he opened his software editing suite. Opening the control file for the OPOV client contact program, he scanned down to where his remark had been added. There he found the polynomial in the exact spot he had left it. Looking for the first letter "A" in the hex code polynomial he replaced it with 1010, the binary equivalent. Then he changed the date on his computer to the same day he accessed the file previously, clocking the time to a few minutes later. He saved the file. Quickly changing his computer date and time back to the present, he allowed himself a deep breath. He had effectively made the polynomial much harder to find. The anomaly could be blamed on a computer error during copying—or at least he hoped that would be the case. He had bought himself and Christen a little time, he thought.

A computer on another desk sat quietly running a system monitor window with four subdirectory windows. File updates to three system directories erratically updated, creating jittery scrolls of information. A fourth directory, the current OPOV external files directory, was not showing activity. Then the listing changed. One of the files in the OPOV subdirectory had been altered. The checksum changed, and the time stamp for the last time it had been saved changed by 8 minutes, but kept the same date. The user pulled up the network activity log for the file. The last ten people to do a "save" appeared. User 1670770 had made the last two changes. Marty Torrance.

Reaching for the phone, Karlovich made a call.

"Hello?" A voice answered.

"There's been a change. It needs to be put back the way it was. Can you fix it?"

"Probably, but..."

"You have his password?" Karlovich interrupted.

"From three days ago, unless he's changed it. This wasn't the plan." The voice responded.

"We have a contingency plan. It's always been in place."

"He'll check again. He'll know it reverted if it's changed."

There was a pause. "Fix it." Karlovich said. "I'll make arrangements for tonight at eight."

"I don't like it." The voice contended.

"Fix it!"

"Not that part. The 'arrangements' part."

"Is there a problem?"

"It's too soon."

"Do it anyway. Tonight. Make it happen."

"Right."

Both parties hung up.

Blair's cellular phone rang. "Yes?" His deep voice resonated.

"We need maintenance...tonight at eight."

"Location."

"Location Tango Echo."

"Location Tango Echo, two-zero-hundred hours. I'll have a maintenance team there."

Both lines went dead.

Chapter 57

Robert's day seemed typical, aside from having both Secret Service and Treasury agents in his office. It was an otherwise average Thursday with the usual duties, including two conference calls, three reports coming in, and two going out. Robert also had received a request for an appearance at a fundraiser—one he'd rather avoid. Then a lunch request for Monday came in from Senator Morgan Farrell, a senior statesman on the Senate Rules Committee. Well, maybe that had been a little unusual. Farrell had a long Senate career, beginning before Robert had been born. He was connected, and subtly powerful. The lunch request was probably a checkup initiated by Gregg, Robert mused, since the two were connected. It had seemed more of a command than an optional meeting. Farrell and Robert had never spoken before. He'd been tempted to turn down the lunch, but finally concluded that it might be useful.

The morning continued with more routine. Robert heard from two State's Attorney Generals who were fighting for states' rights, each with the fervor of a televangelist. Both were writing state laws in defiance of Federal Acts. Robert considered both issues frivolous, and egregious wastes of taxpayer money. He figured these guys were trying to make a name for themselves to further their own political careers. The issues catered to their wealthy campaign contributors' interests, but the money spent fighting the Federal Government came from their taxpayers.

Robert had been looking over an update from Jerry and his team. It was dry stuff—a rehash of what he had done two years ago. He almost stopped Jerry's team from combing through every detail, but he had to see if something had been overlooked. To stop now would invite inquiry later. Methodical research was tedious, but essential to any good legal, or investigative technique. He kept plowing through the summary.

He almost didn't notice when his phone rang.

"Mr. Carlton." Lorraine chimed in on the intercom. "Mr. Davidson is on the line."

"Thank, you. I'll take it." Robert picked up the phone. "Phil, you have something for me?"

"Yes, but I'd like to show it to you. It's a diagram of how I think the accident happened. Can you come over?"

"Phil, can't you bring it over here? I have a lunch meeting coming up, and I'm busy doing some preparation."

"No, it's really too large. I would appreciate it if you could come over here."

Robert looked at his watch and decided he could stop by there on his way to eat. "I'll drop by your place on the way to lunch. Let's say eleven. Will that work?"

"Yes, that would be perfect." Phil hung up.

"Hasn't the guy heard of computers?" Robert wondered as he went back to his reading. Time passed quickly, and before he knew it, it was ten forty-five. He threw the documents into his briefcase along with the computer, grabbed his coat, and headed over to Phil's.

Traffic was surprisingly light. Robert strode into Phil's office, leaving Agent Long in the hallway. The door swung open more easily than he expected and hit the wall firmly, jerking Phil's attention up from the desk.

"Phil, let's see it." Robert felt rushed, and wanted to get through this in the least amount of time possible.

"It's down in the lab." Phil quickly ushered Robert down the hall to the stairs, and into a small, enclosed room with rack after rack of electronic gear. Long followed, and patrolled the hallway outside the electronics room.

Robert looked around. "I don't see any accident layout." He said, blankly.

"I made that up. I couldn't talk over the phone." Phil looked a bit apologetic.

"Why not?" Robert was irritated.

"I found out some things about Hunt."

"Go on." Robert was interested now.

"He works for a lobbyist group," Phil told him. "They work for various special interest groups; all big money."

Robert stared at Phil.

"But here's the important thing, Robert. Hunt was with the Secret Service fifteen years ago." Phil seemed torn between excitement and concern.

"He worked with the Secret Service?" Robert repeated. He couldn't believe what he was hearing.

"No." Phil paused for a moment. "He was *in* the Secret Service. Big difference."

"Phil, people don't just leave the Secret Service," Robert said slowly.

"Actually, they do." Phil was presenting the information at his own pace.

"He was fired?" Robert asked, trying to pull the story out of Phil faster.

Phil answered. "No, no. Hunt was a USSS-1811. Back in 1995, when they opened up the SSA-OIG, he moved over as a manager. That was right after SSA moved out from under HHS. You follow?"

"Not at all." Robert said, gritting his teeth. "You're making this about as cryptic as possible."

"Okay, let me try again." Phil took a breath, and continued. "Hunt was in the Secret Service when they opened a new program with the Office of the Inspector General. They hired almost nothing but 1811s from the Service. The first Inspector General was from the Secret Service, and hired people he knew and trusted. At this point Hunt was a senior agent in the system. He ended up involved with FLETC a couple times. They handle Federal Law Enforcement Training for about ninety agencies. Later, Hunt went to a special group, and the documentation trail gets lost there. Now that is unusual, and I think it means he's still connected to the service."

"The bottom line, though, is that I could find him in the system up to that point," Phil concluded, letting that last bit sink in.

"So, Carey should have found him in the Secret Service files," Robert said slowly.

Phil was clearly becoming more uncomfortable. "Yes, easily. Here's the worst part: Carey didn't have to look him up."

He paused, causing Robert to react. "For Christ sake, Phil! Spit it out!"

Phil made direct eye contact. "Robert, Carey met Hunt at FLETC. He was on Hunt's training team for six months."

Chapter 58

Agent Carey was on the phone with Blair. The secure government line's "green light" glowed reassuringly in the security room.

"I have the track you requested on Barlow," Carey told Blair. He had used Secret Service connections to get what they needed. No one would be the wiser.

"Excellent," Blair answered in his deep voice. "Where is he?"

"He's settled in Henniker, New Hampshire. He's stayed at a place called 'Great Pines B&B' on previous trips to that area, so the odds are good that he's there." Carey read off the address and phone number.

"Where is that in relation to anything on a map?" Blair asked.

"It's about twenty-five miles west of Concord."

"Okay, hold on a second." Blair set the call on speaker. "Can you hear me?"

"Yes," Carey responded.

"Okay, let's see." He pulled up the GPS map on his smart phone, located the nearest airport, and opened a travel app to scan flight schedules. "There's a flight I can catch to Manchester." He hit the button to purchase his ticket. He purchased another for the next flight under a woman's name. "This will work. I'll need you to stand by. I may need you to join in on a delivery tonight."

"Now, wait a minute! I didn't agree to that." Carey was worried about his cover as he considered the idea of another "delivery." Most "deliveries" ended up with strong-arm tactics. He preferred working as a single, since it gave him more control. Pairing up always put his cover at risk.

"It's what you do tonight, if that's what I need you to do." Blair's voice carried venomously across the phone. "I hope I don't need to motivate you."

"I think you know better than that." Carey snapped, making no effort to hide his resentment. He would accomplish whatever task Blair requested, and Blair knew it, but he didn't have to be happy about it. He had no choice; he was in, and he had to stay in.

"I will let you know whether you're required. Stay by the phone for the next hour." Blair hung up.

Carey sat quietly fuming. The relationship with Blair seemed one-sided. The money was worthwhile, but Carey didn't have any options when it came to Blair's demands. The risk of exposure was growing.

Blair punched another number. The phone rang twice.

"Hunt," the man answered.

"I need you to make a delivery tomorrow night in DC." Blair laid out Hunt's instructions. "You will pick up a woman named Carol at eight. I'll send you the address and her photo. Go with her. She'll be making a visit to Senator Farrell. Don't worry about getting in, she'll make that easy."

"Carol will have information for Farrell from Gregg. Exchange it for the packet I'll be sending you," he continued. "Examine what's in my packet when you get it, then give it to Farrell. The data fingers Daniel Gregg for the OPOV conspiracy, and links the NSA. Make sure you memorize it. You may have to help Carlton put the pieces together."

Hunt tried not to show any surprise in his voice when he said, "So, we've switched horses?"

"Yes, we got a better offer," Blair told him.

"Carlton may not be satisfied with only getting Gregg."

"He'll still get the NSA. We're running out of time, and so is he. Gregg will have to be enough. You know what to do with Carlton."

"I do." Hunt felt a little of the old excitement of his job stir. This was more like it. He preferred action. "What about Karlovich?"

"He's still going down. He just doesn't know it, yet." Blair responded. "Pick up your favorite sandwich for lunch tomorrow. The envelope for Farrell will come with it."

"What do you want me to do with Gregg's original packet?" Hunt asked.

"Destroy it." Blair ended the call.

Blair sent a text to Carey. "Not needed for delivery. Take next Peter K. shift."

Tracking Grady had been little trouble for Carey. Grady had made too many mistakes, as most amateurs did. Grady thought he had outsmarted any tracking by setting up a separate answering service. He'd been right to assume he could be traced when he called Robert's office, but he hadn't understood how prepared they were to locate him. Carey had connected into Robert's line the day Robert had called for security—his call had provided the justification. The trace revealed the answering service. The service's records didn't track the number of an incoming phone, but all Carey had to do was request a report from cell carriers that listed every cell phone calling the answering service in the last 48 hours. For the Secret Service it was all too easy.

Grady's cell was not identified specifically on the lists, but four pay-as-you-go phones were displayed. A call to two of the cell companies found that only one of these types of phones had been bought and activated within the last 48 hours. That information led Carey to cell site location maps, showing the location of each call made from the phone. The Homeland Security laws made it simple; no search warrants were needed, and thanks to counter-terrorist laws, he was able to tap the number. Carey had chuckled to himself, thinking that Herbert Hoover would have loved this new world of access to anyone's information under the guise of being a potential "threat."

Carey had pulled the last two years' worth of Grady's credit card bills, matching zip code of charges to the GPS locations of Grady's current calls. There were a couple of restaurants, a ski resort, and one B&B on the list that coordinated with the direction Grady seemed to be heading. The odds were good that Carey had found Grady's hideaway for the night.

Blair, too, was thinking about Grady. He dialed a number on his phone. The woman who answered was annoyed with the short notice, but the money offer guaranteed her acquiescence. Her commitment was expected, as both of them knew, but Blair enjoyed the process of her capitulation.

Blair hoped Grady planned to dig in for several nights. His hunch was that Grady would be vulnerable in his current situation, and most of his hunches were dead right.

Chapter 59

At the NSA building Marty had fidgeted around his cube all morning. Terri had noticed how he avoided walking past her that morning. She also noticed that he couldn't sit still during a half-hour department meeting. Something was up. When Terri asked Marty to lunch he responded positively, and quickly got ready to go—which was definitely not his normal behavior.

When it came their turn to go in the airlock, Terri joked, "You go first. After all, I'm a women's libber."

"Age before beauty, I guess," Marty replied.

"Thanks! And you can get the stuff out of the lockers." She smiled back.

Terri waited until Marty had entered the airlock and the door was closing behind him. Suddenly she spoke aloud to no one in particular, "Damn, I forgot to sign off!"

Moving quickly, Terri went past the opening to her cubical and directly into Marty's. She punched in Marty's access code and password. The network confirmed the password and crosschecked the computer's location. Scanning through Marty's files she located the most recent backup of the file Marty had changed. She verified the date and the correct byte count. Locating the file on the system, she deleted it. She then changed the date and time on Marty's computer. Next she took the backup file and got ready to copy it over. Holding her watch up where she could see it, she waited for the second hand to come full circle then hit the save button. Pulling up the file listing she confirmed that the file date, time, and size matched with the way it was yesterday, but still added the 8 minutes. The only way Marty would notice her change was if he checked his own editing, the checksum, or the network time log.

Resetting the date and time, she signed him off and went back to the airlock.

"Hey, where did you go?" Marty asked her as she came out of the airlock; his arms outstretched with their locker items separated into each hand.

"Sorry, I forgot to sign off. You know how touchy Karlovich can be." Terri responded. "Then I got stuck in line..."

"Tell me about it. Let's go for pizza. I could use a beer." Marty's hangover was threatening to come back, but the feeling of taking action against his blackmailers was a relief.

Chapter 60

Mulling over the day's events as he sat at home, Robert was frustrated. He had been hoping to fit a few more pieces into the puzzle. He couldn't escape the feeling that he might not be able to prove anything in his investigation. Those trying to compromise OPOV might very well succeed.

Robert continued to list possible motives and perpetrators in his head. Terrorists, anarchists, and lobbyist groups clicked through his brain. His mental gymnastics ground down to the three most likely reasons to target the system: one, to gain money or power from the effort; two, to break down confidence in the OPOV program; or three, to make the President look inept.

But this plot also required opportunity, and long-term strategy. Infiltrating the NSA, and destroying a program like OPOV was a subtle infiltration. Foreign interests usually targeted economic factors, and terrorists were prone to bold acts that created panic. Lobbyists' strategies played out in different arenas.

This type of manipulation surrounding OPOV was a combination of expensive technical cyber warfare, and old-fashioned Mafia-type techniques. Deep pockets were behind it all.

What about the money angle, Robert thought? If this was all about money, it would have to be a very big financial issue. It would have to be something that could bring down a large corporation or industry. Something that was significant enough to damage the country's economy. Robert couldn't see how manipulating the vote would change an economic disaster, or a company's specific earnings. Even changing the outcome of who'd been elected President couldn't have changed the rolling momentum of the Great Recession, or the years that followed.

OPOV had been the President's campaign promise, and a failure of the system would make his promises look empty. Oddly enough, this seemed the most likely answer among the motives. The act of crippling the President's pet program would result in a decline in public support for his administration. If the President looked weak, it would transfer power to his opponents.

Robert wondered whether his conclusion was valid. Undermining OPOV was a risky political play. A scandal would be cheaper, and easier by far to create; real or not.

And assuming that he'd hit on the answer, he still didn't know who would be behind this effort. Robert shook his head. The numbers were overwhelming. Undermining the President's plans was the full-time job of at least half of Congress, plenty of political groups and lobbyists, many large companies, and at least two major news networks. And those were just the groups from within the United States. Throw in foreign interests, and the list exploded in size.

Robert had come full circle in his analysis. While the motivation might be to undermine the President, or even confidence in the government, this was about controlling the outcome of many votes. Controlling the software in OPOV would mean political influence over many voting issues, over a period of years. It was about long-term control of the country from within, invisible and untraceable.

Robert knew one thing was undeniable: the upcoming vote was only a rehearsal for bigger issues.

The Carey/Hunt connection continued to bother Robert. Why was Carey editing his reports to Robert? Was Hunt still associated with some classified operation in the Secret Service? Was Hunt, or Carey for that matter, acting outside his position in the Service, or was he acting in accordance with instructions from a superior?

Robert's mind hashed and re-hashed the question until he got a headache. Finally he left the study in search of Ibuprofen to release his stiffening neck.

Chapter 61

Sitting in her cubicle at the NSA, Terri had been listening to Marty's movements since lunch. He had done nothing unusual. He'd been very quiet; exactly what she expected. She'd regularly pulled up the activity listing to see if the computer file had been modified again, or if Marty's name showed on the activity list. Since he had changed the bite count last time, she hoped he would make the same mistake if he tried to change the program again. It would make any changes easier to catch.

At quarter 'til five, Karlovich emerged from his office to do his bed-check rounds through the cubicles. As always, he talked only to those who made eye contact with him. Marty had been an exception to this last time, but Karlovich only gave Marty a visual once over today, and continued on. Arriving at Terri's cube, their eyes met.

"Terri, life still treating you well?" He asked jovially.

Terri turned around the rest of the way in her chair, both legs exposed right up to mid-thigh. "My life is still in turmoil. My neighbor is a peeping Tom." Her skirt slid up a little farther as she moved in her chair. "I think he's peeking into my bathroom at night, but it's okay." She added, sounding as though she was discussing the weather.

"That sounds great. If you need something, I'm always available to help." Karlovich answered in his usual manner, seemingly oblivious to her commentary. His eyes never left her thighs and the edge of her skirt.

Terri smiled and turned back to her computer screen.

Karlovich broke off his stare and finished his rounds, heading back to his office. Terri sprinted over to Marty's cube. "He's such a sleaze. I could get him out on a sexual harassment charge in a heartbeat. What do you think?"

Marty grunted a little, but that was the extent of his reaction.

"So, what are you working on?" She leaned over his shoulder toward the computer screen.

"Nothing, just some stats." The screen was full of keystroke counts and access figures. It was a chart that would bore or confuse most people. Marty was working it into a nice-looking graph that Karlovich would use to justify the department budgets.

"Close it out, and let's get out of here." Terri coaxed.

"You go on ahead, I'll finish up here in a little bit." Marty sounded distracted, but he was feeling emotionally exhausted. The stress, pressure, relief and anxiety were taking a huge toll.

Terri had to make this work. She couldn't afford to be subtle, but Marty wouldn't know how to handle it if she came on too strong.

"I'm bored, and I'll bet you are, too. Let's go to dinner. I know this new restaurant that's opened up. It's supposed to be the best Italian you've ever tasted. I've heard they have a linguini in clam sauce to die for."

She knew that would get him. Rich, creamy sauces were his weakness, and he loved Italian. His head moved back from the monitor slightly. She had gotten his attention.

"They also have a special frozen drink made with amaretto, peach schnapps and something else that everyone is raving about. Oh, and the cheesecake sounds fabulous..."

"All right, but I'll pass on the frozen whatever it is." Marty acquiesced.

Terri was visibly pleased. "Great, let's go. We can hang out in the bar 'til we get hungry."

"I'm kind of hungry now," Marty said dolefully. He was starting to worry about the change he'd made. He had spent the entire afternoon wrestling with his anxieties. When the kidnappers tried to access the file he was told to modify, would his change be discovered? His only hope was that Karlovich, or someone in the office would spot it first, and take it out on him publicly enough that Christen's kidnappers would know that he'd tried, but had been discovered. He desperately hoped they wouldn't take it out on Christen. He was silently begging them to let her go.

He knew that his odds of making this work were worse than they'd be for winning the lottery twice in a row, but it was all he had. He had to take the risk in order to delay them. If for some reason they didn't test the change before the vote next Tuesday, Marty would have more time to think of some way out of this mess. They still needed him, since he was the senior programmer on that section of code. That meant he could make changes without getting approvals. He was the only one who could. He hoped that would be enough to protect his and Christen's lives.

Marty needed an escape. Dinner with Terri sounded better than obsessing over this mess.

"Hello!" Terri stood behind Marty's chair with her coat on. "Anybody home?"

Marty snapped out of his self-absorption. "Sorry, I was just thinking."

"Think while you put your coat on. I need a drink."

They didn't talk until they reached the parking lot.

"Let's take your car," Terri suggested.

"Sure. Where is this place?" Marty was so mentally overwhelmed with his problem that he had to ask directions twice. He felt like his head was in a fog.

They arrived at the restaurant about fifteen minutes later. The bar was already getting busy with happy-hour patrons. Everything was two for one, and Terri had two of the popular frozen Bellinis. Marty had two, very tall beer steins filled with honey brown ale.

"Isn't this great?" Terri seemed pleased with her surroundings. The quietly elegant décor was understated. The bar and chairs were finished in fine mahogany, and oil paintings hung from the expansive walls, but the environment felt open and spacious. It was upscale yuppie heaven.

"Very nice," Marty answered reflexively.

"It talks!" Terri smiled at Marty. "And they said it couldn't be done."

Marty broke a small smile back. "Sorry, I'm just wrapped up in something."

"Well, get over it! Relax a little. You might enjoy it. Here try these." She slid the appetizer of fried calamari toward him. "They're delicious."

Marty wrinkled his nose at the golden rings.

Terri was clearly enjoying herself. "It's great. You'll like it," she insisted.

"I've had it before. It was tough, tasteless, and fishy." Marty protested.

"This is different. Try it." Terri nudged them a little closer.

Marty slowly picked up a piece as if it was radioactive, and dipped it in the eye-catching, flamingo-colored sauce. Paprika, mayonnaise, and mustard filled his mouth along with crispy squid. He slowly chewed the tidbit, and was surprised at how much he liked it. Before long, he and Terri were racing each other to the last one.

The bar was packed now, and they realized the tables were filling up. The second set of double happy-hour drinks arrived just when the hostess told them their dinner table was available. With a drink in each hand, they followed her to their table.

Terri had been right. The food was excellent. Marty was thoroughly enjoying himself. Her carefree laughter and the drinks were drawing him in, and warming him up. Marty was happily ignoring his problems, and slurring his words just a little.

They skipped the cheesecake. They were both too full, and the after dinner drinks sounded better. They ordered two Keoki coffees. They were smooth and warm, just perfect for facing the winter weather outside. Terri insisted on picking up the check.

"You can get it next time," she said with a laugh. "We'll make it more expensive." The bill was well over a hundred dollars. Marty didn't even notice. He was definitely not in any condition to drive. As they walked out, Terri glibly told the hostess. "Don't worry, I'm driving."

Marty's car was nearby. He didn't protest when Terri held out her hand for the keys. She adjusted the seat and mirror, then off they went. Terri drove Marty's car with as much reckless abandon as she drove her own. She had been drinking just as much as he had, but in the glow of alcohol and conversation Marty didn't notice. When the car stopped, he realized they'd arrived at Terri's house.

Chapter 62

Arcing across the Northeast, clouds muted the landscape into a deep gray. The wind below them was relatively calm. Snowflakes fell silently, coming to rest in light, fluffy mounds.

Grady woke in time for the last breakfast seating in Sue's dining room. Sue's breakfasts alone were worth the trip to her B&B. He threw on some clothes, ran his hands over his hair, then used the toothbrush and toothpaste he'd purchased. He'd forgotten to buy a razor, but fortunately Sue had stashed a throw-away razor in with some courtesy supplies by the sink. That was lucky, he thought. The last time he tried to grow a beard it had looked horrible. He left the cottage for the main house.

As promised there were Lingonberry stuffed waffles, plus Canadian bacon, fresh squeezed orange juice, and beautiful pastries in a dainty lace-lined basket. Scrambled cheese egg blintzes rounded out the meal. Grady dug in, ignoring the calorie count.

The only drawback to breakfast was the chitchat that came with staying in a B&B. Everyone seemed to want to talk to everyone else around the breakfast table. It was the only thing Grady didn't like about the place, but he felt pleasantly sociable today. A few curious stares reminded him that his face was still looking bruised, so he casually mentioned a recent car accident in conversation. He mentioned resting up at the B&B, and soon escaped to the solitude of his cottage.

Grady lounged in his room the rest of the morning, relaxing and letting the TV drone in the background. Hunger pains set in around lunchtime, and he went forth in search of food. The front had passed, and sunshine cast its light everywhere, so he decided to wander around the outcropping of stores and restaurants scattered beneath the Pats Peak Ski Resort. The sun made the day feel warmer than it actually was, and made the snow sparkle. It was the perfect ski village setting. As he strolled along the street, nothing in takeout or fast food looked appealing, so Grady chose a sit-down restaurant.

He seated himself in a sunny corner of a small café and scanned the menu. A friendly waitress supplied him with coffee, and a personal-sized warm loaf of banana-nut bread to munch while he made his choice.

"Salmon Wrap or Blue Bacon Burger?" Grady asked when she came back to take his order.

"Both are great," she responded. "With the salmon, I'd recommend our lemon sauce. The Blue Bacon Burger is legendary."

"Then the burger it is." Grady smiled.

"Fries, Sweet potato fries, red boiled potatoes, or steamed vegetables?" the waitress asked him.

"Sweet potato fries." He'd get back to watching fat grams later.

The burger was amazing. Grady figured an extra five-mile run should make up for it—or maybe ten miles. He read a local newspaper while he ate, thinking how far removed this place seemed from DC, and reflecting on what he'd left behind.

Pushing his plate aside, he pulled out his cell phone and dialed the service. They reported that he had no messages. Then he pulled out his key chain code device and asked to be transferred. At the beep he put in the second code.

The phone connection clicked in. "John? It's Barlow."

"Colonel; glad to see you're alive." John quipped.

"What do you mean?" Grady realized he sounded abrupt, and tried to sound more casual. "Know something I don't know?" His comfortable lunch mood waned quickly, as he wondered what John had been told.

"Just an expression, Colonel." John answered, moving on with the conversation. "I found something that may interest you. Modifying that file I told you about would work for a while, but the safeguards would eventually catch it. That's the good news. The bad news is they could keep setting up new files. If it was done inside, we'd always be a day late, and a dollar short when we caught up to the change."

"I'm following you." Grady told him.

"Good. Here is where it gets interesting: imagine you're the guy in charge of this operation. You don't want to have to depend on your inside man, right?" John asked.

"Right," Grady answered cautiously.

"So, you build something that's self-perpetuating, like a virus." John sounded confident.

Grady thought about that concept. "If someone did that, wouldn't a virus checking program stop it?'

"They're only set to stop unauthorized actions," John answered. "If your computer is expecting a legitimate change, and the action becomes part of the valid software, virus software will never catch it. At least, not in this case. Pat has figured out that much already. You see, once it is authorized inside the firewall, the anti-virus system ignores the virus, unless it tries to modify a program it is not related to, or the program is flagged to not allow changes. So, unless someone anticipates or spots a problem, the automatic system will run as 'normal,' and will ignore it."

He continued, "The beauty of this scheme is that no one will know the system is doing something wrong. If someone found a way to do this, it would be practically invisible the first time, and from then on it would be impossible to find, except in the software code. I don't think anyone would ever check there. At least not until it had screwed things up a number of times, or for some reason the results misaligned in some very visible way."

Grady thought about it to make sure he had a clear picture. "I think I've got it. You have anything else?"

"Not at this point," John answered.

"Any suggestions about how to determine whether this is occurring?" Grady felt that this conversation wasn't giving him a trail to follow.

"Yes. Have an expert team evaluate every program in the project for changes, particularly those interface files just outside the last firewall, and look for something similar to a virus." John directed.

"Thanks. Sounds simple, but time-consuming." Grady answered, wondering if Robert had a team ready to do this.

"Not that simple. But done right, it will appear to be. Most truly complex things are." John answered cheerfully.

"Good job, John. Pass on my thanks. I'll send the information on, and make sure we plug this hole." Grady assured him.

"Good luck. Oh...don't forget, you can't use any experts who are already inside." John reminded him.

"Why?" Grady questioned, realizing the answer even as he spoke.

"Because one or more of them may be corrupted," John told him.

"Great. Who can be used to second-guess these guys?" Grady asked, thinking out loud.

"Good question," John answered. "Good luck." He hung up.

Grady called the answering service again. This time he had his service dial the call and introduce him.

"Associate Attorney General's office. Lorraine speaking, may I help you?" Lorraine answered.

"Thirteen calling for Mr. Carlton," the woman at the service intoned.

If Lorraine was unnerved or surprised by the use of the number, or by the woman's voice, she didn't show it. She quickly put the call through to Robert as Grady thanked the service secretary, and took over the call.

Robert was on the line in a flash. "Grady! God, I was wondering if you were still with us."

"So far, so good. You might want to think about lowering your voice, instead of shouting out my name. Remember, I'm still dead as far as anyone else is concerned." Grady said wryly, trying to instill some cautionary discipline. "I have some information for you." He continued.

"I need to ask you something," Robert interrupted. "Who was in the car?"

"In the car?" Grady asked blankly.

"Fire, police and the ATF assume you died at your house, and the Secret Service is assuming you died in the car explosion on Roosevelt Island. It's only a matter of a time before they complete a check on the dental records. I need to know who was in the car," Robert explained.

"One of the guys who attacked me at the house," Grady answered. "And what's this about the ATF?"

"A fireman found parts of an incendiary grenade at your house, so now it is all about arson, murder, and explosives. The ATF has jurisdiction on explosives, and we're assuming that Homeland Security will be involved soon. So, the guy in the car—you took him with you from the house? They found the other guy in the house, or at least what was left of him. He and the house are ashes." Robert told him.

"I didn't plan to take the other guy. Actually, I didn't know he was in the car until I looked in the trunk. I guess you don't have any idea who these guys are?" Grady asked.

"That hasn't come to light. Like I said, everyone involved has a different perspective and theory, even on the simple things—like where you died. So nobody's questioned who the bodies are, yet. Different groups are both assuming they are your remains."

"And you aren't asking, either. That's probably good. A little confusion may help keep them off my trail." Grady told him.

"So, do you always keep Thermate grenades around for special occasions?" Robert asked curiously.

"Those guys brought them," Grady said. "They had the grenades ready to use when they came to see me. The one that blew up my house was their idea. I found the second one, and put it to good use."

"That makes more sense than you having them. ATF and the Fire Marshal are assuming arson as a minimum. Inventive, blowing up your own car." Robert commented, sounding a little dazed. Never would he have believed a conversation like this would sound so casual.

"Look, we've already been on the phone too long. You'd better let me get to the point." Grady proceeded to tell Robert what John had told him, as accurately as he remembered. "Some computer expert could make better practical use of that information."

"I think I've got what you're telling me straight." Robert was making notes while Grady talked. "I need to get some computer whiz to dig into this, and then we'll have that possibility covered. It will be a problem finding someone with both the expertise and security clearance to watchdog the NSA."

"You just said, 'we'll have that possibility covered.' *That possibility*? I thought this was it—the hole in the operation that we needed to plug." Grady asked, irritated.

"Well, we can't count on that being the only thing someone might try," Robert said reasonably. "It sounds like a strong conclusion, and certainly it's a logical path to follow if our problem is inside the NSA, but we're still guessing that this is where someone would strike."

"Yeah, I see what you mean." Grady felt a little deflated. He'd been so intent on getting this thing wrapped up that he'd hoped John's information would lead to an immediate conclusion.

"I wish I could say that this thing is going to be over soon, Grady." Robert sounded sincerely concerned about leaving Grady hanging. "You don't know how much I appreciate your help. I hope this is the answer, but until we know for sure, and until we find out who's behind this, we need to keep digging. I wish I could tell you to lay low, Grady, but I still need your help. Keep checking on this, and call in if anything new comes up. We still don't know why this is important enough to kill somebody. You're undoubtedly still a target. I think you had the right idea about getting out of town. It's not feeling very safe here anymore." Robert advised him worriedly.

"Believe me, I wish you had never gotten me into this—and I'm not so sure you're safe, either. Do you know who you can actually trust?"

"I have concerns. I need to check something out, and then I'll let you know which way it leads, but don't take any calls from anyone you don't know. That includes my security detail, since you'd have no way to verify that you are hearing from verifiable agents."

"Something, or someone?" Grady sighed. "Perfect. Is someone trying to blow up *your* house?"

"I'm covered," Robert assured him. "I've got the Secret Service for roommates." Robert had just lied to Grady about being covered. Knowing that Carey had omitted information about Hunt had compromised his faith in the Secret Service.

"I'll call again later." Grady hung up the phone. He decided he would grab a much-needed nap. He still hadn't caught up on his rest, and the big lunch was making him sleepy. He drove back to the cottage. Before he fell asleep, his thoughts fell on the call with Robert, and *"the possibility"* that they would never find out who might want him dead.

Chapter 63

"Where are we?" Marty had questioned, looking around. He wanted to know if he was right about it being Terri's house before he said anything else.

"My place," Terri answered. "Come on, I want you to see it. I can make us some coffee. I think I have some Kahlua, too." She got out of the car and headed for the door. Marty could do nothing but follow. He didn't feel like saying no anyway.

The house had a wide, comfortable living room. It was well appointed, with reasonably nice furniture. Terri hung their coats in the hall closet, after they shut the door on the nighttime chill.

"Kona, or Hazelnut?" She said as she went into the kitchen.

"Both are fine." Marty tried to look at ease, leaning unsteadily against the kitchen counter. "I like your place."

"Thanks. I haven't been here long, but it's coming around." The coffee maker began making gurgling sounds. "Kahlua?"

"I better not," Marty answered unsteadily, wondering if he'd sober up enough to drive home.

"Oh, live a little!" Terri poured a small amount into each mug. "It's just for flavor. Do you want milk?" She asked as she reached for the coffeepot.

"No, thanks."

"Bailey's?"

"Definitely not." He smiled, suddenly. He felt like he was on a first date. He was enjoying the sensation.

"Go pick out a CD," Terri told him. "The stereo is in the living room."

Marty dutifully headed in to make a selection. Terri poured more Kahlua into his coffee.

He picked some light jazz CDs from the top of a stack. The stereo blasted out saxophone notes, and Marty quickly turned the volume down. Terri apparently listened to very loud music from time to time. Turning, he found her behind him with the coffee.

"Here you go, have a seat." She indicated the couch. When he had settled in, she sat cozily beside him.

The conversation died away as the warmth of the room, coffee, and soft music set in.

"I really like this music. I listen to it all the time." She said softly.

Marty would have felt his eyelids getting heavy if he hadn't been concentrating on Terri's hand casually resting on his thigh. It had been on his knee at first, but was slowly working its way up. He drained his cup. When she had asked him if he wanted more, he declined. She got up to get herself some, and took his empty cup with her. When she returned, she had poured more coffee and Kahlua in both cups, despite his protest. She settled back into the couch right next to him. She sighed quietly, and nestled against him.

"Don't you love this music? It's one of my favorites." Her hand slid up to touch where his leg and hip joined.

Marty could feel a rush run through his body. "Yes, I like this music very much," he said. He raised his arm and put it around her, surprised at how bold he was, and wondering why he felt so comfortable.

Rolling a little to her side, Terri looked up into his face. As she stretched up to place her lips on his neck, her hand ran up between his legs. He flushed from head to toe, fully aroused. The alcohol had filled him with confidence. He set down his coffee cup, and drew his free hand across her young, flat stomach. From there he moved upward to her breasts. They were firm and full. She nibbled his neck harder, her tongue sliding up to his ear, and her hand pressing into him aggressively.

"I think we should go in the bedroom." She said in a throaty voice. Marty was overwhelmed at how ready he was to be with her. They stood as one, refusing to let go of each other.

She giggled and broke the clinch. "Come on." She said with a wide, sensual smile. Taking his hand, she led him to her bedroom.

She had a four-poster bed with a sheer awning over it. She threw off the comforter and coming over to him, started unbuttoning his shirt. He did the same to her.

Her breasts hid momentarily behind the delicate white lace of her demi bra, which unfastened easily from the front. Their clothing fell to the floor as one. The dark pink nipples of her breasts accented the remnants of last summer's tan line. Marty felt no inhibition as he caressed and kissed her body. Terri didn't seem to notice or care that his body was soft and pale, as she wrestled his pants off. Soon they were both on the floor tugging playfully at each other's shoes and socks.

They rolled over the floor naked together. Marty was thoroughly aroused, and Terri seemed to know how to keep him that way, with an occasional touch, or long delicate stroke. He teased her with smooth circular motions of his fingertips. Her whole body seemed to be covered with erogenous zones, and he happily touched every part.

The pressure was too much for Marty. He fell onto her in a frenzy of sexual extravagance. Her cry of exultation followed closely behind his as he collapsed onto her, beads of sweat turning chilly in the winter-cooled air.

"God, that was great." She said.

"Pretty amazing." He murmured back.

They lay there for several minutes just feeling each other inside and out. The exertion and booze were taking its toll. Marty's eyes were dipping lower and lower.

"Oh no, you don't." Terri gleefully chided him. "I'm not done with you, yet."

"I'm not falling asleep." Marty insisted, trying to reawaken himself.

"No, and you're not going to." Terri rolled him off her. "Go start the shower, I'll be right in. I'm in the mood to feel slippery." She giggled as she headed out of the bedroom almost skipping toward the kitchen.

Marty smiled at her departing naked backside, then hopped into the adjoining bathroom, and turned on the hot water. He hadn't felt this good in a long time. Terri ran into the kitchen and unlocked the backdoor. Coming back into the bedroom she heard Marty ask, "Are you coming in?"

"I'll be right there. Go ahead and get in." She called back.

She reached into her nightstand drawer and pulled out a black object. When she heard the shower door close she went in. Marty was turning in circles under the water.

"Hi." He said when he saw her naked form through the mottled translucent glass. "Come on in! The water's great."

She reached her hand forward and opened the shower door a few inches. Throwing the switch on the electric stun gun in her hand, she tossed it into the shower.

The high current battery discharged completely, as the water formed a conductor over Marty's body. Marty convulsed, falling down into the basin, his arms and legs flailing with the massive electric shock. The gun had been modified to discharge high amperage as well as volts.

When she could tell the battery was dead and the sparks finished, Terri reached into the shower and turned off the water. Marty lay crumpled in the bottom. His breathing was raspy, and getting shallower by the moment. He jerked a couple of times, then fell silent.

Two men stood in the doorway behind her.

"He's dead?"

"Yes," she said as she grabbed a towel and wrapped it around herself. She reached forward and checked for a pulse in his neck. "Yes, he's dead. Take him out. I'll be along in a minute."

The men dumped him in the trunk of their car along with his clothes. One of the two men checked to make sure Marty was definitely dead, callously jabbing a small knife blade into the meat of his leg. Marty made no move. Only a single half-drop of blood formed. Convinced, the man slammed the trunk shut.

Terri came out, dressed as she had been before. One of the men went toward Marty's car and got in the driver's seat. Terri got in with him, and both cars drove away, in opposite directions.

Pulling into the NSA parking lot, the man let Terri out near the front lobby just like Marty had done before, then drove away. Terri went inside, used the bathroom, then went to her car and drove home. Once there, she cleaned up, and climbed into bed. She fell asleep with a satisfied smile.

Chapter 64

Grady had failed to get the nap he wanted, and needed. He hadn't been able to sleep, resorting to flipping channels on the television. He felt stiff. No pillow position seemed comfortable. Eventually he got up to do some stretching.

The weather had settled back to gray and miserable. The forecast refused to change no matter how many times he flipped past the weather channel. When dusk finally arrived, he decided it was time to seek out dinner.

As he drove out of the B&B driveway, a man in a nondescript white rental car watched him make the turn and head for town. The man followed.

Grady was looking for a place where he could hide in the crowd. Going straight to an après-ski tavern and grill, he parked across the street, walking over to the restaurant. The tables were jam packed with skiers laughing about the day's escapades, but there was room at the bar. That suited him fine. He sat on a stool far around the corner of the bar, facing the door, and ordered an amber ale.

The place continued to fill. He had been there for several minutes, and was thinking of ordering a rib-eye to eat at the bar when an eye-catching woman walked in. She was about five-foot eight, standing on her calf-high boot heels. She had a magnificent figure of curves. Her full shapely hips rose to a small waist, shown off by a tight waistband and short jacket. Her tapered legs looked strong and athletic. Her black stirrup pants were tucked inside the fur-trimmed boots. There was a noticeable dip in the bar's noise level as male attention re-focused on her. She stood on display in the entry for a moment, surveying the room with bright energetic eyes. The hostess came up and took her name for a table, then pointed to the bar, presumably offering her a place to wait.

Her bright green eyes looked straight through the bar patrons. Grady noticed that her tight après ski gear and light jacket were only warm enough for going around town. The jacket's accents of gold and dark red caught the lights in metallic brilliance.

Grady counted himself lucky to have a seat where he could look at her without being conspicuous. Another guy down the bar was almost drooling onto his shirt, staring at the woman. She had no trouble getting the bartender's attention, ordering a Cosmopolitan. Two guys stood, offering her their seats, and she reluctantly accepted. She smoothly placed her jacket on the tall stool back, revealing a matching gold and red accented turtleneck that hugged her form nicely. Her hair caught the light, showing glinting gold and red highlights running through satiny dark brown waves. Both men hovered behind the vacated seat next to her. Grady could hear their casual conversation, as the men tried to strike up a connection with the woman.

"Did you come up for the skiing?" The taller of the two queried.

"Yes. How is the snow?" She wasn't showing any particular interest in the two men, just being polite, but everyone noticed her engaging smile. Her voice was easy to listen to.

"It's excellent!" Chimed in the second man. "Have you skied here before?"

"Yes, I have. This is my favorite resort." Her eyes continued to survey the room, the people, décor, and the food coming out of the kitchen. Neither of the two suitors noticed her lack of interest in them.

Grady kept watching the exchange, amused by the men's attempts. She was sitting six chairs down from him. She certainly was sparking his imagination, as appeared to be the case with most of the men around her. He found himself enjoying the scene.

She talked to her admirers, which now included the bartender, and two newcomers who had boldly taken up positions near her. She declined all offers of drinks, or dinner, and maneuvered gracefully through the onslaught of one-liners, innuendos, and ice-breaking jokes. One by one, the men admitted defeat. They disengaged, started talking to each other as before, but hung around the general area, hoping for a second chance. The original two continued their attempts to engage her.

Grady ordered a second ale, content to view the show. He had to admit she was worth watching. Her skill with the circling men drew him in. She was a warrior, parrying and thrusting, defeating each maneuver, but remaining desirable. She was clearly enjoying herself. Grady liked those qualities more than anything in a woman.

Grady was caught by surprise and slightly embarrassed when her green eyes suddenly met his, and locked in place. He didn't look away, though, and this made her gaze more intense. Her smile brightened slightly. The room felt suddenly warmer to him.

Still looking directly into his eyes, she said, "Hello." The natural shade of her shining lips was captivating when she moved her mouth.

Grady saw the word more than heard it. The room had become noisier, so he could no longer discern most of what was being said near her, but anyone could have deciphered the movement of her lips. He said, "Hello," back, slightly nodding his head. The eye contact broke as the hostess approached and indicated that her table was ready.

The guys at the bar put up some minor show of disappointment as she rose from the stool, cordially thanking them for lending her a seat. Their loss became absolute as she moved away from them and down the bar. Rather than following the hostess directly, she stopped next to Grady. Leaning over, she looked directly into his eyes.

"I have a table, and I hate to eat alone. Would you like to join me?" She asked.

Grady found he was nodding up and down like a toy dog in the back of '67 Chevy.

Grady tended to approach women with chivalry. He'd never been much of a wolf. He was aggressive enough when a woman was interested, but until then he always let the girl set the pace. This girl had surprised him. He tried his best to look calm as he followed her to her table. The walk was just long enough for Grady to regain his composure. She paused, allowing him to pull out her chair.

He forced his voice to sound casual, as he made the movement and deftly slid the chair back. "May I?"

"Thank you." She smiled and sat down as Grady slid the chair forward, seating her.

"My name is Grady," he offered, attempting some normal conversation while he sat in the chair across from her.

"Melanie." She responded brightly and easily. She offered her hand, which Grady accepted in a firm handshake. "Are you here to ski?"

"Usually, but not this trip." Grady rolled out his napkin and utensils. "This was kind of an impromptu getaway." She hadn't mentioned his face, but he'd seen her eyes taking in his bruises. "I had a little car accident, and decided to take some time off to recuperate."

"That's a shame," she said languidly. "It would be a shame to miss out on some skiing. The rumor is that there'll be fresh snow in the morning." Her smile poured over him.

Their conversation flowed steadily, and Grady gradually became more relaxed with her natural beauty. She had everything: face, body, hair, eyes, smile, and brains. She was marvelously conversational, fun and high energy. They laughed over dinner as if they had been friends for years. She seemed genuinely attracted to him, rather than having chosen him as a 'safe' dinner companion to keep the vultures at bay. He felt welcome.

They talked about everything and nothing. Mostly they talked about skiing. Grady was an excellent skier, comfortable on any slope. Apparently she was quite proficient as well, and before long she had convinced him to go skiing with her the next morning. Grady rationalized that there was little he could occupy himself with at the cottage, other than a few phone calls. He'd have to buy some ski clothes, but that seemed easy enough. Something about almost getting blown up made him feel that life was too short to miss an opportunity with this kind of companionship.

Their conversation continued until nine-thirty, when she adroitly let the conversation lull. She told Grady it was time for her to get some rest if they were going to hit the slopes in the morning. They argued briefly about the check, but finally agreed to split the bill. Grady offered to escort her to her car, and she accepted.

It wasn't far. She remotely beeped the door locks open. Turning, she said, "Eight-thirty at the Peak double-chair?" She reached out as if to shake hands, but grasped both his forearms instead. With a light pull, she drew him a little closer. It wasn't suggestive, but her soft lips on his cheek made the moment seem intimate.

The smell of her hair lingered in the air as Grady watched her tail lights reflecting off the slick spots on the icy road. His heart was beating a little harder as he walked toward his car.

The nondescript white rental car sat nearby. The man inside watched as Grady finally made his way to his vehicle. He could see Grady was enticed by the girl, exactly as planned. He cracked a grim smile.

Chapter 65

Fearful of every sound she heard, Christen had spent the day cowering on the couch. The meals came on schedule. Each time Mary would say a single word, "Eat," and Christen would dutifully force the food down, then return to her place. She sat with her knees up, both arms wrapped around them, and her right arm pressed against the side of the couch. Her eyes held a fixed, hollow gaze on the opening to the kitchen. Her deep eye sockets showed yellowish purple bruises, trimmed by black blood crusted through the center of her cuts. Her hair was in disarray. She had been going through the motions of surviving, breathing in and out. She only moved occasionally to the bathroom. Then an idea had come to her and with fanatical concentration, she could think of nothing else.

When dinner arrived, Christen ate as fast as she could, wolfing down every scrap. She took great care to make no sound as she pushed the food down. Rising silently, she went into the bathroom. She was only gone for a few seconds. Slinking back to the couch, Christen waited.

In the other room, the cell phone rang. Christen could hear Mary answer it. Her voice was muffled and unintelligible.

Mary held the phone close to her ear and cupped her hand over the mouthpiece so Christen couldn't overhear. The voice on the other end was deep and emotionless.

"Mary?"

"Yes."

"The schedule has been moved up. Removal will be necessary."

"Removal?" She confirmed.

"Yes." The man said. "Removal."

"Understood." Mary hit the end button, and set the telephone down. She had a strange smile on her lips. Christen heard the back door open. She could feel cold air rolling in across the floor from the open door, but couldn't hear or see what Mary was doing. Christen wondered what was going on, but did not move as she gripped her plan with crazed determination.

Mary went back and forth outside twice, carrying in four large metal gas cans. She set them on the floor in the kitchen with a dull metal on wood sound. Unscrewing each of the lids, she jostled the cans, sloshing the gas to see the level inside. Satisfied, she set the lids down over the openings, then headed for the living room.

Christen sat in her huddled position as Mary appeared in the doorway. The bright lights from the kitchen behind Mary silhouetted her body as she moved forward to the empty food containers. Christen's grip tightened around the towel bar from the bathroom. She held it in her right hand, tucked between the seat cushion and arm of the couch.

The cheap towel bar had been easy to remove from its mounts. Its tubular shape ended in rough, sharp ends. As Mary bent over to grab and move the tray, Christen made a small helpless sound. Mary instinctively looked up, leaning closer, a sour look forming across her face.

At that moment, Christen lurched forward, the silver tube flashing in her hand as she jabbed it like an extension of her thumb, directly into Mary's eye.

Screaming and clutching her face, Mary crashed backward to get away from the assault. Blood streamed from her mangled eyelid and brutally lacerated socket. As she rushed backward, Christen charged forward, bent on finishing her foe. Mary's arm came up to protect her face as she fell back over the television stand, bashing her head on the corner of the doorway. She fell unconscious, slumping to the floor, her hand falling away to reveal the carnage Christen had wrought.

Christen dropped the metal tube and began tugging frantically at her chain. She had no plan for getting it off, she only knew she had to fight back. The chain was attached solidly to the frame of the couch. She rummaged through Mary's pockets for the key and found nothing. Spinning around, Christen looked through the doorway into the kitchen.

She ran back to the couch and tugged at it with all her strength. It moved with each convulsive heave until the leg ran up against Mary's stomach and could go no further. Christen yanked and pushed at it, but Mary's body still blocked the way.

Running to the full length of the chain, Christen frantically opened cabinets and pulled out drawers, throwing their contents over the floor. She had emptied them all except the last drawer and cabinet, which she couldn't quite reach. Still there was no key.

Crying, she yanked viciously at the chain, the skin around her wrist tore away, making her scream as the blood began trickling down her fingers. She pushed the couch back from Mary's limp body, yanking her by her arm, and dragging her heavy weight into the kitchen. Her body now out of the way, Christen, gasping from the exertion, went back to the far end of the couch. She put everything she had left into pushing it, and rammed it half into the kitchen doorway.

Jumping over the couch she reached the final drawer. She spotted an old manual can opener with straight metal handle. Grabbing the chain she realized that the links were large, and not welded. She pulled the can opener out, and wedged the handle into one of the links, but could get no leverage. It twisted away again, and again. Spotting the heavy gas cans, she pulled the nearest one to her and tried to wedge the can opener handle and chain against the gas can handle. It seemed like it might work, but she lost her grasp and the can fell over. The lid fell away, sending gas gushing across the floor.

Fumbling with the awkward can, she finally lifted it back up. Most of the fuel had emptied out. Again she jammed the opener handle into the link and pried at it.

Mary suddenly made a gruesome sound, almost a gurgling as her arm moved across her chest. Christen's eyes flashed toward Mary's body. Her mind raced as she frantically looked around the room for a weapon.

As Mary's eyes began to open, Christen brought the metal gas can over her shoulder with every ounce of her strength and crashed it down hard on Mary's skull. The hideous sound of crushing bone and exhausting lungs echoed in the room.

Christen turned back to the chain, jamming the can opener into the handle of a full gas can. She frantically twisted the link. One fraction of an inch at a time, the link spread. She tried to feed the other link through it and failed. She twisted it again, and screamed with the exertion. The can opener slipped again, slicing her finger, but the link had opened just enough. She fought with the bent link, and pulled it free from the chain.

The blood stained handcuff dangled impotently from her wrist as she ran across the house to burst out the front door into the cold dark night. Inside the gas had flowed across the floor, its acrid fumes rolling toward the hot water heater, the propane pilot light softly hissing. When the fumes reached the pilot light they burst into flames, rushing back along the floor toward the overturned can. The vapors trapped in the can exploded, knocking the other cans over. Christen, standing just in front of the open door, was pushed to the ground in the frozen snow.

Scrambling away on her hands and knees, she had reached some small leafless scrub brush next to the fence when the remaining cans blasted the back half of the cabin into fragments. Flames erupted over the whole structure. She sat on the icy ground, sobbing, as the flames grew higher. She almost stood up at the sight of headlights coming down the long drive toward the house. Gathering her wits just in time, she shrank back behind the tiny bush. In daylight she would have been easily spotted, but the glare of the headlights, flames from the burning cabin, and flashing brilliance of the snow made her appear as a dark smudge on the landscape. The car pulled up as close as it could, the front tires crossing her path of footprints from the front door. The driver swung the car back and forth, using its headlights to pan the building. The tires obliterated Christen's tracks. She shrank into the snow behind the bush as deeply as she could to hide from the bright red and white taillights. The flames from the building were rapidly engulfing it. It would be burned to the ground in minutes. The driver walked once around the house, waited for a moment, then got back into the car, speeding away.

Christen was too frightened, hurt, and cold to cry. She pulled herself onto her feet and began trudging through the snow toward a distant light in the opposite direction of the road.

Chapter 66

Sitting in his car at the light as they approached the Four Seasons Hotel, Hunt laid out instructions again for Carol.

"I get it! Okay?" She was understandably frustrated. This would be the end of a long and profitable relationship for her, but she had no choice. When they pulled up to the valet, Carol opened the car door and got out. Heads turned as she entered the lobby. She was used to it, and ignored the stares. Silky blonde hair, expertly cut and styled, covered her head and shoulders. Her fur coat wafted from side to side as she walked, exposing a long, black, designer dress, which appeared to have been made just for her body. A slit ran up the front between her smooth legs, and the neckline dipped to her substantial cleavage. She had a walk that drew men's eyes. She looked stylish, sexy, alluring, and more than anything, expensive.

As she entered, the bellman discreetly handed her an electronic key card. Behind her, at a distance, came Hunt. He had taken care of the car and valet, but he didn't want anyone to notice him following the girl. He lagged behind her, but arrived in time to get into her elevator.

The key unlocked the floor. When they arrived, Hunt let Carol go into the hall first. The suites on this floor catered to the elite, and it was possible that someone would have security standing outside their door. Hunt was lucky; that didn't appear to be the case this evening. He followed Carol to Senator Farrell's sumptuous suite.

Opening the door, Carol could see that room service had set up a tray in the living area. Champagne stood in a silver bucket, and Strawberries Romanov adorned a china platter. She left the door ajar, and headed into the bedroom. Hunt entered the room behind her.

Senator Farrell had arrived much earlier, and was relaxing in the spacious marble bathroom's tub.

"Carol, my beauty," he called, seeing her approach the doorway. "Why don't you relieve yourself of those clothes, and come join me."

Carol entered the bathroom. "Hello, Morgan." She smiled. Draping her fur on the makeup stool, she perched on the edge of the large tub.

"Did you bring it?" Farrell had a hungry look.

"It's right here." She patted her purse. Leaning away, she set the purse on top of the fur. "Wouldn't you like to have some champagne first?"

"It can wait. Jump in here, and bring the purse with you." He told her.

"You sure? The strawberries look terrific." She stood up to leave.

Hunt rushed through the door grabbing Carol harshly by the upper arm, forcing her down onto the hard tub edge.

"Stop squirming!" Hunt growled at Carol. ""Hello, Senator." Hunt said conversationally. Farrell made a weak attempt at rising. "You just stay right there in the tub." Hunt's gun sat comfortably in his hand, pointing at Farrell. Hunt's fingers were biting into Carol's arm, making her wince.

"What the hell are you doing here?" Farrell asked irritably, annoyance causing his voice to crack slightly.

"Now, is that any way to greet a business associate, Senator?" Hunt said with intimidating confidence. "You've been enjoying yourself," he continued with a nod toward Carol, "and it's time to pay something back. I need a little favor from you."

Farrell made a move to get out of the tub again. Hunt, still holding Carol, leaned forward and pushed Farrell back in with the point of his barrel. His grip brought a pained whimper from Carol. "Don't press your luck with me, Senator."

Farrell let out a huff of indignation. "I don't know why you think you can talk to me like this, Hunt. I don't owe you, or anyone else, anything. You should know better than to barge in here and make demands on..." he began.

"I know exactly who and what I'm dealing with, Senator." Hunt interrupted. "I think our past dealings together may have misled you about me. Let me explain the situation to you, Senator." Hunt yanked Carol off the tub edge and pushed her to the floor, her arm twisting awkwardly in his grip. Hunt was enjoying himself immensely.

Knocking Carol's purse off onto the floor with his gun, he watched Farrell's eyes followed it as it fell. "My associates and I have the ability to make you quite miserable. These little luxuries you enjoy? If you want to keep them, you're going to do a favor for us. You're going to turn Senator Daniel Gregg over to the U.S. Attorney General. Are you listening to me?"

Farrell had been distracted by Carol's purse, staring at it throughout Hunt's speech. He slowly tore his eyes away, trying to focus on what Hunt was saying.

"You will 'out' Gregg as the key man behind the attempt to sabotage and take control of the OPOV system." Hunt continued. "You will do this by handing over supporting evidence to Robert Carlton, the Associate Attorney General, when you have lunch. You'll need to move that lunch up, by the way. It'll have to be tomorrow."

"I can't do that! Gregg's..." Farrell stammered. His face flushed with a mix of anger, anxiety, and high blood pressure.

"Yes, you can. And you definitely will." Hunt interrupted. He was in control and he liked it. Pressing his foot into Carol's waist, he pinned her against the cabinet and floor. Hunt let go of her arm. "You'll give Carlton these two recordings." He pulled a memory stick and yellow envelope out of his side coat pocket and set it on the makeup counter. "If you don't, I cut off your supply permanently." Nodding in the direction of the purse, Hunt gave Carol a nudge with his foot. "Open it." He told her.

Struggling against the pressure of his foot, she leaned over, and opened the purse. She took out a vial of white powder, handing it to Hunt.

Farrell watched each movement. He mustered every ounce of confidence he had to lean casually back in the tub, suppressing his need for the powder. "You can't cut me off from anything. I can get that anywhere. You don't understand who you're tangling with."

"Really, Senator?" Hunt replied casually. "I think I know exactly who I'm 'tangling' with. I know about your oil lobbyist—the one you've been kissing up to for those fat bankrolls you've been enjoying. Believe me, I can cut you off from that, and from this type of perk." Hunt said, gesturing to the luxury suite. "And I know your fetishes, and your indulgences," Hunt said, nodding toward Carol and the vial. "I have plenty of information that will discredit you with your public, your supporters, and your family, if you want to play hardball. If you choose to cooperate, however, everything can be just like it was. Plus, we'll supply some extra benefits." Hunt was careful to keep the gun trained on Farrell. "Take a look at that envelope. Make sure you look closely." He picked up the envelope and laid it on the edge of the tub.

The first signs of nervousness crept into Farrell's expression. He took a moment to glance through the few pictures, and then read through a list of documents Hunt claimed to have. A copy of one was in the envelope. It was a damning list. Farrell knew that Hunt was serious. If any of this got out, the scandal wouldn't be survivable.

"Who's behind this?" He demanded. Farrell decided he wasn't going down unless somebody a lot bigger was pulling the strings. He knew there weren't many that fit that description, and he could influence most of them.

"Senator, you have my guarantee that this is far too big for you to fight, and those involved are too significant for me to name names," Hunt answered easily. He paused, then continued in a meaningful tone, "Believe me when I say you have no choice. If we don't have your assurance of 'support,' you'll wish you weren't walking out of here in the morning. You won't like the reception outside."

Farrell sputtered, as words failed him. His face began turning very pale.

"Nicely said," Hunt commented. "So, turn the evidence on Gregg over tomorrow at the lunch. That's all you have to do." He opened the vial and tapped out some of the powder on the counter. "I don't want you forgetting, so I'm keeping the rest of this for now." He dropped the vial into the purse. "I locked out your connections for more, so unless you want to go to the street searching for some...well, that wouldn't be very smart, would it? I'm pretty sure you'd be photographed, especially since it would be my operative doing the picture taking. I'll turn your supply back on when I hear the door slam on Gregg. Not before. Oh, and don't think you can get help from anyone without my hearing about it. Besides..." He cracked a thin-lipped grin, "I'm quite sure you don't want to talk to anyone else, do you?"

He stood up and tossed the fur to Carol who stood up slowly. "You're leaving with me." Carol looked scared. Hunt had not warned Carol about anything he'd planned to do. He'd wanted her reactions to be genuine.

"That craving you feel now will turn into the shakes once that little taste I left wears off." He told Farrell. "So, I'd get moving if I were you. We swept your house and office clean of those emergency stashes you keep around. Oh, and we got the one from your secretary's desk. Yes, I know about you taping it under her drawer. That's not very nice. What if she were to get busted in a sweep?"

Hunt turned and closed his hand around Carol's arm, leading her to the door. Putting his gun away and picking up a towel with his other hand, he threw it into the water. He looked back over his shoulder, telling Farrell, "Get out. Your romantic evening is over." Hunt left with Carol, leaving the bathroom door open.

Farrell clambered out of the water, pulling the wet towel out onto the floor. He rushed naked to the counter to inhale the small stripe of cocaine.

Driving away from the hotel, Hunt broke the silence first. "You did well. I'll drop you at another hotel. From there you can catch a cab."

"You scared me." Carol's weakened voice was barely audible.

"Yeah, well, it was important that he think you had nothing to do with it." He pulled a thick wad of money from his pocket and handed it to her.

They drove several blocks away. Arriving at a lesser hotel that had self-parking, Hunt pulled in, driving to a top-level parking spot. The lights in the corner of the garage he chose weren't working. Hunt turned off the engine, and the car lights.

"Turn around." He commanded Carol.

She was surprised, but turned her back to him compliantly, simultaneously placing the money into her purse. He pulled down the zipper of her dress. Carol flinched a little at his touch.

"There's an extra thousand there." Hunt said dryly, pulling the top of her dress forward and off her shoulders. Her fair skin looked pale in the poorly lit garage. As she reached both hands backward to unclasp her bra, Hunt pulled a garrote from between the seats. The cold wire looped around her head in one silent, quick movement. Hunt tightened and relaxed his grip a couple of times, allowing her to gasp for air repeatedly before he finished her prolonged death struggle. The confines of the car made her kicking and flailing useless. He grinned through clenched teeth as her nails bit into the backs of his hands. His head went back in a spasm of demented ecstasy.

The wire was thick enough to strangle without cutting, so there was no blood, just a deep red line of broken capillaries and damaged skin. The strangulation turned the blood vessels in her eyes brilliant red. She made no sound as her throat collapsed, and her air gave out.

Hunt didn't like loose ends. In his business, no one did.

Chapter 67

Blair followed Grady back to the bed and breakfast cottage. He kept plenty of distance between his car and Grady's, knowing where Grady was likely to be headed. He was making sure there were no surprises, and no slip-ups. He stopped along the road before reaching the B&B, where his car wouldn't draw attention. The car rapidly became an icebox as the inside temperature dipped below freezing, forcing him to periodically crank up the engine to get warm. He'd coated the windows with a thin layer of soap as an anti-fogger, allowing him a clear view.

He picked up his night vision binoculars and scanned the cottages. The area was devoid of movement. A few of the bungalows still had lights on, but most were dark. All the snow and ice would make his car noisy if he drove into the complex, and walking in made for a bad exit strategy. He'd rather get this done tonight, before he left, but that didn't look feasible. He picked up the phone.

"Hello?" The woman's voice sounded groggy.

"I need you to close out the job tomorrow." He told her.

"That soon?" She asked, sounding more alert.

"We need to finish this job. I've got more work for you to do. Do you think you can get him to the back road?"

"No problem. But short notice costs extra." She informed him.

"You're confident he'll show in the morning?" Blair wanted to be sure this got done.

"Yes. Absolutely." She affirmed.

"Then I'll arrange the car and reception." Blair thought that was at least one thing he could make sure got done.

"And my bonus?" She reminded him.

"If you get him there. The guys will take care of the rest. If for some reason they don't show, you'll have to do it. Your bonus will be five percent."

"Ten." She bargained.

"Five and you take over the watch...now. I have to head back." Blair said firmly.

"He's not going anywhere." After a pause; "Five percent." She sighed.

"The minute you hand him off, you catch a flight back. I need you on the other job right away."

"I'm at your service," she answered.

They both hung up.

Grady rose when his alarm clock chimed. He had slept soundly. A quick glance through each window verified sunny skies. After a quick shower he headed out the door. The ski shops wouldn't open for more than an hour, so he figured he'd stop for food. Turning onto the main road, Grady didn't notice the car discreetly following him.

Grady found a familiar coffee shop near a rental and clothing store, and sat back to comfortably enjoy his espresso. He ordered a ham and egg bagel.

When he saw the ski shop open up, he strolled in behind a couple of college guys. A girl at the counter set about helping the boys get boots and skis.

Grady approached the counter. A twenty-something guy behind it asked, "Looking for a rental package?"

"Do you have a set that's been recently tuned up? Fresh wax?" Grady asked directly.

"Yeah, I tune the skis. I just set up two new GS pairs, and three pairs for all-around." The guy answered comfortably.

"Excellent." Grady smiled. "I would like the all-around ones closest to 175, and a set of better quality boots. I don't know if we will be on the moguls, or in the back bowl, and I need to be able to beat my friend down the hill. I want the bindings locked down tight, and the wax brushed so it's hot on the first run. Do you know what I mean?"

The guy's interest had perked up from the moment Grady had asked about tuned skis, but now he was excited. "Cool!" He enthused. "Yeah, they're a little extra, but I think you'll like these." Walking back, he pulled a colorful pair from the hanging rack. "They're choice, if you're between a 10 or 12. I put a coat of 'White Gold' on them using a copper brush, then a nylon brush, tip to tail on each coat, and..."

"You know your stuff." Grady interrupted, laughing. "Let's say I'm an 11. And I'll need stiff, tall boots."

"I'm on it, Dude." The tech was clearly happy to be putting together something more interesting than the cheap, standard rental.

Grady went to the overpriced clothing section, and picked through the trendy gear. Fortunately, there was a partial rack from last year on sale for half-off. He found a nice jacket, a set of long underwear, gloves, and hat. His jeans would do fine in this weather. The rental paperwork needed ID, and a charge card. Grady wasn't worried about the ID; it wouldn't be broadcasted anywhere. The charge card was the problem. He'd disposed of his attacker's cards and ID, and if he used his own it would become a trail when swiped through the machine. He decided that the excuse of forgetting his card and a generous tip would get him past that hurdle. He was right. The guy tuning his demos didn't need to be asked twice. He didn't peg Grady as the type to steal the skis, and he needed the extra money. It all took a bite out of Grady's dwindling cash. He changed into the new gear at the shop, then picked up his boots and skis.

Proceeding to the ski resort, Grady rolled into the upper parking lot. With his boots finally on, and the skis balanced on his shoulder, he began his trek to the main ticket booth.

Grady deftly adapted to walking in the tall, stiff boots. He found himself enjoying the moment. The day felt fresh, and the ground was covered in bright white patches of sunlight. The chilled air super-cooled his face. He found himself anticipating a pleasant day.

Once he arrived at the ticket booth, he propped up his skis and got his ticket. With the ticket safely secured to his jacket, he snapped on his skis and skated to the Peak double. He waited, watching the path that came up from the parking area. He didn't have to wait long. Walking toward him was the most fantastic woman he could have imagined. She wore almost solid white, with a few vibrant yellow accents. Even her boots and skis were almost all white. Her hair cascaded across her shoulders, framing her face perfectly as she smiled at him.

"Good Morning, Grady!" She sounded genuinely excited to see him.

"Melanie...you look fantastic!" Grady was overcome by her appearance. She looked more beautiful than she had last night. Even in the insulated ski clothes her spectacular figure was evident. Maybe more so, with her tightly cinched waist belt emphasizing her curves. He recovered himself. "Are you ready to go?"

"Yep, my lift pass was part of my hotel package." She flipped the ticket hanging from her jacket.

"Well, let's head for the chair." Grady helped her with her skis by setting them on the snow, next to her feet. She snapped in easily and they polled the last few feet to the lift line.

"It's a perfect day. I'm glad you talked me into this." Grady felt awkward. Not with the skis, but with the woman. He looked up and around to orient himself. It really was a beautiful day, he thought, admiring the bright blue sky between the white clouds.

The sun beamed down on the snow, sending multicolored sparks of light in every direction, and glinting off Melanie's shiny hair.

"Too bad it didn't snow more. This will all be packed down on the runs in no time." Melanie added, not sounding too disappointed. "But the base looks good, and I can work on my technique for packed powder."

Grady was having a tough time concentrating on the thought of skiing. This woman had captivated him. The voice in his head was beginning to wonder what was wrong with this picture. He usually took his time with relationships, forming connections based on joint interests and conversation, holding back his smoldering passions until he felt there was more than basic physical attraction. There had been no one special in his life since his wife had passed away. Girls hit on him occasionally, but he was frequently oblivious to their charms. His friends usually ribbed him about it.

"Want to start right off, or take a warm-up run?" he asked, dragging his thoughts back to the slopes.

"Let's take a quick warm-up run, and then head up top to avoid the crowd." She responded.

"Sounds good." Grady felt more confident as they slid their skis to the chair. Out of the corner of his eye, he caught the leering gazes other guys were giving Melanie. He had to admit it felt good.

They ended up taking their warm-up run on an intermediate blue named "Duster." Melanie was a good skier, but didn't seem quite as experienced as Grady. She almost lost her balance once, but recovered well. They ran alongside each other, almost matching turn for turn each other's movements on the wide, smooth slopes. The fresh show had indeed been packed down, and the groomed run had lost its moguls.

Stopping while they were still above several lifts, Grady asked, "Ready to try something tougher?"

"Sure." Melanie pulled out her ski run map, and they picked an expert slope up top.

They were almost level with the Vortex lift, so they skied over and took it to the top. From there they skied over to the right, and then came to a stop. Pulling out her map again, Melanie confirmed that they should run across the ridge past the two double-diamonds until they reached the single-diamond slope called "Twister." They both slid forward so they could look over the side of the mountain. This was the starting point of one of the double diamonds, as it ran under the lift.

"Whoa, I don't think I'm ready for that, just yet." Melanie said with a grin as she looked over the precipice.

Grady was glad she felt that way. He was a good skier, but the mountain seemed to drop away like a cliff, and he was still a little stiff. The snow was crusty and chopped up from skiers, with little new snow. It looked like a difficult run even with perfect snow, but the crusty stuff could catch a tip. Grady didn't want to finish the rest of the trip on his backside, or on his recovering face.

"Yeah, looks like a lot of crust, and chop underneath. Maybe after the sun softens it up it'll look better." Grady offered. He wasn't sure it would, but he wanted to sound optimistic.

"Maybe," Melanie responded, but not very enthusiastically.

They slid back from the edge, and Melanie called out, "Last one to the run buys lunch!" She pushed away down the ridge.

Grady jammed his poles into the snow and sped after her. He was gaining rapidly as they reached the top of the second double-diamond. It looked just as bad as the first, but Grady was concentrating on catching Melanie. The run was still in shadow and full of early morning frozen ruts. His skis were bouncing around wildly. They had picked up a reckless amount of speed, and there were no good places to stop without crashing.

"Wheee!" She cried as she bent her knees to absorb a bump, and launched off the ground from the other side.

Grady had come up beside her and was about to pass. The exhilaration ran through him as the icy wind blasted his face. Just as they approached the trees marking the far edge of the double-diamond run, Melanie abruptly stood up from her crouch and slammed into Grady's shoulder. The sudden move knocked him off balance, and he careened over the edge into the crusty snow. The slope was terrifyingly steep. His speed shot up. Clumps of ice bashed into his skis. It was all he could do to stay standing. He should have fallen, but he didn't, obstinately trying to pull out. His path took him directly through the slope they wanted and into the trees, as he rapidly traversed across the run. He frantically tried to keep from splitting his legs around scrub brush as the cleared slope ended, and trees began. As they got thicker, the snow became softer and deeper. Grady's speed slowed rapidly.

Grady was worrying about a hidden root catching him under the powder when a limb caught his right pole, yanking his arm backward. He spun completely around and into a small pine, ice crystals flying around him as branches dumped their snow. He fell away from the tree, dazed. Both skis released and were gone, hidden under the surface powder. One of his legs was jammed into the snow, and his arms were flared out. He lay silently for a moment, staring up at the tree.

Reaching a hand to his head he quietly said, "Ow". Apparently he'd hit his head on something, but his hat had stayed on. Rising up on one elbow to a sitting position, he found one leg was trapped, and buried beneath him.

He had not seen Melanie as she calmly skied through the trees behind him. She had followed at a smooth, controlled speed, and was handling the slope like a ski patroller. Sliding up behind him, she said. "I'm so sorry! Are you all right?"

"Man, what a crash." Grady groaned back.

Melanie quickly looked around. They were deep in the trees, completely hidden.

"Here let me help you." She was uphill and behind him, her skis and feet planted sideways to his back. Bending way over, she grabbed under his arms and together they struggled until he regained his feet, or at least got them evenly under him as his boots repeatedly sank in the snow.

It was quite a process getting his skis back on, but eventually he was able to traverse thru the trees to an open space. Looking up, he saw clearly that it wasn't a good direction to ski, but the distance and steep drop made sidestepping back up the hill a ridiculous idea. They both looked across and down, but only saw more trees.

"Well," Grady said after a minute or two, "looks like there's not much choice. It's across, or down. Down doesn't look too good."

Melanie pulled out the map. They may have run half the length of 'Twister', but it was hard to tell. "We aren't on the map anymore." She smiled and laughed at the idea. "Seriously, this isn't a run, but I know people take it all the time to get untracked powder over the ridge." She ran her finger along a valley in the picture. "I think if we go along here," she continued, "we'll come out near the ski-in lodges, and we can traverse back to the lifts, or catch the lodge bus."

"I think you're right." Grady sounded confident, but he wondered whether she was right. "Don't they have a rope-tow down there?"

"Yes, I think they do." She was pointing to a spot further down the mountain. "Let's go that way."

"You lead. I haven't been down this side." Grady poled forward to give her an open path so she could maneuver, and get them started down the hill.

Melanie picked a traverse path going gently down through the trees. It looked like a deer trail. The branches and limbs seldom crossed, and were small and flexible. They slid a little as they knocked twigs out of their way with their polls.

After a short distance the slope of the hillside relaxed, and the trail headed downhill, allowing them to stop polling and pick up a little speed from gravity. The trees thinned into fewer and fewer clumps. Grady started having fun again, and Melanie was laughing.

They both celebrated little bumps and turns on the makeshift path. A couple of times he had to edge out of her tracks to avoid running into her from behind, while she broke the trail. Before long they were rushing along the side of the valley on the backside of the ridge, headed away from the resort.

Below them was a snow-covered stream. Occasional spots of water appeared where the water was too wide, or too fast for the snow to completely cover it. Melanie spotted what looked like a hiker's bridge. She turned abruptly, and raced across it, the tips of her skis leaving the snow as she came off the other side.

Grady followed with a little more speed that made the lift at the end exciting. His extra speed sent him into a drift and stopped him instantly. Melanie didn't notice. She was swiftly skiing down the trail.

Pushing back with his polls, Grady stomped around to get his skis back in Melanie's tracks. He pushed hard on the poles to get some speed to catch up, and slid after her, following her trail.

Every now and then he caught a glimpse of her through the trees, but the terrain and soft snow kept him from gaining much ground. Gradually the valley became steeper again, and he had to concentrate to avoid catching an edge or snagging a tree. His breath began to wheeze with the exertion. The burn in his thighs was growing, and each new bump made his legs weaker. When he suddenly burst through the scrub oak on the edge of the road he found Melanie standing almost across his path.

Making a hard left to avoid her, the change from soft to hard pack and the burning in his legs turned a sloppy stop into a spinout crash. He half fell, half slid to a crunching, twisting stop, ending up on his back at the side of the road. Grady's skis had rattled across some gravel on the exposed blacktop where the sun melted the snow. With his polls crossed, skis at odd angles, sunglasses crooked, and panting for air, Grady looked up from the ground to find two men standing over him with guns drawn.

"Good morning, Colonel." One of them said.

Chapter 68

Christen sat with her arms protectively crossed on the heavily worn office chair. Her eyes were looking down at the old green cushion, and the chipped paint of the metal legs resting on faded commercial linoleum tiles. Across the gray metal table from her sat a female deputy, and the Sheriff of Summit County, Utah.

The Sheriff had been the first one to arrive at the Harris' farm. It had been a few minutes past midnight when the call had come in. Christen had been unable to speak at first, but Frank Harris knew a crime when he saw it. Mrs. Harris had been trying to get Christen to drink some hot chocolate while he called the police.

The first faltering words from Christen sent Frank to the upstairs window at the side of the house. From there he could clearly see the flames in the distance. There would be nothing to save, but he called the fire department anyway.

By the time the Sheriff arrived Christen had stopped shaking, but the story of her ordeal came out stuttering and disjointed. They had to keep going over the events of the past week with her to get it straight. Now she sat in the interrogation room, exhausted. Warmer clothes, heavy socks, soft snow boots, and new bandages from the EMT had helped clear her mind. The cold deep in her body was fading. Breakfast had helped.

The deputy at the front desk had already called the University dormitory, and was now on the phone with the police near Marty's house. Christen's file was thickening rapidly. The Sheriff ran a tight ship. Usually his cases were simple to unravel. This was the biggest crime he'd dealt with in years.

"So, you can't remember any names besides 'Mary?'" He had been methodically retracing every part of her statement for what seemed like hours to Christen.

"No, Sir." She said again.

"What else can you recall? Was there anything unusual in the last few weeks at school? Any new people on your floor, or in your classes? Maybe a new teacher?" He probed.

"No, Sir. I can't remember anything that was different. I was just sitting there. I've told you everything." Christen was swaying a little in the chair. It was clear she needed to sleep. The Sheriff finally relented.

"Okay, Christen. If anything comes to mind, I want you to tell us right away. Officer Morgan is going to take you to a nice safe cell, so you can lie down and rest while we take care of some things. If there is anything you need, just ask, but I want you to relax—take a nap if you can. You've been a brave girl, and you're safe now. Give sleep a try."

They all stood up. The female officer gently took Christen's arm, leading her out through the desk area. Mr. and Mrs. Harris were sitting on the lobby benches, and saw Christen go by.

"Is she going to be all right?" Mrs. Harris worriedly asked the Sheriff as he came over to them.

"She'll be fine, now. We've got your statements, so you two can go home. We'll call you if a question comes up. Thank you for all your help."

Christen had heard them and looked back, smiling weakly, and mouthing the words, "Thank you" to the couple.

They waved to her, and left after Christen disappeared down the hall.

Christen laid down on the bunk. She fell asleep before the deputy quietly closed the door.

Chapter 69

Grady lay on the hard-packed side of the road. He lifted himself up, using his elbow, and looked into the muzzle of a Sig forty-caliber. Melanie shuffled over, still on her skis, catching his attention.

Grady was twisted away from her, but looking back over his shoulder he saw her smile at him.

"It was fun. Sorry we didn't get a few more runs in." Her smile was a cross between genuine regret and sly victory. It even contained a little attraction.

"Thanks for the lesson. Would you consider best two out of three?" Grady gibed.

Melanie shrugged her shoulders a little as her green eyes narrowed.

"It's really too bad. I would rather have taken my time." She turned and pushed away, running her skis along the road toward the lodges. She disappeared quickly around the bend of the curving mountain lane.

Grady watched her ski away, then turned back to the pistol.

"Can I help you gentlemen?" He asked conversationally.

"Let's start with you getting up." One of the men said. The second man started walking toward a car parked up the road, almost out of sight.

Motioning with the tip of the gun barrel, Grady's captor indicated his interest in seeing Grady stand. Visibly struggling, Grady pushed up to a sitting position, then to a deep crouch, so he could prop himself up to a standing position with his pole.

With both hands on one pole Grady started to get up. The gunman watching him didn't notice the angle of the second pole as it rose up from the ground. It appeared that Grady was suffering a normal skier's struggle to stand until the moment the rising pole tip jabbed viciously at the gunman's face. Grady's desperation and full weight heaved into the pole. The metal tip penetrated deep into the gunman's upper lip, ricocheting off his teeth, upper jaw, and the bones below his nose. The force of the thrust continued pushing the sharp point until it tore through the soft nasal cavity, and only stopped as the basket prevented the spike from traveling to the gunman's eye.

His head snapped backward, blood gushing over his face and pouring down his throat, choking off his voice. Frantically trying to grab the pole and pull it out of his face, he flailed and fell backwards, dropping his gun. Falling on his back, he thrashed against the pain and embedded ski pole.

Grady let go of the pole, pushing hard with his remaining pole and on the opposite ski. The skating action propelled him across the small road into the trees covering the steep slope on the other side. He was completely off balance, trying to bring his skis back together.

The gunman at the car looked up in time to see his partner go down, and Grady skiing toward the tree cover. He pulled out his pistol to fire, but only got two shots off before Grady was deep into the trees. Running toward the trees he saw Grady go straight down, then sharply to the right on the steep, forest covered hillside. He fired until his clip ran empty. Grady's angle and erratic movements through the thick trees blocked his shots. He was an impossible target. Each bullet missed, hitting branches, snow, and rocks.

All of Grady's concentration was focused on surviving. He rapidly accelerated directly into the forest. Miraculously, he kept finding enough room to squeeze through the tightly growing trees. He broke branches with both sides of his body, and lost his pole after snagging a tree. His hat had been torn off. Blocking limbs from his face with his arms, he tore long rents in his jacket sleeves. His jeans snagged on twigs flashing by.

When he reached the bottom of the narrow valley, the tips of his skis dove directly into the rocks of a small stream, and he fell headfirst into the bank on the other side. The snow broke his fall. He'd missed a rock by inches. He got to his feet, fumbling frantically with one ski to snap on the released binding. He pulled hard on a branch to start moving again, and continued skiing along the stream edge. No shots rang out behind him, but he wondered if his breath, coming in haggard gasps, and pounding heart were blocking outside sounds.

As he grappled with the terrain and trees, Grady fought his way downhill, and away from where he thought the road existed. Emerging into the open, he was relieved to see the resort downhill from him. He pointed his skis to go as fast as he could handle to the crowded area.

Grady's wild entrance caught the attention of many skiers standing nearby. His aching legs could no longer hold him up as he slid, half-crashed into a standing rack of skis.

As quickly as his throbbing, exhausted muscles could handle, he popped loose his bindings, and stood the rental skis in the rack. He stumbled awkwardly into the lodge. Finding a bench, he pulled off his ski boots and left them. Walking down the hall in his socks, he realized that his torn clothes didn't fit in with the casual hotel guests. He took off the jacket, and entered the lodge's clothing and ski gear shop. He bought a white turtleneck shirt, a plain lightweight black parka, black gloves, black running shoes, and black jeans. Changing in the nearby restroom, he stuffed his ski clothes into a large trashcan, and headed for the most expensive restaurant in town.

From a distance Grady observed the restaurant entry and parking valet. When it neared prime time for lunch, he walked up to the entrance just as the attendant drove away to park a car. Stepping up to the valet stand, he graciously accepted a restaurant patron's car keys, handing the owner one of the paper claim numbers sitting on the stand. He drove off in the patron's silver SUV. In an hour he would be in Massachusetts.

Chapter 70

Hunt joined the Saturday workaholics arriving at Justice. Security glanced at his pass, and accepted it without a second glance. Practice and skill made it appear that he had a key when he easily picked the lock on Robert's main office door.

Sitting in Robert's chair, Hunt placed an envelope on the center of the desk. He casually pushed everything away to clear a large round space, making the bright envelope more obvious. He leaned back, studying the effect. This sort of operation felt good. Just like old times. A corner of his mouth rose in a half grin, as he slowly snuffed out his burning cigar in the leather of Robert's chair arm.

He decided it was time for breakfast. Hunt rose, leaving a curl of smoke wafting through the room. Passing a few people on his way out, he thought about the perfect place for steak, eggs, and a great cup of coffee.

Robert's phone lay silent. Friday had been quiet. Too quiet, Robert thought, but it had given him the time he needed to get thinking clearly again. With each tick of his watch, he knew the plans to compromise OPOV were moving forward. He was no closer to stopping them. Until he figured out how to put the brakes on all of this Grady would be on the run, and his life with Tracie and the boys would be unsettled. "Unsettled...that's an understated way of putting it," he thought.

He wanted to make sense of things. He sat at the desk in his home study, trying to untangle his notes. He had to figure out some new angle, or a line of questioning that would lead to an answer. His jaw was cramped from clenching his teeth, his head hurt, and his neck was painfully stiff.

He had spent most of Friday's evening hours going over his files and notes, trying to see a connection or pattern that would lead to the answers he needed. Who would willingly commit murder to remove his former boss, Brady? Who would then have Chris killed, and try to get rid of Grady?

Robert couldn't fathom how any acquisition of power could make murder justifiable. Logic demanded there be more motivation, and yet the same facts and conclusions existed when he reviewed his notes.

Robert forced himself to think outside his comfort zone. He knew that people would often commit heinous acts based on three criteria: first, the belief that they needed something; second, having opportunity present itself; and third, their belief that the odds of getting caught were negligible. Desire, greed, and envy were strong, but often uncontrollable human emotions. The idea of "need" was sometimes based on a skewed or sociopathic impression. If "need" existed, opportunity could be created, but it generally took an impression of power to be sure that an individual wouldn't be caught.

He slapped his pen down on the desk in disgust. This analysis wasn't getting him anywhere. He wanted to slam his fist down on the hard wood, but that would only give him sore knuckles to add to his list of frustrations.

Reining in his irritation, Robert tried to think. He had to think. The vote was scheduled for Tuesday. He kept telling himself that if something went wrong, the resulting vote wouldn't create a crisis. He was still convinced that the infiltration was either to discredit the President and his Administration, or that the first use was simply a test, in preparation for distorting the outcome of a bigger voting issue. The first vote was unimportant, but any failure would undermine public confidence in OPOV—if the failure became public information. If it didn't reach the public's ears, then the whole operation would be kept running in secret. It would be ready to use for some other purpose. That was a much bigger concern.

Robert had too many problems. He had no direct evidence of an infiltration, he had no evidentiary link between the murders and Grady's attack, and he had too many people expecting quick results for what still was labeled an "unofficial" investigation. The President and his father were his biggest problems. He had to deliver if he didn't want to see his career go down the drain.

Tracie called at six that evening. The kids were fine. She had no intention of coming back, and she didn't want to talk about it to Robert. The call was short. Robert had expected her to be nurturing anger all day. He figured she'd be ready to unload on him, but she hadn't, which left him even more annoyed. She had gone into deep-freeze mode. He knew her cold demeanor could last for months.

Robert's empty frozen food boxes were stacking up in the garbage three at a time. The agents had offered to bring in food, but defrosting frozen was the easiest option. He suddenly felt suffocated at home. He thought about going into the office, but there was nothing productive he could accomplish there—especially on the weekend. He paced back and forth by his desk, in the hall, and on the back patio, but it was too cold for his thoughts to process. He soon returned to the study.

Agent Carey stood nearby. He had shown up for the day shift, commenting that Peter wasn't feeling well. Robert kept glancing toward Carey, wondering what his role was in all of this, and why he was covering for Hunt.

Robert wanted to interrogate Carey, but instead he watched and waited for Carey to show his hand. Carey remained enigmatic. He was distant, even disinterested.

When the night shift came on, Carey left without a word. Robert spent the night in and out of sleep, tossing in bed.

With the Saturday morning shift change, Carey was back. When Robert asked about Agent Karelonski, Carey said he assumed that Peter was still sick. Robert watched as Carey and the other agent, John, walked through the house checking every nook and cranny. That action was repeated with every shift change.

When the phone rang Carey was standing just outside Robert's study. Robert read the cell phone display. The caller ID showed "Blocked." Robert hesitated; normally he would avoid unidentified callers. Then he remembered Grady and grabbed the receiver.

"Yes?" He said quickly.

"Mr. Carlton, I'm glad I caught you." Senator Farrell's somewhat strained sounding voice answered. "I need to talk with you. I'd like you to meet me for lunch today, instead of Monday."

Robert was a little stunned. Farrell? Calling him on a Saturday to meet for lunch? Whatever the Senator wanted couldn't be good. "Senator, I've got a full schedule right now with OPOV debuting Tuesday," he parried. "Could we stay with Monday?"

Farrell cleared his throat. "I'm sorry, Robert," the Senator said, dropping the formality and sounding firm. "I know it's the weekend, but this can't wait, and I can't discuss it over the phone. We must meet today. Believe me, you will be glad we got together." Farrell had started off solidly, but began to sound rushed, and anxious. "Can you suggest somewhere off the beaten track, so that we won't be disturbed?"

Robert was surprised again. This wasn't the Senator's reputed style of operation. What about this meeting could be so important? Robert considered refusing. It was always risky meeting with a Senator when unprepared. They rarely brought "gifts." More often than not they brought trouble. Robert had to balance an appearance of control with his lack of knowledge. It was a challenge anytime, but right now it felt like a stroll along a cliff edge.

Robert decided to roll the dice. Farrell and Gregg tended to run together in political arenas, but Farrell sometimes talked a little too much. It was possible that Robert could get information about this OPOV issue from Farrell that Gregg wouldn't provide.

"How about the Key Bridge Marriott on sixty-six?" Robert had been thinking about Grady, so the place popped easily into his mind.

"The Marriott?" Farrell looked toward the corner of the room. The man standing in the shadows shook his head. Looking down at a list on the table, Farrell countered with, "How about Carl's? It's that barbecue place near The Marriott?" The man nodded his approval.

"Yes, I've seen it." Robert responded. "I can be there at 11:30. Does that work for you?"

"That's fine, Robert." Farrell said, and hung up.

From the corner shadow of Farrell's room a deep voice spoke. "That was excellent work, Senator. Continue as I've instructed, and everything will be taken care of." Blair stepped from the shadow. "You'll leave at 11."

Robert thought Farrell had sounded odd. The abrupt hang up seemed out of character for the suave Senator. Robert wondered if Gregg had told him to find out what Robert had come up with on the investigation. Was he so much under Gregg's thumb? Robert always considered Farrell to be equally as powerful as Gregg, but perhaps he'd been misled. Robert's heart began to beat a little faster as he considered another possibility. Was Farrell directly involved with the OPOV problem?

"Carey, get the car ready. We'll leave just before 11." Robert went back to his study to gather up his work.

Carey had driven, while John texted an update to their command. Robert sat in the back of the nondescript Secret Service vehicle. They encountered normal weekend traffic on the way to Carl's. Arriving ten minutes early, they had to wait for the restaurant to open. Carey had been quiet on the drive, and was now standing silently inside the restaurant's front door. Robert had followed the hostess to a table. John was still going through the kitchen, and looking around every corner. Carey stood watching the parking lot through the door's side light.

Robert hadn't been waiting long when the senator arrived. Robert recognized his tall, lanky form immediately. Carey remained standing near the door, and pointed Farrell toward the table. Robert was seated in the back corner at John's suggestion. John now stood nearby. The place wasn't busy. They had the room almost to themselves. The few patrons paid no attention to Robert. Farrell came over and sat down.

Carey stayed by the entrance. From his vantage point he could watch the doors and still see the table. The entrance was a typical cold-weather entry, with two sets of doors and a foyer between them. There was one sidelight window by each door, showing a narrow portion of the parking lot. It wasn't an ideal situation for a secure meeting, but the parking lot was relatively quiet.

Farrell seemed uncomfortable. He greeted Robert with some of his usual aplomb, but appeared distracted. Robert decided to take control of the meeting. He leaned forward, his hands interlaced.

"Senator, you called this meeting. Would you like to get to the point and tell me what we're doing here?" Robert narrowed his eyes, concentrating on the Senator's face. He intentionally lowered his voice tone to sound authoritative, and slowed his speech to make himself sound calm. In his chest, his heart was pounding, pulse high and palms sweaty. The trip over, riding with the silent Carey, had heightened his anxiety. The more he'd thought about it, the more he'd decided that Farrell might have some connection to the plan to undermine OPOV. Farrell was known to have some dubious connections. He'd managed to keep his public image clean, but Washington insiders muttered that he was in the pockets of certain lobbyists, and had underworld connections. Robert kept worrying that he was going to be thrown another curve ball. That was one thing this investigation didn't need.

Farrell was struggling. Perspiration beaded lightly near his hairline. He pressed his left hand down on his shaking leg to make it stop moving. Farrell hadn't realized how much he needed a fix. He had to cross his ankles to keep his knee from bouncing up and down. It was freezing outside, and chilly in the restaurant, but his shirt was soaked under his arms. Sweat began to bead lower on his forehead as he pulled out the envelope, and set it on the table. He looked around nervously.

Farrell decided to get this over with. He pushed the envelope toward Robert. "The information in there implicates Gregg in your investigation of the OPOV penetration."

Robert was stunned. Placing his hand on it, he said unbelievingly, "Senator Gregg?" Robert had not expected anything like this. Questions were racing through his mind. Robert took a breath to regain his composure before continuing. He decided he'd had enough of the subterfuge. Farrell was going to give him some answers.

"Senator, I don't understand." Robert said directly. "Out of the blue you contact me, and now you're dropping Gregg's name, implicating him in a possible crime? How is this evidence relevant, and why are you giving it to me? Why would the Senator perpetrate an offense against OPOV? Senator Gregg actually helped begin the investigation into how OPOV might be compromised. Why would he initiate an action that would uncover his own involvement?"

Farrell was looking sick, dark-reddish blotches lay under his eyes. "He's been keeping tabs on you the whole time, hasn't he? Been a step ahead at every turn?" He questioned, sounding harried. "Did it ever cross your mind that Gregg might have an agenda? That he might be the puppet master in this thing?" Farrell watched Robert's reactions. He could see the questions running through Robert's head. He suddenly felt more comfortable. This was going to be easier than he'd thought. "You missed that one, didn't you? Everybody's got an agenda, Robert. If Gregg wanted to keep control, then he'd have to control the investigation. You've been in Washington long enough to know that. Hell, look at your own father! Nobody follows the legal version of right and wrong. We work the gray areas every day, and when we head into questionable territory, we divert the attention away from ourselves. That's politics. It's not easy to cross the line, it's inevitable, and the only way to get anything done." Farrell's voice was still agitated, but now became quieter. In almost a whisper he said, "Look, Gregg is behind compromising the OPOV system. It's as simple as that."

Robert began opening the envelope.

"Not here." Farrell hissed. His hand and his insistence stopped Robert.

"What's in here?" Robert wanted to yank out the contents and look.

"There's enough in there to finish Gregg. He'd have to step down if it became public. It's not a direct link to OPOV, but you can use it as leverage. It's not the kind of thing you can use in court, and you'll have to handle it alone. I can't be involved."

Robert was angry now. He wanted evidence he could use. He needed it, in fact, to protect himself, and to make this an official investigation. "Then, Senator, this stuff's no good to me." He shoved the envelope back toward Farrell. "I need legally obtained evidence that's admissible in court."

"What I'm giving you will help you get it. Listen to what I'm telling you." Farrell looked at Robert with a sudden harshness. "You can stop these people in their tracks, and give the President what he needs. That's what you want, isn't it? This won't get you your headlines, but it will lead you to what you need to solve your problem."

Robert suddenly realized that he wanted more. He was feeling an emotion that he hadn't felt since law school. This wasn't about being recognized for his work, or about getting his promotion; he wanted to know everything. He wanted to hold these men accountable because they were corrupting the people's right to choose. In fact, they were corrupting the core principles of democracy that had created the U.S. republic. He wanted to know why Chris had died. He wanted to prosecute the perpetrators, and he wanted Grady's attackers brought down. He wanted justice.

Farrell interrupted his thoughts, sounding nervous again. "This is all you're getting from me, Robert. No public statement; no witness for the prosecution. My name stays out of this. Period. I'm doing you a favor, but I'm not putting my neck on the line." Farrell was looking paler, as if he might collapse, but he was firm.

Robert was thinking quickly. Farrell knew as well as he did that it was commonplace to use inadmissible, but damaging information to get answers, and to manipulate, so the envelope probably contained something useful. If he accepted the envelope, would there be enough inside to either lead him to evidence, or to push the perpetrators out of their spheres of influence? If Gregg was leading the infiltration, could he be brought down? Would there be enough to satisfy the President?

Robert knew that if OPOV was compromised, a public conviction might be useful in deflecting the problem away from The President. Played well, the President could be the hero, along with everyone in the Justice Department. He was sure that was what his father had been thinking with the mention of indictments.

The President didn't want to undermine public confidence in OPOV with a scandal, however; any issue that became public might reflect badly on his administration.

Robert tried to stall. "You're talking corruption and extortion. Call it political pressure if you like, but you're apparently not providing anything I can use, legally. I still need admissible evidence, or the situation could still be in play."

"Don't be naïve, Robert! This is how it's done. This gets you what you need. You can use it to get your proof, but you may not need the proof to get what you want." Farrell responded, sliding the envelope across the table again.

Robert put on his best poker face, and pushed the envelope back. "That's not what Justice does, Senator. You'll have to handle this yourself. Otherwise you'll open yourself up to being investigated."

Farrell's eyes filled with panic. He tried hard to regain his normally commanding tone, but ended up with a harsh whisper. "You have to do this! He's got to be stopped, and you're letting him go if you don't take action. What about the citizens' right to be heard? What about keeping the vote in the hands of the people?"

Robert shook his head mockingly. "Nice sound bite, Senator, but I don't believe for a minute that you are worried about Joe Blow's right to vote. What's your motivation in all of this? What do you get? And just how is Gregg involved? Have you got some score you're trying to settle with him?" Robert hoped to make Farrell talk more.

"Look, you don't need to know why, or how, and you don't need a courtroom to do what's right. You want to wrap up your investigation? You want your promotion? Use this." He pushed the envelope back at Robert and stood up abruptly. "Sometimes you have to do what's right for yourself. Screw the rest." His lanky stride pushed him quickly toward the door.

"Like you're doing now?" Robert called after him.

Farrell halted for a second, looking back. "Yes. Exactly like I'm doing right now." He turned and was out the door.

Robert had the impression that the envelope held a live rattlesnake. He was torn between ethics, politics, and getting the job done. Farrell's rhetoric aside, he had a problem to solve. Whatever was in the envelope might help get answers, or it might create more problems. He didn't like the idea of exerting pressure on a powerful Senator. A move like that could backfire more easily than it might succeed.

Carey came over as the Senator went out the restaurant door. "The Senator looks guiltier than usual. That guy has a hand in every DC pocket," he snarked.

Robert was startled. Carey's inscrutable Secret Service manner had uncharacteristically disappeared. "It's neither of our places to consider Senator Farrell's appearance as 'guilty' looking," Robert reprimanded, wondering what had prompted Carey's comment. Did Carey have some axe to grind with Farrell? He tried to casually slide the envelope over the side of the table. "As far as I know, Senator Farrell hasn't been accused of, or charged with any crime. If he has a hand in anyone's pocket, I haven't been presented with evidence of that."

"Understood." Carey answered, reacquiring his reserved demeanor. "I'll get the car." He left for the parking lot.

Robert watched him for a moment. He realized, too late, that he'd made his meeting with Farrell sound important. The last thing he wanted was Carey reporting to Hunt, or anyone else for that matter, that he'd received information from Farrell. He fumed at himself for the error as he opened the envelope.

He found that it contained one memory stick, along with three pictures. Gregg was in the pictures. Only an arm showed that another man had been with Gregg. Robert stuffed the photos back into the envelope, closing it securely.

Blair sat in the parking lot. He had watched Farrell rush out and drive away. He now watched Carey go to his car. Everything was falling into place. He'd taken care of Karelonski earlier, in order to put Carey in position for departure. Karelonski had made himself a liability by reporting a break in department procedure by another agent—one of Blair's recruits. He hadn't told a superior, just the agent himself, but the agent had reported the incident to Blair. Blair had decided that Karelonski was getting in the way.

It had been surprisingly easy to take him out of action. Peter made the mistake of taking the same route home each day. Blair's man pulled out in front of Peter in traffic and drove just slowly enough to build a gap between their cars and any traffic in front of them. An accomplice was waiting down the two-lane road at a convenient curve, with a tire-puncturing strip he quickly unrolled across half the lane. In the early winter darkness it was nearly impossible to see on the blacktopped surface.

Blair's man kept Peter close behind him, pulling off onto a side street just before the curve to avoid the narrow row of spikes. Peter had accelerated into them. His front tire hit the spikes. The spikes sank into the rubber, then were yanked free by a tether tied to a tree. The spike strip was thrown off the road and out of sight.

The tire had immediately gone flat, causing Peter to pull over. He stood on the side of the road, trying to examine the tread in the failing light. Blair's second man waited for another gap in the thinning traffic, then pulled up alongside. He rolled down his window and leaned over.

"Need any help?" He called out.

Peter turned to face the man's car, realizing too late that a silenced pistol pointed at him. The shot ripped through Peter's forehead, killing him instantly.

Karelonski's body slumped to the ground beside his car. It was a simple process to pull the accomplice's car in front of him, and block any remaining view of the body. The first driver had parked on the side road. He walked over to the scene. The two men waited for a car to go by, then heaved Peter into the trunk. Blood, skin, and hair evidence was irrelevant. The car was going to be completely dismantled. One man drove away as the other calmly changed Peter's tire, subsequently driving the car away to be cleaned and sold to a parts dealer.

Blair loved simple and direct plans. They worked reliably, leaving no loose strings. Farrell had delivered. This plan was proceeding nicely. Now he had another detail to manage. It was time to finish the day's chores.

As Carey approached the Secret Service car, Blair started to count quietly to himself.

A smile almost formed across his tight lips as he watched Carey pull the vehicle up to the restaurant. He knew Robert would wait inside until the car was out front. Standard Secret Service procedure was so predictable. It was a factor he counted on. When he reached the count of thirty, he pressed the remote button.

Robert saw the front bumper of the car through the restaurant window as it slowly rolled up to the outer door of the restaurant. As he walked toward the inner set of doors, reaching for the handle, Carey's car exploded violently, sending large chunks of metal into the air. Fiery pieces landed on the employees' parked cars, and far out into the road. A chunk hit the door to the restaurant. The impact shattered windows and cracked the doors, blasting them open.

Robert was slammed backward into the wall. He slid down to the floor, stunned. Flame and smoke burst through the open doors as waitresses ran for cover. Their screams were matched in pitch by two car alarms squealing and honking outside.

The inner doors of the restaurant had protected Robert, blocking most of the impact before they swung open. The outer door hung by one hinge, flames rolling up both sides, blackening the ceiling above it. Dark smoke billowed into the room past jagged remnants of window glass.

Robert was groggily lifting himself up on one elbow when a second explosion ripped through the car. Its fuel tank burst in red flames. The blast launched the car's back end over the front, landing the vehicle onto its roof, and collapsing it to the ground. More debris flew into the air, while another blast of hot air shot into the restaurant. Robert fell back hard on the linoleum floor again, shielding his face from the heat.

The partially open trunk lid could be seen through the shattered entrance windows. As the black smoke lifted, it revealed an arm hanging from within the trunk. Robert watched from the floor in shock, as flames wafted back and forth across the car, charring the arm's pale flesh to a black and cracking macabre sculpture. The hand's fingers curled up like a withered flower. Robert couldn't tear his eyes away from the burning flesh.

It had been a busy twenty-four hours for Blair. It felt like old times—like the days when he had been the "go-to" operative. He didn't do his own work often these days, but it was gratifying to know he still had his touch.

He didn't stay to gloat, driving away as soon as he'd hit the button that would detonate the car. No one had noticed the dark sedan leave amid the commotion. He smiled as he drove. It was too bad he couldn't stay and watch the fun of seeing how the Secret Service would handle the police and fire fighters. Blair's men had delivered Agent Karelonski and Carol to Carey's car while Blair kept watch. It had pleased him to watch their efficient work. It would have been entertaining to see a swarm of Secret Service trying to explain a dead agent, with another in his trunk, along with a high-priced call girl.

Blair's satisfaction was short-lived. With a busy schedule, he now had other concerns.

Chapter 71

Robert was still shaking. Agent John was rolling past on a gurney after being hit by several chunks of flaming debris. He was severely injured, but not fatally. Robert had not even noticed John in the alcove between the two doors. The firemen had lifted a section of ceiling and found him underneath. The ceiling, collapsing onto him, had probably saved John from burning alive.

The scene was incredible. Fire trucks and police cars filled the parking lot. The entry to the restaurant had caught fire, but the nearby firehouse responded in minutes. They didn't need a 911 call. The explosion and smoke had brought them out. The car was a smoldering wreck. Plumes of black smoke still rose from the tires pointing up towards the sky. Acrid fumes stunk up the air. Everything nearby was scorched and blackened. The police were holding everyone in the area while they investigated the incident.

Despite his injuries, John had managed to hit his panic button. His GPS locator and distress signal had brought another agent to the scene. Agent Brown had arrived, ascertaining the condition of his fellow agents, and calling for a Secret Service investigator. He'd then managed to get Robert checked over by the paramedics. Robert was told to see a doctor, but the paramedics released him to Brown. Robert just wanted to get out of there.

Agent Brown drove Robert back to his house. Two more agents and a doctor were there when they arrived. Brown had been busy making arrangements while Robert had been detained.

Robert now sat in his study. His ears were still ringing from the blast, but a shower and fresh clothes had proved soul cleansing. Robert refused a trip to the ER. After using a portable sonogram device, the doctor pronounced Robert sound, but left instructions with the agents on how to spot internal bleeding symptoms. Brown was back in the hallway in his usual location for evening duty. One of the other agents paced outside Robert's window. Robert hadn't asked his name. Carey's fiery death was too fresh. He didn't want to know any other agents at the moment.

Driving back with Brown, Robert had overheard that Agent Karelonski was AWOL. He was not at his house, and his car was missing. He was considered to have disappeared under suspicious circumstances. Robert wondered about that briefly. Still disoriented from the explosion, he wondered if he was being paranoid when he thought that Karelonski's disappearance was too coincidental. Could the Agent have been involved in setting up the explosion?

The death toll surrounding Robert was mounting up. He felt that it had become overwhelming. He had called Tracie twice, but only got the answering machine.

Brown called Agent Crandall, who was with Tracie and the boys. He brought Crandall up to speed, which apparently activated a more secure procedure that included not taking anymore outside calls, even from Robert. Agent Crandall would have to listen in during their calls, after confirming the source.

Robert asked to speak with Tracie. She told Agent Crandall she didn't want to talk to him. The cold war still raged.

Robert sat, holding the phone, with Crandall still on the open line. He had to admit that some of Tracie's anger was justifiable. There were things about this situation he might not ever be able to tell her. She would either make up her mind to forgive him, or not. He hoped the agents would successfully protect her and the kids. That thought made him queasy, and an odd feeling swept over him. He managed to say to Crandall, "Tell her I love her, and the kids." The echo of that statement sounded lame. He wasn't even sure he meant it. He turned toward the picture of Tracie and the kids on his desk. She seemed to be glaring at him. Robert turned the picture away from his view as he hung up the phone.

Pulling the manila envelope out of his coat, Robert placed it on the desk and stared at its curled corners for several minutes, thinking. Opening the envelope, he slid out the contents and looked at the photographs again. The first two showed a slightly younger Gregg on what seemed to be a large motor yacht. He was standing near the transom of the boat, and looked as though he had just accepted a small white envelope from a man's hand. The man's face and body were outside the frame of the picture. The envelope was clearly filled with a stack of greenbacks, visible through the envelope's open flap.

Robert dispassionately considered the photo. While the money appeared to be a payoff, or perhaps a bribe, the picture could be explained many ways. The sequence in the two photos was unclear. It was possible that Gregg was preparing to hand the envelope to the other man. Without context, the photographs were at best suspicious, and possibly damaging, but not criminal.

The third photograph was of a more current Gregg at an event of some kind, shaking hands with a man Robert did not recognize. On Gregg's other side stood Chris Stoker. Robert sat back and pondered. How had Chris ended up at an event with Gregg? He racked his brain, but couldn't imagine any situation that would put Chris and Senator Gregg anywhere near each other. The photo was curious, and frustrating, but meaningless as far as implications, or conclusions.

Snatching up the memory stick he went to the computer and plugged it in. It had two short voice files recorded on it.

Robert played the first one. It was easy to recognize Gregg's voice. The other man's voice was garbled. It had been electronically modified, and was not familiar. Robert guessed that the voice was male, and would originally have sounded deep. It had little or no accent.

The key sentence seemed to be Gregg's voice saying, "You handle security, let Robert handle the money."

Robert could not connect this statement to anything. Money? Money for what? He didn't have anything to do with money, and Gregg had not mentioned the subject around him. Robert drew a blank. Why had Gregg used his name in that conversation?

In the second conversation, Gregg was speaking to the same man, his voice still disguised, and as before, Gregg's voice was clear and easy to recognize.

Gregg: "We have to move up the schedule."

Other: "Why?"

Gregg: "Don't ask stupid questions. Just do it."

Other: "We don't have the information, or know who all his contacts are."

Gregg: "That doesn't matter. The run will go as planned. That's all set. We don't need him, and he could cause problems. I want you back here to take care of it personally."

Other: "What about Barlow?"

Gregg: "Have it done tomorrow. Make it look like an accident, or whatever makes sense, but you get back here."

Other: "I'll take care of it."

Robert stared at the memory stick. No date showed on the recording. Had it been made before Grady's attack, or did they know where he was?

Farrell had been sitting alone in his Georgetown home all day, shaking. He had seen nothing of the explosion. The envelope situation and the lack of a fix had him drinking heavily, but the booze wasn't helping. His hands quivered uncontrollably. Hunt had been true to his word. There was nothing left anywhere. He'd searched everything. Drawers throughout the house lay scattered, along with their contents. He had torn the place apart looking for even a little of the white powder to ease his craving. He rocked back and forth talking to himself, "I did what he asked. He promised I'd get it."

The doorbell rang, sending him stumbling across the room to answer it. He looked through the peephole. A blonde of impeccable shapeliness faced away from the door, the bright sun illuminating her body. "Carol," he whispered as he unlocked the door quickly and swung it open.

"Carol, thank God…" Farrell almost sobbed, then cut himself off. Staring, he stepped back, saying, "Who are you? What do you want?"

"Hello, Morgan." The woman said calmly. "Carol couldn't make it. She asked me to bring you something."

Farrell looked skeptical. He hesitated. His instincts for survival still remained intact. Something seemed wrong about this. He tried to focus, but his forced drug withdrawal and excessive alcohol consumption were rapidly eroding his self-control. The woman was beautiful. Athletic legs, slender waist, long blonde hair and bright green eyes made her a stand out. She'd dressed to show off her figure. She was standing on very high heels, with her coat now open to show a form-fitting dress. Carol knew what he liked, and he needed what this woman had undoubtedly brought him. He knew what that was—what it absolutely must be.

Farrell must have been staring too long, and too silently, without acknowledging her.

"I understand." She smiled gently, and turned slightly away. "I'm sure Carol will be able to come by later."

"No. No!" Farrell's initial defensive paranoia dissolved at the thought of the drug that must be in this woman's designer purse. He couldn't stand the thought of waiting a second longer for his fix. "You've got it wrong. Come in!" Farrell grabbed her gloved hand and pulled her into the entryway. "Where is it?" He reached for her handbag.

"Not so fast, Morgan." She pulled the bag away from him. Walking past him to the living room she prodded, "Where are your manners? You haven't offered me a drink."

Farrell looked around the room, saying, "What do you want? I've got everything. Just tell me...." He realized that he hadn't asked her name.

"Melanie," she intoned.

"Yes, of course, Melanie. I'm happy to get you whatever you want." Farrell became servile in his attempt to make sure she didn't leave. "Just tell me what you want."

"I hope it's not too early for Champagne." She purred.

"Yes! Of course!" He raced to the bar and pulled out a bottle of Crystal.

"Oooh, that's nice, Morgan. I appreciate a man who knows what to serve a lady." She seemed to be enjoying his discomfiture. She sat down on the couch, luxuriously stretching her legs down the length of it. The skirt of her dress rode up high.

Farrell pulled out a champagne flute, placing it next to the bottle.

"Not joining me?" She looked disappointed.

"No...yes. Of course." He quickly grabbed a second glass.

"Did you bring enough?" Farrell asked. "Let's have some now with the champagne." His hand shook as he attempted to remove the foil from the bottle, almost knocking over a glass with his arm.

"Here, take it, Morgan." She pulled a small vial out of a pouch in her purse and set it on the coffee table. "You're making me nervous."

A small sound, almost a giggle emanated from Farrell's throat as he hastily put the Champagne bottle down. He rushed over to grab the vial. His shaking hands spilled a little onto the table as he dropped to his knees on the rug. He tapped the bottle on its edge to dump out more. He made no attempt to make nicely formed lines, simply dropping his face to the table and inhaling. The white powder stuck to the end of his nose as he breathed in the drug. His hands rapidly collected the residual, rubbing it onto his gums. He fell back onto the floor with a thud, and loud sigh of relief combined with anticipation. The drug sank quickly into his system. A broad smile formed as his head leaned back, and closed his eyes.

"Feeling better, Honey?" The woman asked with a grin.

"I'll show you just how good in a few minutes," Morgan told her, recovering enough to wink at her. He rolled up on his elbow. "Now for the champagne," he said, stretching out his arm toward the bottle. "Interested in a little romp on…?" The sentence faded as his eyes suddenly widened and he coughed violently.

The pure, uncut drug had invaded every organ in his body. His bloodstream pulsed violently as his heart seized and released with built up pressure. He convulsed, hitting the coffee table with his leg, knocking some small decorative art onto the carpet. The woman stood and moved away from his pitching body. Farrell vomited across the floor.

Once he stopped moving, she watched for his convulsive breathing to ebb. His wheezing finally ended with a long, gurgling exhale.

Tucking the drug vial back into the pouch in her purse, she pulled out a small plastic bag of cocaine. She opened it, and tapped out a dusting of the normal strength powder to the side of the table. She dropped the packet next to Farrell's hand. Moving to the bar she put the wine bottle back into the refrigerator, and the glasses back on the shelf. Behind the bar she pressed on a portion of the wainscoting. The picture frame molding hid a door that clicked open. Inside was a pair of security recorders. She popped out the disks and placed them in her purse. Placing fresh disks on the sliding drawers, she gave her blonde wig a reassuring tug to make sure it was straight. After a glance around the room, she pushed the "close" buttons on both machines and shut the hidden cabinet door. As the machines booted the disks she exited the brownstone, closing the door behind her, and calmly walked away. The camera equipment began recording just in time to capture her from the back.

Chapter 72

Sitting in their office in the lowest level of The Pentagon, Pat and Gail watched three computer monitors. They had been trying to break into the NSA OPOV security system ever since Grady had visited them. Hooked on the project, they'd kept working through the weekend. Gail had succeeded in breaking into the moderately secure area just outside the main OPOV firewall. Pat had set up two machines identical to the voting servers used by the individual states. It took several code breaks to get all the downloaded software he needed, but breaking codes was his business. His computers now looked like carbon copies of North and South Dakota's.

The OPOV schedule called for a system wide check and verification at 1 p.m. Saturday. This would give the NSA time to fix any apparent problems before the vote on Tuesday. This was the standard test procedure, according to the manual Gail had located. Pat and Gail now watched the monitors, waiting.

At 1:15 the North Dakota server signed on remotely, and the code started running across the screen. Pat's set-up would record every command string. A few minutes later, the South Dakota system signed on. Pat smiled at Gail. Now they could analyze the data.

Pat concentrated on the system comparison. He had selected the Dakotas because they were so similar in population, time zone, number of counties, and number of elected officials, making it easier to spot any variations between the two sets of data. It didn't take long. He now had four lines of code that did not match. The first looked like the state ID he had used to copy them, so it had been easy to spot. The second lines each looked like a long polynomial. The third and fourth were decimal numbers.

He handed over the polynomials to Gail, who began crosschecking them. Pat wrote the decimal numbers on the wallboard.

"Vote counts!" Pat suddenly exclaimed.

"Really?" Gail turned around.

"Yep, these are vote counts. 'Yes,' and 'No'. They match up with typical Dakotas' ballot turnout."

Gail came over and looked at the numbers. A quick comparison to the state's voter demographics confirmed it. "They seem a bit inflated, even for a national ballot. Could it be a ratio?" She suggested.

"Hmmmm." Pat made some calculations on the board. "It could be a ratio. Does either of the polynomials use these numbers?"

"Yes, the first poly confirms activation, and reads two variables." Gail confirmed. "The second compares the results of the first poly with these two numbers, and then adjusts the output."

Pat did a search routine on the download. "The comparison numbers look like the right number of votes for each state within a standard deviation of normal. I think this thing adjusts the vote count." He said, pointing to one of the polynomials.

"It sure does," said Gail. "It adjusts it by a ratio in the direction given by the activation code. Then the software reports an adjusted vote count."

"Look here." Pat pointed to the computer screen. "This part right here is the confirmation code, and the last two characters are 01. That would drive the vote count slightly negative bringing the results closer together. If they made it, say 09, the vote would have swung the other way by a tiny margin." Pat was clearly enjoying this. "How about that! A landslide vote result wouldn't change, but if it was a close vote, it could be swung either way."

"I recognize the format of the activation code." Gail looked over at Pat.

"Really?" Pat asked eagerly.

Gail nodded. "It's the same sequence we used back when I did work on the new Senate and House systems. One capital letter, two numbers, and then five of anything you want. It's the same size and configuration as one of those passwords. Back then we didn't have as much flexibility in the security code." Gail went to an old file on her computer and pulled up an archive of passwords used to verify that the users were not repeating or using their old passwords. No one could use a password for more than ninety days, and then never again—the system would check it against the list. She looked up at Pat. "There's only one match, Pat," she said slowly. "It's from six years ago. It belonged to Senator Tom Baxter."

Robert couldn't take the quiet at home. He'd paced around his study a few times, and then distracted himself by looking at the photos on the wall. Something about the pictures was bothering him. There was a familiar feeling about the scene in one of them, but he couldn't put his finger on why it was disturbing.

His pulse was still spiking from adrenaline, and he felt edgy. He kept hoping that Grady would call. He needed to know that Grady was still alive.

After listening to the recording again, he'd decided to confront Gregg. It was a dangerous move with such limited information, but he'd run into too many brick walls in this investigation. His time was running out. He was going to have to bluff Gregg into thinking he knew more than he did.

Robert logged into the government system from his computer, and checked the Congressional calendar. It looked like there was a chance he could catch Gregg in the office today, given the Saturday meetings he saw listed. He left a message for the Senator, and told Agent Brown to get the car.

Robert worked while Brown drove. He left another message for Senator Gregg, and continued making notes on his computer pad. He jumped slightly when his phone rang.

"Robert?" Gregg's voice boomed.

"Yes." Robert took a deep breath, thinking about how he was going to approach the Senator.

"We seem to be talking more often these days, Robert. Do you have something for me?" The Senator asked.

"I need to meet with you right away. I know it's Saturday, but I was hoping you might be available."

"It's getting late, Robert, but I am in the office right now. If you can get here in the next half hour, I can spare you a few minutes." Gregg stated.

"Getting there won't be a problem," Robert answered, thinking that getting there in time was the least of his troubles. This conversation could be a huge problem. "I'll see you in 20 minutes."

Robert and Brown got out at the front steps of the Russell Senate Office Building, even though the Agent had objected to not using the underground parking. The car sat in the loading zone, a portable flashing blue light running on the dash.

Going through security was much faster than on weekdays. It was late afternoon, so most people were thinking about leaving, and some were already heading home. Tours were done for the day, and most workers had left to enjoy what remained of their Saturday.

The Russell Building's classically straight rectangular exterior hid a massive round rotunda from view. Its two-story ring of columns above a white and dark-grey swirled marble floor never failed to impress visitors. Robert found himself listening to the heels striking the rotunda floor as visitors headed out, pounding past him. He walked out of the circle, heading up the stairs and into the hallway on the right.

The senatorial office corridors were cold and impressive. Dark wood doors lined the halls, with large, freestanding federal and state flags marking each Senator's office. The flags stood in colorful contrast to the white walls, dark doors and white crushed marble terrazzo floor. Black POW/MIA flags also flanked some doorways.

Robert felt some surprise that he was noticing these things. He felt no sense of the intimidation he used to experience in these halls, but the stark contrast and bareness of the place seemed significant today.

Stepping into Senator Gregg's reception area, he expected a tactical waiting period. An assistant surprised him by immediately saying, "Mr. Carlton, the Senator is ready for you."

Startled, Robert wondered how much of what he had to say was being anticipated. His cynical side kicked in, and he began thinking about the Senator's manipulative tactics. He deliberately slowed his breathing, projecting a calm, confident demeanor as he entered the office. Agent Brown stood in the outer office as the assistant closed the door behind Robert.

"Deputy Attorney General Carlton." Gregg was sitting behind his desk, but rose to extend his hand. "I have a difficult schedule remaining today. I assume you will get straight to the point."

Robert nodded, but did not reach for Gregg's hand. Gregg raised an eyebrow, and gestured to the chair next to Robert. Both men sat.

Robert sat as straight as possible, his back barely touching the chair. The Senator's large desk set the two men unusually far apart. "I'd be happy to get to the point, Senator," Robert said, diving in. "I have information implicating you in receiving a bribe, and involving you in a possible murder investigation in an attempt to derail OPOV." Robert opened his briefcase. From his smart phone he played the recording of Gregg's voice.

Gregg held his hands together in front of his stomach, his elbows on the chair arms. His index fingers were pointing up and touching. His face had paled slightly after hearing his voice, but he sounded solidly in control. "That's not evidence," he stated flatly.

"If my information is accurate," Robert continued, as if he hadn't heard Gregg, "there will be more than enough evidence for a trial, and for a conviction."

Gregg's voice grew a little louder. He was clearly discomfited by Robert's accusation. "Is this what you are wasting my time with today, Robert? You can't possibly think you have anything on me. That so-called 'recording' is garbage."

Robert interjected quietly. "Then you deny its validity."

"Of course I deny it!" Gregg's face was now suffused with color. He looked understandably angry. "That could easily have been fabricated from other conversations. And, as you well know, it's inadmissible. You have nothing there, and I very much resent your attacking me in this way. I would think you'd know better by now than to approach someone without more substantive evidence."

"This is the beginning of 'more,' Senator," Robert said, and placed the photographs onto the desk.

Gregg glanced fleetingly at the pictures, and then glared at him.

"Do you recognize anyone in these pictures, besides yourself, of course," Robert pursued.

"You are well aware that I meet many people, Robert. I don't remember them all, and neither do I want to," the Senator said carefully.

"Senator, being evasive is rather pointless. You realize where I'm going with this. You are clearly..." Robert began.

"Shut up, Robbie." Gregg commanded harshly. He gave the top picture a flip with his finger. He quietly fumed for a couple of minutes, then said, "No matter what you think you've got, you have nothing on me. You can't indict everyone involved in this—you know that. You can't pick and choose when it comes to an investigation like this. When you're forced to issue subpoenas, how do you think you'll manage to avoid serving everyone? You may think you've got a case, but think about it: you can't attack me without burning the bridge under your own feet. Did you dig deep enough to find that out? You're showing me a few pictures that could be interpreted a hundred different ways, and a recording that could have been created with some electronic magic. It's not enough to scare someone like me." The Senator was beginning to regain his confidence. He looked Robert squarely in the eye. "All in all, you've got nothing, and I have nothing to explain." He shoved away the pictures contemptuously as he sat solidly back in his chair. "Alone, these pictures are completely out of context. You'd be a fool to release them into an investigation. Where did you think you were going with this?"

Robert stayed silent, maintaining direct eye contact. He hardly blinked, leaning back slightly in his seat. He displayed a confidence that he hoped gave him the appearance of having another card up his sleeve.

Gregg, too, stayed silent for a very long time. He had regained his normal demeanor, and was obviously thinking...calculating. "But I suppose you wouldn't be here if you didn't have something more significant than this paltry offering. What is it?" he tried, fishing for something that would indicate what Robert might know. "More photos? More recordings? Perhaps some pathetic copy of a document?"

Robert stayed silent for almost a minute, silently counting the seconds, then said, "I think you know what I have access to at this point, Senator. My...connections... have provided me with some interesting data, once I found the trail." He held his breath, hoping his bluff would work. If Gregg thought he had more, he might just slip. He might even give Robert enough to hang him.

Gregg was silent for almost three minutes, staring hard at Robert. Robert wondered how long they could both play this game. He carefully cocked one eyebrow at Gregg, and leaned a little farther back in his seat, indicating he was in this for as long as it took Gregg to figure out what he might have discovered.

"You're very much like your father, Robert, and I see now that you've finally learned to play your cards as he does," Gregg spoke, sighing almost imperceptibly. "Perhaps," he said, carefully gauging the effect of his words on Robert, "you are willing to use your information as leverage, since you came to me before taking any action? Perhaps that was the advice you were given?"

Robert was trying to maintain his poker face, but he was startled. He'd been literally biting his tongue, trying to keep from talking for as long as possible. He'd thought he could provoke Gregg into an admission. This was not what he'd expected. Gregg was ready to make a deal? Without verifying the extent of Robert's discovery? Robert knew he must have bumped into something big. Gregg must have thought Robert had found what could cripple his Senatorial position—maybe something he'd masterminded.

"As always, Senator, you are astute." Robert complimented him, assuming that was the best way to continue his charade. "What do you have in mind?"

"I suspect, Robert," Gregg suggested, "that you'd rather not bring all of this into the light of day. Perhaps your 'connections' mentioned that I might be amenable to a trade?"

"I think we are beyond that, Senator." Robert suddenly felt that he had been too heavy handed in that remark. He almost winced, thinking about it. Could he have overplayed his hand?

"Think I'm through, Robert? That I'm reaching retirement age, and want to spend more time fishing, and golfing? Maybe I should finish my term in a reserved and dignified manner? Would that fit nicely for all of you?" Gregg almost sounded mocking while extending his carefully worded offer.

Robert was reeling. Gregg was capitulating? Without a fight? What was going on? What had he stumbled into? He cleared his throat, trying to conjure up a response, but Gregg was continuing.

"I have to admit that I didn't expect this, Robert. I don't know how you were able to ferret this out. I'm sure you know what your role was supposed to be, now, but let me show you how we can both benefit from your findings. You have, shall we say…an opportunity." Gregg stood up, moving towards the picture hanging just beyond his desk. "Your career has been hanging in the balance, and you're trying to figure out how to ensure that your career path eventually gives you Jack's job. I can get us both what we want, and satisfy your 'connections,' as well. You'll have a successful outcome to your investigation, accolades, and career insurance, and I'll enjoy the rewards for my many years of service and influence."

There was a long silence. The Senator had paused, and was facing Robert. Robert's shoulders twitched, and his neck stiffened. He was thinking hard. There was no way that he was going to get anything admissible out of Gregg without agreeing. He had no other cards to play. Gregg clearly thought that he had discovered whatever and whomever were behind this situation.

Robert had known that in coming here he would have to cut some kind of deal with Gregg. Seeing Gregg's corrupt influence brought out in a very public venue would have been satisfying, but Robert knew it was a layman's fantasy. He liked the idea, but couldn't flesh out the actual events, or put together a complete picture without Gregg's help. If he could bluff Gregg into a retirement deal while getting more information, it might be the best choice.

"You're a consummate negotiator, Senator. I'm willing to proceed on that basis," he finally answered.

Gregg now felt he had the upper hand. He acted upon it with smooth confidence.

"I can give you what you want, Robert. I can hand you Farrell and Karlovich on a platter, with enough admissible evidence to make your case. The proof will be complete, without any embarrassing connections, and it will satisfy everyone."

Robert thought it over quickly. Robert now knew for a fact that Gregg had become involved in the OPOV investigation knowing most of the answers before the investigation had ever hit Robert's desk—before Chris Stoker had called. What Robert didn't know was why Gregg was capitulating so completely, and who else might be involved. Who were the associates who wanted to remain out of the limelight, but could be powerful enough to intimidate Gregg?

To get what the President wanted, Robert was going to have to take Gregg's deal. Gregg might give him more than he'd hoped for. It was a gamble, but Robert wasn't going to get Gregg anyway.

"That sounds acceptable, Senator. Let's see what you've got." He agreed.

Gregg pulled the painting away from the back wall. After quickly punching in the lock code, he opened the hidden safe, and removed two folders. "I have materials here relating to the infiltration of the OPOV system. Watch your step, Robbie. This is dangerous stuff. You're on the big boys' playground now." He handed the two folders to Robert, then looked toward Robert's folder, and lifted a questioning eyebrow.

Robert decided to use his upper hand for a change. "Tit for tat, Senator? I'll be happy to hand over my information to you, once this investigation is complete, but not until then."

"Robert, that's not how this works, but I'll allow for some variations if you will agree to not use that," Gregg said, pointing to Robert's pictures. "I will agree to give you whatever you need. We know we both have copies of this information, so there's no point in me destroying what you leave. You understand that we have a commitment based on mutual trust."

"Trust?" Robert said, a tinge of sarcasm in his tone. He stood up.

"Yes, trust." Gregg smiled. "This trust is based on what we know we each can accomplish, and upon what we choose not to do. Leverage." Gregg told him. "You haven't heard a few stipulations that I'm going to make. Take a minute and look through those folders."

Robert opened the folders and scanned through the documents, feeling an increasing sense of elation, tainted with growing nervousness. The information was shocking. The specifics outlining Senator Farrell's and NSA Director Karlovich's involvement were damning. Robert wondered how much of this kind of information Gregg had stored away. He'd been involved with multiple programs and many people in high-ranking circles. If his data was this complete on this subject, there must be a warehouse somewhere filled with files like these on his other potential victims.

Since these two folders rested with only a few others in the safe, Robert also knew that Gregg had been prepared for his visit. His elation quickly faded to concern. Was he being played again?

"You've been prepared for this for some time," Robert said, his eyes narrowing.

"When one plays in the big game," the Senator said, "One had better protect oneself. Be grateful, Robert. You'll still have to do a little legwork, but that information should give you most of the specifics."

Gregg sat back down. "Now...here's what I want: this investigation ends with Farrell. No watchdog sub committee crap, except where I direct; no investigating down the line. You will ask for an oversight mandate of the government agencies involved in OPOV, and you will recommend that the House Committee on Rules, along with Homeland Security convene a subcommittee to investigate the viability of OPOV in the current cyber-terrorism geopolitical climate. Obviously, I'm not your source."

Robert shook his head in disbelief. The Senator wasn't asking for peanuts. His stipulations weren't going to be easy to achieve— and what was he getting at, with investigating the "viability of OPOV? "Is that it, Senator? No laws you want rewritten? No Presidential appointments?" Robert asked, his sarcasm clear now.

"Laws control the lesser man, Robert, and I make my own deals with the President. These aren't big requests, considering what you're getting in return. Let's face it Robert, it would have taken you months to get this background data that I'm handing you. You may need more information that you will only be able to get from me." Gregg sat comfortably in his chair, his fingers laced together over the top of his stomach. He was confident and arrogant once again. Robert had to admit that the guy was skilled at manipulation.

"Robert, you now have a place at the adult table. I'm willing to make sure you stay there. Be careful what you say, and to whom you say it. When you aren't sure, ask me. I'll guide you. You only get one shot at this level. You will need allies, and somehow I don't think your father is going to be one of them. Don't mess this up." Gregg stood and gestured toward the door.

Robert took Gregg's folders, left his, and walked out without saying a word. What did his father have to do with this conversation? Was Gregg referring to his father's influence with the President? He didn't dare ask. It would reveal too much about what Robert didn't know.

Robert thought about the information in Gregg's file. Had Farrell and Gregg each been trying to get rid of the other? If so, they were both losing something. Gregg would still have his influence and money, even if he no longer had his office. Farrell and Karlovich would fry. There were names, dates, places, and money exchanges. A Marty Torrance at the NSA figured prominently with the perpetrators, and Chris Stoker was named. Robert was feeling queasy.

Agent Brown drove Robert home. Strangely, while Robert had become used to being chauffeured, he'd found that he wasn't entirely comfortable. It didn't feel good, sitting in the passenger seat while someone else handled traffic. Having the opportunity to work or relax during the commute was not the benefit it should have been. It was a reminder that nothing was normal, or safe. The last government car he had ridden in was a wreck, actively burning in his mind. He felt distanced from, but not numb to the shocks that had added up over the last week. Logically, he could assess and deal with them, but part of his brain was slower to feel the full implications of what had happened.

When they got to his house another agent was standing in the garage. Robert didn't ask his name. He just walked inside and went to his study. When asked, he agreed easily to Chinese food being ordered, and didn't give it another thought. He sat studying the evidence from Gregg, a glass of dark, red wine within easy reach.

<u>Chapter 73</u>

Grady had been driving his stolen car for less than an hour. He knew exactly what he had to do. Whoever these guys were, they weren't going to stop trying to kill him.

He took the back road path through Goffstown to avoid the freeway. It was easy enough to park the car at the Manchester, New Hampshire regional airport, and walk into the terminal. A small airport like Manchester was unlikely to have the license plate scanners at their toll booths that the big airports were getting. That made the odds low that, if it had been reported stolen, the car would get matched up to the big database in the Cloud. It was possible that the car's owner, eating a leisurely lunch, hadn't yet realized that the car was gone. They'd get it back unharmed eventually.

A quick check at the information desk in the airport, and Grady had an Amtrak pamphlet. Grady then checked the bus connection at the Manchester transportation center. An hour and a half bus ride to Boston, and then taking the train would put him in DC at about 7 a.m.

There was a Sam Adams pub outside of security at the airport. Grady settled in with a Boston Lager, a burger, fries and football recaps on the TV. After relaxing for a couple of hours, he took a cab to the bus station. He bought a ticket. With no security checks, Grady's departure would be hard to trace. He figured they wouldn't think of him going back to DC.

Chapter 74

Robert woke up early Monday. The clock said 5:30. He'd slept surprisingly well. The contents of Gregg's file were spread all over his bed and floor. He hadn't expected to sleep. He'd spent all Sunday coordinating the information that Gregg had given him. The pen still in his hand certainly spoke to the idea that he'd passed out while working. With a quick shower, an espresso, and bagel from a batch one of the agents had brought in, he was back in his study crosschecking his evidence.

Grady had also slept soundly. When the train pulled into Union Station in DC at 7 a.m. he was awake and rested, despite a slightly stiff neck from sleeping in a chair. A quick eye-opener, plus a breakfast burrito, and he was on the Washington Metro. He changed lines twice, ending up at National. There he grabbed a hotel shuttle, figuring that was the best place to hide out until he could get the information he needed on Monday, and then see Robert.

Grady was back at National, catching the Metro again Monday morning. Switching lines, he decided to stop at the Pentagon barbershop for a trim and shave. His next stop was the Pentagon uniform store. A fresh set of Class A's, new ribbons, and high gloss shoes made him feel much more like himself. He carried a second uniform in a hanging bag, with two additional shirts. The jackets and shirts would have to be tailored later.

Grady didn't go to his office. The deluge of work that would have piled up during his absence would have to wait. He proceeded directly to Phase Shifted Crypto, and John McGarrity's office. Entering through the outer door, he walked back to John's office. It was empty. He heard Gail's voice from around the corner, and found her talking with Pat.

"Lt. Colonel! How nice to see you again." She said. "John's not here."

"I noticed. I looked in his office. I'm sorry for barging in, but John was going to give me a list of the critical findings, perhaps you have them?"

Gail and Pat both looked hesitant. Providing findings was a rarity, but this project had been special.

"I think...hang on." Gail got up and went past Grady down the hall to another room. When she returned she was carrying a dark manila folder with a metal, two-hole clip at the top. The front cover read "Confidential" in red letters. It did not say "SECRET," or "TOP SECRET" Grady noticed.

"I think this is what he was planning to give you." She handed Grady the report folder.

"Just 'confidential'?" Grady asked with a smile.

"Yes, amazingly, all that information was gained via the open internet, so only the method of finding it is 'secret.' We didn't disclose the method in the write ups."

Grady opened the file and gave it a quick glance. The second page, the one behind the confidential qualification statements, shocked him, but it was precisely the kind of information he'd hoped to find.

"Yes, this is what I needed." Grady looked up. His air was decisive and confident. "Do you have a sign-out sheet for this?"

Pat hesitated only long enough to say, "I can make one up. It will take a minute."

Gail spoke as Pat got up to create a tracking form. "I suppose you've already made sense of it all."

"Yes." Grady sounded confident. "I need to complete the files now, and the members need to review this. Then we're done."

Pat returned. "Here we are, Colonel. John checked your clearance already. You are obviously approved for carry at this level outside the 'reservation.' No copies without review approval, and you cannot release possession of the original. Pretty standard. In the back you'll find associated IPs that have clearly related code. We ran a regional cache-file-sweep routine. It turned up some interesting links."

Grady gave a thorough look at the last page. "The same password was within each transmission."

"Yes, on the subject line." Gail answered.

"This was over the VPN. How can that be on the open internet?" Grady queried.

"VPNs are used when outside the buildings; therefore, they run through Internet services. Usually these transmissions pass through at least one buffer on a server farm. These particular communications were still sitting in memory at a hub, kind of like a copying machine or fax keeps a copy until you deliberately clear the memory, or overwrite it using FIFO—you know, 'first in, first out.' Technically speaking we never left the open domain to find these."

"You're not making me feel good about our security." Grady shook his head.

Gail beamed. "Not just anyone could have found it."

"Where is the rest of the email to go with title line?"

"There isn't one," Pat replied. "Either there was no email content, or it wasn't actually an e-mail. It may have been a link transfer of some kind. Or, maybe a command statement to a reader file we haven't located yet. It might just be a signal to go look at something else. In each case, all they needed was the subject line. We're still trying to work that out."

"Outstanding." Grady signed the top slot on the freshly minted check-out sheet.

"You're allowed thirty days." Pat was going by the book. Grady was okay with that. Some things, at least, were as they should be.

"Excellent. Thanks." Grady put the folder in his shiny new black valise. It was empty except for two pens that were equally new.

"Then I guess we will be seeing more of you?" Gail smiled.

"Absolutely." Grady smiled back. "Thanks for expediting this." He raised the valise slightly, and turned away.

As Grady walked down the hallway he knew he needed to go directly to Robert's office, and fast.

Chapter 75

Robert called Lorraine on his way into the office Monday morning.

"Yes, Sir." Lorraine answered, sounding as efficient as ever. Her typical voice mannerisms seemed to be returning.

"Lorraine. I need to you call the West Wing and get me an appointment with Buchanan, Chief of Staff, or McCray, Deputy Chief of Staff for Operations regarding the OPOV investigation. Track down Jerry and have him meet me for the appointment. And get hold of Phil Davis for me. Have him call my cell."

"Yes, Sir." Lorraine hung up.

It was a calculated move—or maybe a gamble. By going to the West Wing right away, he could establish a timeline. He didn't expect to get a meeting with the Chief of Staff, but the request might get him bumped up the list enough to meet with the Operations Deputy. McCray administered the inner workings of the Presidential offices, and a number of the President's temporary oversight teams, including OPOV. If he could see the Deputy Chief of Staff, he could effectively get multiple support functions investigating at the same time, and free up his team to concentrate on prosecution.

Lorraine called back a few minutes later. "Mr. Carlton? Lorraine."

"Yes, Lorraine."

"You have a fifteen-minute appointment with the Chief of Staff this morning at 9:15. I have notified Mr. Turner who will meet you at 8:30 in the lobby. I left a message for Mr. Davidson to call you as soon as possible on your cell."

"Thank you, Lorraine." He hung up the phone.

Agent Brown got Robert through traffic in time for him to meet Jerry at 8:30 in the lobby area of the West Wing. Robert set to work with Jerry, giving him an edited summary of the evidence and loose ends. Robert had compared the information Gregg had provided with what Jerry and his team had researched. The timing matched, showing how each player had set the changes in motion, based on Farrell depositing funds in accounts, or coercing participants through fear. The probability of convictions looked good.

Not being able to use Gregg as the source of their information was a problem. Jerry voiced discomfort over having an anonymous source—inadmissibility in court could become a huge problem. They would have to corroborate Gregg's findings with their own research, but at least now they knew where to look. By the time Chief's assistant came out to get them, they felt sure they had a case to present.

The assistant led them through the left door toward the Roosevelt room, instead of the Chief of Staff's office. Jerry gave Robert a glance. This meant that there would be people in the room other than Buchanan. Robert's view was fixed on the assistant who continued walking to the Presidential Secretary's desk. She rose from her chair, extending her hand.

"Mr. Carlton, how good to see you again." The woman told him. Beth Parin had been an associate of the President's for years. Her organizational skills and ability to keep the President on schedule was legendary.

"Thank you, Mrs. Parin. Good to see you, too." Robert said, shaking her hand.

"Both of you are scheduled to see the Chief of Staff in a moment, but Mr. Carlton, the President has asked to speak with you first, if you don't mind."

"Of course not. It's my pleasure." Robert waited as she moved to the oval office door and knocked twice. She didn't wait for a response to the knock, and swung open the door for Robert to pass into the Oval Office. Jerry waited silently behind.

The President sat looking toward the door from the far couch. Facing the President with his back to the door was Robert's father.

"Robert, good to see you. Here, have a seat." The President indicated the spot next to Robert's father, who turned his head, smiling toward Robert. "I suspect you have brought me some answers to the OPOV trouble." The President sounded congenial.

"Yes, sir." Robert was surprised. He didn't want to discuss this in front of his father. He wasn't sure it was the best time to present his evidence.

Robert's discomfort showed as he sat down next to his father. The two of them looked similar in body style, features, and coloring, but beyond that, they couldn't have been more disparate. His father sat back, relaxed and comfortable. Robert sat erect and stiff, feeling the acolyte beside his revered patriarch.

"What have you got?" The President asked Robert.

Robert cleared his throat and told the President about Farrell, Karlovich, and the others implicated in Gregg's files. It was a shorthand version, identifying the perpetrators, and explaining the admissible evidence, and that which would have to be obtained in order to make solid convictions. Robert wasn't sure that courtroom guilty verdicts were necessary to achieve The President's goals, but it felt good to be able to state that they might be possible.

As he spoke, Robert felt an absurd sense of the anticlimactic. Robert's newly discovered evidence suddenly seemed thin...predictable. Sitting next to his father made him feel like he was giving a book report to a teacher—a teacher who had read the book many times before. The President wasn't responding as though he was surprised at any of Robert's statements.

"So, you could go forward with charges?" The President was asking.

"Against Senator Farrell, NSA Director Karlovich, and Dr. Torrance, yes, Sir." Robert nodded. "We have enough to indict, even perhaps to convict, but I haven't had time to thoroughly investigate. This is the beginning, but it's clear that we've located key individuals involved in the operation."

"Are we sure that Karlovich and the others were aware that they were involved in an operation to compromise the OPOV system?" The President probed.

"They had to know that they were compromising security, Sir, but the extent of their knowledge was probably limited to their portion of the undertaking. Certainly Senator Farrell knew, but according to what we've discovered, he was more interested in supplementing his lifestyle than in issues of national security. They all seemed to have received payoffs, or had been threatened in some way. These people didn't initiate the actions themselves. Ultimately we will have to make our arrests to find out how they were originally recruited, and by whom. The odds are that anyone under the level of the NSA Director doesn't know who was at the top."

"What about OPOV? Was the system compromised?" The President asked directly.

"Yes, sir, the indications are good that the system has been seriously compromised. Now that we have the perpetrators I'm sure we can repair the system, and get started again." Robert proposed Gregg's stipulated requests as his own. "I would say an investigation of OPOV election fraud by the House Committee on Rules would make sense. Perhaps they should ask Homeland Security to look into its cyber-security viability."

"A good idea." The president looked pleased. "See that your office puts forth a formal recommendation to that effect. Karlovich and Torrance are part of the NSA programming team?"

"Yes, sir. Karlovich is the Director, and Torrance is a key programmer. Both are directly involved. It's more than a casual security break. Only the best talents could have spotted it, even when knowing what to look for."

The President thought about it for a while. "I tell you what, Robert: the vote is Tuesday, so you're going to have to write up a statement for the press. State everything as 'persons to be named, since the investigation is underway'—you know the approach. We'll use today's press meeting. Put in just enough detail to make halting the scheduled vote the right thing to do. Give the statement to my secretary. I'll have my guys tweak it. When will you make arrests?"

"As soon as we can get the warrants. We should be able to accomplish it today—tomorrow at the latest, with arrests following immediately." Robert answered.

"Good. Keep me posted." The President stood, signaling the end of the meeting. Robert and his father also stood.

Robert's father offered his hand to Robert with a broad smile.

"Proud of you, Son." He said. "You really came up to scratch on this one."

Robert barely made eye contact with his father. He was still wondering why the President had discussed this with his father in the room. Robert was also trying to sort out why the President was so quickly ordering a shutdown of OPOV. It had been his "baby" from the start. Robert had thought he'd want to know if a patch job would be possible, so that the vote could continue.

The President put an arm around Robert's shoulder, and walked him toward the door. "You've done a great job, Robert. I won't forget it." With that he closed the door behind him. Robert's father stayed in the office.

<u>Chapter 76</u>

There was, in fact, no meeting with the Chief of Staff. Instead the Press Secretary worked with Robert and Jerry to put together the press announcement for the President. They were careful to indicate the importance of the situation with regard to the OPOV system, but revealed no key details, and no names. After reading it three times, they left it with the President's secretary. In the Deputy's office they received a full update from the Secret Service team leader on what had happened over the past twenty-four hours, including the car explosion. ID on Carey had confirmed he was driving, and there were not two, but three bodies in the car. Two had been in the trunk.

"Are you kidding?" Robert asked, unbelieving and dismayed.

"No, Sir." The team leader continued, "A man and a woman were in the trunk. We have no ID on the bodies, yet."

"That news may impact another problem I'm looking into." Robert paused, trying to think of the implications this might have for his investigation. "Let me know what your team uncovers."

"Yes, Sir." The man told him.

That was when it hit him. Neither the President nor his father had asked about the car explosion.

Robert and Jerry started to head back to their building, but concluded that there was not quite enough time to make that practical before the press meeting.

The ball was already rolling. While Robert had talked with the President, Jerry had used the secure lines to assign his team the problem of getting warrants for Farrell, Karlovich, and Torrance. Now in the pressroom waiting area, Robert and Jerry were both making follow-up calls. Federal Marshals would serve the Karlovich and Torrance warrants. Farrell would require special handling.

Robert was making calls to facilitate this delicate, non-public arrest. Robert began feeling better, since he could at last take some action.

Once the calls stopped, Robert had a few minutes to reflect. Something was bothering him. He hashed and rehashed the week. His elation at getting the information from Gregg was fading. The adrenaline rush from talking to the President passed. He slowly came to the conclusion that he'd missed some key point. Something was wrong with this whole picture. He knew he didn't completely understand Gregg's involvement, but something else was wrong. He tried to figure out how Farrell might have masterminded this project. The evidence from Gregg made Farrell look like the big fish, but Farrell had dished the same type of dirt on Gregg. Could either of them really have the connections to have Chris killed, and to arrange Grady's death? Assassins weren't generally listed for hire in the yellow pages, or on the internet. He rethought that; maybe one could find an assassin on the internet, but wasn't it a huge risk to hire anyone for a job like that?

The files had shown that Farrell and Karlovich had some large bank accounts aside from their personal accounts, directly and indirectly grown from what looked like subversive groups' deposits. They'd have to spend some time tracing those, but Robert wondered whether Farrell's expensive habits had been enough to make him a target for insurgents, or if Farrell was the one with an agenda. Farrell hadn't been a supporter of the President, so it was possible that he'd intended to damage his credibility by corrupting OPOV. Some of Farrell's colleagues would have found that useful. But Gregg was no fan of Baxter, either, Robert reflected.

Torrance was a weak link in the chain, when it came to money. He didn't have a bank account swelled by strange deposits. He appeared to have been threatened in some way. Robert would have to investigate that further.

He checked in with Lorraine. "Any messages?"

"Yes, you just got a call from Colonel Barlow." She gave Robert the number. Robert didn't wait for the rest of his messages. He hung up, and began dialing.

"Robert?" Grady answered cheerfully.

"Grady?" Robert answered. "Are you all right?"

"Yeah, I'm back in DC, and I'm about to get on the Metro to your office. I've got to tell you what we found."

"Wait," Robert stopped him. "Where have you been? What's happened?"

"We can talk about that later, over a beer. You're buying." Grady responded.

"Fine, but if you're here, you must have found something important," Robert said.

"I did," Grady said firmly. "I can tell you in the office."

"No time for that. I'm not there now." Robert said as he looked at the clock. There were only a few minutes left before the press conference. He decided to take a chance.

"I need to know now, Grady—it can't wait."

"Get a pen. I'm on a brand new cell phone I just bought from a machine here at the station, so I hope that helps." Grady walked to a quieter spot in the station that still had a signal, and laid out the information to Robert. "OPOV has been manipulated to report fake vote counts, Robert. It can increase or decrease them by any ratio, depending on what the guys behind this want." He briefly explained what McGarrity's team had discovered. "There's more, Robert. "The link in all of this is the activation code that drives the whole system." Grady took a deep breath. "You know how all the networks, like the Senate and House systems, won't let anyone use the same code twice?"

"Sure, our system is set up the same way." Robert confirmed. "That's standard."

Grady stopped talking as a man walked close by him, then continued, "The activation code used to break into OPOV is Senator Tom Baxter's six-year old password." Grady paused. He let Robert take that in before moving on. "Robert, either the President's involved, or someone awfully close to him is. It's unlikely that his code would be stolen. The list of old passwords is quite definitely not public. It must be him, or someone intimately involved with him. Whichever it is, you need to watch your back."

"Was it the President's, I mean the Senator's *personal* password?" Robert asked quickly.

"It was his official access password to the Senate network. My guys can only see it because it is supposed to be inactive, and one of them was involved in the design of that program. Even at that, they had to break in to get it. I can't imagine anyone letting someone use an important password like that. So like I said...watch your back."

"Can you get a hard copy of any of this?" Robert queried. He knew this was dangerous ground, but he had to have the hard evidence.

"Already did, I'm on my way with it, so I'd better get moving." Grady answered, sounding ready to hang up. "I need to stay in a secure area as much as possible."

"More trouble?"

"You have no idea how much more."

"Wait a minute. Why are you in DC? What about laying low?" Robert asked.

"Didn't work worth a damn. So, I decided to man-up, and get this job done. See you at your office." Grady hung up the phone.

Holding the disconnected phone in his hand, Robert fleetingly wondered what had made Grady decide to come out of hiding. He didn't have much time to dwell on the thought. He had to decide what to do about Grady's information.

President Baxter's former password being used to infiltrate the security on OPOV made everything more complicated. The scenarios racing through Robert's mind were politically dangerous. The President would be furious if it was made public that his password had been used in this way. Robert could easily imagine how, as a Senator, Baxter might have been sloppy about giving someone on his staff the password. Discovering, quietly and quickly, who had used the password was essential. Robert had to do something, but what and how, he wasn't sure.

Robert grabbed Gregg's folders and looked again through the information on Farrell, Karlovich, Torrance, and Stoker, carefully reading each detail. The material in the folders was damning, and not all of it was related to OPOV. Drugs, payoffs, prostitutes, lobbyist influences, and extortion were all tools Farrell had used in high-level political deal making. Farrell had links to some important names—the President would have to be consulted about some of them. Farrell's manipulations to control OPOV were clear. The President was going to get a very visible scapegoat out of this, unless Farrell was able to cut a deal.

Stoker was dead, but it hurt Robert to know that his name would be publicly trashed. He winced as he read of Chris' involvement, but it was small compared to the others. His family would suffer a little shame, and the confiscation of a secret bank account that they probably knew nothing about. Maybe Chris hadn't known, either. The links looked strong on paper, but why would Chris blow the whistle on something he was involved in? It was possible that Chris had been set up to look guilty after he'd discovered and leaked the information on the conspiracy. Robert hoped that was what had happened, and that the evidence would clear Chris as they investigated.

Robert glanced one more time over the material to find something that made a link to Baxter's password understandable. He knew that the odds of someone accidentally duplicating the six-year-old password were extraordinarily remote.

Six years before those passwords had been required to have random capitals, lowercase letters, and numbers. Even if they were based on something easily remembered the odds were hugely against random discovery. The system had required a change to the password every three months, with no duplications. Most people ran out of ideas for passwords within a year or two. So the passwords became less personal, and more obscure over time. Security regularly swept all offices, so the chance of it being discovered on a sticky note under the desk was remote. Unless Baxter had broken the rules and given it to someone, the most likely scenario was that it had been stolen. This pointed to an insider within the then Senator's office.

An assistant to the Press Secretary came out to lead Robert and Jerry to the hallway outside the pressroom. They now stood watching the Presidential Seal come up on the monitors. The Press Secretary walked up to Robert's shoulder.

"Thank you for coming." He told him. "I'll need you to stand over here."

Robert was surprised to be ushered onto the elevated platform. He was shown where to stand, just behind the President's right shoulder, opposite the press secretary.

The press secretary stepped forward to introduce the President. "Ladies and Gentlemen, the President of the United States."

The press corps stood as the President walked in confidently, briefly shaking Robert's hand before taking command of the podium.

"Good afternoon. Thank you all for being here." The President began. The press took their seats following his gesture to sit down. "As you know, my administration has fought hard to put the 'One Person, One Vote' system in place. It has been my personal mission to bring each and every citizen direct access to government deliberations through voting. I believe in following the framers of our Constitution's intention to support every citizen's right to be heard, but which, until now, resulted in representation that didn't always reflect public interest. We've worked hard to put a more direct voting system in place. This easily accessible method of voting has been designed to put the public's wishes before Congress, knock out the lobbyist influence, and to give everyone a voice in their government.

Today I am saddened to inform you that multiple agencies, in cooperation with the Department of Justice, have uncovered an attempt to undermine that system. Key perpetrators have been identified, and are being taken into custody. It is unfortunate that this crime will delay the One Person, One Vote system. This is disappointing to all of us. Be assured, we will not rest until we deliver to all citizens the kind of voting that belongs in the greatest democracy in the world. Now, I'll take a few questions."

He pointed to the sixth chair. "Yes, Mary."

Mary Rutherford was a favorite with the President, and a long-time White House correspondent. "Thank you, Mr. President. Is it true that this announcement comes as part of an investigation initiated by the Justice Department, and that as a result you have named Robert Carlton as Deputy Attorney General?" The question was obviously planted. Robert was reeling. He'd worried the President might direct some questions to him since he was on the stage, but this was completely unexpected.

"Yes," the President beamed. "Mr. Carlton discovered the breach, and immediately brought it to my personal attention. His efforts have been unparalleled in uncovering the perpetrators of this crime against the citizens of this country, and in protecting our rights. Come up here, Robert."

Robert tried to maintain his composure in spite of the multiple shocks he had received in the last few hours. His pulse was out the roof. He knew his hands were visibly shaking, so he had been holding them together. Robert quickly hid his left behind him as he accepted the President's handshake firmly for the cameras. They both smiled. Robert marveled at how steady the President's hands were as he grabbed Robert's forearm for a double handshake, stabilizing Robert from head to toe.

"It is my pleasure to announce that Robert Carlton will be taking over the duties of Deputy Attorney General immediately. His leadership and resolve will continue to protect our country. His team will continue to bring offenders to justice, under the auspices of Attorney General Jack Crain. We couldn't have done it without you, Robert." Robert suddenly realized that Jack had come in behind him, and had also stepped forward to shake Robert's hand. He and Jack automatically stepped back as the President turned back to the podium.

In all the turmoil, Robert had completely missed the public announcement of Jack Crain's appointment to Attorney General. Tracie would be livid at Robert's failure to be the first to congratulate Jack.

"Next question," The President was saying, pointing to another reporter in the crowd.

"Mr. President, can you confirm that a high ranking director at the National Security Agency has been named in the OPOV investigation, and that a warrant has been issued for his arrest?"

Another shock shook Robert. He had not released that information, nor would he have done so. This would put Karlovich on the defensive before they had time to issue a warrant. Had this question been planted, as well?

"The specifics of the investigation will be released in a statement by the Attorney General. Until then we will have no further comment about this ongoing investigation." The President answered, scanning the room. "One last question. "Yes?" He pointed to a reporter in the second row.

"Mr. President, do you have any information regarding the sudden death of Senator Farrell?" The reporter asked.

Robert was caught completely off guard. He kept his face rigid, and avoided looking at Jack. Farrell was dead? Why hadn't he been told? He didn't know how the President was going to field that question.

"The only information I have for you is that Senator Farrell was found dead from an apparent heart attack." The President answered smoothly. "My family and I wish to extend our sympathies to his family. He faithfully served our country for many years. The Press Secretary can tell you about funeral arrangements as soon as the details become available."

He stepped away from the podium, and began talking to Jack and Robert, dragging them with him toward the Oval Office. The Press Secretary was left behind to handle the reporters. "Those are all the questions the President has time for..." His voice was cut off as the door closed behind them.

They walked quickly down the hall. "So, Mr. Deputy Attorney General, congratulations." The President was saying to Robert.

"How does it feel, Robert?" Jack smiled as he placed his hand on Robert's shoulder.

"Fantastic," Robert answered, trying to absorb everything that had just happened. "Thank you, Mr. President; Jack. I'm sorry I didn't get a chance to congratulate you earlier, Jack."

Jack smiled. "You were busy—and busy on one of the most important topics of the day. Good job."

The President broke in. "I assume you will be wrapping up your investigation?"

"We still have a few things to sort out, Mr. President," Robert answered. "I was unaware of Senator Farrell's death..." Robert instantly regretted that admission, but continued, "which may complicate tying up some details." Robert said as they entered the oval office.

"Let me explain something, Robert." The President held up his hand, silencing him, as he shut the door. Once it was firmly shut he continued. "You have done an outstanding job, but you and Jack have a presentation to make. You need to be fully on the same page before then. I'm sure you do have some work to do in order to finish this, but here's what I want you to do first."

Robert stood by a chair in front of the President's desk. President Baxter went behind the desk, and seated himself. The President rocked back slightly in his high-backed leather chair, thinking for a moment, then indicated that Robert and Jack should be seated.

"Robert, you will announce, through Jack, the results of the investigation." The President stated. "You will name Karlovich, Torrance, and anyone else you need to pin this on as the perpetrators," he continued. "Farrell's dead, and his involvement would needlessly complicate the situation, so we'll leave him out of it. You will also, regretfully, announce that the rollout of OPOV is on indefinite hold. Make this short and sweet. Don't say anything about the program being compromised, broken, or refer to rebuilding it. Use the same language I did. We'll just let the marketing types take it from there."

"Sir," Robert hesitated. He was headed into dangerous territory—political suicide, in fact, if he approached this the wrong way. Did he even want to ask? A smart man would just put the documentation on Baxter's password in his wall safe to use someday when it was needed. But he could feel his lips start to move. He couldn't seem to stop his himself from speaking. "Mr. President, there's something else."

"Yes?" The President asked.

Listening to himself in horror, Robert heard words coming out of his mouth. "To activate the break-in software, they were using an old password."

"Hang on a second," President Baxter interrupted. He hit the buzzer on his desk and his secretary came in the door instantly. "Mrs. Parin. Has that file arrived from the Joint Chiefs yet?"

"Yes, Sir."

"Good. The Attorney General will be right out." Releasing the button he turned to Jack. "That is the file I mentioned. You and Jim need to drive a strategy. Bring me a proposal as soon as you can."

Without a word Jack rose and left to join the Chief of Staff, Jim Buchanan, closing the door behind him.

"Sorry for the interruption. Can you make this fast, Robert?"

Robert's pulse had been high since he arrived. The pace of the West Wing was never calm, but this particular day seemed too intense. Gathering his words quickly, he tried to organize his thoughts. "Yes, Sir. To activate their access to OPOV the perpetrators appear to be using a code that is identical to an old Senate password. Your old password, Sir." Robert's breathing stopped. His heart pounded. He wondered if he had just put a gun to his own head.

"Okay, and...?" The President leaned forward.

Robert didn't know what to do. He didn't know how to proceed, and he couldn't take back the words. Something in him needed to know the answer, and kept pursuing the subject. "Sir, it's a password you used as a Senator six years ago. We need to know how that password was obtained." Robert waited.

"Interesting coincidence." The President didn't seem concerned. Robert wondered about that, but he found himself pressing the matter.

"The odds of it being a coincidence, Sir, are extremely low. We need to find out..."

"You know Robert," The President held up a hand, and stopped Robert mid-sentence. "This is a bad situation. I agree that we need to understand how this happened, and fix the problem so that it doesn't occur again. The first question I have is: how could it possibly have been so easy for you to find my six-year old password? Then I wonder whether the NSA has the same access, and if they found it the same way? Obviously there was a breach, and just as obviously this was a heavy-handed effort to implicate me. How absurd! But the fact is that we shouldn't talk openly about any of this. It's bad enough that OPOV was compromised; now we have a leak or breach in another location, too."

The President stood, signifying that this meeting was coming to an end, "Send me a proposal for an investigation into general access security for the Legislative and Executive branches, Robert. Let cybersecurity drive this one, and let's get this buttoned up."

Robert wasn't convinced that a breach had been the problem. He started to ask the President whether it was possible that one of his aides had been able to access the password when flashing white lights erupted in four directions. Instantly a high-pitched whooping sound filled the air. Baxter was moving toward the side door before Robert noticed that four Secret Service men were storming into the room. Two were already obstructing the view of the President from the windows. Their huge shoulders looked like walls in dark gray wool suits. The other two had lifted Robert from his chair by his elbows, locking them against his sides. His feet barely touched the floor as he was whisked bodily to stand near the President. The six men pressed together as one, blocking Robert and the President from even the room's light.

The alarm sounded again, and the President was gone from sight as Robert's feet once more left the ground.

He found himself taken down a couple of hallways into an unfamiliar room with the President. About twenty people were inside the room with them. No one spoke. The Secret Service agents showed no emotion, simply standing guard and waiting. Then the flashing lights in the building blinked blue, while the alarm chirped lightly twice.

"Well, wasn't that fun?" The President joked with a smile, following the audible sighs of everyone in the room beginning to breathe again. "Fence jumper?" He asked an Agent. He turned to Robert. "It's a common fraternity prank this time of year. You'd think word would get around that it ends up with the prankster being arrested, but apparently that's not a topic discussed at college these days."

"Yes, Sir, we think that's the case." The lead agent responded. "It may be a few minutes before we're clear."

"Robert," The President was saying, "What I'm telling you is that we need to have you wrap this investigation up, and get us back on track to building voter confidence. It's more important than ever. We have to set aside issues that might be confusing to the public. This is a critical time, and the world is watching how we handle it."

Most of the people in the room were also continuing their conversations. They all used low volume in the tight space, as they returned to business as usual.

Robert felt a touch of relief. Instead of being reprimanded for his probing, he was getting a new assignment. Assignments generally indicated job security. It would have been frustrating to be promoted and fired in the same day.

"We're clear." The agents released the doors and Robert found himself in a hall by the Roosevelt room. The lead agent briefed the President. "It was a fence jump attempt. He was apprehended quickly, and the perimeter is clear."

"Happens way too often." The President stated flatly as he headed to his office, indicating that Robert should follow.

"Robert, this is why the founding fathers were so amazing in their construction of our government. Sure, they could see the lack of education and pathetic communications of their day. They also envisioned that relative education levels would never get better. They understood that people would want to focus on their lives, their children, and jobs. They saw how our people could never directly lead themselves, so they structured leadership through representation. A federal republic was born. We listen to our constituency, but we must also guide them."

Robert was confused. Was the President explaining that OPOV would be shelved? He found himself asking, "Are you saying we're going to abandon the system?"

"Don't worry about that, Robert. OPOV is only on hold. We'll fire it up again just after the midterms as a constituency polling system."

Robert was having a flashback to the Senator's election campaign. Baxter had never once given any indication that OPOV was a ploy to endear himself to the public. What was he saying now? "But what about your idea of bringing the vote directly to the people, Sir, since so many have indicated that they aren't being represented by Congress?"

President Baxter had returned to his seat in the Oval Office, but had not given Robert a signal to sit down again. "Seriously, Robert; after all that you've seen and heard you can't possibly in good conscience want to turn this country over to the misinformed, poorly educated public? They don't care about the business we deal with each day. Half of them get their news from Tweets and political comedians, and the other half is cowering under the covers because conservative talk-show hosts tell them that religious extremists are coming to get them. Of course we can't give them the power to make decisions about issues they don't understand. That crazy fence jumper just now—do you want his vote to count? I think not." He paused. "No, we must continue to lead the people. We just want to do it more effectively."

Robert was reeling. Every thought he'd had about this man had suddenly been turned inside out. Everything he'd worked for since Baxter's election as President had been destroyed. He had believed Baxter when he'd said that the people needed a stronger voice.

Robert suddenly felt tired—exhausted. "Mr. President," he almost choked out, "You campaigned on One Person, One Vote. It's why I and most of your staff supported, campaigned, and voted for you."

"Robbie," the President almost sounded like he was chuckling at Robert's naivety. "Listen to what the people are saying that they want. So-called 'reality shows,' faster Internet, and the freedom to enjoy football and video games. Oh, I know that's oversimplifying a bit, but they don't want the responsibility of running the country, and it's clear that the majority don't know much about it. They want us to take care of it for them. They're afraid to step too far out of the box, so they vote in the same people, year after year, convinced that they'll make their lives better. The idea of OPOV gave them confidence that we are looking out for their interests. That's what we needed to do."

Robert was stunned. Words had failed him.

"So, get this buttoned up." The President repeated. "The public needs a nice, uncomplicated package to focus on." He stood and took three steps towards the door. "Keep up the good work, Robert. You've shown that we can count on you."

"Thank you, Sir." Robert shook hands automatically as he left the Oval Office.

Chapter 77

Robert headed to his office along with Jerry and Agent Brown. He needed to think, and that was as good a place as any to do it. "Coincidence" Baxter had called it. He might as well have stated that it was irrelevant—that the whole "investigation" was irrelevant.

Robert felt utterly outmaneuvered on every front. He had exposed himself as naïve—and he had been. He'd thought he'd learned about Washington politics, and he'd thought he'd been working toward a better government. The President, instead of exhibiting concern for breaches in the system, had repositioned everything Robert had thought he'd known.

Robert felt he had been a pawn in this game. Why had they even involved him? The investigation hadn't been about fixing OPOV; it had suddenly become a test of loyalty. He understood that there were always concessions in law, and in politics. He also knew that some of Baxter's discourse was valid—the public generally wasn't well informed about what their government representatives were doing. Some of them didn't even understand how their government operated. They didn't vote often, and when they did, it was often fear-based, without research or understanding.

Robert had thought he could count on Baxter's public and personal commitment to return the vote to the people. He'd agreed when Senator Baxter had said that the public was apathetic because they'd been too far removed from decision making for too long. Involve the public more, he'd said, and they will recognize that their participation is changing their lives for the better. The people would become interested in their government again. Politics would capture and absorb their attention. The country would become stronger because people would learn through participation. Now that speech was so much empty rhetoric.

Robert felt deceived and used. He had two choices: accept the situation, and continue in his job; or commit career suicide. He could expose the President as a liar, and walk away from politics—along with any chance of joining a prominent law firm. He'd be quickly forgotten, and it was doubtful that anything would change.

As Gregg had said, Robert was only going to get one chance at this level. He could keep rising, or hold onto an idealistic dream of blind justice. Which was it going to be?

Robert had asked Jerry to work on the cybersecurity proposal. When Robert came through the door of his office with Agent Brown by his side, Lorraine was there, uncharacteristically smiling. A man was aligning a metallic decal of Robert's name in gold vinyl on the door, under the freshly added "United States Deputy Attorney General." Robert was staring at the lettering as Lorraine handed him a sheet of paper.

"What's this?" He asked, then stared at the paper. It was an order for the name change on the door—with his signature.

"It's the copy of the work order," Lorraine told him. "They told me it was supposed to be a surprise, but Mr. Crain wasn't available to sign for the work, so I shuffled it in with some other papers you were signing the other day. By the way, they said that we'll be switching offices later. There's some complicated rearranging they have to do."

Robert turned to look at the door. His name was shining with gold gilt. Lorraine had said, "the other day"—his promotion had been decided days ago?

"Guess I'll have to pay a little more attention to what I'm signing in the future," he said, lifting an eyebrow at Lorraine. "I understand the situation, Lorraine, but I'd prefer that you not do that again. I'm willing to forgo the surprise factor."

"I understand, Sir," Lorraine answered, looking abashed. "And Mr. Carlton, Senior, is waiting in your office."

Robert didn't answer. He just stared at the open door, visualizing its gaping maw widening and sucking him in, as though he was in a horror movie. He could feel the effect. His father was the last person he wanted to see. He wanted nothing more than to run away.

He went in and closed the door behind him.

His father didn't turn to look at him as he entered. Without moving from his seat he begin speaking. "Robert, I got a call from Tom."

Robert felt the reprimand in his Father's voice. What was left of his energy evaporated. As he walked around to his desk chair, he saw in his father's face an imminent verbal lashing.

Sitting down, he awaited the lesson he knew his father would deliver.

"You made a mistake. You've given Tom the impression that you don't understand what's been decided." His father started flatly. He paused for what seemed to Robert an eternity. "It's not as difficult a situation as you may think, Son." He stood up, and began moving around the office. "Robert, maybe I should have explained this years ago. I thought you understood that you're dealing with influence here. This is bigger than money or power. Power can get money, and money can buy power, but both of them come from influence. Life is all about compromise, and understanding the trade-offs that make it possible to achieve greatness. You *are* part of this. Tom sees that you can contribute. If he didn't, you wouldn't have this promotion—you'd be out. But you have this chance. If you don't grab it now, I can't, and I won't help you again."

"This situation is incredibly wrong." Robert spat out, despite his intention to keep silent. "Sure, I can keep moving forward, as long as I'm willing to knuckle under, and accept that I've been lied to, and used. I have to accept that a program and a man I worked hard to promote are both filled with deceits." Robert was completely conflicted. He was having a hard time making eye contact with his father, looking down at the desk. An envelope centered in the middle of it, sitting apart from the clutter, seemed to be staring back at him.

"That's exactly where you need to alter your thinking." His father told him.

Just what I need, Robert thought; more lectures.

His father continued his tutorial. "You think the President is wrong, but that is because you've narrowed your focus to absolutes. One Person, One Vote was a solid platform, but not practical. Think. Be realistic about this. If 'the people' got to vote on everything Congress considers, there would be no taxes, no defense appropriations, and eventually no country. Those are obvious examples, but consider the hundreds of issues that people don't understand, and don't take time to study. Roads, water, air; the people think that they want to make decisions about things, but they really want to get back to their mindless pastimes. If they were genuinely interested, they'd do more to learn the facts. They'd be more interested in what their Representatives and Senators are doing, and how their money is being spent.

Most people in this country don't have any idea what their elected officials do, or how they vote. They whine over how much they're paid, or about who has a better pension plan, and insurance. They understand that their taxes are paying for the schools their kids go to, and the local cops. What they don't understand is that they're paying for pension plans and insurance for their government representatives, which are better than anything they'll ever have. They don't get that Congress doesn't live by the same rules they do. They don't know that their Congressional representatives are busy lining their pockets with lobbyists' bribes, and that their political parties are only interested in power, not in serving the people." Robert's father was pacing as he spoke.

"And the truth is that they don't want to know. We've been living in the 'all about me' society for some time, now, Son. You and Tracie would be part of it, if you weren't working here. The people don't care what's happening to anyone else. They care more about the newest smartphone gadget than about what any level of their government is doing."

"I do understand that, Father. And I just heard the President say essentially the same thing," Robert muttered, still staring at the envelope. The envelope had no address, just his last name in its center.

His father walked casually toward the bookshelves lined with old Corpus Juris Secundum volumes. "And we're both right. You need to take your thinking further, and recognize the greater good when you see it. You can't make the people smarter. You can't force them to wise up. It is, and always will be a politician's game."

Robert's attention came back. "I was almost killed as a result of this investigation. Other people *were* killed. Where's the greater good in that?" Robert's voice gained strength.

"You were always protected, Robbie. You played your part well, and did what you were supposed to do. Now it's time to get past all of this. You need to officially take down the perpetrators, and punish them for those deaths."

Robert's head was clearing. "Okay." Robert figured this was his last chance to get some answers. "Explain the President's password being used. I'm sure he told you about that." Robert sat back in his chair and waited.

"What makes you think that? You're an attorney, Robert. Focus on the facts. Think about what you do know." Remarkably, his father was holding himself in check. He sounded merely annoyed, rather than angry. "If you were the Senator, and surrounded by trusted advisors who had been with you for years, what are the odds you'd need to give someone access to get your work done?"

Yes, Robert thought; it was understandable how that might occur, but that answer only led to other problems. If the then Senator had breached protocol, and given his password to an assistant or advisor, who was that person? Had they knowingly passed on the password? Had they used it themselves, and been involved in the OPOV scheme?

Robert was tired. He knew that if he persisted he'd only have the dubious success of enraging his father. He decided to concede in the hope this conversation would end, and he'd have time to sort this all out.

His Father, sensing victory, became more generous, bringing Robert's skills into the discussion. "Remember your courtroom experience, Robert. You have good litigation skills. You never ask a question unless you know, beyond a doubt, the answer. It's not important which side you argue, only how often you win." He lifted his coat from the back of the chair.

"Pick the battles that are worth fighting. From those, pick the ones you can win. You can win this one if you are on Tom's side. You have the opportunity of a lifetime—an opportunity most never see." He twisted the door handle. "Don't waste it." He walked out leaving the door open behind him.

Chapter 78

Grady was standing just beyond Lorraine's desk, facing the window. When Robert's father came out of the office he appeared to take no notice of him.

Lorraine bid Robert's father a good evening, getting a slight head nod in return as the hall door closed behind him. She turned to Grady and told him he could go in Robert's office.

Grady walked into the office, closing the door behind him. Robert stood to the side of his desk looking out the window, much as Grady had just been doing.

"Hello, Robert." Grady greeted him.

"Grady!" Robert turned immediately. He was honestly glad to see Grady. He uncharacteristically grabbed Grady's broad shoulders with both hands and shook him. "I'm really glad to see you—alive!" He added as an afterthought.

"Thanks. Glad to be that." Grady's natural smile came back. "Got a minute?"

"You're kidding, right?" Robert shook his head. "I haven't had a minute to myself since this thing started, but if I don't find out what you know, I'll never get any of this straight in my head. Start at the beginning, and tell me what's been happening to you." Robert had almost forgotten about Grady's research.

"Plenty of time for that and a beer, too...later. Right now, I need you to look at this." Grady opened his valise. "You can't keep it, or make copies, but you need to know what's inside." He handed the "Confidential" folder to Robert, who opened it under his desk lamp.

Robert quickly passed the cover sheet, and read the second page. He scanned the rest, which seemed to be mostly charts of information.

Grady pointed to the folder. "Take a close look at the last page."

Robert flipped to the back and read the title line, "Search results keyword 2". The chart showed three Internet connections that linked to each other on three occasions. The links were based on IP addresses with VPN passcode accesses.

Robert read the chart and looked up at Grady.

Pointing at the chart, Grady said. "All three used 'key fob' generated VPN sign-on passwords that gave them Virtual Private Network access with time-generated numbers. You probably have a software version of the key fob on your computer for less sensitive things like e-mail these days. I'll bet for really sensitive things you still use a physical device."

Robert pulled open his desk drawer where a roughly key-shaped plastic device sat. The LCD display showed six numbers that would change every thirty seconds. "That's mine." Robert pointed. "I need it to access case files, but stopped needing it for emails about a year ago."

Grady clearly disapproved. "You're supposed to keep that with you, or in a safe place. Anyway, on this list three VPNs assigned to three different people were used within 24 hours, and none of the assigned owners reported a missing fob or computer. This happened just over a year ago."

Grady pointed. "See on the last column? The assigned VPNs are for Director Karlovich on an NSA e-mail server, Rick Marsten on a White House server, and Senator Daniel Gregg on the Senate system. The key word used in this search is the password previously used by Senator Baxter, and found in the suspect OPOV file."

Robert stayed quiet as he thought about the information from the file. He flipped to an earlier chronologically sorted page showing Senator Baxter's password used in links that went from Marsten to Gregg, and then from Gregg to Karlovich. There was a response back on each connection within a few minutes, but without the keyword. At the bottom was a tally of communications between the three of them. There were very few from Marsten to Gregg and back, and even fewer from Gregg to Karlovich. He could find none from Marsten to Karlovich. Robert looked up at Grady as though he didn't see him there.

Grady asked pointedly. "So, what are you going to do with this?"

Robert focused on Grady, thinking for a long minute. "Grady," he finally said, "We need to see the President."

Chapter 79

Lorraine had been on the phone with the White House scheduling administrator for some time. She'd had no luck in getting even a moment for Robert to meet with the President. Robert and Grady had continued to compare notes in Robert's office.

After almost an hour their conversation had lagged. They'd rehashed the details too many times. Grady broke the silence.

"So where's your bodyguard?" he inquired. "I didn't see him when I came in."

"That's odd," Robert told him. "They've been planted in the office since I was assigned the detail." He hit the intercom button. "Lorraine, where is Agent Brown?"

"He is in the hallway talking with building security," she told him.

"Could you ask him to come in please?" Robert requested.

"Just a moment, Sir." Lorraine got up and went to the main door. Looking out to the left, she asked, "Agent Brown, could you come in for a moment? Mr. Carlton would like to see you."

Brown walked into Robert's office, along with the Justice Protective Service Officer. "Yes, Sir?"

Seeing the uniform of the normal building security officer, Robert asked. "Is there anything happening that I should know about?"

"Yes, Sir." Brown answered. "I've been asked to notify you that we will be returning your security to the JPS team. We're supposed to stand down in forty-eight hours and report for new duty."

Robert was stunned. "The car I was riding in blew up with Agent Carey in it, and you're to report to other duty? The Secret Service is being reassigned? Has some new information been released?"

"I'm not aware of any new data, Sir, but I checked for confirmation of the orders." Brown answered.

"That makes no sense." Robert was flabbergasted. "And my wife?"

"They will escort her back, if she wishes. That team has seventy-two hours before they are required to report back for new assignments."

"Has my wife been told this?" Robert asked, wondering about Tracie's reaction.

"Not yet, Sir. I was just informed. I was told to await your instructions on how to proceed. My team leader felt you might want to inform Mrs. Carlton personally." Brown said neutrally.

"I'm sure he hoped I would," Robert commented sarcastically. He wondered why someone apparently thought he was no longer a target. He turned toward Grady. "We don't have answers to what's been happening, but apparently we're supposed to return to everyday, normal life. How nice for us," he commented acerbically. "What do you think of that, Colonel?"

"I have to confess that I'm amazed!" Grady responded in an equally mocking tone. "I suppose I can simply go back to my house now. There is that little problem with it having been blown to smithereens, along with my vehicles, and with the fact that someone apparently wants me dead, but I suppose that's of no consequence in the big scheme of things." Grady shook his head, and got up, walking to the window.

Brown's poker face showed no reaction. The JPS Officer stood by, looking slightly uncomfortable.

"Could you both wait in the outer office for a moment?" Robert said to Brown and the officer. They nodded and walked out, shutting the door behind them.

Grady turned back to Robert as the door clicked shut. "Are you kidding me? What is going on around here?"

"Just hang on. Something doesn't add up." Robert said, thinking hard.

"Really, counselor! I'm shocked to hear you say that. Perhaps I should just give my insurance agent a ring and get this all straightened out, since we're out of danger now." Grady told him acidly, sitting down hard in one of the leather chairs.

Robert was still thinking, while watching Grady. Grady's smooth, unwrinkled jacket and crisp pants seemed at odds with his temperament. Robert had always imagined that military uniforms were like formal guards. They appeared to be carved out of stone, and somehow the men in them didn't crease or crumple.

Robert pulled himself out of this digression and back to the matter at hand. "Just hang on a second, Grady. Let me try something here."

"What?" Grady asked.

Pressing the intercom Robert asked, "Lorraine, could you please get Phil Davidson on the phone. Tell him it's urgent."

"Yes, Sir."

They sat silently. Robert tapped his finger as he looked through a couple of pages in the file on his desk for the fiftieth time. Grady was glaring but not moving. They didn't have to wait long.

The phone chimed. It was Lorraine. "Yes?" Robert answered.

"I have Mr. Davidson on the line." She hung up when Robert was connected.

"Phil," Robert said.

"Mr. Deputy Attorney General. Congratulations!" Phil sounded chipper.

"News travels fast. Thank you. Phil, I have a favor to ask." Robert wanted to get right to the point.

"Certainly. What can I help with?" Phil answered quickly.

"I need you to trace bank accounts for Senator Daniel Gregg, Presidential Special Assistant Rick Marsten, NSA Director Bill Karlovich, and NSA software programmer Chris Stoker. I need anything on any recent bank account increases, or any new accounts that look suspicious."

"I can get to the Gregg, Karlovich, and Marsten accounts, and link to anything they didn't hide well, but Stoker is probably not part of our public record," Phil cautioned.

"That's okay Phil. Do what you can. Also see if the four sent payments to any of the others, or to an account within their own bank. Start with these dates, plus or minus ten days." He rattled off the dates that coordinated with e-mails that contained the old Baxter password.

"I'll see what I can do," Phil told him. "How fast do you want this?"

"Can you do it now?" Robert asked.

"You don't ask for much, do you?" Phil sighed. "Okay, I'm on it. I'll call you in a few minutes."

"Great. Thanks, Phil. Oh, call on my cell. I'm headed up the hill." Robert hung up.

"You think he can do that?" Grady asked in disbelief.

"You'd be surprised," Robert told him.

"So, we're going to see the President?" Grady asked.

"No, I think we are headed somewhere else, first," Robert answered cryptically. He had turned toward the intercom when the mysterious envelope on his desk caught his eye again.

Picking it up and swiftly tearing it open, Robert dumped out the contents. Pictures on a contact sheet spilled onto the desk, along with a memory stick. The pictures were in order, dated, and time-stamped. He popped the memory stick into his USB port, and yanked open a drawer to get his magnifying glass to examine the pictures at closer range.

The pictures were of Gregg on the yacht. The framing covered more area than the two pictures he had gotten earlier from Farrell, but they were the same photos. Robert stared at one picture, understanding now what had seemed familiar. Gregg was on Robert's father's boat. His father was in the picture, standing with what looked like his usual scotch in hand. His back was turned while he talked to a man who was almost out of frame. Farrell's pictures had been cropped to leave out the man. The hand giving Gregg the money was fully visible now. The man was young—maybe 28. Robert realized that it was Marsten, the President's aide.

The computer had loaded the memory stick. It had the series of photo images stored on it, and one video file. Robert double clicked the video and the player window opened up.

It was the source of the pictures. The pictures were screen captures from the video, taken from a cell phone. Robert watched as the envelope came out of Gregg's jacket and was handed to Marsten, who put it into his jacket. It wasn't Gregg getting the money. It was Marsten, which meant the money wasn't a campaign contribution.

Robert copied the memory stick contents to his computer. Putting the stick and the pictures back in the envelope, he looked up at Grady.

Grady had been watching the video as it played. "Looks like a payoff. Who's that young guy?"

"Rick Marsten, the President's special assistant," Robert answered.

"That other guy looks like your father," Grady said cautiously.

"Yes, and that is our yacht." Robert knew how bad that sounded.

Robert's phone rang. Lorraine picked it up in the outer office, and almost immediately beeped the intercom in Robert's office.

"Mr. Davidson for you." Lorraine's voice told Robert.

Robert picked up the extension. "That was fast," he told Phil.

"Thanks," Phil answered. "Actually I found a common thread linking electronic transfers through Marsten, so it wasn't very difficult. All four have obvious transfers of over ten-thousand dollars each; some multiple times."

"You're serious?" Robert was actually shocked. He had hoped for a link to confirm his theory, but hadn't expected to find it so easily.

"Yep." Phil sounded like he was smiling. "Four weeks earlier, and then again two weeks before the dates you gave me Marsten's account jumped by ten-thousand. Then the week before the e-mails, it went up ten thousand each day for seven days. Cash deposits. Gregg's accounts showed large, consistent cash withdrawals from his "leadership" PAC. No annotations showed where they went. Now, get this: I thought of a question of my own, and searched the Secret Service background check for Mr. Marsten. He had a roommate at his Ivy League college. His roommate was Daniel Gregg's son by Gregg's first wife, who used her maiden name for herself and the son after she and Gregg divorced," Phil finished.

"And I'll bet if we check," Robert mused aloud, "we'll find that Marsten had recommendations from the 'Who's Who of Congress' to get on Senator Baxter's campaign staff, and into the White House. He may even have brought in some interesting campaign funding." Robert paused a minute, then said, "We can research that all later, but right now I would say Grady and I need to talk with Gregg. Thanks, Phil. You're a miracle worker. Keep digging and make sure you document this research. We may need this in court."

"Glad I could help. I'll dig a little more on this, and get back to you." Phil hung up.

Robert held the envelope in his hand, and grabbed his coat, herding Grady along with him through the office door.

Brown and the JPS Officer stood as he and Grady entered the outer office. Robert looked at them, remembering that Brown was waiting for an answer.

"Agent Brown," Robert addressed him, "Tell your team leader that he may have the pleasure of informing my wife that her security detail will be released. I'll leave it to her to decide whether she wants them to escort her home."

Robert turned toward Lorraine's desk. "Lorraine, see if you can track down Senator Gregg. Tell him I'm on my way, whether it's a convenient time to see him, or not."

Chapter 80

As Robert and Grady drove up Independence towards Gregg's office in the Russell Senate Office building, Robert got a call from Lorraine. It hadn't taken her long to find out that Gregg was not in his office, but in a meeting at the Capitol building. She gave Robert the room number, and told him where it was located.

Robert's new position gave him some of the privileges he'd been waiting for, so he parked in the Russell garage. They took the underground Capital subway, since it was quicker and warmer than walking. Robert figured his badge had automatically been updated with the credentials to use it, and to take a guest. He was correct. Clearing security again at the Capital, Robert and Grady found the room they needed. The doors to the room swung open as they walked up. Apparently Gregg's meeting had just adjourned.

Gregg stopped when he saw Robert, and stepped back into the room. A few cordial words with departing members later, Gregg, Robert, and Grady had the room to themselves.

"Gentlemen." Displaying some mild annoyance at seeing them, and glancing at his watch pointedly, Gregg asked, "to what do I owe the pleasure?"

"Senator, I believe you know Lt. Col. Barlow," Robert said, a touch of sarcasm flecking his words.

"We've met," the Senator said shortly, hardly sparing Grady a glance. "It's getting late, Robert. Would you like to tell me why you're here, and why I'm seeing you again so soon?"

"You're right, Senator; it is late, and I'm a little late figuring all of this out. You'll have to take some of the blame for that, since you complicated the situation." Gregg raised an eyebrow, but turned and seated himself in a chair. Robert and Grady remained standing. "I'll get to the point, Senator," Robert continued. "I played a recording for you during our previous conversation. In that recording your voice appeared to be ordering Colonel Barlow's death."

Grady's spine stiffened, making him seem taller. He stared at Senator Gregg, barely restraining himself from attacking the man. Gregg remained silent, ignoring Grady.

"Since then I've realized that Hunt was your man," Robert continued. "All those little hints leading me toward the NSA were coming from you. I was slow to pick up on that, but I do know that Hunt was with the Secret Service, and he's now what, OIG? Homeland Security? You and your cohorts created a nice plan, Senator. You thought you'd distract me; that you'd be the man behind the curtain whom no one would ever see. You pointed the blame toward Karlovich and Farrell, figuring they'd be nailed for the crime, while you controlled OPOV. But something went wrong, didn't it? I wasn't supposed to find out about your involvement. And Hunt's man Carey wasn't supposed to die. Yes, I know that Hunt knew Carey from FLETC. I doubt that he intended to get rid of Carey—he was too useful a tool. So there had to be someone else in the loop." Robert began to pace as he talked. "The picture of you and the men you didn't remember? One works for Karlovich. He's dead." Robert paused for Gregg's reaction.

"I'm not impressed, Robert," Gregg said dismissively. "What is the basis for this wild speculation? I'm not sure what it is that I'm supposed to get out of this. You and I already have an agreement. Let's just keep it at that, before you overstep your bounds and cause me to reconsider." Gregg stood up and moved toward the door to leave.

Grady wasn't standing near Gregg, but with one step he blocked Gregg's direct line to the exit. Gregg's face snapped toward Robert. "Call off your dog, Robert. You've got what you want from me."

"I'm not sure I do, Senator." Robert sounded very sure of himself. He felt confident as he continued, "I discovered some things today that I'd like to share with you. Perhaps you'd like to take your chair again?" Robert gestured toward Gregg's chair. Gregg ignored him, and remained where he stood.

Robert held up the confidential folder from Grady. "I have proof that your dedicated VPN connected with the President's Assistant, Marsten, and with Karlovich in a sequence, and that the President's personal password was transferred to Karlovich, through you. That password, which the President no longer uses, was later applied in software designed to infiltrate the OPOV system." Robert stopped again, waiting for Gregg to speak.

Gregg smiled as he calmly walked around to the end of the table, and sat with an air of exaggerated patience at the head of the table. "Go on, Robert. Let's hear you make a complete fool of yourself."

"I'm happy to oblige, Senator," Robert continued, "But I believe that the jury is still out on which of us may be more foolish. Rick Marsten, the President's Special Assistant went to school with your son, Senator Gregg."

"As did many others." Gregg snarled. "Out with it, Robbie. You have to do better than this. I'm losing my patience." Gregg looked at his watch again, and tapped the desk with his finger.

"I've reached the part where I explain how that fact is connected to this situation, Senator," Robert said smoothly. "That password was used in the software to break OPOV security, and you paid Marsten to get it. It was easy to convince him. He wouldn't have his job without your help, or without the recommendations you got for him. And yes, Senator, I do have proof that you were paying for his assistance." Robert hit the play button on his smart phone, playing the video from the yacht. He held it out for Gregg to see.

Gregg stared down at the video as Robert continued. "You paid him tens of thousands in cash from your Leadership PAC, and he was foolish enough to make lump deposits of that cash. You thought it wouldn't be traceable, because it was cash, but his deposits are timed with your e-mails and these pictures. You thought you were untouchable—too bad you didn't advise Marsten to be a little smarter with where he put the money." Robert felt stronger with every word. He knew he had Gregg's attention.

"Are you done, Robert?" Gregg growled, dropping his pretense of annoyed tolerance. "You seem to be a little too impressed with your promotion. I'm reminding you again that we have already agreed on a strategy. So what if I paid off Marsten? I've given you scapegoats. What's your point with all of this? If you try to publicly take me down, your career will nose dive—I'll make sure of that. There's no profit in it for any of us that way, Robert. I've given you a nice, neat package to close this case, and to keep everybody happy, including the President."

Robert smiled coldly. "I have more, but perhaps you would like to admit your involvement, again? I've been recording this conversation," Robert said, lifting his cell phone into view.

"Inadmissible, as you should know." Gregg snapped. "I didn't, and don't agree to any recording of this session." Gregg smiled sardonically at Robert, trying to re-attain his nonchalance.

Robert smiled. "It doesn't matter, Senator. I don't need it for court."

"You're right it doesn't matter." Gregg stood up again. He was angry. "What do you think you've got? The President's password and payments to his personal aid, some pictures, Baxter's voting system, and the nation's electronic security-controlled communications—have I covered the points that you think implicate me? No one will let you publicly prosecute this, Robert. If you're thinking of changing our deal, you should understand that no one would want the press this would generate. They'll bury it. If they don't your own father will be exposed. You know that, too, so what's your objective?" Gregg was making a show of leaving again, but it was clear that he was waiting to see what else Robert was going to reveal.

"My next stop is the White House." Robert picked up his phone. "I have no plans to take this public, Senator. I told you that I didn't need the recording for court; I need it for the President. I intend to end your career earlier than you planned." He walked toward Grady and the door. "You're retiring—now. You just made the decision, Senator. Today. And those little stipulations you had for me? I'll keep them, because you've proved we need some oversight—but, Senator, if I were you, I'd hustle right over to my office and start packing up. You'll have to clear out by the end of the day. I'll have your security clearance pulled after that."

Gregg had stopped moving, and was staring at him. Robert continued. "You can still become a highly paid consultant. You'll get richer, but you won't represent your constituency for one more day. You deserve jail; but, yes, I do understand how this works. I understand that courtroom publicly won't benefit the country. I'm willing to make things more public if necessary, but I don't think I'll have to do that, do you?" Robert asked rhetorically. He turned and walked by Grady, grabbing the door handle.

Gregg's face had reddened as beads of sweat dotted his forehead. "You have no idea of the power I have, Robert. You can't do this to me. Laws control the lesser man, and I certainly am not lesser to *you*!"

"Right conduct controls the greater man." Robert said. "Finish your quotes, Senator. You might learn something. Again, I suggest you get over to your office before I have security change the locks."

Robert and Grady were out the door in an instant, leaving Gregg alone. As they headed back to the car, Robert asked, "Ready for that beer? We've got one stop to make first, but after that my time is yours."

"About time you offered." Grady smiled. "What stop?"

"Your hotel, to pick up your stuff. You're staying with me."

"No way." Grady protested, shaking his head. "I'm fine at the hotel. Really."

"Grady, after all this, it's the least I can do. Besides, I have the place to myself. The guest room is comfortable and has its own bathroom with a big shower." Robert smiled.

"Fine. I'm too tired to argue anyway." Grady opened the car door and settled in. "What kind of beer do you have?"

Chapter 81

Robert and Grady stood in Robert's driveway staring. Tracie, the boys, and a crowd of people were pouring out of the house, cheering. Tracie raced to Robert, arms wide, and grinning from ear to ear. A huge banner painted by the boys hung from the house. "Welcome Home, Mr. Deputy Attorney General" it read. It was big enough to impress everyone in the surrounding area. It was apparent that they'd had plenty of time to work on it. Tracie must have heard of his promotion even before Robert had known about it. It flashed through Robert's mind that his father must have told her. That would explain her presence, too. His father somehow had explained away the Secret Service cloak and dagger, and now all Tracie could see was the glory of his new position. Others saw it, too. Tracie's friends, the Kennedy Center Hostesses, had rushed over champagne, a sumptuous display of catered food, and festive trimmings that had been thrown up in record time. The hostesses were amongst the crowd.

After Robert convinced everyone to go into the house ahead of him, he turned to Grady. "Still want that beer?"

"Champagne's fine," Grady responded, grinning. "But maybe a hotel would be better than the guest room."

"Stay. This will wear off soon enough. Until it does, let's celebrate a little. I think we deserve it." Robert grinned at Grady as they walked up the steps and headed in the door.

Once inside, Robert was greeted with an endlessly enthusiastic series of handshakes and smiles. Some even came from people he knew. Glasses and forks clinked as conversations broke out all over the living room, hallway, and kitchen. Grady quickly found himself the center of attention in a group of single women, clearly having been pointed in his direction by the talented Kennedy hostesses. For a moment Robert stood alone, watching the circus, then Tracie swooped in to grab his arm and hug it to her.

"I'm so proud of you," she whispered in his ear. "It's so exciting, and I got so many congratulations from people who couldn't be here."

"Thanks for putting this together. It's great." Being congratulated felt nice, but Robert didn't get much out of soirees such as these. He was genuinely glad that Tracie and the boys were home, though, so he was willing to go along with her celebration.

"Oh, it's just a little thing." Tracie brimmed with self-satisfaction. There was a short pause as they looked over the happy throng. "Your father is here, by the way. In the study."

The air quietly left Robert's chest. It was a reflex reaction. Without a word, he let go of Tracie's arm. Robert walked the few feet toward the office door and entered, closing it behind him. His father stood admiring Tracie's gallery of trophy photos.

"Congratulations Robbie, you've done well." He didn't turn around.

"Thanks," Robert answered neutrally.

"Despite the fact you took too many chances," his father continued. He turned to face Robert, the ice tinkling in his scotch. "What were you thinking? One minute you're not being aggressive enough, and the next you've gone in over your head. You went too far, Son."

Robert stood silently, thinking about the picture of his father's yacht.

"I raised you to be better than that," Robert Carlton, senior, admonished. "You got lucky, and it paid off, but you need to be more careful from now on. Smarter would be better."

Robert felt a surge of adrenaline, but it was a different feeling than he'd had when his father berated him in the past.

"You need to understand..." his father was saying, warming to his theme.

"No, Father, *you* need to understand." Robert was almost shocked to hear his own voice sound so commanding. He went on before his father could respond. "I could have implicated you. You were sloppy, and you exposed yourself in a criminal capacity. It's clear that you had a significant hand in this, and I have the proof."

Robert casually took a sip of his champagne, before continuing. "I have video that implicates you in a bribe on your yacht. Don't bother denying it, or trying to explain your 'business' dealings. It's quite clear that you hung yourself out to dry on this one, but you should be grateful that I didn't follow suit, and nail you with the crime."

His father was seething, his knuckles white on the scotch glass. "Meaningless!" He spat out at Robert. "You don't know what you're talking about. You wouldn't be able to get any mileage out of your video, or anything else. You don't have that kind of power."

Robert's heart was racing. He was still a little amazed at his own audacity, but his anger pushed him onward. "I don't think your board of directors and those lobbyists who fill your pockets would be happy to see that video, or the bad publicity that would come with it. It isn't likely that you'd keep your position in the current business climate, with a scandal like that exposed. That will be especially true when the story breaks on Senator Farrell, and when the President's aide resigns. You got what you wanted, Father. By the way, Gregg will be resigning immediately.

You should remember that I saved you, Father; that has me thinking that I should see a lot less judgment coming from you, and a little more gratitude." He wanted to say more but didn't dare.

From the moment Robert had realized that his father had orchestrated this operation, he'd wanted to blurt out a speech full of righteous indignation. The President had decided to take down his own system, and with Robert's father's help he had done it. In the process they'd gotten rid of key opponents of the President, and left a trail of fall guys and victims for Robert to find. With the adrenaline surging through his veins Robert couldn't trust himself to say more. He clamped down on his jaw, and held his champagne glass tightly.

Robert's father lowered his glass to within an inch of the desk slowly and deliberately. He paused, and then said unsmilingly, "So, you've decided you're a man. About damn time, but you should be careful whom you go up against. You got something out of this—don't forget that." The glass came down on the desk with a thump.

"Yes, I did, Father. And it seems that you should be careful, as well, since I have a much better understanding of you and the President. I'm holding some cards that neither of you would like laid on the table," Robert told him.

The two men glared at each other. Robert felt seconds tick away as though they were hours. His father finally turned, and walked out of the room without another word.

Robert stood with his heart pounding in his head. The champagne glass was still clenched in his hand. He put it down on the desk, and found his hand was shaking a little.

Grady confidently came through the open door with a bottle in his hand. "Some party out there, Robert. Congratulations! Run out of champagne in that glass, yet?" His glowing smile warmed the room instantly, and Robert immediately felt better.

"Yes! Thanks." Robert said.

Grady dumped some champagne into Robert's glass. "You ought to taste some of the food out there," Grady told him. "Those friends of your wife know how to put out a spread."

Robert's face broke into a smile. "Yes, Tracie and the Kennedy Center Hostesses throw a great party."

The phone rang loudly on the desk.

"Excuse me just a second, Grady. Don't move." Robert leaned over and grabbed the phone. "Robert Carlton. Yes, Mr. Secretary. Yes. Certainly. The day after tomorrow?" There was a gap as Robert listened and Grady emptied his glass. Robert gestured for him to hang on another second. "Of course, I'd be glad to represent us. Debriefing with your staff tomorrow morning at 9 a.m. I'll be there." Robert hung up.

"That was quick. Not much on pleasantries." Grady commented.

"Vance never is." Robert said thoughtfully.

"Secretary of State Vance?" Grady almost dropped the bottle. "Wait. Seriously, that was Secretary Vance? What's going on? Why would he be calling here?"

Robert didn't answer for a moment. Something was clearly churning in his brain. "Grady, how would you like to take a trip to the Caribbean?"

"Sure, when?"

"The day after tomorrow." Robert smiled. Grady choked on his champagne. "I'd like you to be the liaison to an investigating team I'm setting up." Robert grinned. "I could use your help."

"Mind if I freshen my drink first?" Grady was smiling. "You know I'm still assigned to the Pentagon. What's this team of yours going to do?"

"I've just started thinking about this, but I'd like to form a multi-departmental team with members from the NSA, the Pentagon, and the DOJ. This won't be the last time we have an investigation like this, so it's clear to me that we need a group that has the connections to get answers."

Grady's face changed, and he groaned. "Wait a minute, Robert! I seem to remember that the last time you asked for my help, I ended up in some explosive situations. Are we talking about *that* kind of investigating?"

"I'm not making any promises, Grady," Robert laughed, "but one thing I know is that you're the guy I can trust with state secrets. I'll tell you all about it if you're willing."

Grady stood still for a moment, considering. "Well, it's probably better than the desk duty I'll end up with. I'm in, but let's try to keep the super-spy stuff to a minimum, okay?"

"You've got a deal." The two men clinked glasses. "Let's go back to the party and try to forget the last couple of weeks," Robert told him.

Grady shook his head and laughed. "Robert, I suspect that the only thing I'm likely to forget is how much trouble you're going to land me in this time."

Chapter 82

Sitting in a quiet crab shack far down the bay on the Maryland side, Blair slowly drank his beer. The steam from the crabs was gone; the chill afternoon air had cooled them quickly. He sat at the rail of the outdoor deck that reached over the water, his back to the inlet. The waitress only brought out two crabs at a time so they would stay warm. The few other patrons preferred indoor heat.

He had been reviewing details of the last job. The end result was good, but too much of his plan had been altered. Things seldom went precisely as planned when dealing with the complexities of humans and their behaviors, but Blair hated mistakes.

The girl had escaped. That was irritating. Somehow she had gotten the better of Mary, and escaped. He'd read that the authorities had found Mary's remains in the burned rubble of the house. They couldn't identify her, so she was still on ice as a crispy Jane Doe. Christen had been traumatized, according to the papers. All she could remember was two young men whose descriptions fit almost anyone. The police drawings were no threat to his operatives; they were too generic. The police had already stopped working the kidnapping, although the file remained open.

The girl had seen Blair, but having been under the influence of the drug it was unlikely she could recognize him. Still, he would have to delegate activities like that from now on. A pity; he enjoyed his field work.

After spending time with her mother, Christen had returned to school—this time sharing a room with another girl. Her father's death had been ruled an accident when he was found at home in his bathroom. It was assumed he'd tripped and fallen into his wet shower while holding the hair dryer that lay next to him. They'd ruled out foul play.

Blair's operatives hadn't subdued Barlow. Instead, Blair's two men had been killed. Maybe they weren't as good as he'd thought. He'd have to recruit better. Barlow had proven a surprise—or perhaps he'd just been lucky. Melanie was expert at what she did, but overall the team had failed. He'd have to think about that.

He'd received instructions yesterday to shut down the operation. So that was that. Blair never held grudges. It was all strictly business. Nevertheless, he would keep an eye on Carlton and Barlow for a while. If they kept nosing around...well, that would be personal. His personal business.

In between bites, he watched the driveway. It was the only way into the restaurant. A white car pulled into the lot. A bright green rental agency and airport tag showed on the rear bumper. A stocky man got out and headed his way. Hunt.

The waitress came out with two more crabs. Blair ordered a beer and two more crabs, plus the check. As she went toward the building, Hunt came out, holding the door until she'd gone inside. Seating himself on the picnic table bench across from Blair he waited.

"You did well, considering," Blair said.

"He needed more pushing than I anticipated," Hunt replied. He knew that Blair was not interested in excuses. Admitting difficulty was usually safer ground, particularly on a job that had not gone smoothly.

"Yes," Blair responded, focusing on the crab.

The waitress came out with the beer and set it down near Blair. "The crabs will be ready in a moment. Can I get you something?" She asked Hunt.

"He's not staying." Blair pushed the beer to Hunt. "I know you don't like the crab much."

"Well, if I can get you gentlemen anything, just let me know. I'll be right out with those crabs for you, Sir." She smiled and left.

Blair pulled one of the crabs over, and hit it with the wooden mallet.

"I have another job for you. It's a short one, but interesting. The particulars are in the bag along with what you earned." He pushed a black gym bag along the deck to Hunt.

Hunt reached down to grab the handles and pull it closer. "When do we start?" Hunt asked.

"You'll be told," Blair said.

Hunt took a long draft of his beer, then stood up, holding the black bag. He walked away toward the restaurant shack. Inside, he passed the waitress as she was coming out with the two fresh crabs. "Never mind those two. Get him a dozen on me." He handed her a hundred. "It's a surprise. Keep the change."

She smiled and went excitedly back to the kitchen.

Blair watched Hunt head for the parking lot. A grin stretched across his face. He pulled a remote from his pocket and counted.

From the moment Hunt had left the building, he also started counting. He tried not to look awkward walking in his suddenly flatter shoes. The heels had detached easily when he pressed them together under the deck table. They sat unnoticed beneath the bench, a few inches from Blair. When Hunt reached the count of twenty, he pressed his own remote. The wooden bench and table exploded up into Blair's face, sending thousands of flaming splinters into the sky. Blair's torn and charred body was blasted into the water. It floated face down, surrounded by riven shards of scorched wood. A plume of red flame and black smoke rose where the table had been.

Hunt drove calmly away, shaking his head as he said out loud, "You shouldn't always count to thirty. People start noticing."

<u>Did you like the book? Tell your friends and the world.</u>

Reviews are the easiest way to say thank you to an author. Books with more reviews get more views on sites like Amazon and reach more readers. Post a review! Readers want to see what you thought about my book, and I do, too. It can be short. Just type this link into your browser and it'll take you directly to Amazon reviews.

Amazon Review: http://amzn.to/1J7GBQW

Now please enjoy chapter one
from my new thriller.

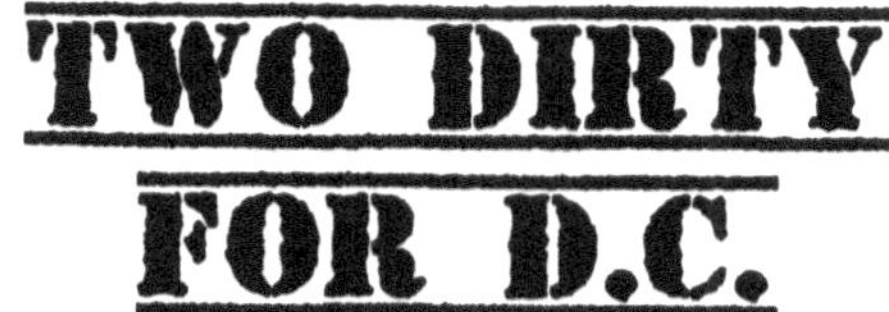

The Washington D.C. Series Book #2!

Chapter 1

Moving unheard through the cargo ship was easy. With all the noises around him, he could shout and never be heard. Passing unseen was another matter. Exposed ladders, narrow gangways, hidden corners, and very few paths to choose from made avoiding the crew difficult and dangerous, even at night. The hold was dark, which helped him hide, but so dark that he could barely see. There were a few sparsely spaced dim lights, covered in a film of diesel and dirt. Craig crept slowly down the aft starboard ladder into the hold. The ladder, made of bent rebar crudely welded to the side wall, was rusted and brittle. A rung under his foot creaked loudly, hinting it might break. He hesitated even though he knew the noise was drowned away in the general cacophony of stressed metal and machinery. The thrumming of the engine and frequent groans of steel joints twisting in the rough seas masked other sounds. Craig paused again when he reached the last rung. Peering through the gloom, he stepped off into the maze of corridors made by thousands of crates and the chains that bound them. He could barely see, but he didn't want to turn on his flashlight. Trusting his instincts, he moved forward through the cavernous hold.

The ship had seemed small and fragile crossing the last of the Atlantic. It had pitched and yawed unceasingly. Even here, in what should be calmer waters as they approached the southernmost Caribbean Sea, it rolled from side to side. Heavy wood boxes, teetering over his head in the deep belly of the ship, strained against their chains with each pounding wave.

Weighing in at about eight thousand tons, the ship was a converted tanker from the fifties. Rust, age, and general abuse disguised its purpose. The engine was in prime condition under blotchy, deliberately aged paint. The propeller shaft spun smoothly in its bearings, surrounded by rusted mounts. Dented and chipped, the propeller itself was carefully balanced and tapered. Its brass had been washed in acid to hide its newness.

Craig was on board because this was a smuggling ship. A former Soviet government smuggling ship. Walking slowly through the aisles of wooden containers, Craig reached his marker. He had made three trips below in three nights over six days, when the laziest crewman had the night watch, and when the fewest sailors were about. Pulling his old chewing gum from the chain, he tossed it between the floor slats into the lower bilge. This was the spot where he'd left off the last time. Reaching into his back pocket, he took out his thin flashlight and a new stick of gum. He didn't switch on the flashlight; instead, he pulled on the end cap. It had a push-pull safety cap, requiring a twisting action. Drawing out smoothly, the casing telescoped almost a foot as he turned the cap. The flashlight contained a normal looking halogen bulb, but inside there was also a small LED hidden to the side. It now blinked faintly and went dark.

Craig had activated his very sensitive Geiger counter, the only hi-tech tool he had in his cover as a Venezuelan merchant sailor. He put the gum in his mouth, tossing the wrapper through the slats below his feet. The gum tasted sweet and minty in his dry mouth, turning it suddenly wet with saliva.

Making his way forward down the starboard side, he thought he saw a glimmer from the flashlight's LED. Swinging to his left, he saw the flicker appear again. As he stepped between two huge crates the ship lurched from a big rolling wave. The boxes above him shifted against their chains. Craig ducked instinctively, but the chains held and he moved on. The LED began to beat a slow, regular rhythm, as the Geiger counter picked up radioactive traces. Craig's breathing quickened as he approached five boxes of similar size and construction. The wand in his hand beat a faster rhythm of red flashes from the LED. They rushed to a frantic pulse each time he waved it near one of the boxes. Closing the Geiger counter back into its flashlight form, he switched on its white light.

The five crates were made of stained and battered wood. They measured roughly three-by-three by four feet. They lay on their long sides, stacked on top of a single pallet. The Russian and

Spanish markings indicated that the boxes contained machine parts. Seemingly older markings read something about plastic parts, but these had been scratched out as if the boxes had been reused.

Pulling a crowbar from his belt, Craig stepped up on the edge of an adjoining stack and jammed the iron blade under the edge of the top box lid. Prying against the lid, he felt the chain which held the crates steady in the rocking ship strain against his efforts. He gained only the barest glimpse of the inside packing material before his belt was grabbed and he was pulled off balance. Bouncing hard off the corner of a box, his head split as he was thrown to the oily floor. His flashlight careened between the boxes and dropped through the slats into the bilge.

"So," a man spoke from the darkness in deep, grating Russian. "You are looking for something." He held the beam of his large metal baton-shaped flashlight in Craig's eyes.

Craig's training kept him from responding quickly. The small delay gave him time to think--to stay safe; disguised. The simultaneous shocks of pain, being discovered, and hot blood oozing down his head pulled at his ability to maintain his cover. Craig couldn't make out the man's face in the dark, but the voice was easy enough to recognize. It was the Second Mate, Vlad. Craig had not seen him do anything on board except walk around, listening and watching. Craig avoided him and the two large men that stayed near him. All the crew avoided them.

"I don't understand," Craig responded in halting Russian, keeping up the impression that his knowledge of the language was limited. "Let me explain, Sir," Craig tried answering in Spanish, while he attempted to regain his feet.

The crowbar, freed from the box and now held by one of the bodyguards, crashed down on his shoulder, slamming him back to the ground. The loud crack of his breaking collarbone echoed in Craig's head. Searing pain shot up his neck and into his skull.

"Silence!" The Russian came closer, shining the flashlight into Craig's face again. "I know you speak Russian. You try my patience, Arnulfo."

Craig had worked in the Venezuelan merchant marine for three years as Arnulfo. His American accent hid nicely behind the guise of a Castilian-speaking Venezuelan, sounding like the Spanish spoken around the Canary Islands. The Venezuelans on the ship thought he was avoiding arrest somewhere. They didn't care where he was from. It was easy to buy their silence and deepen his cover. The Russians thought the crew all sounded alike, with their lightning fast clipped forms of Spanish. Until now Craig had thought his cover was solid, and that his identity remained hidden.

"I don't understand." Craig's voice cracked as the Russian words came out slowly. The broken bone digging into the meat of his neck continued to bring fresh pain with any movement.

Vlad pressed the bell head of his heavy flashlight under Craig's chin. The Russian asked slowly in Spanish. "Who sent you?"

Free now to respond in Spanish Craig said, "I was just checking the cargo tie downs."

The flashlight fell away as a hand crashed against Craig's cheek, snapping his head to one side. Craig cried out, his face contorted in agony as the muscles in his chest and shoulder cramped around the snapped collar bone. The ragged and sharp splinters at the end of the bone threatened to pierce through his skin from underneath.

"I think you found what you have been looking for." The Russian stood up. "Bring him!" His hand waved aft as he stepped away. The two men grabbed Craig by his arms and lifted him.

"Ahhg!" Craig felt his broken collar bones pushing through the skin as the men dragged his body face up and backwards through the boxed corridors to the engine control room. His heels slammed into the elevated water-tight door sill. Craig didn't notice. The pain in his head from bone jutting through his skin was overwhelming.

Pushing the heavy door mostly closed, Vlad switched on the bright white overhead lights. Craig was dropped to the floor, his head bouncing hard against a gray, rusted-looking controls cabinet. Hidden inside, the new modern electronic control circuitry quietly managed the engine and wheelhouse equipment. Craig's neck bent forward against the box, his chin to his chest, choking the air in his windpipe.

"Now, why are you here?" Vlad pressed his flashlight against Craig's broken collar bone. The pain shot through him, increasing as Vlad pushed harder, making the raw, splintered end of bone jut further out of his chest. A slow stream of blood ran from the torn skin and spread around the collar of Craig's dirty t-shirt.

"Gahhh." Craig responded with a guttural sound of pain.

Vlad lifted the flashlight away. The drop in pain felt like pleasure. A relieved sigh poured from Craig's lips.

"Who do you work for?" There was a long pause, then agony exploded through Craig's head as he felt the heavy flashlight slam fiercely into his jaw, cracking it in half. He felt his teeth shift as his jaw deformed into an angular shape. Blood coursed from his mouth.

"Who sent you?" Vlad asked in Russian again. He'd lost his temper and his patience.

Craig struggled to translate Russian through his pain-mangled mind, but it wasn't working. The throbbing and numbness alternately swept in between spikes of agony. He was slipping rapidly into unconsciousness.

"I know you understand me! I'll not ask again!" The Russian punched Craig's face on the remaining good side and switched back to Spanish. "Who sent you?"

Craig lifted his head and glared through the bright lights at the cloudy vision of the Russian. A hint of a smile came to the still intact corner of his mouth, but the pain from his badly broken jaw twisted it, creating a grotesquely disfigured expression.

He managed to croak out, "Ffffk uoo."

The Russian nodded at one of the men who then reached over and squeezed Craig's jaw.

"Auuuuuurg." Craig's pain was unbelievable. He passed out briefly, but the man held his head up to face him and slapped him back to consciousness.

Changing to English the Russian asked one last time, his voice thick with his Russian accent and anger mixed together, "I won't give you another chance. I know you understand me, American. Who sent you? CIA?"

Craig spat blood at his face.

Standing up the Russian wiped his cheek. He spoke Spanish to the men holding Craig. "He will tell us nothing. Kill him, and throw him overboard."

Craig felt the impact of the crowbar on his head and blacked out. He was unconscious, but breathing, as they heaved his limp body into a cargo net beneath the small hatch. The hoist lifted him easily out of the bay into the open air and ocean spray. A wave hit the bow hard enough to send a blast of sea water over the deck, splashing Craig in the face. The water seemed cold after the heat from below decks, despite its almost eighty-degree temperature. The salt water stung angrily in his wounds, waking him just enough to open his eyes in thin slits. One of the ruffians noticed.

"Hey, he's waking up!" he shouted over the wind.

"Who cares?" The other answered with a grimace of bad teeth. "Dump him over. I'm getting soaked out here." They both fell silent as they saw Vlad emerge from the hold, glaring at them.

They lowered the net and released all the loops but one from the hook. Raising the net again they spilled Craig out on the deck.

"Get his shoulder." With one man on each side, they hefted Craig up against the rail, his chest striking the hard steel. The exposed bone sticking out of his shoulder should have forced a scream, but there was nothing left in him to cry out.

He could see the ocean whitecaps below, illuminated more by the moon than the dim ship lights. He could hear the wind and the grunts of the two men as they each grabbed a leg and lifted. His chest slid against the rail as they forcefully heaved him overboard. His face scraped down the rusted gunwale as he fell.

Vlad turned, marching off to search Craig's berth. He would find nothing. The only hard evidence of Craig's mission lay in the oily water sloshing in the bilge. The GPS locator transmitter in the flashlight lay useless beneath the heavy steel of the ship.

One man watched as Craig's body dropped down the ship's side into the water. The other walked away toward the crew quarters and the dryness inside. The white splash of water was all that could be seen under the moon as Craig's body hit the ocean. There was no sound of the splash over the engine noise and wind.

The warm water wasn't enough of a shock to wake Craig fully. He couldn't seem to move. He knew he was sinking and instinctively held his breath. It was a futile action. He knew that the deep, black water would soon consume him.

Sinking slowly; his arms and legs wouldn't function, but his mind held on defiantly. His descent was not fast enough to pull him down past the churning propeller. The last thing he felt was the pull of the blades sucking him in, the heavy brass hacking his body into ragged chunks. The gore of blood and meat spread like a slick behind the ship in the darkness. Small and large fish quickly converged on the unexpected midnight buffet. The few chunks that made it to the sea bottom were picked over by crabs. Craig no longer existed.

<u>Did you like One Man Two Votes? Tell your friends.</u>

Reviews are the easiest way to say thank you to an author. Books with more reviews get more views on sites like Amazon and reach more readers. Post a review! Readers want to see what you thought about my book, and I do, too. It can be short. Just type this link into your browser and it'll take you directly to Amazon reviews.

Amazon Review: http://amzn.to/1J7GBQW

The Washington D.C. Series Book #2 read now!

TWO DIRTY FOR D.C.

The Washington D.C. Series Book #3 is coming!

THREE STRIKES YOU'RE DEAD

Want to be the first to know when it is released?
Go to www.jrussbriley.com and register.

To know more about me and my books:

On Amazon   http://bit.ly/BrileyonAmazon
On Goodreads   http://bit.ly/BrileyonGoodreads

Thank you,
J Russ

www.ingramcontent.com/pod-product-compliance
Lightning Source LLC
Chambersburg PA
CBHW032155180726
48284CB00001B/52